beloved

CORINNE MICHAELS

Beloved
Copyright © 2014 Corinne Michaels
All rights reserved.
ISBN: 9781682306215

Cover design:
Cover Design: Okay Creations
Cover photo © Perrywinkle Photography

Interior design and formatting:
Christine Borgford, Perfectly Publishable
www.perfectlypublishable.com

Editor:
Megan Ward, Megan Ward Editing
www.meganwardediting.com

dedication

To my husband, my anchor, my beloved.

prologue

$\mathcal{J}$O BELONG TO someone.

All I've ever wanted is to be loved. I crave it—need it, desire it—more than food and water. I long for undying love and affection. The kind of love that bonds souls. The kind of love that's so deep two become one.

To be someone's beloved.

As a child I had my father, who adored and worshipped me—I was his perfect little daughter. He held me when I was sad, kissed my knee when I fell and got hurt, and read me bedtime stories. I was his princess, his daughter, his entire world.

What happens to a little girl when all of that stops? When she's no longer her father's perfect angel, but *instead* a painful reminder of his past. What happens to her when he pushes her aside and shows her he doesn't want her anymore?

"I just can't stay, Catherine. It hurts too much." His eyes are filled with pain and regret.

"Daddy, I love you! Please don't go. I won't cry anymore. I'll be good," I plead as I look into the dark brown eyes that mirror mine. My heart is begging for understanding from all this confusion and change. It's my ninth birthday, we finished cake and presents, and he's leaving. If only I could go back in time and change my wish. I'd forget about the silly bike and wish for him to stay.

"It's not you, baby girl. You have to understand—it's too much. Your mom and I don't love each other anymore." He looks into my eyes, unwavering, as I continue to plead.

"Don't you love me, Daddy?" I ask the man who is supposed to love me forever, the man who's supposed to never

leave me.

"I do, but I have to go now. You be good. Good-bye, Catherine." *He kisses the top of my head and I grab onto his leg for dear life. I know, even at this age, this will be the last time I see my father.*

He pries me off his leg and turns without another word.

And I watch the man who promised to always be there leave me behind without another glance.

He broke me.

He ruined me.

And he won't be the last man to do so.

chapter

one

"ASHTON, I'M RUNNING over to Neil's house. I'll be back in a bit!"

Our wedding invitations arrived. They're beautiful, everything I could've hoped for. I can't wait to show him. Not that he's really into the details, but we spent a lot of time choosing these. It'll be such a relief when we finally move in together and stop all this back and forth. Ashton and I signed our lease a month before Neil proposed, so I couldn't leave and screw her out of half the rent. Though I adore my best friend, I would've loved to have lived with Neil as we planned the wedding. Thankfully, the big day is in four months and we'll finally be under one roof. I'm excited and anxious to make everything official.

"Okay. I'll be here," she says, walking toward me.

"Don't get into any trouble while I'm gone." I wink as I grab my purse and rush out the door. Once I get in the car I send him a quick text.

Me: On my way. I have a surprise!

Ten minutes later, I'm pulling into a parking space in front of his cozy two-bedroom townhome in the trendy section of Hoboken. This area is all older homes on cobblestone streets. It's a place I look forward to building a life and starting a family in. I gather my purse and the invitations and hop out, excited to share this piece of our future with him. His car is in the driveway, but the door is locked. Digging for my keys, my bag topples over, spilling all my belongings on the stairs. After collecting everything, I use my key to get into his house.

As the door opens I hear a low moan. Slowly I lift my eyes. Nothing could've prepared me for the sight before me. I freeze, watching my worst nightmare unfold.

The shock ripples through me, coming in waves of horror and pain.

And no matter how much I want to ... I can't look away.

The man I love, the man I'm going to marry, is having sex with one of my friends.

Neil has Piper bent over on the couch—the couch *I* picked out—and is taking her from behind. His head is turned toward the door, his eyes are closed, and his face is pure ecstasy as he drives into her, enjoying every second of it while my world crumbles. With each thrust I feel the floor falling out from under me. I can hear them, see them, smell the sex in the air. Each slap of skin on skin, each grunt and moan tears through me like a knife slicing my veins open. I'm bleeding out, and there's no stopping it.

I close my eyes, begging for this not to be real, hoping this is a sick joke or a bad dream, praying that when I open them again, this cruel vision will fade away. When I gather the strength to look at them, I realize this isn't a joke or a dream—it's reality.

Piper's head is thrown back as she moans. "More. Harder!"

His hands grip her hips as he rears back and rams into her.

"Neil, yes!" Her loud, high-pitched voice screams out, "Oh! I'm coming. Oh. My. God. Neil! Fuck!"

Unable to control the shaking of my hands, the invitations fall to the floor. My sob breaks through the sounds of their pleasure, alerting them to my presence. The air punches through me as both their heads snap up and Neil's eyes lock on mine.

"Catherine." He stops moving, staring at me with wide eyes. "I can explain."

He grabs the blanket off the back of the couch and covers himself, hastily throwing another one at Piper.

"Explain? You can't fucking explain!" I choke out as the tears begin to flood my vision. "Oh my God! You ... you ..."

My limbs are tingling and my breathing is shallow as I try to remain standing. Everything around me is fading, but cruelly, my mind keeps the two people in front of me crystal clear. I close my eyes, hoping to give myself a reprieve.

Neil speaks as I grip the doorway for support. "Give me a minute and we can talk."

I don't want to talk. I want to pour bleach in my eyes and rip out my heart so it will stop hurting so much. Nothing he can say will erase this. Ever. My heart will never be the same. Cheating is bad enough, but for me to witness it—with one of my friends, no less—is torture.

And she was my friend, or at least I thought she was. Sure, she was never in my inner circle and we drifted apart after college but I never saw this coming. I didn't know she was even capable of such a vile betrayal. Piper was the one who introduced me to Neil. She dated one of his frat brothers and the four of us used to spend a lot of time together. I knew they broke up a few months ago, but never in a million years did I expect her to go after Neil.

When I look back up, the smug smile on Piper's face says it all. She wanted this to happen. She's enjoying my humiliation. Standing here shocked and horrified, watching her with my fiancé while she grins, obviously convinced she's won whatever game this is ... I snap.

I turn, slamming the door, and run as fast as I can. Shakily, I turn the car on and speed out of the driveway. All the good times we had, beautiful memories tarnished by his act of betrayal. As I drive the memories besiege me one by one—good and bad, love and hate, happy and sad.

Our first date ice-skating in Rockefeller Center, Neil skating backward holding my hands so I wouldn't fall. Two months later, going to the bed and breakfast on the Jersey shore and making love for the first time. He was tender and caring. The love and adoration he had in his eyes as we looked at each other during intimacy. I swipe the tears streaming down my face. It was all a lie. You can't respect someone then turn around and deceive them.

The memories keep coming.

The ride to the city, playing stupid car games and laughing until my sides hurt and Neil trying to convince me that the Jets would win the Superbowl. When he took me to Little Italy in July and got down on one knee and proposed in the middle of the street. The tears become too much. I can't see the road, so I pull over. In the confines of my car I lose it. I cry and sob for everything I saw and will never forget. I call Ashton hoping she can calm me.

"Hey, Biffle," Ash answers.

At the sound of her voice, any emotion I was holding back breaks free. A choked sound rips from my chest and the tears come faster.

"Catherine? What's wrong?" Her voice changes from sing-song to concerned.

"Neil ... He cheated on me! I saw it! I ... I."

"What do you mean?"

"I w-went there and he was f-fucking her on the c-couch. I-I can't-t bre-athe," I stutter as the phone shakes against my wet cheek and ear.

"Okay, calm down. Where are you?" she asks.

"I d-don't know! I couldn't s-stand there and w-watch it," I cry, weeping on the side of some unknown road.

Ashton takes a deep breath before speaking. "I'm coming to get you. Where are you?"

"Why?" I croak, letting the pain take over.

"Catherine," she says, authority ringing through the phone.

"Listen to me. Can you drive?"

"I g-gotta go," I say and hang up, right before I throw the phone against the dash.

I can't talk anymore. I can't even think. My head is a mess. I want to forget and stop seeing that moment of betrayal on replay.

I grip my hair, screaming in frustration as I try to form coherent thoughts through my agony.

Why? Why after all this time? Why?

Seconds, minutes, hours are lost to me. As the tears begin to ebb, even though the pain doesn't, I pull myself together enough to drive.

After driving around in circles for hours, my phone has over thirty missed calls and voicemails. I have no idea who they're from and I don't care. There are no words of comfort anyone can give me. My life, my future, my everything— ... is gone.

Somehow I find my way back to my apartment where Neil is waiting for me in the hall outside. Seeing him brings me up short. The last few hours come right back, slamming into me with the force of a thousand bricks, piling around me and threatening to bury me under their weight.

He stands there, staring at me. "Hey."

"How long have you been here?" My voice is quiet, but there's no mistaking the undertone of disgust.

"A while. Ashton wouldn't let me inside."

My eyes close of their own accord as I try to find any ounce of strength I have left to handle this. The nausea hits me full force and I hunch over, trying to keep the bile down. Looking at him, being around him again, makes me physically sick. He's destroyed every good memory we've ever had. Five years of love is gone. I want to crawl into a hole and never come out. The pain of the last few hours has left me empty.

"Catherine, please." Neil comes forward and places his hand on my back.

I snap back up, throwing his arm off me. "Do *not* touch me!"

"I didn't want you to find out this way." Neil runs his hands through his sandy blond hair as he huffs.

"Really? How would you have preferred? After the wedding maybe? Or maybe at Christmas?" I glare as moisture returns to my eyes, threatening to spill over.

The tension rolling off of him shifts and he snaps, "I wanted to talk to you weeks ago, but I couldn't do it. I didn't want this." He gestures between us, apparently indicating the "this." Gone is the apologetic man from a few moments ago. His eyes are cold and devoid of the love that once shined brightly in them.

"You think *I* did?" I scream in his face. "I don't deserve this!"

"I need more," he bites out, completely uncaring that he's ripping my heart out—again.

"More? What more do you need? I can't believe this. You cheated on me!"

He steps back, averting his hard stare at the elevator. "It's been over for a while. I think we both knew this was coming."

My eyes widen in shock and disbelief. "You're kidding me, right? Because I didn't know anything. We were getting *married*, Neil. How is that knowing this was coming? How many months of planning and building a life together shows me you were done?"

"I've been unhappy for months." He sighs, running his hands through his hair. "I didn't know what to do."

"I'll tell you what you could've done. You could have told me! You could have not slept with my friend!" I shout, but my words don't even penetrate. He stands there, completely apathetic. "So that's it? You're going to walk away after five years?"

"Why fight what we both know isn't going to work?"

I step back, shaken by his words. And then it sinks in: he's not here to make it right; he came here to end it. To further damage my beaten heart—the heart he bruised and battered with his infidelity.

"This is why you're here? To tell me this. Now?" I ask with fear choking me.

His voice is empty as the words tumble out of his mouth. "What we have just isn't enough, Catherine. It's better this way."

Without another word he turns and walks away, ending the last five years of what I thought was the beginning of our life together. The elevator door closes and my heart shatters into a million pieces. Broken. This can't be happening. We were getting married. We were going to have children, a life, a future! *No!*

I gasp for air, trying to fill my suffocating lungs. Ashton opens the door and pulls me inside while I lose everything I ever thought mattered.

"Shhh, it's okay." She holds me close to her chest. "It's going to be okay," she murmurs quietly in my ear.

There is nothing to hold me together as I crumble to the ground in complete devastation.

Not enough.

All over again.

chapter

two

Three months later

"EVER WONDER WHAT makes these people think they're going to find love on these stupid reality shows?" Ashton asks as she plops on the couch next to me.

We're watching another episode of this show where random women try to find their one true love through a series of dates with multiple people.

"No. But maybe we should sign up since the traditional route isn't working so much." I laugh, shoveling another spoonful of ice cream into my mouth.

It's a three-day weekend and we've been lazy, drinking wine and watching trashy television and movies. After spending the first month post-breakup wallowing, Ashton put her foot down and forced me to function outside of work. I believed my life was just beginning and there was a happily ever after in sight, but I should've known better. This is real life: there is no prince charming, and I'm definitely not a princess. No more illusions of fairy-tale endings. He's gone, and I'm alone.

"Could you imagine? All these girls are hot too. They're dumb, but at least they're pretty. Your company should represent them."

"I don't represent celebrities, Ash. You know that. I like being a publicist in the business world. Way less drama dealing with companies versus people." She tries to snatch the ice cream but I move it out of her grasp. "Can we change the channel? Let's watch something about blowing people up, or shooting people! I have no desire to watch people fall in love. I'd rather pretend everyone's miserable like me," I say, grabbing for the remote as my phone vibrates with a text.

Ashton slaps my hand. "Don't change the channel. I want to see her cry and be all sad when he picks the other idiot."

"You don't want to watch the other girl be happy?"

"Are you crazy? This is better than watching someone get blown up!" Ashton sits up, animated and excited. "She's going to be all 'I thought what we had was real.' We can change it after the first girl gets dumped." She looks down at the phone and her jaw falls slack. "Neil's still texting you?"

"If so many people didn't have my number for work purposes, I'd change it." I groan and grab the phone.

For two weeks after he chose another woman, I didn't hear a word from him. Then I started getting periodic text messages. Initially I thought he was concerned, considering he broke my heart and ran over it a few times with an eighteen-wheeler. However, I figured out pretty quickly that he wanted something. His texts were usually about issues with cancelling wedding vendors. But lately, his texting has become more frequent and has focused on us exchanging belongings.

Neil: I have a few things I found of yours. Also, I think I left some stuff at your place.

I'm sure he did, but a few weeks after I found him and Piper together, I burned it. I took everything and anything I could find of his and set it on fire.

At first, I wanted to hold on to anything that was his. Even with how our breakup happened, I loved him. A part of me hoped we could reconnect, find a way to get past everything and move forward. But he never called. I held on to the false ideas of what our life was like—how we loved once and how wonderful he had been. All of those memories I latched on to so tight, hoping if I squeezed hard enough, they'd be enough. But they weren't.

"You know none of this is your fault, right? He did all of this," Ashton says while snatching the ice cream from my grasp.

"I know, I know. I want to stop thinking about him and move on, but he was my life for five years. I hate him so much, but then there's this small piece of me that won't let go."

The worst part was when I was depressed. I was barely eating, forgetting things all the time, and the tears were pretty much constant. Days were lost like that. Work was the only place I could function, the only place that wasn't tainted by memories of Neil and Piper. I could be me there, or at least some semi-normal version of me.

Now I'm in the anger stage, which is working out just fine. Every time I've had to explain why I cancelled the wedding, I've relived what he did. It's been humiliating. I'd rather deal with a hundred rabid reporters than call my family to explain how my fiancé cheated and then broke up with me because he needed "more." I remember the way he was so callous, so emotionless. The Neil I fell in love with wasn't the same person at the end.

The memory floods back, barreling through my anger, which quickly morphs into sadness as I recall the pain. A tear forms, but I swipe it away before it can descend. Crying is for the weak, and I will not let him break me again.

Ashton smiles and places her hand on mine. "I'm sure there's a part of you that will always love him. But I'll help you hold on to the hate because that's the only emotion that douchebag is worthy of." Her blue eyes are blazing.

"I know, Ash. I'm ..." I try to find the right words. The bottom line is I'm not really sure what I am anymore. At first I worked so hard to hide it all, putting it aside so I could continue on with my life, not wanting anyone to see how badly it hurt. No one wants to be the girl that was stood up at the altar—even though we never made it there, the context is the same.

Her jaw sets and she narrows her eyes, trying to ensure

that I'm listening as she says, "I say the prick did you a favor. Guys like him are never content. He would've done it sooner or later."

"I'm tired. All I want is to enjoy our weekend and not think about him anymore." I sigh and lay my head in Ashton's lap. "It'll get easier, won't it?" I ask with a touch of hope.

She stares back and shakes her head. "It's already easier. One day you won't be sad or angry, you'll only feel pity for him."

"I'd like that day to be now. And I'd like him to stop texting me." I half laugh.

Ashton swipes the hair off my face with a sad smile. "Do you remember in high school when I swore I was going to marry Stephen? I thought he was perfect. I mean he was the captain of the football team, smart, funny, fucked like an animal." Her arched brow rises with amusement.

I laugh. "Yes, I remember Stephen the Stallion."

I used to laugh so hard when she would call him that. She thought she'd marry him based solely on his ability to do things to her she never knew were actually possible. He doted on her, but we later found out he had a few other girls who were also receiving the benefits of his talents.

"What I wouldn't give for another ride on that pony." She reminisces, laughing as she returns her attention to me. "I digress. My point is he was the one who lost out. I didn't cry. I punched him in the face, walked away, and found myself a better horse to ride."

"I didn't want another horse, Ash. I thought I'd finally found my white knight," I say as a flash of loneliness stabs through my heart.

Ashton isn't the wallowing type. She breaks up, moves on, and finds greener pastures. I've seen her go through her share of breakups, but she always bounces back quickly. Thing is, she doesn't know what it's like to get engaged, plan a wedding, and think you're going to spend your life with someone only to have it all taken away from you.

"Well your horse wound up being a donkey. Time to put his ass where it belongs—outside."

She's crazy, but I love her. I smile, shaking my head at another one of her off-the-wall retorts. "You and your metaphors."

"Okay, enough of this. Tonight's Gretchen's birthday. We need to get ready," Ashton says and slaps my ass. "We have dinner plans in the city."

"Crap!" I say, sitting up quickly. I haven't seen Gretchen since my engagement party. She, Ashton, and I grew up together. We've been friends since we were eight. Gretchen lives in Manhattan and even though Ash and I work in the city, we live in New Jersey, so we barely see her.

"You better not try to back out." She glares indignantly.

I raise my hands in mock surrender. "I'm not. I forgot. I'll go get ready."

"That's my biffle!" She jumps up off the couch with a gleam in her blue eyes.

"Don't call me that around Gretchen. You know how she feels about it since 'she's our best friend for life too,'" I say, imitating Gretchen's sweet voice. She gets a little touchy when she feels we're not including her.

Ashton grins. "She'll be fine. I'll call her now and let her know we're taking a train in. Go! Move it, sister!" She grabs my hand, pulls me up, and pushes me toward my room. "We don't have time for your shenanigans. Now go take a shower. You smell!"

"You're a real bitch and I hate you," I lie.

"Well, I love your smelly ass." She giggles and runs off.

"I do not smell!" I say to her back. Then I head into my room to start getting ready.

An hour later, Ashton busts through my door looking breathtaking. She's wearing her long hair pin straight, the fiery red strands compliment the emerald top she has on. Her black eyeliner makes her blue eyes look bolder, bring out the cobalt in the depths of her irises.

I'm wearing my dark blue dress paired with my four-inch silver stilettos. At least I'll get an extra few inches on my five-foot-four, vertically challenged self. Ashton and Gretchen were both graced with being tall and slender, so I always feel tiny around them. My makeup is minimal, but I spent extra time curling my long brown hair into loose curls, which tumble down my back.

"Well hello, sexy! Where have you been hiding? You don't look like you'll be turning the big three-oh in a few months." She nudges me as she appraises my outfit.

Maybe I have been hiding, pretending things were okay while I was finding a way to be on my own. But today is a new day.

"I'll forever remain twenty-nine, thank you very much."

"Sure you will. And I'm still a virgin." She laughs and grabs the eye shadow from my bag.

My phone buzzes again.

Neil: I'll be around tomorrow if you can meet.

I decide to respond because he's apparently not taking the hint, no matter how hard I try.

Me: No. I'm busy.

"I'm changing my damn number."

Ashton grabs my phone and powers it off. "No phone. No Neil. You, my love, are beautiful and we're going to focus on that!" She places a kiss on my cheek and heads out to finish getting ready.

Dressed to the nines and excited to be going out tonight—though I'll never admit that to Ashton—I look for the finishing touches. I rifle through the beautiful mahogany jewelry box that my father gave me for my ninth birthday. I finally find my diamond studs and go to close the lid, but my eyes get caught on the light shimmering off my engagement ring snuggly sitting in the ring slot. I pull it out and look at it, remembering all the promise it once held, before putting it back in its place.

After my breakup with Neil, I started wearing a sapphire ring instead. When I took off my beautiful diamond engagement ring, my finger felt awkward, naked. Ashton convinced me that I deserved an apology gift, and since Neil and I still had a joint bank account, we went and spent a little of his money. It's a one-carat sapphire surrounded by diamonds in a platinum setting. It's vintage and beautiful. We call it the "Fuck You" ring.

"Let's go, Catherine! Dinner's in an hour and we have to get into Manhattan," Ashton yells from the hall.

I grab my clutch and rush out of the room, ready to start putting the past where it belongs.

Behind me.

"Cat?" Gretchen jumps up when she sees me walk in with Ashton.

"Hi, Gretch!" I rush over, throwing my arms around her.

God, I've missed hanging out with my friends. No matter how many years or miles there are between the three of us, we've always been constant. When everything went down with Neil, they both rallied behind me and took care of cancelling everything. I, on the other hand, have been a shitty friend. When I'm not at work, I'm at home, so I see Ashton all the time. But I always find a way to get out of any parties or anything requiring me to leave the house.

"Hello to you too!" Ashton feigns being hurt.

"Oh Ashton, always the drama queen." Gretchen giggles and pulls her into a giant hug. "Both my girls are here! Tonight's already a great night."

It's so easy to make her happy. She's a lawyer in one of the most affluent firms in New York City, and she's aiming for partner within the next two years. There was a time we didn't see her more than a few times a year because she was inundated with work, but I always understood. Work is something the three of us thrive on, always have. I'm a publicist for one of the premier companies in Manhattan, and Ashton works as an embryologist. Who would've thought the three of us would each find a career we love and excel at?

I look around the restaurant, taking in the unique design. I'm instantly in love with the old-world charm and kind of Tuscan feel it's got going on. Judging from the interior, you'd never guess it was located right in the middle of the West Village.

"Any new clients, Cat?" Gretchen asks while sipping her beer.

"I have a meeting on Tuesday with a possible new client. We're pitching against Boyce PR for this one. It's a cosmetics company looking to expand their brand. I'm really excited. If I can land it, I think I'd be up for promotion."

"That's great! I'm sure you'll get it," Ashton says, smiling.

We laugh, catching up on work and any good gossip about people from back home.

Ashton and Gretchen are babbling on about some movie they're both dying to see, so I glance around the room and take in the crowd. When I hear a boisterous laugh, I turn, searching for the source of the sound. When I see him my breath catches. He's sitting at a table to my left with a few guys. There's something about him that's mesmerizing, something that prevents me from tearing my eyes away. His entire presence pulses with energy, demanding my attention without saying a word. He has dark hair, styled—or maybe not—in sexy disarray. His strong jaw is covered in stubble, only adding to his attraction. Though I can't see his eyes clearly from here, I can imagine the virility within them. But it's not just his looks, which are more than any man should be allowed to have. There's more ...

He's commanding even in a relaxed state: confident bordering on arrogant. Every part of him is captivating.

"Earth to Catherine!" Ashton waves her hands in front of

me, breaking my trance on the sexy stranger across the room. "Sorry ... too much wine." I laugh and grab my glass, trying to keep my attention off him.

We finish our dinner and polish off another bottle. It's been a wonderful night, filled with laughter and tons of memories of our crazy childhood. I'm glad we could spend this time together.

Gretchen clears her throat. "So ... I got a call from Piper the other day. She called the office asking if we could talk. She said she needed legal advice."

I was about to take a sip but freeze midway. My heart accelerates at the sound of her name. We all became friends with Piper during college. She was in my marketing class and also in one of Ashton's labs. Over the years, we grew apart, but until three months ago we all considered her a friend. After what happened though, no one has spoken to her again. If hateful is what I feel toward Neil, murderous is what I feel toward Piper. What she did to me is reprehensible. No woman should ever go after someone else's man. Which brings us to the burning question: Why, after three months, has she decided she needs legal advice from Gretchen?

Ashton chimes in quickly, "I hope you told her to take her fake-ass bullshit and shove it, and the only thing you'd represent is a case against her."

"Oh honey, I told her that and a whole lot more. I still can't believe she was so devious about everything. I always knew she was jealous of you and Neil, Cat, but I never believed she was capable of being so disgusting."

Air ... I need air. "I'm gonna go to the bathroom. Be right back."

"Cat," Ashton calls out, empathy swimming in her eyes.

"It's fine. I'm okay." I smile and pat her arm before heading toward the bathroom.

As I'm sliding through the tiny aisle, a chair juts out and slams into me, throwing me backward. My arms shoot out in an effort to brace myself from the inevitable fall, but two arms wrap around my torso, saving me from hitting the ground. However, I'm now sitting in a stranger's lap.

"You okay?" a deep, throaty voice asks from behind me. The sound of his rasp stills me, awakening all of my senses as it reverberates through my body. "Yes, thank you," I say, trying to calm my heart rate.

"Glad I caught you." Before I can move, his large hands grasp my hips to lift me up. His fingers wrapping around my waist may as well be flipping an internal switch inside of me. My heart kicks up, beating erratically from the warmth of his hands on my body.

I stand and turn, locking eyes with the most hypnotizing blue-green eyes I've ever seen. If I thought he was handsome from across the room, up close he redefines the word. He's rendered me speechless. My eyes devour him, my mind cataloging every feature. A dimple on his left cheek, a square jaw, and an angular nose give him a rugged, almost beautiful face. Everything about him screams masculinity.

I start to wobble on my heels and he stands, placing his hands on my shoulders to steady me. I take a deep breath, inhaling the scent of crisp linen and cologne—his scent. It fills my mind, practically overwhelming me, as I commit it to memory.

"I'm so sorry," I murmur, barely able to form words.

"No need to apologize. That asshole should've been more careful. Can't say I minded, though." His eyes crinkle in amusement.

Is he flirting with me? How sad that I don't know for sure.

"Well ..." I give a shy smile. "Thank you again for catching me."

He stares at me, looking me up and down. Something about his gaze makes me feel naked, exposed. Here I am, standing before him, fully dressed but completely bare.

"So since I saved you from a rather embarrassing moment, how about you tell me your name?" the drop-dead gorgeous man asks in that low rasp of his.

And though every part of me feels inexplicably drawn to him, something in the back of my mind, the part that knows how off-kilter he's knocked me, is telling me not to give it to him. I have no reason in the world to want this man, but I do and I can't explain it, which means it's time to walk away.

Trying to find an excuse, I look over at Gretchen and Ashton. "Sorry. I have friends waiting." I shrug.

"Well tell them to come join us."

I smile, looking at the two guys who keep volleying their eyes between him and me. "I'll let you boys get back to your dinner."

I start to walk away, but he grips my arm. His touch sends shockwaves through my system, momentarily stunning me again. "Wait. Sit. Have a drink with us. This is Nathan, that's Garrett, and I'm Jackson."

Even his name is sexy. *I'm in so much trouble.* I need to get away from him and quick, before I say or do something stupid. Oh wait. I already did. As much as I would love nothing more than to sit, I'm not ready. I know exactly where this will end up—I'll be hurt and he'll be leaving.

"It was nice meeting you, Jackson, but I have a table waiting."

"Don't you think you owe me your name at least?" Jackson asks, his eyes bright with mischief.

I look down, spotting the ring on my finger. It gives me the perfect excuse to run and avoid this bizarre encounter. "I'm getting married, but thanks again for catching me." I show Jackson my ring finger and shrug. "Sorry, I have to go," I say and turn to leave. Who knew Neil would be good for something?

"Lucky guy," I hear him say as I'm walking away.

I walk back to the table, forgoing the bathroom. There's no way I'm walking past him again. Thankfully, Ashton and Gretchen are oblivious to what happened or they'd both be grilling me. My heart is racing and my body is tingling every-where he touched. I slouch in the seat, feeling as though I've run a marathon. It's been so long since a man sparked any emotion or arousal within me. I feel unmistakably alive, which scares the hell out of me.

"You okay?" Ashton asks.

"Yeah, do you think we could head out? I'm not feeling so good."

I want to get away from this place and get myself under control. Unease is running through my veins. Foolishly, I look over and catch him smiling in my direction.

Deciding I'm not waiting for Ashton, I grab my bag and run out the door, away from a man who reminds me how easy it would be to fall all over again—only this time I don't think I'd survive.

chapter

three

BACK TO WORK today and my mask is back in place, so everyone will believe I'm the put-together Catherine Pope. My commute on the train from New Jersey into Manhattan gives me time to prepare. I've been restless since the night we went to dinner and I literally fell on that guy. Jackson. I swear I can feel his hands, hear his voice, smell his cologne everywhere I turn. Until that night, it'd been months since a man had touched me. I've not allowed myself to get caught up in any kind of relationship. Men have asked me out, but I knew I wasn't ready for that yet. Plus, there was nothing pulling me toward them. However, the other night I wasn't just pulled, I felt bound. He awakened me—my body, my emotions, my mind—and I still haven't recovered.

Shaking my head, I chastise myself. Today I have to be on my A-game. I have an important meeting across town and if it goes well, I'll be solidifying a promotion in my company. I don't have time to fantasize about a man I'll probably never see again.

Once I get into the city, I walk the four blocks to my office at CJJ Public Relations. In this building, I'm more than *enough*. My skills, my smarts, my vision, me—I'm worth something and it's well known. Instantly I'm stronger. For the last six years I've worked my ass off to become a top publicist. I've climbed the corporate ladder fast and proven myself account after account.

I enter my office, smiling and saying hello to my assistant, Taylor. If it weren't for her, I'm pretty certain I would've lost my job by now. The first week back after things ended with Neil, I was a mess. One time I wore my shirt inside out. Taylor came over and pointed me toward the bathroom with one word: shirt. She's kind, caring, and always ensures my schedule is perfect. More than that, she's a friend. I love her. One day she'll realize she can do my job and I'll be lost. But for now, I have her and I'm thankful.

I have all my notes and I've gone over every possible scenario in my mind. Usually before we go into a meeting we know the client. We study them and learn as much as we can to gain the upper hand. In this case, we couldn't get as much information as I would've liked, but I'm confident, even with what little knowledge I've obtained, I'll come out victorious. Boyce PR is my only competition for the account, and they usually don't invest their time in research like I do. They typically send the same two reps to bid meetings, and they've only won an account over me a few times.

"All right. The meeting's in an hour and it'll probably be about a fifteen-minute cab ride to get over there." Taylor smiles and throws some lip gloss on my desk.

"Thanks, Tay. I need to print out some files I emailed myself last night."

"I found out that you're going to be dealing with two people: the assistant and another member of their team."

I seriously couldn't do this without her. "I'm pretty sure I'm in love with you."

The people at Raven Cosmetics are anxious to get a publicist on board quickly. The more I learn about them, the more my confidence grows. I know I'd represent them well. I know this demographic. Plus, with my vast amount of contacts in this particular industry, I'd be able to get them in the spotlight easily.

Taylor turns to me, giving me the remainder of the files and presentation boards she had mocked up. Her sweet, timid voice is now firm, making sure I'm ready. "Were you able to find out any more information on the CEO?"

"No. And I despise the secrets behind this account. I asked around again. All I found out was that Mr. Cole recently took over. Whoever was running things early on left, and the interim CEO didn't want to stay on." I let out a frustrated sigh.

Taylor and I scoured the Internet and questioned all our contacts to learn anything we could about Raven Cosmetics. The company is only about four years old, but they've changed CEOs three times already. Even so, they've grown extremely fast in the industry. They have a line of natural eye products that exploded and skyrocketed them to the top.

The rumors floating around are that when the first CEO and co-owner left abruptly, someone stepped in as acting CEO. I don't know what happened with the acting CEO, but the silent partner, Mr. Cole, stepped in, apparently worried about the image of his company. As he should be. A young company needs to portray strength and consistency to its consumers and investors. That's why they decided to seek out a publicist to help clean up their chaotic, and relatively unstable, image.

"It doesn't matter, though. We're the right firm. Despite the lack of information, we'll still have the best strategies," I say. I straighten my back, gathering my confidence as I go over my notes, making sure I'm fully prepared.

"Agreed. Time to get going. Your cab's waiting. By the way, I wasn't able to find out who's representing Boyce PR. My friend said the original rep got sick and they're sending someone else in their place."

"Really?" I ask, surprised. It doesn't sit particularly well with me, but there's nothing I can do about it at this point. I collect my things and head for the elevator. "As always, you amaze me. Wish me luck!" I say over my shoulder.

"Good luck! Even though you don't need it. You'll be

great!" she shouts behind me.

On the ride to the lobby, I can't stop my mind from wandering to the fact that Neil works for Boyce. Over the years, it was part of what solidified our relationship—us both working in the same field. We understood each other's need to be number one and how demanding the industry is. There was friendly competition between us, but more than anything we supported and encouraged each other, even sharing tips and ideas. It was fun talking about our day and what accounts we were working on. At least, I thought it worked well. Maybe that was why Neil did what he did. Maybe his tiny ego couldn't handle his future wife being better in business than he was. Or it could be he's just a fucking cheater.

He sent another text yesterday about needing to get a deposit back from the reception hall. Apparently, they won't refund him the money. I don't know why he thinks I care. I lost money too. If anyone should be trying to recoup their losses, it's me. I've been a bitch, then nice, then I ignored him, but the texts haven't stopped. I'm beyond irritated. And, of course, my phone has been chirping all morning. Against my better judgment, I decide to check it.

Neil: We should talk. See you soon.

Me: No, Neil, I won't see you soon. Stop messaging me.

Neil: I'm sorry, Cat.

I have no idea why he's apologizing. Games—all he does is play games. I hate him for everything he's done and all he keeps doing. I'd like to put this behind me, but he continues to infiltrate my life.

The elevator dings and I walk out toward the waiting car, pushing thoughts of Neil out of my head as I get in the cab. I have a good feeling about today. I'm dressed in my favorite outfit—a black pencil skirt that ends right at my knee, my white blouse tucked into my skirt, and my favorite pearl earrings and necklace. My red heels finish off the ensemble. They're a power color, which is what I exude in the boardroom. As we near the building, I grab my purse and pull out my compact, checking one last time to make sure my makeup is flawless. The cab stops. I put my compact away, swipe my credit card, and head in to Raven Cosmetics' headquarters.

Heading straight for the receptionist, I introduce myself, "Hi, I'm Catherine Pope from CJJ PR. I have a twelve o'clock meeting."

"Yes, Ms. Pope, they're expecting you. I'll bring you right back." She smiles and walks me to the conference room.

"Thank you so much," I say as she retreats back to the reception area.

Steeling myself, I place my hand on the door handle. The scent assaulting my senses stops me dead in my tracks. I know that smell—clean soap and cologne. I'm instantly taken back to the night I fell into Jackson's lap. It's like I can feel his strong hands setting my body on fire, see his enthralling god-like face, as his eyes penetrate my soul. I shiver, trying to compose myself. I look around expecting to see him, but I don't. Someone else must wear the same cologne. I'm dreaming. That's what this is because there is no way in hell he's here. I need to focus, but it's kind of hard when my stomach is in knots. Shaking my head to release the memory, I draw a calming breath and open the door.

Entering the conference room, I look around, taking in the floor to ceiling windows, the long dark table, the small woman in a suit with short blond hair, and the two people talking over to the side near a refreshment area. All I can see of the two people is the man's back, but as he turns his head his eyes lock on mine, and the past hits me all over again.

I close my eyes and take a deep breath. *Please, God, let me get through this.* Of all the people at Boyce PR, they chose Neil to take over this account. I should've known.

He gives me a smug smile before he shifts, revealing the

person behind him.

Piper.

My stomach plummets as the floor drops from beneath me.

Her eyes peruse me as a snide smile forms on her plastic face. My chest hurts. It literally hurts to breath. *I can do this.* I have to do this. It's only my ex and the woman he cheated on me with—easy day. Right. Just another meeting.

The small woman approaches with her hand extended. "Hi, I'm Danielle Masters, the assistant to the CEO of Raven Cosmetics. You must be Catherine. This is Piper Carlson. She's consulting with us. And that's Neil Mullins with Boyce PR," she says, pointing toward Neil and Piper.

If karma is paying me back for something I did in a past life, I'd like to say after this my debt is fully paid. My professional sense kicks in immediately. I straighten myself, and prepare to kick some ass. If I fail, they win, and that's not an option.

"Danielle, it's a pleasure to meet you." I extend my hand and shake hers. She has kind eyes and a brief but genuine smile.

"Nice to meet you as well. I apologize that Mr. Cole isn't able to attend. He had an emergency, which is why we called in Ms. Carlson's firm to assist us in deciding the best publicist to help us achieve our vision," she replies.

"Of course. I understand." I smile and place my bag on the table. I'm going to lose my mind before today is over. I glance up, looking at Neil and Piper, who are now standing in front of me.

"Catherine, you look lovely as ever." Neil smiles, but I know him well enough to see the underlying sarcasm.

"Neil, good to see you again so soon." I'm biting my tongue so hard I swear I'm going to taste blood. Right now I'm anything but good.

Neil turns his attention to Piper, and I have to choke down the bile climbing up my throat. I try not to look at her. Though

I knew she was an independent marketing consultant, I had no idea either of them would be at this meeting. A few years back, Piper formed her own company. Basically, she acts as neutral third party who evaluates an agency's ideas and then helps the client find the one best suited for their vision. So, of course she's here. *I can kiss this account good-bye.*

I turn to Piper and try to refrain from wrapping my hands around her neck. "Piper, I'm surprised to see you here." That's all I'm able to manage in terms of niceties.

"I wasn't aware you'd be presenting," she retorts.

Sure she wasn't. I'm sure Danielle filled her in on the details of the account and was told CJJ would be here. I guess lying comes second nature to her. Seems she and Neil have a few things in common.

Neil places his hand on her lower back and she smiles at him before walking over to stand by Danielle. Gathering my confidence and all strength I have left, I smile and mentally roll my eyes. They deserve each other. Assholes.

Danielle points to the chairs, instructing us to have a seat as she and Piper sit opposite us. "Let's begin. Who would like to go first?"

I quickly yet politely jump in to gain the upper hand. "I'm happy to go second, Neil. Since this is a last-minute meeting for you, I'm sure you have other clients that need your attention," I say in a saccharine voice, putting on my best fake smile.

"That's very considerate of you." He knows he can't argue, or he would look like an asshole. Well, more of an asshole than he already is.

Let the games begin.

Danielle steps in. "Yes, Neil, we don't want to keep you. Please begin. I'm sure Catherine and I can continue without you if you need be somewhere."

Neil takes over forty minutes to present—in my opinion—a mediocre presentation. He obviously didn't prepare as much as I have, but that's typical of him. He and Piper keep sharing tender glances, making me want to gouge my eyes out. Judging from their body language, I'd guess their relationship has progressed. Clearly they're still together. I don't want to be here and now I'm having difficulty focusing, but this is my chance and I can't blow it. He drones on and on and I've mostly tuned him out, until I notice the words he's speaking sound extremely familiar.

"The number one market segment we need to reach are the young girls starting to wear makeup. My company will use several targeted social media campaigns as well as television spots to engage these consumers. Girls between the ages of fourteen and nineteen spend at least 78% of their time..." This is *exactly* my pitch. He goes on, meeting my eyes and silently confirming that he's somehow gotten my presentation. I look over at Danielle and Piper to see how engaged they are—Piper is hanging on his every word, but Danielle doesn't seem impressed. He's cocky and condescending, talking to her as though he's above her because she's only an assistant.

My head is spinning. I can't believe this. *How* did this jackass get my files? How did he get my social media stats and all my graphics? I did everything at home and then emailed my graph and presentation to myself. There's no way he could have gotten them.

I'm trying to contain my rage and maintain my professionalism, but right now I could tear him limb from limb. I've never wanted to inflict bodily harm on someone as much as I do in this moment—hell, I could kill him with the rage coursing through me. Once again, Neil has stolen something from me and there's not a damn thing I can do about it. Thankfully, I always have a backup plan. My hands are shaking with barely contained anger as Neil finishes and sits.

Danielle turns to me. "Ms. Pope, if you would like to begin, please."

I smile, harnessing my indignation so that I can use it. "Thank you, Danielle." I gather my now useless boards and set them aside.

My eyes are sharp as I look over at Neil, and my voice is strong and steady. "Well, Neil, it sounds like you and I are in agreement for once." I stand up, moving over to the projection screen to set up the video I put together.

"Danielle, let me show you the mock-up on what CJJ would want to hit the sites with. I won't bore you with statistics and numbers—we all know this market. Instead, I've prepared a video to showcase how we'll approach the campaign." I go on explaining how I'd work with Raven's marketing people and the press to strengthen the brand and image of the company. While I talk, I try to hit on points Neil didn't mention to differentiate my presentation from his.

I finish my initial pitch, press the start button, and watch, hoping the video is enough to sway the vote to my side. It's short and raw, and it certainly isn't flawless, but it's powerful. Part of being a publicist is marketing and helping clients create a plan. Whether I secure this or not, I know that I've shown my dedication and ability to think outside the box.

As the video ends, I look at Neil with my eyebrow raised and a smile that clearly says, "Screw you, asshole."

I turn to Danielle and Piper, giving them my final pitch. "I assure you that my ability to work with the press along with my vast experience in marketing will help us skyrocket Raven to the top." I'm completely composed because, like it or not, Piper is going to have a say on whether or not I get this project. It's out of my hands now. I have faith that I did enough. If not, there's nothing I could've done differently. Neil, on the other hand, better pray for mercy—I'm going to rip him to shreds.

When Danielle speaks again, I wonder if she's more than an assistant. I can't put my finger on it, but she seems assertive, not at all intimidated by handling a big meeting like this. Taylor is one of the best assistants I've ever known, but I'd still never send her into a meeting of this magnitude. "Thank you both for your presentations. I have a contingency that Mr. Cole needs to be in agreement before we make a final decision." She looks at both of us for confirmation.

Neil cuts me off before I can speak. "Danielle, we're prepared for whatever your company needs."

"Both of your presentations were quite similar, but Piper and I will speak with Mr. Cole about our impressions. Typically, he isn't involved in these projects, but this campaign is important to him. He's aware that he needs to be the face of Raven now. We want the publicist to be available whenever necessary. That person will also need to travel on short notice at times."

I nod in agreement. "Yes, of course, that's all included in our contract. My schedule is open to Mr. Cole and the team here at Raven." My eyes don't waver from hers, which I hope assures her of my sincerity.

"Thank you both. We'll be in touch." She and Piper stand to shake our hands. "I truly appreciate your time."

Now the waiting game begins. As for Neil, he should start running because my patience has reached its max. It's about time he pays for his sins.

chapter

four

I STEP OUT of Raven's building into the warm air, but a chill settles over me. I can't believe what happened in the meeting. Of all the possible scenarios I was prepared for, Neil being the other publicist and Piper being a consultant was not one of them. I heard she'd been busy with her firm, but her attempt at surprise when she saw me was complete bullshit.

Then to have my research stolen by Neil? I'm at a loss on what to do. All I know is there's no way I'll allow him to get away with this. I've never been aggressive with him—I was always the perfect girlfriend, quiet and supportive. Good thing I'm not his girlfriend anymore. I deserve an explanation for this, among many other things.

I stand off to the side of the main entrance, waiting for Neil to exit. I hear him before I see him. He's talking on his phone as he walks out, so I stand and wait. With each passing second my anger grows more and more. Who does that to someone? It's so unethical. So ... fucked-up. I'm about to lose it. He continues talking to whoever's on the other line while I stare incredulously at this man I loved with every fiber of my being. The man with warm brown eyes, a smile that could light up a room, and soft sandy brown hair, which I used to run my hands through to put him to sleep. That was then. Right now all I see is a liar and a thief. I'm ready to get this confrontation over with. I walk over, grab his phone out of his hand, and end his call.

"What the—" Neil starts to say, whipping his head up. When he realizes it's me, his mouth quirks into a self-satisfied grin.

That's all I need to release the fury I was barely holding on to.

"How *dare* you? You son of a bitch!"

"Now Cat, you need to calm down. I'm not sure why you're so upset." A red haze begins to take over my vision.

"Not sure? Are you stupid? Oh wait! I already know the answer to that, you prick!" The scales deciding whether or not to inflict bodily harm are tipping decidedly toward inflicting. If I were on a seesaw, I'd be on the downside, heading to hell.

He looks at me as though I'm insane. I'm sure I appear to be to anyone passing us on the streets of New York City.

He raises one eyebrow and smirks. "You should really be more careful. I hear it's very easy to forget things when you're not paying attention. Like the funny way passwords save when you login on someone else's computer."

"Wow! You have some balls. You hack into my email, steal and use my presentation, and this is what you say to me? No 'I'm sorry?'" I'm trying to control myself, but each time he speaks the fight is leaving me.

"Well, love, it's not hacking if I have a password. Plus, we were going to share a life together. I didn't think you'd mind sharing a few statistics for old times' sake," he replies smugly.

That's it. I raise my hand, rear it back, and slap him across the face, enjoying the bite as it connects. The sound reverberates, causing a few people to stop and stare. My palm stings, but it reminds me that this is real. I've hit him. Finally. I've done what I wanted to for far too long and it feels damn good. Considering I had to sit through a two-hour meeting next to his self-righteous, project-stealing ass, I've earned the right to do a lot worse.

The shock blankets his face before he recovers, rubbing his

now reddened skin. "Well that wasn't very nice."

I continue forward, pure hatred flowing through my body—it's red, ugly, and can no longer be controlled. He's quick, though, and anticipates my next move. His arms wrap around my shoulders, pulling me against him. Using whatever strength I have, I punch him in the chest over and over again. I know I'm not causing any damage, but I can't stop. Each blow is a release of the pain he's inflicted on my life. The cheating, stealing, lying, and the way he makes me feel worthless expels with each fist I land.

"I hate you! Don't touch me! You *asshole!*" I scream and continue my assault. Neil grabs my arms, pinning them to my sides so that I can't hit him any more. I'm flush against his body. My brain ceases to make rational decisions as I sink into him. Memories of being in his arms surround me. I remember the strength and love they once held for me, the way they used to hold me for hours after making love, how he would wrap them around me from behind when I would do dishes. Why am I leaning into him? I close my eyes, pretending I'm his fiancé again and that the last three months were just a misunderstanding, a bad dream. As angry as I was a few minutes ago, it's gone now, morphed into pain and sadness. I wanted him to love me. I needed him. He promised to cherish me. I inhale, taking in the scent that's all Neil—cinnamon and coffee. Losing myself in the past, a tear falls from my lashes and slowly glides down my cheek to rest upon my lip.

I turn my head into his chest as his grip tightens around my arm. "You don't hate me. You're just pissed because you want me back."

The words force me to remember he's not the man I loved—this is the man who destroyed my world. He took from me and made no apologies for hurting anyone. This person has allowed me to spend my time wondering what I did wrong and why I wasn't worthy while he moved on with Piper. He's not a man—he's a coward.

Gathering the hate and anger I previously held, I shove back against him. "No, Neil, that's where you're wrong. I want to be around when karma finds you so I can sit back and watch with a big bowl of popcorn."

"You should save your energy, love. You'll need it if you think you're going to get this account," he scoffs.

I lean in close and whisper, "Let's be crystal clear, you cheating bastard. You fuck with me again, I'll ruin you, *love*." I kiss his cheek and lift my knee straight into his balls. With him hunched over and clutching his junk, I turn and walk away before he can reply.

I start walking as adrenaline floods my system. Oh my God, I physically assaulted him. While I'm relieved that I stood up for myself, I can't believe I actually slapped him, punched him, and then kneed him where it hurts. I've never in my entire life hit someone, and I'm not sure how to handle the high I'm on right now. I need Ashton and I need a drink.

I walk another few blocks, letting my pulse return to normal, before I hail a cab. Once my hands are steady, I grab my phone and text Ashton.

Me: I swear you're never gonna believe this shit!

Ashton: You got the account???

How I wish that were the case. It would at least make this day worth it.

Me: No decision yet. Will you be home tonight?

Ashton: Be there by 6 xoxo

I call Taylor and let her know I'm going home instead of heading back to the office. I can do a few things remotely anyway. She almost goes postal when she hears Piper was in the meeting. I relay the turn of events to a stunned Taylor—everything from Neil stealing my presentation to our showdown outside the building. There are times in your life you wish there were a reset button—this is one of those times. My anxiety is starting to rise again. What if Piper's involved with the entire project? There's no way I could deal with her day in and day out, pretending she doesn't bother me. I head to the station, anxious to get home and glean some wisdom from Ash. She always knows how to talk me down.

With perfect timing, I catch the train back to Hoboken—luckily, there was one leaving in five minutes. I have a three-seat row all to myself, which almost never happens. I'm usually crammed in a middle seat, trying to avoid people touching me. However, this ride I'm going to stretch out and enjoy the peace.

The conductor's voice comes overhead, informing us the train will be delayed. Fine by me. I close my eyes and sink into the seat. I'm spent from the meeting and my confrontation with Neil. He deserved to be dealt with, even if it did cost me the account and my possible promotion. Whichever way the account goes, this day has been overwhelming. I'm going to use this time to relax, not think, and clear my mind of all the drama I just endured.

"Hello." I hear a familiar voice and open my eyes. Scanning the train car, I see him. Jackson. He's one row back, and he's staring right at me with a dimpled grin.

This day keeps getting better and better.

"I'll call you back," he says into his phone. He ends the call and stands, smiling over at me. "I thought that was you." The timbre of his voice travels straight to my core.

God, he's even more handsome than I remember. The sight of him dressed in dark blue jeans and a tight olive green T-shirt, which makes his eyes more green than blue today, causes my heart to flutter in my chest. He reaches up and grabs his bag from the rack above his head. As he moves, his shirt lifts so I can see his ripped abs.

Wow.

"Mind if I join you?" he asks, snapping me out of my dreaming.

"Ummm, sure. I have room." I scoot over to the window,

looking down and allowing my hair to create a veil. If I can control my blushing, I'll be shocked. Hiding my emotions has never been something I've excelled at outside of work. Hard as I try, people usually see right through me. The last three months have given me some practice, but here I sit, red-faced and wide-eyed because of him.

"Thanks. I'm Jackson, in case you forgot." Jackson's hand extends, his eyes soft and warm as he waits to shake my hand.

"Catherine. I remember you, though," I say, placing my tiny hand in his.

My arm feels like it's been shocked—the current running from his body to mine feels as if I've grabbed a live electrical wire. I gasp and pull my hand from his. The sensation was so strong and intense that my fingers are tingling.

I look to Jackson, who is opening and closing his hand. I wonder if he felt it too.

"So you do have a name. I like it. Nice to meet you *again,* Catherine."

"Yes, what are the odds?" I seem to be on some kind of eternal karmic payback plan. Why not? Keep piling more on top of my already ridiculous day. At least if it all comes on at once, I can get a reprieve ... eventually.

Jackson clears his throat, which draws my attention to his beautiful face. "Fall into any more handsome strangers' laps since I last saw you?" His grin is playful. It seems to melt any irritation I'd begun to feel over my luck.

"Who said you're handsome?"

"Lots of people. What do you think?" Jackson asks and I burst out laughing.

"I think you're ... " I look around, trying to appear allusive before responding, "Funny." There. He can take that however he wants.

"You know, I'm more than just handsome and funny."

"I bet you are, but I never said handsome." I smile and shake my head.

Jackson shifts in his seat. "Yes, but you haven't said I'm not." His brow rises. "Well? Any more casualties?"

"Anyone ever tell you you're a pain in the ass?"

He shrugs and leans closer to me. "I've been called worse." His voice drops to a low rasp. "I didn't mind having your ass on me. It's not every day I get to save a beautiful woman."

"I wasn't talking about my ass. I was saying you *are* an ass."

He's an expert at twisting my words. Typically, I can banter better than most people. Sarcasm is my first language. I'm either off my game today or Jackson's thrown me—I'm not sure which.

Jackson smirks and his gravelly voice stirs the butterflies in my stomach. "I think you're afraid of how handsome I am."

"I think we can add frustrating to the list of your attributes."

Jackson clears his throat. "So where's your ring?"

"Oh, ummm, I left it home."

The train starts moving. I only have about ten more minutes with him before we arrive at my station. I'm hoping there will be another delay so I can talk to him longer, or stare—either works for me.

"So what's his name?" I scrunch my brows, confused by his question. "Your fiancé?"

"I should've said I left it home because he's not my fiancé anymore," I reply.

"Sorry to hear that, but I'm sure he's much more sorry than I am." Jackson grins, showing me that adorable dimple of his. For the first time, I get a strong whiff of his cologne. Why didn't I notice it before? Now that I have, the thought crosses my mind that I could inhale it all day and be perfectly happy.

"Thanks. I'm not so sure he's sorry at all, but I appreciate you saying that." I smile.

His face changes and his now serious gaze locks on mine. It's intense, so much so that I can't look anywhere but into his captivating eyes. "I can assure you, Catherine, if he's not sorry yet, he will be someday. Any man would be an idiot to let someone as gorgeous as you go," he says, and his eyes dart to my lips.

"Jackson," I say in a breathy whisper, unsure of whether or not I can say anything more than his name. My mind is scattered, invaded by thoughts of his lips touching mine, the feel of his mouth on mine, and all the ways I want to explore him. No one has ever confused me like this. I don't know anything about him, but I crave his touch, his words, his presence. Something about him stirs feelings deep within me. Maybe it's not something at all. Maybe it's just him.

I turn to say more, but the train stops. Shit!

"I have to go. This is my stop." I fail to keep the disappointment out of my voice.

I step past him into the aisle. As I'm about to walk away, he grabs my hand and places a kiss against my knuckles. "Until next time."

Though I only have a minute before the train leaves again, I have to say something. I go with the only reply I'm capable of. "Good-bye, Jackson."

I exit the train feeling off balance. Between Neil's antics and seeing Jackson unexpectedly, I need to talk to Ashton more than ever. I feel like I'm one of those Stretch Armstrong dolls being pulled so taut I'm about to snap. I'm digging through my bag, looking for my keys, when someone grabs my shoulder, startling me.

I gasp and turn only to be gazing back into Jackson's eyes.

"Hey." He smiles and drops his hand.

"Hi," I reply, bemused.

"Sorry, I realized you dropped your keys. Didn't want you to have another disaster." Jackson smiles warmly.

"How noble of you to save me *again*," I say, moving through the parking lot toward my car.

"I guess this is our *thing*."

"Oh, we have a thing, do we?" I ask with a smile.

"Are you asking about my thing?"

I gasp, immediately feeling my face flame red. "What? No! I never said anything about your thing."

He laughs out loud, full-on belly laughing at me. After he recovers, his voice drops as he says, "So you do want to see my *thing*." He winks and leans in close to me. So close I can smell the mint on his breath. "I wouldn't mind."

I take another step toward my car, flustered by him and my incapability to handle him. "Again I revisit the list—definitely a pain in the ass."

"You just have to ask."

My pulse is so loud I'm sure he can hear it. "I guess it's a good thing I'm not asking," I manage to reply. I wonder if I sound as frazzled as I feel.

Jackson takes a step closer to me, stalking me like I'm his prey, and I counter with another step back. Once my back hits the car door ... that's it. He has me pinned and we both know it. He raises his arms, placing them on the frame and caging me in.

His lips brush against my ear when he whispers, "Oh, but your body says otherwise." His body closes in on mine and the last remaining space between us disappears. Heat floods my core, my face, my body—my lids flutter closed and I take a shaky breath. "Open your eyes, Catherine."

I submit to his command, watching how his pupils dilate as his eyes seem to go from solid to liquid. Colors blend together in a sea of blue and green lust. He leans forward, removing one of his arms from the car and placing it on my arm. Slowly his fingers trail my bare skin. The current flowing between us is even more powerful than before. While my common sense dies a slow death, every other part of me is alive under his touch. My body and mind are at war with each other, both trying to gain the upper hand—right now my body is winning.

He licks his lips slowly, torturously, until I'm unable to take another second of this suffering. I snap, grabbing his shirt and yanking him toward me. My lips meet his with a passion that borders on hostile. He pushes us backward, pressing me against the car. The cold metal bites through my shirt, but I don't care. I can barely feel it. His tongue licks the seam of my lips, and when I grant him access, he plunges it in. With every swipe of his tongue against mine, he's igniting the lust I was smothering.

I'm losing myself in his incredibly skilled mouth, feeling lighter, as though I'm floating away. The only thing tying me to this earth is Jackson. He's taken over every part of me. All that exists are his hands and his lips and him, but I want more. I kiss him deeper and harder as he moans against me. Releasing his shirt, I run my hands down across his chest and then lower over his abs, taking in every dent and ridge. His arms pull me tighter, securing me against the front of him. I gasp at his excitement pressed against my stomach, and his mouth moves to my ear.

"Next stop Hoboken Station."

"What?" I ask breathlessly as his nips at my earlobe.

"Now arriving at Hoboken Station."

My eyes flutter open, expecting to see Jackson's sexy face, but ... no. I'm on the train.

Holy shit! I was dreaming. It was so real. My palms are sweating and my pulse is racing, and if I'm being honest, I'm panting a little. But none of it happened. Oh, how I wish it had.

I gather my belongings, grab my keys out of my purse, and head out to my car. That drink is looking better and better.

chapter

five

THE DRIVE BACK to my apartment is short thanks to the lack of traffic at this time of day. It's odd being home so early. I have about an hour until Ashton is due home, which gives me enough time to change and check my emails. Throwing my hair into a messy bun, I opt for my leggings, a gray tunic, and my mint-green lace leg warmers—cute and sassy, as Ashton would say. I can't wait to unload all the stuff going on in my messed-up brain—nothing seems to make sense.

I step out into the living room and stop dead in my tracks. This place is a mess! Papers are everywhere, mail's lying around, dirty dishes sit on the table, and clothes are strewn over the back of the couch. Between both our schedules, the house is rarely spotless, but we've never let things get this bad. I decide to skip the emails and pick up a little. We pay way too much money for this place to allow it be this out of control. Ashton and I looked for an apartment in Manhattan. We had always wanted to be like the girls on television, but once we saw the going rate for apartments and sublets we opted for New Jersey. Our high-rise is on the river, overlooking the city, so our rent is high, but it's worth it. We both make a good salary, so we decided to live comfortably and have an apartment with security.

Me: Hey. Gonna start dinner.

Ashton: K. I'll be leaving the city soon.

I look through the kitchen and realize we're out of pretty much anything edible. I can either head to the store or order in. The sensible choice would be to go to the store, but after the day I've had, I decide to say screw it.

There's a knock at the door. Weird. The doorman usually calls if we have visitors.

"Open up, Cat," a bubbly voice says. Gretchen.

With a huge grin, I throw the door open.

"What are you doing on this side of the river?" I ask.

"I had a case here in Jersey, so I figured I'd see if my two crazy-ass friends were around. And lucky me, I get you!" She grins as she walks through the apartment.

"At least it's lucky for one of us," I snort.

"Honestly, I didn't think you'd be here. What gives?" she says, assessing my outfit and facial expressions.

"I had my meeting today for that prospective new client. I finished early. Figured I'd work from home." I shrug, attempting nonchalance.

Gretchen glares, giving me her lawyer look. The one that sees through you as she weighs each word you say and interprets your tone. She does that and then she chews you up. I should've remembered who I'm dealing with. Even fielding questions from crazy reporters hasn't properly prepared me for her.

"So why do you look like shit? Why don't you tell me what's really going on, Cat? Considering I don't believe you for a second." Her voice is stern but sympathetic. She knows the nightmare I went through. I knew it would only be a matter of time until she started pushing me to talk.

We head into the kitchen and sit at the table. I look down, trying to find a way to put into words what's jumbled in my head, as my fingers trace the grain of the wood. "I'm a mess, Gretch. It's been three months since Neil cheated on me, and sometimes it feels like it happened yesterday. Sometimes it hurts so much it's hard to breathe, but I have to pretend I'm great.

"Then today I had to present against him at the client meeting I told you about. Not only was Piper there ..." I trail off, looking up to see her reaction.

"What? Oh wow," she says, stunned, before recovering. "You've had quite a day, babe."

"You could say that. And then I find out he stole my presentation." My head falls to my hands and I release the flood of emotions I've been restraining. "This is the man I was supposed to marry?" I drop my hands, letting out a ragged breath. My voice trembles when I ask, "How can I still love him, Gretch?"

"Do you really love him?"

"Yes ... No ... I don't know. I'm so stupid! I don't understand how he could have loved me and then done such messed-up things. I thought I knew him. I trusted him, gave my heart to him—only to have it ripped out of my chest. Why did I let him do this to me?" The tears I've been fighting threaten to spill over.

"I feel like something changed about a year ago. At least that's when I noticed it. He got distant and moody and started skipping out on things."

"I remember. I noticed too. When I questioned him about it, he proposed. I figured he was nervous about taking such a big leap."

"You never really know someone. But the more you sit here and question yourself, the more you'll drive yourself bat-shit crazy. Trust me. My mother used to say this to me and I think you should hear it: love is a verb—it's an action. Can you tell me what he did to *show* you he loved you? Anyone can say the words, but they need to prove it. His choices are his choices and now you have to make yours." Gretchen grabs my hand and holds it tight.

In the beginning he did show me. He cared and did things to make sure I felt special. It was the little things that meant the most—the handholding, the stolen moments between us, an unexpected note or text—but slowly that all changed.

"I know I'm not to blame for his choices, but *his* choices affected the rest of *my* life," I reply, my voice filled with bitterness and hurt.

"That's where you're wrong, hun. What he did affects today—but *you* decide if it affects tomorrow. The only power he has is the power you give him. You know how brave and strong I think you are. Not many people could handle what you saw and dealt with. Sure, you cried, but you still went to work, kicked ass, and found a way to smile."

It's liberating finally letting it all out. With Ashton I always guard a small part of myself—the vulnerable side. Sure, we share everything, for the most part, but she's so much stronger than me. Gretchen would let me sulk and mope forever, but Ashton doesn't play that game.

"Oh, if you would have seen me, I don't think you'd be saying that." I laugh and squeeze her hand.

Gretchen smiles with warmth and love. "I did see you. I saw the mess you were, but I saw the strength behind it too. Look at you now. You had a fucked-up day, but you're not sitting here sobbing. You're surviving, and you're up for yet another promotion. Of course there are going to be bad days, but you dictate how many. I don't want to mother you, but anytime you want to talk, you know I'm here."

My phone rings, interrupting our heart-to-heart. Taylor's name flashes across the screen, which is odd because we usually text or email. She never calls, not unless it's an emergency.

"I gotta grab this."

"No worries. I have to get going anyway. I love you! Remember what I said, though." She stands, giving me a kiss on the cheek before heading to the door. I smile at how great our impromptu visit was, waving as the door closes behind her and the phone rings again.

"Hi, Tay."

"Sorry to bother you, but I thought you'd want to know immediately," she replies excitedly.

"Okay, what's going on?"

"Raven Cosmetics called. They'd like to speak with you first thing tomorrow morning. They asked if you'd be available for an 8 a.m. phone conference with the CEO. I said absolutely. I hope that's okay," she says nervously.

"Yes, of course. I hope this is a good thing."

"I'm sure it is. I'll confirm the meeting and email you the details."

"Thanks. I'll work from home in the morning and be in the office around eleven," I tell her.

"See you then. Let me know if you need anything before you come in."

"I will. Have a great night."

I hang up the phone, surprised that we're having a conference call instead of another meeting. I don't know what that means, but I need to stay positive. I did the best I could, and all in all I feel good about how I presented. Even with Piper being in my face and unwanted thoughts of her and Neil resurfacing every time I looked at them, I kept it together.

There's a part of me that still doesn't understand how it all happened. What could possibly have brought them together? Sure, she has beautiful blond hair and bright blue eyes, but I never thought Neil saw her as more than a friend. I never imagined she'd be the demise of our relationship.

I hear my phone chirp and look down, hoping it's Ash letting me know she's close.

Ashton: Hey. I got tied up at work.

Me: It's fine.

Ashton: I think I'm staying in the city tonight. You ok?

Me: I'll be fine.

Of course she's not going to come home the one time I

need her to. Is anything going to go my way today? I needed my ex-fiancé to act like an adult, I needed him to leave me alone and not make an attempt to further obliterate me, and I needed my best friend to help me cope when said ex asshole ignored my needs completely and behaved like a selfish bastard.

My phone starts ringing and I see Ashton's face pop up on my screen.

I smile to myself, swiping to answer. "I'm okay, Ash."

She giggles. "Liar. I can tell by your text message that you're not. What happened today?"

"Well, let's see. First, Piper consults for Raven Cosmetics, so she was in the meeting."

"What?" she shouts. "Did you punch her in the throat? Or bitch-slap her? I wish I could've seen that."

"Yeah, Ashton, that's what I did in a client meeting. No, I didn't, although I wanted to." I take a deep breath and quickly tell her the story of my afternoon with all the sordid details and drama.

"What did you do to piss God off? I've never met anyone who has such shitty luck." Ash laughs. "No matter what happens, this will work out. If not, we'll get drunk and make fun of people."

"I still don't know why the hell I keep you around. I gotta go. I have an early phone meeting with the Raven people and I need to be prepared."

"Okay. I probably won't make it home. The new doctor is up my ass about the clinical trials he's running. I need to be in the lab in case something happens. I'm sorry I can't be home for you today, but please promise me you won't eat a pint of ice cream. Just break out the old rabbit and—"

"And that's where we hang up. Thanks for the advice. I love you."

"Love you too. Seriously, an orgasm will totally—"

I disconnect before she can finish, laughing at her ability

to change my mood. There are no words for that girl. She really is my twisted sister. I decide it's time to throw myself into work.

As I sit at the table, I replay the day's events. If I were an outsider, they'd be hilarious. Since I'm the one involved, however, they're not. I have two choices: either I do my best and win the only way I can, or I lie down and let Neil win. Right now, I'm more eager than ever to nail this phone interview and win this job. I go straight to my desk, change my email password, along with the passwords for any other account I may have logged in to from his computer, and get to work on my Raven project.

When I finally look at the clock, two hours have passed and I've accomplished a lot. I crunched numbers with an intensity I haven't felt in a long time. I'm ready for tomorrow.

As I step into my room, all the confidence I built up working over the past few hours vanishes. I look around, feeling uncomfortable and ashamed. It looks like a disaster zone in here. This isn't me. I've always been neat and organized, ready to tackle the world. But the person living here is anything but that. My side table is covered in dirty dishes, piles of clothes are scattered everywhere, the trashcan is overflowing with tissues, and empty ice cream containers and candy wrappers litter the floor. Is this what I've become?

Feeling determined to pull myself together and start rebuilding my life, I begin cleaning up my room, finding my strength through cleanliness and organization. Sometimes putting things in their rightful place is therapeutic. Right now, it's giving me some small measure of control. The hurt and pain are still there, but I need to put this behind me. I need to move on.

Today has reminded me that the life I thought I had and the man I thought I loved aren't things I should want anymore. The future I dream of doesn't look like this. It's full of devotion and happiness, not sadness and betrayal. I deserve more.

Silently, I promise myself to guard my heart from now on. Love is a gift, and I will not give it freely to anyone.

Just as I'm thinking this, I accidentally knock over a frame, which crashes to the ground. Though the glass doesn't shatter, when I pick it up I see a huge crack down the center between Neil's face and mine. Broken—like we are. It's the photo from our first anniversary. I'm clinging to his back and he's looking adoringly at me with a huge smile on his face. We were so happy and in love. It shone through our eyes as we laughed at whatever joke we shared. We were always playful and silly in the beginning—he brought that out in me. But at some point it stopped. We went from happy to comfortable, and then he made his choices.

I can't keep thinking about this. All I want is freedom from him and this idea of what our relationship was or could have been. Alone in my room, I let it all go. Silent rivers of tears stream down my face as the weight of the last three months comes crashing around me. All the lies, hurt, and infidelity, the broken promises ... it's destroyed a part of me. I know that even when I'm fully over everything, there's a part of my heart that will never be repaired. There's a fissure that will always be there, a wound that will one day heal and scar over, but it will never be forgotten.

Grabbing an empty box, I start to place the pictures and the memories that accompany them away. I'll never heal if I keep pretending he'll come back. I glance at our engagement photo. It's amazing the difference between this picture and our first anniversary shot. He's not looking at me like he did in the first photo. In this one he's barely smiling—his eyes look empty, as though he's looking past me, not at me. Why didn't I ever notice that? I was so blinded by my need to be loved that I overlooked the truths that were staring at me every day.

Intent on putting things away, I eye the jewelry box that holds my engagement ring. Tentatively, I open the lid and stare at the shiny diamond nestled in the ring slot. I place it on my finger one last time, and the light creates prisms that bounce off the walls as I twist it around. Tears continue, but instead of feeling weighted by them, I feel as though each one is cleansing me. Reluctantly, I take it off my finger and tuck it back in the ring slot. Back in the box that I received from the other man in my life that I wasn't enough for. I pull out my "Fuck You" ring that I purchased for myself with Neil's money and slide it on my finger. Even though the purpose of the ring was to distract me from Neil and my empty ring finger, when I look at it now I remember Neil. I don't want to remember anymore. I take the sapphire ring off, placing it next to my engagement ring. They are a symbol of the past going where it needs to go—away.

While I'm clearing out my heart, I decide that my father's last gift and the belongings inside it need to be put to rest. These are two men who've caused me tremendous pain—their love was tainted, if it ever was love, and I have no room for it anymore.

Glancing around the room, feeling better about the way it looks, I grab the jewelry box representing my father and Neil and place it on the top shelf in my closet. Staring at the ornate box for a moment, I allow a few final tears to fall as I say good-bye. Then I close my closet door and lie in bed, noticing as I drift off to sleep how my heart feels lighter and how breathing isn't quite as hard as it has been.

chapter

six

*T*HE ALARM BLARES at six the next morning. I roll over, hit the off button, and shuffle into the kitchen to start my Keurig. It's amazing how much better I feel after having a night of restful sleep. Grabbing my cup of coffee, I head to my desk to prepare for my phone call with the people from Raven.

With coffee in hand, I fire up my laptop and get to work. The new email alert sounds off so long that it almost seems as if I've held my finger down on a keyboard for a minute or so. Great. I'm out of the office half a day and I have over one hundred new emails. I skim through and see a few new possible client assignments that look promising and one that I'd love to grab if Raven Cosmetics doesn't work out. I open the email from Taylor, which goes over the details for today's call, and see that she's attached a few files with updated sales figures for the company. They show a small decline from last month's figures but nothing too drastic.

After going through the remainder of my emails and taking care of some mundane things around the house, the conference call reminder pops up on my phone. Dialing in, I mentally prepare myself to hear Piper's and Neil's voices so I won't be blindsided by them. I hear the beep and announce my name and company.

"Hello, Ms. Pope. This is Danielle."

"Good morning, Danielle. I hope your morning is good so

far."

"Yes, thank you. We appreciate you fitting us in last-minute," she replies.

"As I promised in our meeting, I haven't taken on any other accounts in hopes that you'll select CJJ to represent you," I say, projecting my strength through the phone.

"I'm glad to hear that. After we conclude our call, we have a call scheduled with Boyce PR. Mr. Cole should be on in about two minutes. We were advised by Piper of her opinion, and we want to be one hundred percent sure we choose the right person."

"I understand completely. Do you have anything you'd like me to clear up prior to Mr. Cole joining us?" I ask earnestly.

"Our questions this morning will focus on you and your company. I think either company would provide a similar approach, but we would like to know more about you since you would be the person primarily responsible for ensuring clear and consistent branding. Also, I wanted to let you know that I'm not an assistant—I'm actually the director of product development. I'm sorry I wasn't honest, but I wanted to get a feel for both you and Neil without either of you being influenced by my title."

"Honestly, Danielle, I never believed you were an assistant, but thank you for being frank." I let out a short laugh. "I assure you—"

A tone cuts me off, alerting us that someone has joined the call.

"Good morning." A deep, hoarse voice fills my ears. My body tenses and something stirs deep inside. "Danielle?" he asks.

"Yes, Mr. Cole, good morning. I have Catherine Pope on the call, sir. She's with CJJ Public Relations," Danielle informs him.

I shake my head, trying to release the tension triggered by his voice, and prepare to impress him. "Good morning, Mr.

Cole. It's a pleasure."

"Ms. Pope, thank you for joining us. Danielle was impressed by your presentation. I asked to have a call with you since I was out of the area and couldn't make it to the meeting yesterday. I wanted to speak with you and the other candidate before I make my final decision." The strong, sexy timbre of his voice exudes confidence.

"I'm more than happy to go over any questions you may have."

The call continues for about thirty minutes as we discuss my professional background and the company's growth expectations. The sound of his voice pulls at me, though I can't quite place it. With each question he asks, I field and answer appropriately, reaffirming that I'm the right choice.

Mr. Cole breaks in right before we're about to wrap things up. "I'd like to know one more thing."

"Ask away." I smile, hoping it shines through the phone.

"Why should we hire you?" he asks point-blank.

I anticipated this question. It's pretty typical and I honestly love to answer it. There's no real reason other than what I always answer. "Because I'm the best. I work hard, and I don't fail. Ever," I say confidently.

His deep voice vibrates through the phone. "We'll be in touch by the end of the day with our final answer. Thank you, Catherine."

When he says my first name, a familiar feeling washes over me. Though I'd love to take the time to analyze why that is, my professionalism prevents me from dwelling. "I look forward to hearing from you. Have a wonderful day."

"Thank you, Ms. Pope," Danielle replies.

Then the line goes dead.

And I wait.

Again.

After taking a long shower, I stand in front of my closet debating what to wear. The warm water helped ease my residual anxiety from the phone call, but I need something that will make me feel sexy and strong. It's still warm out, so I opt for my navy blue empire dress and pair it with my dark crimson heels. I smile at my reflection in the mirror—I look good. I decide to take some extra time on my makeup and hair. Large barrel curls soften the ends of my dark brown hair, and I leave them hanging loosely down my back. For my makeup, I choose a really soft smoky eye, which gives me that coveted mysterious look. Not bad. This is the Catherine Pope I know and remember.

Once I arrive at the office, I settle into my desk and ... feel useless. I don't know if I won the account yet and my last two clients finished last week. I cleared out most of my emails at home, so I have nothing to work on. My ambition and work ethic won't allow for me to sit around, so I decide to look at the open bids board and start mock-ups for a pitch. I have no idea if I'll get the Raven account and I don't want to waste any time getting to work on the next possible account coming in. Plus, my coworker Elle is the only other person competing with me for the upcoming promotion. I can't let her get ahead, so I need to focus and act as though I've lost this one.

I head over to the board to see what's there, and Elle looks up, grinning broadly at me. "Already looking for a new account, Cat?" Her high-pitched voice pierces through the room.

I give her a fake smile. "No, just looking to see what came in. What about you?"

"Oh, you know, I've got some new models coming in for a shoot. Atelier Clothing wants to do a tour with hot guys. You should stop by and see the eye candy I have coming in!" She's practically bouncing. I have no desire to see the "hot" guys she has lined up. She has the worst taste, especially when it comes to the way she does ads and press releases. I can only imagine what the guys will look like. I'll never understand her choices. They always seem overdone to me.

"Oh, I wish I could." I feign disappointment and stifle the

comments rolling around in my mind. "I have a few things that need my attention, but I'm *sure* they're drool worthy." I can't stop myself. "You sure know how to pick 'em."

She smiles, thinking I'm complimenting her. "I know! I love the one I found today. His name is Colin, and he's just ... wow!"

I smile and look back to the board. "Good luck, Elle. I gotta get back to work."

I add my name to the next best account on the board and head back to my office. When I get there, I send Taylor an email to be in my office in fifteen minutes to start research.

I hear a knock on the door and look up.

"Hey. You want to do research for a new company looking for representation?" Taylor is standing against the doorframe looking baffled.

"Yes, we can't have all our eggs in one basket," I reply and gesture for her to sit in the chair.

"Okay, but doesn't that seem hasty?" she asks tentatively. "You should hear back by the end of the day, right?"

"I don't think so. It's been over three hours since the call ended, and I haven't heard anything. For all I know they've offered Boyce the account and are waiting until they settle the deal before they call me. I can't sit here and do nothing. You know me." I shrug with a smile. "Anyway, the promotion is still up for grabs and I refuse to let Elle get a leg up. Are you ready to get to work?"

"Of course. Let's dig in." Taylor smiles and we get to work on researching the new company.

We're immersed in our iPads and computers and have completely lost track of time when I look at the clock, realizing it's almost five. I start to stretch but jump midway as the phone rings, startling me.

Taylor runs to her desk, grabs the receiver, and pokes her head around. "Cat, it's Raven. Want me to shut the door?"

"Yes. Thank you."

This is it. I grab the phone and take a deep breath before

pushing the blinking button that will finally end the waiting.

"Hello, this is Catherine Pope."

"Hi, Catherine. It's Danielle. I wanted to let you know we've made our decision." Her voice is steady, giving nothing away.

"Wonderful, I hope you're calling with good news."

"Yes, we'd like CJJ to be our new PR firm. Congratulations."

I let out a huge breath and stop myself from dancing around the room. "Oh! Thank you, I'm glad you chose us. I look forward to working with you."

"Us too. We're very excited about your vision. I know this is last-minute but Mr. Cole arrived back in the city today. He would like you to meet him tonight at the office if possible," she responds hesitantly.

I've already stated I would be available for this project, and even though I want to celebrate, I can't wait to get started. There's a new feeling of determination and excitement coursing through my veins. I could probably run the forty blocks to Raven Cosmetics with all the energy I have right now, but not in these heels. I want to hit the ground running, impress him and everyone else, and then land the promotion.

"Yes, that would be fine. What time would he like to meet?"

"Can you be here around six? I have to leave the office to head to our production facility tomorrow, so I'll be heading home to pack, but I'll leave your information with security."

"Perfect. I'll be there." We say our good-byes and I can't help the smile stretched across my face. I message Taylor to come into my office.

She enters with a tentative smile, as if she wasn't listening at the door. Inside I'm doing cartwheels—I needed this. I feel strong, confident, and again—I beat Neil. Even though I don't want to think of him, I enjoy this victory and relish the fact that despite his efforts to sabotage me, I still won.

My smile widens, if that's even possible. "We got it! Oh my

God, Tay! We got the account!"

"Ahhh! I knew it!" she squeals with as much excitement as I'm feeling and rushes over, giving me a huge hug. She pulls back, keeping her arms on my shoulders. "I never doubted you! So what happens next?"

"I have to meet Mr. Cole at six. Can you call and have a cab or a car waiting? I want to make sure I'm on time." She nods and zooms back out of my office. I only have thirty minutes to get there, and it's at least a twenty-minute cab ride with the traffic at this hour.

I start to pace. The adrenaline and excitement is starting to ebb—I'm anxious because now that I have the account, I have to implement all my ideas and gain the trust of the CEO. Nervous energy fills my body and I grab my iPad to start taking notes on all the things I want to lobby for.

Taylor buzzes the intercom. "I have a cab downstairs. Good luck and congrats again. Now go kick some ass." She giggles and disconnects.

I grab my purse and rush out of the office, throwing a quick good-bye over my shoulder. Throughout the ride to Raven Cosmetics I go over my key notes, examine some of my earlier sales figures, and plan to spend the next few days really honing in on the company's core values. When I get there, I hop out of the cab, prepared to make one hell of an impression.

Entering the building, I make my way over to security. The guard hands me the badge that Danielle left for me and calls Mr. Cole, letting him know I've arrived. I'm told to head straight to the office, where he'll be waiting for me.

Luckily the elevator is empty, so I have a minute to mentally prepare. Taking a few deep breaths, I start to form some ideas on how to best sell him on my plan. I also wonder about the man himself. I've met a lot of executives, but there's something about his voice. The deep, raspy sound has me curious as to what triggered the familiarity. I haven't really had time to think about it until now. Surely I would remember if we'd met or spent any significant amount of time together. I'm pretty good at remembering people and small details; it's part of why I excel at my job. As the elevator ascends, so does my anxiety.

Before I have another second to think about it, the door opens. My eyes immediately lock on familiar blue-green ones and the breathtaking face of the man who I've dreamed of for the last week.

chapter

seven

My FREE HAND flies to my mouth in disbelief. "Jackson," I say, barely audible.

Jackson stands there looking absolutely magnificent—he's everything I remember and more. He's wearing a crisp white dress shirt with the sleeves rolled up—the top two buttons undone—and dark gray, perfectly tailored dress pants. His hair is disheveled, like he's been running his hands through the dark brown locks. He steps forward and places his hands on the elevator doors to prevent them from closing. His eyes haven't left mine, and the cocky grin I remember is present as he processes who I am. He shakes his head back and forth in disbelief and gives a small half laugh. I look down and shift my weight, afraid to speak and unable to move forward.

He clears his throat, forcing me to look up. He finally speaks first. "You're Catherine Pope?" he asks, sounding amused as he tries to smother his grin.

I nod my head in response.

He extends his hand, inviting me to exit and reminding me that I'm still standing on the elevator. I place my hand in his and the electric current, which I've tried to convince myself I'd imagined, buzzes through my entire body, energizing every nerve from head to toe. Jackson pulls me forward, still unspeaking.

He's unbelievably sexy and try as I might, my eyes refuse

to look away while he measures his next words. Jackson steps back, pulling me with him toward the office. What are the odds? I never thought I'd see this man again, and now he's standing in front of me, smiling and shaking his head, almost mirroring my own response. Of all the accounts and all the men *he* had to be Jackson Cole.

Jackson clears his throat again, breaking into my thoughts. "You're even more beautiful than I remember." He looks down at our hands and the shift in his attitude is unmistakable, as if he's considering the current relationship we now share.

I remove my hand from his and pull myself together. He's my client. I'm a professional.

"Thank you, Mr. Cole. CJJ is proud that you chose our vision to take your company forward." I smile and mentally high-five myself for saying that without stuttering.

He chuckles at my attempt at professionalism. "Oh, let me assure you, this project is quickly becoming my favorite," he says with amusement, looking me up and down. His deep, sexy voice travels straight to my core. "The more I think about it, the more I think I'm going to enjoy working with you."

I lick my lips as I stare at his mouth. I need to get it together. This is my job. He's just a man, a very sexy and fuckable man, but still—he's my client. I'm not about to be seduced by his gorgeous face or ripped abs and defined arms—nope, not going to happen.

Bring on the delusions.

I smile tentatively. "Shall we get to our meeting?" I ask as my voice shakes, betraying my nerves.

"We're going to play it that way, are we?" He smirks, obviously amused. "Okay, Ms. Pope. Right this way," he says as he looks directly into my eyes, saying so much more with his body than with his mouth. His perfectly formed, totally kissable—

My thoughts are scattered. I want to run back into the elevator and tell him to give the account to Boyce. I don't know how I'm going to be around him for days on end. We've spent a total of five minutes together and he already has me in hyperdrive.

"Thank you," I mumble.

He extends his arm, showing me where to go. I shift my purse on my shoulder and begin walking. When he places his hand on the small of my back, I shiver inadvertently. I feel his warmth through my shirt, burning my skin. I'm mentally berating myself for acting like this.

"Are you cold?" he asks with humor in his voice, somehow aware his touch is wreaking havoc on me.

I turn and look directly in his eyes, hoping to convey my own message of strength and defiance. "No, I'm fine. Thank you." I was strong and confident this morning, but now I feel like I'm on the edge of a cliff. I smile and straighten my back, trying to walk past him as he stands in the doorway. He's left me very little room to get through, though, so I shift to the side, scooting by without touching him. Of course, it's impossible and my arm slides against his, causing goose bumps to form in the wake of our skin-to-skin contact.

His office is nothing like I would have imagined. It has a feminine feel to it. He has a glass desk table with a high-back chair. The walls are cream and the couch is a light lilac color. There are no photos, no personal touches throughout the room. I fight the urge to laugh—this is definitely not a man's office.

Jackson clears his throat again and I wonder if it's a nervous habit of his. Could he be as nervous as I am? "I just moved into this office," he begins, pausing as if carefully weighing his next words. "The person before me was obviously a female. Danielle was the acting CEO for the last ten months. I haven't had time to change anything." He closes his eyes, looking almost pained. I have the strangest urge to comfort him, but I resist.

"I understand. But for the record, purple's not your color." I sit in one of the chairs in front of his desk and start to get out my mock boards and planning sheet.

"No? And what color would you recommend, Ms. Pope?" Jackson asks, smiling.

"Hmmm, I'd say pink." I look around before returning my gaze to him. "Definitely pink."

Jackson comes around and sits in the chair next to me instead of behind the desk. His cologne assaults my senses as I inhale, breathing in all its masculinity. It's even better than I remember and so much stronger.

I open my eyes to see him staring at me with a wide smile. He shifts in his seat and props his arm on the back of mine. "Pink, huh? Well only real men wear pink, and I assure you, Catherine, I'm all the real you'll ever need."

I cough, trying to regain my focus as his eyes bore into me.

"So, fall on any more men at dinner lately?"

And there it is.

"Actually, no. Thanks for being concerned, though." I laugh while shaking my head.

"Good to know. I'd be jealous if you had."

"Anyway, I brought the mock-up and I emailed Danielle the video."

"I saw the video. It's the reason you're here now and not the other company." His compliment washes over me. He didn't hire me because he knew me, no. It was because of my vision and my plan for his company.

"I'm glad I impressed you."

Jackson shifts in his chair and crosses his leg, getting closer to me. "I'm hoping there are many ways you'll endeavor to impress me." His tone is light and joking, but his eyes suggest the truth in his words.

He can't touch me or I'll crack. I try to move back in my chair, but there's nowhere to go. I stand and start to pace. I'm nervous, wound up, and out of my element.

"Mr. Cole—"

"Jackson. You should call me Jackson. We'll be together

a lot," he cuts me off. I turn to look out the window, trying to gather my thoughts.

I'm freaking out. I can't do my job and work with *him*. I can't think straight around him—he's too much. Too sexy. Too intense. Too all-consuming. How am I going to do this? I can't focus around him and if Jackson touches me, I'll crumble. On the other hand, if I walk away from this account, I'll never get the promotion. Shit. I could lose my job. Wouldn't that be the icing on Neil's cake? He would get the account and I'd be unemployed. No. No way. I can do this. I have to be strong.

I really need a vacation from my life.

I turn and he's standing so close behind me that I almost collide with him. "Mr.—Jackson, I think we should go over your company's goals and make a plan. It's getting late."

Jackson walks over behind his desk and sits in his chair. I follow, returning to the chair I was in before, thankful for the desk between us. If I can maintain distance and space with zero physical contact, then I can keep the account and my job. Let's see how long this plan will last.

"How about we grab dinner?" he casually says.

"Dinner?"

"Yes, you know that meal that comes after lunch. I haven't eaten yet and you probably haven't either." His eyes don't waver from mine.

"I can't. I have to do—"

"I'm pretty sure the stipulation was that you're available whenever I need you." He raises his brow as he taps his fingers on his desk.

"Yes, but we've yet to sign our contract." I smile sweetly, but I can't keep the exasperation out of my voice.

He stands and walks around the desk slowly. Each step is measured and deliberate. Every moment stirs something within me. My anxiety is already sky-high. I can't take much more of this tonight. When he's finally in front of me, he leans back on his desk and his voice drops when he asks, "Where's the contract?"

I reach into my bag and pull out the paperwork that will solidify the deal. This is my last chance to walk away from him. I'll have to see him, smell him, be around him, and there will be no backing out without me losing everything. Once he signs this, it's over. I hold the papers in my hand, which is visibly shaking from my poorly concealed unease. Jackson reaches out, silently asking me to hand it over.

I stand and walk toward him with the contract extended between us. He grabs it and leans on his desk, signing on the dotted line without even reading it. Jackson puts the pen down and turns back to me. Though he doesn't voice it, his expression says, "Gotcha."

"Well, Ms. Pope, there's no turning back now."

I bite my bottom lip and my stomach drops as Jackson hands me back the signed contract. Oh God, what did I just do? I'm so stupid and in so much trouble. It's as if he has some inside knowledge of what makes me tick, like he sees right through my layers of bullshit, straight to my libido. No man has ever made me this unbalanced. Even when Neil and I first started dating, I don't think I was ever this scattered. But with Jackson I'm a mess.

I stare into his beautiful eyes. They're dancing with humor. He smirks and holds my gaze, unwilling to break away first. Both of us struggle to gain the upper hand, knowing whomever breaks first is somehow showing they're weaker than the other. I hold my eyes steady and smile, hoping they aren't showing the internal war going on inside my head. I need to say something and put an end to this. "Mr. Cole, thank you for signing the contract. I really do need to go now."

"We just made a deal and I told you to call me Jackson, twice. Now, let's head to dinner," he commands, his voice leaving no room for discussion.

"Jackson, please." I take a deep breath, my eyes begging for understanding. "I really can't tonight." I have no good reason and if he pushes me, I'll cave. My only reason is he scares me. I don't trust myself around him.

He stands and walks over to my chair again. He grasps my chin between his finger and rough thumb. The feel of his skin against mine causes my pulse to race. I'm sure he can hear it. Just like the first night we met, he holds my face steady as he stares into my eyes, searching for something. "Fine, not tonight. However, I need you to meet me here Monday by 9 a.m. There are a few meetings I want you to sit in on with the production team and then we leave for Virginia on Friday."

"Virginia?" I ask, completely thrown off.

"Yes, it's a state a few states below New York." His grin grows and his dimple deepens with his taunting.

"I know where Virginia is." *Ass.* "I wasn't aware you had an office there."

"Our production plant is there. I'd like you to fly out with me this week, see some of the new products that are being developed, and tell me your ideas for future campaigns. If this one goes well, hopefully we can work together on a more permanent basis." He raises an eyebrow suggestively.

I shift in my seat and try to calm my heart, which is threatening to fly out of my chest. Future campaigns? Ugh! This would solidify my career at CJJ. There's no way I can refuse him. Damn him and his gorgeous face. "Okay, next Friday will be fine. I can meet you here Monday morning as well."

Jackson grabs my bag and offers his hand to help me stand. I take it and the contact causes heat to pool in my center, again. A simple touch is all it takes for me to become a puddle at his feet. Who am I kidding? All it took was the sound of his voice. I turn my head away, trying to hide any emotions showing on my face. He gently pulls me up. He's close, so close. It's like he's everywhere. His cologne, the warmth of his body—it's all encompassing.

Feeling overwhelmed and dizzy, I start to tilt. Jackson moves his hand to my hip to steady me. His deep voice does nothing to calm my nerves. "Easy. You don't want to fall into my arms again."

"Yes, that would be a tragedy." I blink hard, shaking my head and trying not to focus on the way my body is heating from his touch.

"I wouldn't go that far. I can think of far worse places to land. The ground for one."

I laugh and try to take a step back, but I'm stuck. "Right. I have a feeling I'm going to pay for that for a long time."

"What? Me catching you? I would've let it go if you'd stayed and had a drink with us." He smirks.

If there were ever a time I wanted the ground to open and swallow me, this is it. "If this is going to be my punishment, I almost wish you would've let me fall," I kid.

"Now where would the fun in that be?"

I nod and start to head toward the door. "I really have to go. I'll see myself out. Thank you for your time." I turn my back and exit his office.

I should have known he'd follow me. I sense him before I hear him. Deciding to ignore him and get the hell out of here, I start moving quickly, hoping he gives up and goes back to his office. I hear him chuckle behind me as if he can read my mind. Right as I reach the exit, his hand presses against the door so I can't open it.

I huff and turn with my back flush against the door and— Jackson is so close. It's like my dream, only this time I'm not at my car. The cold glass is doing nothing to help the fire burning within me.

He takes a deep breath, and neither of us speaks as his hand slides down the door until it's next to my shoulder. Ever so slowly, he lifts his left hand and caresses it down my arm, stopping at my wrist. Lifting and opening my fingers, he places something in my palm then closes my fingers back around it. Still neither of us has spoken a word, but it feels as if we've had an entire conversation. Jackson leans forward and I think he's going to kiss me. I close my eyes, silently praying that he will. Instead he uses his weight and pushes himself back upright. I feel his warmth evaporate and it takes all my strength not to wrap myself around him and get lost in his touch. Jackson smiles, looks at my hand, and turns away without saying a word.

Somehow I manage to keep myself from collapsing and make my way to the elevator. Once inside with the doors shut, I slide to the floor and close my eyes. I inhale deeply, trying to calm myself. Remembering that he placed something in my hand, I unclench my fingers and look down to find a business card. On the back, scribbled in short, precise strokes, is a message.

Catherine, this is my
personal cell phone.
Call anytime.

"Why didn't you ever tell me about him?" Ashton continues to question me. She's been grilling me for the last hour.

I haven't seen her at all over the last few days. She's been staying at the lab because of the clinical trials, and the one night she was home, I had a dinner meeting with the other publicists from my office. By the time I got back, Ashton was already passed out. Needing some girl time, we decided to spend the weekend relaxing before I have to deal with Jackson again. We're now on our second bottle of wine. During our first bottle, I was a mess—trying to form words while rehashing all the details about Neil and Piper, then about Jackson. She was quiet and listened to me get it all out, constantly filling my glass and offering me silent support. However, during the consumption of bottle number two, we've moved on to complete giddiness and feeling no pain. We're now laughing over all the stuff I was upset about an hour ago. Of course, Ashton finds it highly entertaining—I find it disturbing and unfair.

"I don't know, Ashton. What the hell was I going to say? I tripped over a chair and fell on a ridiculously hot guy? I felt stupid enough. I didn't need your shit too." I laugh and gulp my wine.

"Only you! I swear this shit never happens to anyone else I know. So what are you going to do? I mean he's hot and he's obviously sexually attracted to you." She raises her eyebrow and grins.

"I'm not going to do anything. He's my client."

"So? Who says you can't service your boss?" She winks and giggles.

"I can't believe you. You would never sleep with the doctors in the lab, would you?"

"Who says I haven't? Plus, they're all ugly as shit. If there was a hot one, I'd totally play doctor and let him cure me." She lays her hand across her head in mockery.

"You have issues." I groan at the sheer ridiculousness of my situation. "What the hell am I going to do?"

"You're going to do what you always do—you'll go in there and fight all of your emotions and kick some corporate ass. Then you'll come home and wallow in your Ben & Jerry's, be miserable, and cry yourself to sleep. Eventually, you'll waste all your chances for a real connection and sabotage your own happiness." She shrugs and refuses to break eye contact.

I gasp at the cruelty—and accuracy—of her statement. "What the hell, Ashton?"

"Sorry, Cat, but it's true. You knew things were wrong with Neil, but instead of leaving him, you got engaged. Before him there was Eli. You stayed with him for years because he was safe and you thought you deserved the sheer *hell* he put you through. I'm not trying to hurt you." She scoots over and puts her arm around me, pulling me into a hug. "I'm just telling you that whether this guy was your client or not, you'd find a reason to destroy yourself over him."

My heart clenches at her words. It hurts so much coming from Ashton. I know she loves me, but I hate what she's saying. "I don't understand why every guy I meet or date lets me down."

"You need to stop looking for this perfect guy. You need to get out of your own head and start having fun. Once the product is released, who knows where you and this Jackson guy will be? Maybe you'll like him. Maybe he'll be the world's biggest piece of shit. Either way, you need to figure *you* out before you fret about all this. Monday morning, go to your meeting, be the kick-ass girl I know you are, and blow them all away." She smiles reassuringly before picking up the empty wine glasses and bottles and heading into the kitchen.

I grab a pillow and clutch it to my chest. She's right. It's not like I even know Jackson or have any connection to him, other than this crazy feeling I get when I'm around him. I need to focus on my life for once. I don't have to take anyone else into account. The realization is liberating. Now I need to figure out a way to make my body stop reacting to Jackson and all his sexiness.

chapter

eight

FOR THE THIRD night in a row, I've slept like complete shit. I tossed and turned all night, tormented by images of Jackson and me rolling around in my bed. It was pure heaven. Then I woke up and realized none of the amazing things he just did to me were real. Now I'm all keyed up and have to go to a meeting where I'll spend the majority of my time trying not to stare at his gorgeous face. I groan and roll over, punching my pillow, wishing that I could call in sick today. But I'm no chicken shit, so I throw my covers off and head into the bathroom.

I strip out of my clothes and enter the waterfall shower, turning on the side jets. The hot water relaxes my muscles as my mind wanders to—who else?—Jackson. I need a plan on how to handle him—he makes me feel too much. He's even taken over my subconscious while I sleep. Last night's vivid dream of Jackson touching me, licking me, and claiming me rushes back, rekindling my need for relief. I close my eyes, letting the steam envelop me as I start to remember the way he played with my body, as if he'd been doing it for years.

The warm scent of my vanilla body wash relaxes me as I gently rub the soap over my curves. I lean back against the cold shower tiles and slowly move my hands to my breasts, circling the soap, imagining it's his mouth on me. My nipples harden as I tease myself. I start to gasp and moan, fantasizing that his hands and voice are coaxing me on, telling me how much he wants me. The demand to release becomes stronger as I get lost in the sensations. My hand slides down my slick skin until it finds my clit, circling the bundle of nerves, pushing me further and further into ecstasy. My muscles clench as I envision Jackson's fingers, his body covering mine and entering me. I insert one finger, climbing higher, higher, moaning and quivering. My release comes fast and hard as I increase the friction, finally erupting. I'm panting as bursts of light blur my vision.

Eventually, I come down from my euphoric state, finish my shower, and manage to dress myself without any major catastrophe. Hopefully the release will alleviate some of the tension in my body and make it easier to deal with Jackson. I make it to the train without a minute to spare, but at least it's nice and quiet. I'm hoping I can hold on to this blissful feeling all day.

Once I arrive in Manhattan, a new set of emotions overcomes me. Raw strength and determination flow through me. There's something about working in New York City. You can almost feel the power in the streets. It's a breeding ground for success. Being here, working here, living here—it's invigorating.

Standing in front of Jackson's building, I see my reflection in the glass. I certainly look the part. I have on a soft cream blouse tucked into a pair of high-waisted gray suit pants. My long hair is pin straight, my dark brown eyes look soft with only a wisp of mascara, and sheer lip gloss accentuates my lips. My black heels elongate my tiny frame, making me feel tall and bold. With my posture straight, I enter the office, heading up to face Jackson and start kicking ass.

The same sweet receptionist guides me back to the conference room where my initial meeting was held. I'm a little early, so there isn't anyone else in the room yet. I'm removing items from my bag when I hear the door click open. Jackson's voice floats through the space.

"Yes, I'm aware of your opinion on the matter. However, I've made my choice." He sounds irritated.

A second voice responds, but I can't make out what they're saying. It's a female, though, and by her tone I can tell she's trying to make him listen to her.

"I don't care or agree with you," he responds to whatever the comment was. Another long pause as I strain to hear her response. The door inches open a little more.

"Well, Ms. Carlson, it's a good thing I'm the CEO."

Shit! Piper! My blissful mood drains away.

The door opens and Jackson steps aside to let Piper come in first. She looks up and grimaces when she notices me standing here. Jackson enters. It's as if the world stops moving. His presence would cause the energy in any room to shift, but I can't help wondering if I feel it more intensely than everyone else. It's—he's—intoxicating.

He looks over at me and smiles. "Good morning, Catherine."

"Good morning, Mr. Cole." I smile and look at Piper. "Good morning, Piper. Nice to see you in a color other than nude." The last thing I wish for her is a good morning. However, pleasantries are necessary, and I refuse to let her to take yet another thing from me. But I allow myself the small dig.

She snorts and rolls her eyes.

Bitch.

Jackson doesn't notice her catty behavior. He sits at the head of the table with Piper to his left and me in the chair on his right. He's so close. I can feel the heat radiating from him.

"Okay, let's get started," Jackson says.

We spend the next hour debating and discussing the best way to present the soon-to-be-released makeup line. Piper tries to undermine my opinion at every turn, but I hold my ground. Jackson sits back and interjects only when he feels the need. It seems more like a volleyball game than a meeting. After another hour, she's finally done arguing and agrees with my vision on how to get the company on track.

"Well, ladies, I think we're about done here. It's been rather entertaining." Jackson chuckles and stands, gathering his papers as he does.

Piper leans over to him, trying to keep her voice down. "Mr. Cole, I really think we should talk privately about our options."

A flash of irritation cross his face as he gruffly replies, "Piper, again, I'm well aware of your opinion and the answer is no." Jackson meets my eyes and grins.

I sigh and flush with embarrassment.

"Mr. Cole—"

He raises his hand to stop me. "I asked you to call me Jackson."

Piper stands there slack-jawed with her arms crossed.

"Yes, sorry. Jackson, I've arranged everything for Friday's trip—"

"My secretary will send you the details. I've already arranged to have a car pick you up and take you to the airport. You won't need to worry about anything." He tucks his materials under his arm and pushes in his chair to leave. As he approaches the door he stops, turns to me, and smirks. "Expect to have dinner while we're there." He winks and exits.

Dinner. Of course. I'm never going to avoid this man. He's going to take full advantage of our time together in Virginia. There is no escaping him. If he's persistent enough, I may not be strong enough to resist him. I'm barely hanging on as it is. Except there's the small problem that he's my client, and I could lose everything I've worked for if anything happens between us.

A cough breaks me from my thoughts and I realize I've been staring at the door. I look to see Piper glaring at me. "Are you dating him?" she asks in a condescending tone.

"Excuse me?" I stand so I'm eye level with her, looking at her incredulously. Surely she isn't talking to me like that.

"I asked if you were dating Jackson Cole." She walks toward me and places her hands on the table, leaning in. She raises her eyebrows, waiting for my response.

My eyes widen at her challenge. I glare right back at her with unadulterated hate. "You're insane—and a whore, but we'll revisit that in a minute. Are you seriously talking to me right now?" I'm seething. My body is shaking at her asinine question. She slept with my fiancé and now she's going to stand here and give me shit? I don't think so.

"I'm just surprised, Catherine. Is that how you beat out Neil for this account? *His* numbers were flawless. He deserves to be here, not you," Piper states, tilting her head to the side as she narrows her eyes accusingly.

"Well I'm glad you think so because Neil stole *my* figures!" I step closer to her, radiating anger. First, she has the nerve to insinuate that I won the account because I'm sleeping with Jackson. Then she brings up Neil's stellar figures. "I seriously can't believe you have the balls to address me, let alone accuse me of something. It's none of your business—any of it—but for the record, I got this account because *I'm* the better choice!"

She huffs and rolls her eyes. "Well I guess *I* was the right choice for Neil."

"Wow, Piper, you want to go there? Good, have him! After seeing what he's capable of, I'm glad we're done." I clench my hands, desperate to punch something or someone, like the blond bitch in front of me.

Her eyes flash and venom fills her voice. "You think you're so fucking smart, don't you? You think I give a shit about what *you* think or what you're happy about?" She steps toward me, grinning. "I fucked your fiancé for four months and you had no idea."

My hand flies to my throat. "Four months?" The words slip from my mouth. My stomach plummets and I grab onto the chair for support. Four months of Neil sleeping with her and then sleeping with me? I'm such a fool. I thought it was a one-time thing, not an affair! My chin quivers as I drown in pain and betrayal, but I won't let her see me cry.

"Not so smart now, huh?" A victorious smile spreads from one cheek to the other, and I want to slap it off her arrogant face. That's all it takes for the tightly pulled thread of my control to break. What the actual fuck? Where I was upset a few moments ago, right now my blood is boiling. I won't break down any further in front of this piece of trash.

"I'm not going to stand here and listen to your shit. The only thing you should be saying to me is, 'I'm sorry,' not this bullshit. You went after a man that wasn't yours! You were my friend, or at least I thought you were. Then you try to give me crap about going after Jackson? Fuck you! I'm done here."

"Well I'm not done yet," she sneers.

There's no way this bitch is going to call the shots. "I have nothing left to say to you, and I couldn't give two shits about whatever you want." I take a step toward her and smother the urge to choke her. "I won. I got the account and you got Neil— which was the best fucking thing that could've happened to me."

She lifts her bag and turns to me, her eyes narrowed. "Just so you know, Neil came to me. Not the other way around. I didn't need to go after him. He obviously wasn't happy with what he was getting at home. I think that says something, don't you?" She raises her brow and takes a few steps toward the door. Without looking back, she says, "I wonder how long until Jackson gets bored with you." Then she shrugs and strides out of the office. I guess she couldn't resist digging the knife in a little deeper.

I'm crazy to think I have any shot with a man like Jackson, not that I'm trying for anything with him anyway. If I don't get out of here now, I'm going to break down. I know I shouldn't let her affect me, but she managed to remind me of every insecurity I've ever had in a matter of five minutes.

I grab my belongings and rush out the door only to crash

into a hard chest. All my papers fly out of my bag and flutter around me. As they settle, I let out a sardonic laugh and hear a deep, familiar chuckle, letting me know I've run into Jackson yet again. Will the humiliation ever end? I look up and see his captivating eyes change as he takes me in. I haven't had a chance to school my features, so I have no idea what he's seeing right now. He's close enough that I can feel his chest rise and fall. I can feel his warmth. Neither of us has spoken. He hasn't said anything obnoxious. He's staring at me inquisitively.

"Are you okay?" he asks in a soft voice as he crouches down to collect the papers. His concern makes my heart ache. "What was that about?"

Oh God, did he hear what Piper said? I clear my throat, bend down across from him, and try to force the conversation with Piper—and all the emotions that came along with it—out of my mind. "Yes, I'm fine. It was nothing I can't handle," I say as I pick up the last paper.

His penetrating eyes lock onto mine and he cocks his head to the side, trying to determine if I'm telling the truth. Giving me a half smile, he silently hands me the papers he gathered and we both stand. I stuff them back in my bag and return my gaze to Jackson's. Deciding to break the awkward silence, I speak first. "Well, thank you for helping me. I should go."

"No thanks needed." He looks like he wants to say more but is debating internally. Without another word, he grabs my bag off my shoulder and places his hand on the small of my back to guide me. "I'll walk you out."

When we arrive at the front desk, he hands me back my bag and smiles warmly. "I'll see you in a few days."

I grab his arm, stopping him in his tracks. I'm not sure why—I couldn't let him walk away. Quickly, I try to think of something to say to justify my behavior. "I ... I meant to ask you about ..." I stumble over my words, feeling more and more foolish. "You know what? It's fine." I smile awkwardly, hoping he lets it go.

Jackson leans forward, dropping his voice so only I can hear. His eyes give away nothing, and I can only imagine the myriad of emotions my own eyes show. "I was having a hard time walking away from you too." He leans back and grins at me as his words float into my brain.

"Yeah," I say breathlessly. Wait, what? That isn't what I wanted to say! Dammit! I had a great come back and *that* is what comes out of my mouth? Shoot me now, please.

He raises his eyebrow and gives me a full mega-watt smile, enjoying my discomfort. "This trip is going to be fun. I'll see you soon, Catherine." His voice drips with the promise of things to come.

I smother my groan and decide to try to play it smart and casual. "Good-bye, Jackson." I turn and walk to the elevator, hoping he's watching as I sway my hips a little more than normal. I look over my shoulder, smiling when I see his eyes are exactly where I want them to be.

chapter

nine

"UGH! WHERE THE hell is my black dress?" I yell out my bedroom door. Ashton is sitting on the couch laughing at something on TV.

"Stressed much?" she replies from the other room.

"I need your help! Get your ass off the couch!" I say in my pouty voice and stomp my feet like a twelve-year-old. I need her to calm me down and pack for me. It's been four days since I last saw Jackson. I've gotten almost nothing accomplished because every time I sit to start something, I find myself daydreaming of his face or imagining his lips leaning down to kiss me. Lost in yet another fantasy of Jackson, I sigh and hear Ashton laugh again, only this time she's in my doorway, staring at me.

"Lost in Jacksonland again, are we?" She snorts and heads into my room. "You got it bad."

"Shut up. I do not!"

"Really?" Ashton tilts her head up and taps her finger on her chin as if she's debating something. "Well if that's true, then where's his business card? I could always call him since I'm single." She shrugs, gauging my reaction.

I glare at her. "You wouldn't dare."

"Hmmm. You said he's hot though, right?" She grins before continuing, "I *really* would like to see for myself. Who knows? Maybe we'll hit it off."

"You're so full of shit. You wouldn't do that to me." I turn and look in my drawer for the damn black dress that's not in my closet.

"If you're not interested, why should it matter?" In the mirror I see her raise an eyebrow, goading me.

"I'm not interested, but that doesn't mean I want him hanging around here." I know she'll never buy it, but that's all I've got.

"I'll make sure not to bring him around. I know he's your client and all." I turn and look at her smiling face. She's waiting for me to either have an epic tantrum or call her on it.

Fine. Two can play at this game. "The card is on the dresser," I walk over to the card Jackson placed in my hand last week. "Go ahead and give him a call. I'll be right here." I hold it out to Ashton, willing her to take it, hoping she doesn't.

She grabs the card and reaches for the phone. She types the numbers and smiles the whole time as I gape at her. I can't believe she's calling him. I know what I said, but I never thought she'd actually do it. She knows me better than that. I'm about to say something when I look closer and realize she has *my* phone in her hand. I leap over the pile of clothes on the floor and lunge for the phone. She falls back on the bed, laughing hysterically as I claw my way up and rip it out of her hand. "You bitch!" I try to contain my laughter as I scroll through the call log to see if she dialed. "I'm gonna kill you! Thank God you didn't freaking call him!"

"Nope, I wouldn't call him. That would be *sooo* embarrassing." She stands and heads into my closet.

Just as I'm about to go back to packing, my phone vibrates in my hand. I look down and open the text message from a number I don't recognize.

Unknown: Can't wait to see you either.

Dread seeps through my veins as I grab the business card and check the number. Sure enough, it's Jackson. She's dead!

"Ashton! You've got to be kidding me! You texted him?" I

exclaim.

She peeks her head out from the closet, smiling. "I said I didn't *call* him. Never said anything about other forms of communication." She giggles and goes back into the closet.

I take a deep breath, trying to calm down. *Okay, I can handle this.* I won't respond, and I'll play it off when I see him—although, I might be in a jail cell instead of meeting Jackson tomorrow. I think a judge would understand why I had to murder my best friend. I sink onto my bed and put my pillow over my head, groaning.

Ashton comes over and nudges my leg. I pull the pillow down and glare at her in response. "You're being a drama queen. Look at the message I sent him before you get all stabby." She starts folding clothes and putting them in my suitcase.

I look at the outgoing text message.

Me: Ready for the trip. See you at 8.

Whatever. She should have never sent him a damn text message. Now he probably thinks I sit around thinking about him. He wouldn't be far off in that assumption, but I don't exactly want him to *know* that. Damn Ashton and her stupid interfering. I look over to find her rummaging through my underwear drawer. I snap at her, "What the hell are you doing in there?" I rush over to close the drawer.

"If you're getting naked, you need proper panties." She smiles mischievously.

"There will be no naked!" I sigh and grab out a few pairs of underwear.

"Sure, Cat. Keep telling yourself that. This guy wants in your pants and you can't even try to tell me you're not dying to get in his. So embrace your inner temptress, get some cute panties, and get on it ... or under it." She winks and runs out of my room before I can throw something at her.

Not even ten seconds later she pops her head in my room, giggling. "Oh, your black dress is in the bag. You can thank me later," she says. Then she runs out again.

Sure enough, I look in the suitcase and find my black dress along with one of my negligées. Ashton!

My suitcase is bouncing noisily down the foyer stairs at our apartment complex. I'm exhausted and crabby after being completely unhappy with pretty much anything I had in my closet. Since I have absolutely no idea what we're going to be doing in Virginia, I packed for any scenario. Trying to pick the perfect travel clothes for today, I went for comfortable and cute. I'm wearing a black and white sundress with my black flats. I don't know why I thought a dress would be a good option for being on a plane and going through security, but it doesn't matter now. I'm ten minutes late and don't have time to change. As I make my way outside, my eyes widen in surprise. Jackson is in front of my building, leaning against the door of a black town car sedan and smiling at my reaction.

He walks forward, takes the handle of my bag, and leans toward me, handing me a cup of coffee. "Good morning, Catherine. You look happy to see me."

I groan and roll my eyes, taking the coffee out of his hand. He lets out a deep chuckle at my reaction and hands my bag to the driver.

"Good morning, Jackson." I turn and walk to the other side of the car, open the door, and whisper under my breath, "Yeah, oh so happy." I hear him exhale in a short burst, almost like he's laughing. I look back to see him smiling from ear to ear. Of course he heard me.

He slides his big body into the seat next to me, taking over all the space in the car. We're close. So close that his warmth radiates into me and his cologne fills my nose. He leans down, reaching for something in his bag, and his fingers brush the bare skin of my leg. Tingles shoot up my thighs at the contact. It's too much for me.

I scoot over a little more toward the window. Even though I'd love nothing more than to sit on his lap, I try to avoid touching him. My walls are going to come crumbling down really fast if I don't keep some distance. I look out the window and sip my coffee. Smiling, I glance at him, surprised that he somehow managed to make it the way I like it. I was prepared for it to be black, not light and sweet.

"How did you know?" I lift the cup.

"I have my ways." He grins and turns his attention to the file folder on his lap.

I'm sure he does. I smile reply, "Well, thanks."

"You're welcome." He doesn't glance up and I'm a little disappointed. He has this uncanny way of knowing my thoughts—maybe he's trying to keep his distance so I'm not uncomfortable?

I grab my iPhone and go through my alerts. We have about a thirty-minute drive to the airport.

I notice the voicemail that I've been avoiding—my mother's. She's called eight times, but I keep putting off returning the call. She frustrates me, and lately I don't have the patience to deal with it. I glance at Jackson. He's engrossed in whatever he's reading, so I decide to listen to it.

"Hello, Catherine. It's Mom. I hope all is well." She pauses and I can almost hear her bristle. Her voice is filled with frustration. "I've tried to call you about ten times now, but I guess you're ignoring me again. I'm not sure how to say this, so I'm just going to come out with it." She lets out a deep sigh and goes on, softer now. "I got a letter from a lawyer. They sent notice that your presence is required next week at their office. They need you to—" Another long pause. "—settle your father's estate. He passed away a week ago." She sounds sad, and I can hear her taking short breaths as if she's crying. "You were listed as his beneficiary and this was your last known address. I'm so sorry, sweetie. Please call me. I love you." The line goes dead.

I drop the phone in my lap. The emotions swarming inside

of me are jumbled, all over the place. I haven't spoken to my father in almost twenty years. I don't know why I feel sad. I hate him. He walked away. He deserted me—never called, never cared—so why do I feel like I'm going to cry? What do I do now? I'm supposed to go through his affairs, settle his estate—I don't even know where the hell he's lived all this time. I drop my head in my hands and struggle to catch my breath. I'm so angry. I moved on. I forgot about him. I got over the fact that I wouldn't have someone to walk me down the aisle or dance with me at my wedding. I don't need him or want any part of him, so why do I feel such utter despair? The tightness in my chest has me gasping for air, shaking. I roll down the window frantically—I need air.

Jackson places his hand on my arm and I snap my head up. I kind of forgot about him there beside me. He's staring at me. He squeezes my arm and his eyes soften as if he can sense my panic. "Are you okay?" His voice is concerned.

I shake my head subtly up and down. I don't think I can speak. I avert my eyes, looking at my hands grasped tightly in my lap.

"Catherine," he says softly, looking alarmed by whatever emotions are showing on my face. He reaches for my hand and places his gently over mine. I can't look at him. I need to keep it together. I should have never listened to that damn voicemail. Who tells someone their parent died on a voicemail? Another way my mother and her selfish ways come to light. She could've called again, could've called Taylor—anything other than leave a voicemail.

I need to explain this to him. I have to say something. I look over and whisper, "My father died."

His eyes widen in shock before changing to sympathy. "I'm so sorry," he says, and his sincerity breaks my carefully constructed wall.

"It's fine. I mean, we weren't close. I just—" My chin begins to tremble. I can't speak anymore.

My heart is aching. All these years, all this time—it's all over and I'll never get the answers I so desperately needed. Why did he really leave me? Tears blur my vision. I close my eyes and try to hang on to the anger I had moments ago.

Jackson must sense I'm about to fall apart because he leans in, puts his arm around me, and pulls me to his side. I try to resist, but he's stronger and grips tighter. Not wanting to fight him, I give in, allowing myself this one moment to accept the comfort he's offering. His warmth cocoons me as I curl into his chest and slip my arm around his stomach. He holds me so snug, keeping me together while my mind spins. He does nothing to move me, just tenderly strokes the side of my arm. My heart is pounding and my breathing is shallow, both from the whirlwind of emotions and his closeness. I start to pull away, trying to put some distance between us, but Jackson refuses to relax his hold on me. I have to admit I feel so small and safe in his embrace. Closing my eyes, I lose myself in his touch. I want to cry, but the tears won't come. I focus on the steady sound of his heartbeat. So sure, so strong. The thrumming anchors me and keeps me from falling apart. We stay like this the rest of the car ride, neither of us speaking as I try to understand the numbness I'm feeling.

When we arrive at the airport, Jackson shifts slightly and I sit up. I look out the window and realize we're at Teterboro, which means we're flying on a private jet. I turn to look at Jackson, confused and embarrassed, when he puts his hand on my cheek, softly cradling it. "Are you going to be okay? We can cancel the trip if you need to."

"No!" I say loudly and he startles, dropping his hand from my face.

"I'm serious. You need to deal with—" His brows draw together before he runs his hands down his face.

"No, it's fine." I don't want to deal with any of it. I'm not going to run to take care of a man who never cared enough to take care of me. I take a deep breath and move my hand, placing it tentatively on his. "Please, I don't want to reschedule the trip. I promise, I'm really okay."

He stays quiet for a minute. I'm praying he believes me. Jackson pinches the bridge of his nose, closing his eyes. He blows out a long breath, exits the car, and walks over to speak to the driver. My heart can't take this pain. I hang my head, creating a veil with my dark brown hair so he can't see me falling apart. I need this trip. I want to escape and not go back and have to deal with my dead father who abandoned me. I put him and all the shit he did to me in a box—then I took his box and shoved it away. I have no desire to dust it off and open it again.

I hear my car door open and look up. Jackson is standing there, hand extended, with a sad smile on his face. He tilts his head toward the runway and says, "Come on, we've got a plane to catch."

I place my hand in his and allow him to help me from the car. "Thank you, Jackson." My eyes are soft and my voice is full of emotion. I remove my hand after giving his a small squeeze and head toward the trunk to collect my bag. Jackson walks silently behind me. I've probably scared him with my almost breakdown.

We both reach for my bag's handle at the same time. I giggle as he swats my hand away. I look over at him. His eyes are bright and glossy and his mouth is in a half grin. "I love your laugh."

The way he says it makes my heart feel lighter. "Thanks," I murmur and look away.

Jackson clears his throat and says, "Now, let's head to Virginia." His smile grows as he tilts his head to the side. "You know where that is, right?" He winks and grabs my bag. There's the smug bastard I know.

"Yes, I knew where it was before too." I smile, thankful for the change in topic.

"Sure you did."

"You know I have a master's degree, right? I'm pretty sure

I had a class or two where we discussed the fifty states." I huff, pretending to be irritated with him. In reality, I'm silently awed by how quickly he brought me back.

"Hey, it's not my fault you were confused the first time."

"Gah!" I throw my hands up in mock frustration.

Jackson stops at the bottom steps of the plane, shifting his weight back and forth. My eyes dart between the contemplative look on his face and the plane—I hope he's not going to cancel. As if sensing my distress, he places both hands on my shoulders and waits for me to look at him. Our eyes meet and I can't look away. My breathing stops. My heart accelerates. His eyes are clouded with emotion. For me? For my loss? I can't tell. He looks sad, and it rocks me to my core. Slowly, he pulls me toward him and wraps his arms around me. I return his embrace as he rubs my back. We stand there in each other's arms, giving and receiving comfort from one another. My news was unexpected and so was Jackson's response, but I don't mind it.

I clear my throat and I swear I feel Jackson kiss the top of my head, but it's so light I can't be sure. We break apart and I smile. He reaches for my face but drops his hand before touching me, frowning as his eyes empty of all the emotion present just seconds before. Without a word, he turns and ascends the stairs to the plane. I take a deep breath and follow, praying I can keep it together and remain professional. The lines are blurring, so I need to redraw them and stay on the appropriate side.

chapter

ten

*T*HE PLANE IS breathtaking. It has plush leather seats and a couch against the right wall. There's a wet bar at the back wall and another room in the rear of the plane. I'm assuming it's an office or a bedroom, but I have no intention of finding out. The décor is beautiful. Done in cream and a rich blue, it's striking and regal. Very fitting for the man I'm traveling with.

Jackson walks forward from the bar area looking calm and collected. He's back to being professional. "Make yourself comfortable. It's only about a two-hour flight."

"Is this your plane?" I ask, still looking around the cabin as I sit in one of the captain chairs.

"Yes, I fly back and forth from New York to Virginia a lot. Purchasing a company jet made sense." He looks at the seat across the aisle and then turns and sits in the seat next to me. Why does he insist on sitting so damn close?

"Oh, I didn't know you visited the facility that much."

He looks up, shifting uncomfortably in his seat. "I don't. Well, I didn't. I have a second company, which is why I spent a lot of time in Virginia. Plus, I was stationed there when I was on active duty, so I get to visit the team when I'm there."

"You served?" I never would have thought he was prior military. He looks so young. Finding out he owns a second company throws me as well.

Jackson straightens in his seat and lifts his head, his eyes locking on mine. One side of his mouth lifts revealing that adorable dimple. When he speaks, his voice is laced with pride. "Yes, I served eight years in the Navy."

I smile at this remarkable man, who's accomplished so much, and realize I know nothing about him. I guess this explains the hero complex. A small giggle escapes me, and I slap my hand over my mouth. *Crap!*

He looks at me with amusement. "Why is that funny?"

I smile. "It's not. I'm just laughing at how you seem to like to save people." Great, now I sound stupid.

He lets out a short laugh. "Yeah, well there's a lot about me you don't know." He nudges my arm.

I smirk and shake my head at him. Out of nowhere the plane jerks and I freeze. A sudden burst of anxiety hits me and I grab the arms of the chair, white-knuckling it. He notices, of course, and places a hand on my arm. "Are you afraid of flying?" he asks. His sultry voice does nothing for my nerves.

"N-No," I barely get the word out. My hands are sweating and my heart is pounding as he removes his hand. I've flown hundreds of times. I don't mind it at all, but I've never flown on a private plane. Or flown next to a man who seems to affect me so much.

He leans closer. His clean soap and cologne smell is so hypnotic, I can't stop myself from taking a deep breath. The heat from his body is everywhere, and he's not even touching me. "Don't worry, Catherine, you're safe with me. Just close your eyes."

I glance at him as the plane begins to move again. "I'll be fine. I'm being silly." How many more ways am I going to embarrass myself with this man?

"Relax and close your eyes," he says softly but with an air of authority.

"When did you get so bossy?" I close my eyes and smile, hearing a rustling before I sense him shifting closer.

"Wouldn't you like to know?" he replies, humor dancing in his voice. "Now, stop talking and just breathe."

I take a deep breath and start to sing to myself. My father used to sing this song to me at night whenever I had bad dreams. The lyrics soothed me. Throughout my life, I've always sung that song when I needed strength, even though it was associated with him. Now is no different. My father's voice, singing about me being his one and only sunshine, echoes through my ears and floods my mind. If only it'd been true.

I repeat the song over and over as Jackson's fingers graze my arm. Abruptly, the contact I'd been enjoying vanishes. I shiver from the loss, terrified to open my eyes. What if I'm alone again?

"You're safe now." His warm voice blankets over me.

I'm far from safe, but somehow during that brief moment we managed to become airborne and I didn't even notice. My lids are heavy, so I relax into my seat and think about my morning with Jackson. Within a matter of minutes he put me at ease. He cared for me when he saw my distress. How easy it would be to fall for him. To give myself to someone who looks out for others before himself. But at what cost to my heart? Somewhere before unconsciousness I realize—it's not the plane I should be afraid of, it's the man next to me.

"Catherine..."

No! I don't want to wake up. Damn Ashton and her nudging.

"Catherine." I hear a throaty chuckle. "You're adorable when you sleep."

What?

"Come on. Time to get up. We're in Virginia."

Virginia?

I groan and open my eyes to see Jackson smiling and

leaning over me with both hands on the arm rests. Damn, I'd love waking up to that face every day. I rub my eyes, realizing I slept the entire flight. Between the lack of sleep last night and the events of this morning, it's no wonder I passed out. I try to move but he has me caged between his muscular arms, a huge grin on his face. I clear my throat and look at his hand, hoping my silent cue will register. However, he only seems more amused.

"Could you let me up please?"

He leans back but not enough to give me the space I need. I glare at him until he takes a step back, crosses his arms over his chest, and smiles widely at me.

Now standing, I become extremely self-conscious as he stares at me. "What? Do I have something on my face?" I wipe my face, smooth my hair, and inspect my clothes.

He inches forward, dropping his arms to his sides. His eyes tease me as they travel the length of my body. "Did you know you talk in your sleep?" His voice is full of mischief.

No. Oh no! I'm aware of this, but I've never really thought too much about it. Though, Ashton does make fun of me all the time for the things that come out of my mouth at night. Pink paints my cheeks as I cover my face with my hands. I open my fingers a tiny bit so I can see through them. "Please tell me I didn't say anything embarrassing," I say hesitantly.

Jackson tugs at my hands, pulling them away from my face. His calloused thumbs are rubbing back and forth against my wrists. Taking a deep breath, he gives a small smile. "You said 'Daddy' a few times."

"Oh." I give a deflated huff. "I guess that makes sense ... with everything today." I look down to where he's still holding my arms. I shift my weight and stare at the floor.

Sensing my discomfort, he drops my wrists. "I'm sorry again," he says. And again, I know he is. I can hear the honesty in his voice. It's touching but disconcerting at the same time. I can't afford to form an emotional connection with this man.

The physical one is bad enough.

"I know." I smile. "I'm excited to get to work and see the plant," I say in a polite tone, switching topics. I don't want to discuss my father or anything personal, and I'm not going to think about all the issues waiting for me back in New Jersey. There's business to handle while I'm on this trip, and that is going to be my priority. In the last twenty years, my father never once made me a priority—I'm not about to make him one now.

"We'll head straight there. Then we'll have dinner, since I know you're excited for that too."

"Too?" I straighten my back and snap my eyes to his.

"You might have said something about that." He laughs. "And a few other things," he adds as an afterthought. Jackson turns and cleans up his papers.

Is he serious? I bite my lip and hesitate before asking my next question. "What are you talking about? Did I say anything else?"

He tilts his head to the side, grinning, and then shrugs. What the hell does the shrug mean? I have to know. He grabs his bag and moves past me. I'm stunned, silently praying all I did was mumble.

As he walks by, I grab his arm to stop him. I try for nonchalance, hoping that maybe his good-humored side will play along. My stomach is doing somersaults as I think of all the possible things I could've said in my sleep. In the short time we've known each other I've dreamed of him so often—if my words were anything close to sounding like the two very erotic dreams I've already had, I may die.

His eyes are playful when he looks at me. "Something you want to know?" he asks, raising one eyebrow.

"Me? No." I smile and look contrite.

"Are you sure? You look rather curious." He smirks and pushes my hair off my face.

I laugh, hoping to get him to tell me what I said. "Jackson, I thought you were into saving girls from disastrous situations.

You know, a soldier and all—"

He cuts me off. "No, I was a SEAL, not a soldier. Big difference," he says as he puffs his chest out.

"Okay ... SEAL, then. Didn't know the term meant anything." I tilt my head, smiling and batting my eyelashes. "Anyway, don't you want to tell me whatever it is you think you know?"

He smiles at my blatant attempt at persuasion. Dropping his bag, he says, "Catherine, you don't really think I'm going to give up that easy, do you?" He grins and takes a step closer. I notice his Adam's apple bobbing as he debates his next words. "I'm like a vault, and it's going to take a whole lot more than those gorgeous eyes batting at me to crack this one," he says huskily.

I take a step back and smile. "So there *is* something to spill, then?"

He laughs loudly and steps back. "Come on. We've got places to go."

"Anyone ever tell you you're a frustrating man?"

He taps his finger on his chin as if deep in thought. "Nope, most people find me endearing and charming."

I snort. "Are these people on your payroll by any chance?"

"Maybe, but then again you're on my payroll and seem to disagree with the consensus." He smiles and heads toward the cabin door.

"Good thing I don't work for you. You're just a client, so I don't have to agree."

He stops and turns toward me suggestively. "Good thing I have three days to change your mind about that, then." He winks, leaving me speechless as we exit the plane.

chapter

eleven

*J*ACKSON AND I don't speak much in the car. Both of us are looking at the new sales figures he received from his secretary when we landed. The numbers look promising and show a shift in the market. I look through a few more emails on my phone, not really paying much attention to where we're going. I shoot a quick text to Ashton, letting her know we've landed safely. About fifteen minutes later, we pull up to a large office building that's all windows.

I look over at the Cole Security Forces sign and I'm suddenly confused. Clearly, this isn't the production facility. I glance at Jackson. He's still engrossed in the figures, so he hasn't noticed we've stopped.

I clear my throat. "Jackson, where are we?"

He looks at the building and back at me. "This is my other company. I run a security force that has contracts all over the world. I need to run in and show face for about ten minutes. Would you like to come in?" His eyes shift back and forth and he sounds genuinely nervous.

Well there's a surprise. The man owns a cosmetics company and a security company—talk about polar opposites. My eyes widen at his admission and then I recover, smiling softly. "If you'd like me to, sure."

We both exit the car and head over to the entrance. Jackson places his hand on my shoulder as he opens the door. Just the small touch sends me into overdrive. I tilt my head and give him a small grin as I enter the office.

It's nothing like Raven Cosmetics. Where that office is almost feminine, this one is modern and masculine with clean lines and distinctive colors. The floors are gray concrete and the walls are cream and royal blue, which makes sense based on the décor from the plane. In the center of the room, there are two big cubicle sections that each seats five people. The left wall is taken up by four large offices with huge mahogany doors.

Jackson clears his throat as we make our way into the space. Three guys stand and smile when they see him. A few other guys stick their hands up, acknowledging his presence, but continue to work.

"Hey, Muffin!" A tall, muscular guy with long light blond hair styled back off his face says as he walks over, smiling. He's huge and his arms are covered in tattoos, which might be intimidating if he wasn't so warm and friendly.

"Hey, Mark." He looks happy to see him. The two men shake hands and clap each other on the shoulder. Mark turns his attention to me with wide eyes and a large, appraising grin. Jackson bristles. "Mark, this is Catherine. She's the new publicist for the cosmetics company," he says stiffly.

I smile and extend my hand. "Hi, Mark. Nice to meet you."

Mark shakes my hand. "Catherine, it's a pleasure. Sorry you have to work with this prick all day." He elbows Jackson in the stomach, still smiling at me.

I giggle and reply, "Interesting choice of words. Jackson describes himself a little differently."

Mark raises his eyebrows, looking intrigued by my statement. "Really? What did Muff describe himself as?"

"Muff?" I ask, completely lost.

He howls in laughter. "Yup. That's Jackson! He was always a little soft in the middle,"—he leans in—"whereas the rest of us worked out to keep our amazing physiques." He stands back up, beaming. "So we told him he had a muffin top and that stuck as his call sign."

I giggle at the nickname and glance at Jackson, who's shooting daggers at Mark. Turning back to Mark, I ask, "So what's your call sign?"

Jackson places his hand on the small of my back. "Twilight and I were both on the same team for four years."

"Twilight? Oh, I gotta hear this!" I laugh. Now it's Mark's turn to give Jackson the evil eye.

Jackson chuckles and pulls me against his side. "Notice how pale Mark is?" He asks, jutting his chin out in his direction. I nod. These two are the female versions of Ashton and me. It's comforting, considering the day I've had. "Well he's so white he could glitter in the sun. One of the guys' wives had some kind of obsession with that movie, and he kept telling him he could star in *Twilight*. So Mark here is our glittery, pale Twilight."

Mark scoffs and puffs his chest out. "I'm proud of my name. At least they aren't saying I'm a fat ass. That Edward dude had abs like a rock. Besides, I could kick your ass any day, any time," he challenges, stepping closer to me as he smiles widely.

Jackson raises his chin and addresses me. "He's an asshole but knows his shit, so he stays—for now." He smirks at Mark. "And anyway, he knows who's in charge. Right, Mark?" I can almost smell the testosterone in the room.

Mark laughs and his eyes crinkle. "Keep thinking that, assclown. You need me too much." He puts his arm around my shoulders, taunting Jackson.

"Right, remember who signs your paycheck." Jackson raises a brow.

"Anyway, Catherine, this fucknugget gives you any problems, you call me and I'll kick his ass."

I instantly love this man. He flashes me that ever-present smile one last time before heading back over to his desk.

Jackson grips my hip, grimacing and mumbling something under his breath.

Jackson guides me over to an office and flips on the light before closing the door. It's large and airy. There are photos all over the wall and I walk over to get a closer look. There are a few of Jackson, Mark, and some other guys drinking and laughing. A few of him on a boat with some friends, looking carefree and happy. My stomach clenches at the next one. He's standing in camouflage with a huge gun slung across his body, a menacing look on his face. He looks scary yet unbelievably sexy.

"You know ..." I say, turning, and then I gasp as he startles me.

I was so lost in the photos I didn't even realize he was behind me. "What?" He smiles.

Once my heart settles and I can speak again, I remember what I was going to say. "You looked pretty nice in uniform."

"Nice?" he asks, arching a brow.

"Cute."

"Cute?" Apparently this is even worse than nice.

I look back at the photo, trying to figure out what he seems bothered over. "What? Is cute not a good word?"

I feel him move in behind me, and I struggle not to lean back into him.

"Cute is for babies and puppies. I can think of at least ten other words to better describe me," he says against my ear. A shiver races over my body and I have to consciously work to steady my breathing.

I close my eyes and smother the desire burning through me. "Really?" I ask breathily.

"Hot, sexy, buff, handsome, fucking amazing, God's idea of perfect ... I could go on, but any of those would be acceptable," he says, and I can hear the smile in his voice.

I turn to face him. We're so close physically, but in any other way we're miles apart. Still, I'm battling every cell in my body not to give in to him.

"Jackson," I warn.

He takes a small step forward. "I know you're taken, but I can't stop thinking about you."

My brows furrow in confusion. "Taken?"

He looks down at my left hand and brings it up between us. "Aren't you engaged?" He looks from my eyes back down to my hand where my ring used to sit.

"Oh. Ummm, no. Not anymore. We're over and have been for a while." I don't know what to say. I can't tell him the guy was Neil. I start to feel panic rising at how ridiculously screwed-up my life is and how all of this can come crumbling so easily.

"That certainly changes things." His eyes blaze with un-spoken promises.

"Changes things? No. It doesn't change the fact that you're my client." Or how I'm a mess over the constant screw-ups from the men in my life. And it definitely doesn't change how I know with every ounce of my being that Jackson would ruin me if I let him in.

"Catherine, I can't stay away from you." His voice pene-trates through my thoughts, straight to my heart, and it takes me a second to find my resolve.

He cups my face in his hands, holding me, forcing me to look at him. "Jackson, I'm not with anyone, but this isn't a good—"

Before I can finish my sentence his mouth is on mine. All at once, I'm surrounded by heat, strength, and power—all that is Jackson. The sparks I felt previously are nothing compared to the inferno raging between us right now. I close my eyes and lose myself in the feel of his mouth on mine. My chest presses against him as he pushes me back against the wall and tilts my head to the side. His tongue is against my lips, begging for entrance. I sigh, which is all the permission he needs. Our tongues swirl together as we kiss with fervor. Lifting my hands, I grip his hips and pull him closer. Wanting to touch his body, I trace my hands across the muscles of his taut back, over his hard arms, across the ridges of his abs. The way he feels against my lips, against my body, against my fingers ... it's incredible. I could kiss him forever—his mouth is heaven. Never have I been kissed like this. Jackson shifts and lifts my head to gain better access, and I willingly give it to him. Pushing and pulling each other, trying to get closer and closer, I moan, causing Jackson to break the kiss.

He rests his head against my forehead as we both struggle to catch our breath. I can feel the shift in him as he sighs loudly. "Fuck! I'm sorry." He shakes his head. "I shouldn't have kissed you." He leans back and looks over toward his desk.

I snap my head up, wounded and embarrassed by his sudden rejection. His words, the regret in his voice, and his now distant behavior has me in knots. My stomach flops and I feel sick. He kissed me, and now he's acting like it was a mistake. I don't want to want him, but I do. As much as I want to fight what I feel for him, I'm not sure I'm strong enough. But maybe I don't need to be after all. Maybe my concern was all for nothing. His aloof attitude stings, but I shove down my feelings. I can't let him know he's hurt me. I won't let another man destroy me.

I move over to the side of the room and take a deep breath. "Jackson, it's fine. I should never have crossed that line." I don't know what line I actually crossed, but I'll take the blame. He's my client, and the last thing I need is for him to fire me. Besides, it will only be a matter of time before he sees the real me and decides he's better off. My mind is spinning as the pain of his rejection swells. My God, how many times will I do this to myself? You'd think by now I'd realize that *every* man in my life leaves. They take and take and then I'm left cleaning up the pieces, praying next time will be different.

He moves toward me and stops suddenly. He swallows hard and rubs his hand over his face. He looks sad and angry. "You did nothing wrong!" he snaps and I take a step back. He lifts his head to the ceiling and shakes his head. "You've had a lot of shit happen today. I didn't mean to ..." He takes a step forward with his hands by his side, clenched into tight fists. I'm not sure why he's so angry about it. I thought he enjoyed it, but I guess not.

I put my hands up to stop him—I don't want to hear it. "Please, just stop. Let's forget about it, okay? I'm a lot stronger than you think. I've dealt with a lifetime of this." I turn away and look out the window. I don't trust myself to say any more right now.

"Catherine, please ..." he pleads. I hear him step forward but he doesn't say anything else. It feels like five minutes have passed when I feel his hands on my shoulders. I shrug him off and turn to face him. The look in his eyes stops the hostility I was feeling. He looks devastated, torn. He swallows and his voice is soft, laced with pain. "I've wanted and yet not wanted to kiss you for the last two weeks. It isn't you, I promise. I don't want to take advantage of the grief you're feeling."

I don't know what to believe. "Okay, let's just call it what it was—a mistake. It won't happen again."

"I'm not sure about that—"

"I am. It won't happen aga—"

"It won't happen again on the day you lost a parent," he says with a small smile. "Don't misunderstand what I'm saying. I've been there. I know the pain you're feeling. Okay?" He takes a deep breath and looks at the wall of pictures, staring at one in particular. There are so many, I'm not sure which one he's looking at. However, he was a SEAL—maybe he's lost friends? My heart breaks for him at the thought, and I want to soothe his pain.

"I'm sorry you've lost someone."

"That's not for today. Let's get out of here." He smiles and walks over to his desk, grabbing some papers. I walk back over to the wall, looking at the photo of Jackson—so strong and lethal. A chill runs down my spine. Jackson comes around to where I'm standing and looks at the photo. He's close enough that his arm and chest are touching my back, and I know he positioned himself there on purpose. Every time he touches me I lose the ability to think clearly. I step away from him, trying to keep some space between us.

"You done ogling my picture?" he asks.

My jaw drops at his sudden teasing. "I wasn't ogling. Maybe I was staring at Mark's picture." I lift my eyebrows and challenge him.

"I'm sure he would love that." He smirks and turns to head out of the office.

Before we can leave, Jackson's called over to handle an issue. I meet a few more people in the office as he's dealing with things. Once he finishes, we say our good-byes and Jackson assures them that he'll be back in the office a few times this trip to work over some contracts. Mark and a guy named Ski joke with him, telling him he can only come back if I come with him. He laughs and tells them he'll think about it. I'm captivated by the way he handles two companies—companies that are on such opposite spectrums. It's obvious the security company is his passion and evidently he's good at it, considering some of what I've heard here today.

Once we're back in the car, it appears all the joking and normalcy is gone. He seems distracted. I give him the quiet I assume he's seeking and try to focus on my own emotions. I press my hands to my lips. I swear I can still feel him. I can smell his cologne on my skin. The car is filled with tense energy. I want to say something but I can't. I know what his mouth tastes like, feels like. I'm fighting every part of my self-control to kiss him again. But his small rejection reminds me of the ability he has to hurt me. I don't know if I could handle that again. I promised myself I wouldn't go there until I was sure the guy was worth it. And right now I'm not sure if Jackson is.

chapter

twelve

WE CHECK INTO the upscale Ocean View Hotel. It's chic. The concierge informs us that we both have rooms on the fifteenth floor—right next to each other. Thoughts of how close he'll be float through my mind. I enter my room and the sheer beauty of it takes my breath away. There's a four-poster king size bed that faces the ocean. It's adorned with a fluffy white down comforter and luxurious soft blue linens. However, nothing is as beautiful as the wall of windows that opens to a balcony overlooking the waves. I put my bags down and explore the rest of the room. The bathroom is contemporary but still has the beach feel to it with blue and white accents that match the bedroom area. A huge two-person shower all done in marble is on the left, and in front of it is a square white soaker tub. Everything about this hotel is picture-perfect.

The sound of the hotel phone startles me. I rush over, picking up the receiver.

"Hello," I say, a little breathless.

Jackson's rough voice meets my ear. "Hey, I know we were going to leave right away, but I had something come up at the office that I need to handle." He sounds frustrated. I picture him pacing the room and rubbing his hands over his face.

"Sure, that's fine. Take as long as you need."

"Shouldn't be more than two hours. Sorry, but I have to

go," he says quickly and hangs up.

I flop onto the king size bed in my beautiful hotel room and stare at the ceiling. I'm dead tired, even after my nap. It's only 2 p.m. but I feel like it's 2 a.m. Jackson exhausts me—hell, my life exhausts me. Instead of taking yet another nap, I decide to take this time and call my mother. I'm still beyond pissed that she left a voicemail, but she's all I have left and I need some answers.

I dial her number and press the send button. After two quick rings, I hear her voice come through the line.

"Oh Cat. Hi, honey." She sounds so happy to hear from me.

"Mom." My reply is clipped and full of sadness. I'm trying to control my emotions.

She huffs. "You got my message, I assume."

"Yes, Mom, it was wonderful hearing that on a voicemail." I roll my eyes even though she can't see it. I need to keep calm. I walk over to the balcony overlooking the ocean and stare out at the horizon.

"Catherine, what was I supposed to do? Huh?" she asks and takes a deep breath. "You don't answer your phone. You don't call me back. I do the best I can with your attitude toward me. If *you* answered your damn phone, I wouldn't have to leave you messages." She sounds exasperated. I don't have an answer to that. Talking to her usually ends with one of us upset. We both argue and fight, and most of the time it's about something I'm doing wrong—according to her.

I've always felt second best to my mother. Either I wasn't smart enough, didn't try hard enough, or was too much like *him*. She would cry at night about how I was a constant reminder of my father. My father and I were pretty much identical, so I can understand how looking at me was difficult, but it was even harder having her push me away. The pain of having both parents walk out that day—one physically and one figuratively—was excruciating. I lost every idea I coveted about what my family was like the day he packed and left. He took more than just his belongings with him—he took my childhood. All I've wanted was for her to *see* me without seeing my father.

I let out a deep sigh. "Really, Mom? A voicemail? Why didn't you call Taylor?" I'm trying to restrain my voice, but I'm growing more and more agitated with her.

"I shouldn't have to call your damn secretary!" she yells. Then her voice softens. "I'm still your mother. I don't know why you hate me. You never think of anyone but yourself. I wish just once you cared about what I'm going through."

I choke back the emotion bubbling up. Once again she makes me feel stupid, as though I've done something wrong. I know she means well, but her execution leaves a lot to be desired. "I don't hate you. God. I love you and I don't want to fight. I've been really busy with work. That's why I haven't called." *And it hurts too much.*

"Too busy to call me back? Ten times I called!" She gets frustrated again. This is her thing: she gives me guilt trips and somehow I come out feeling inadequate. She hasn't yet asked me how I'm doing or if I'm okay.

"I'm sorry, Mom. I will try to do better about calling." I soften my voice, knowing we're getting nowhere. I decide to get the answers I need. "So what information did you get from the lawyer?"

"I got a letter stating you're named in his will and you need to call them. I don't know much more than he died last week. Alone." She lets out a puff of air and quickly sucks in another breath as if she's upset. "I'm so sorry, baby girl." She starts sobbing.

"I don't understand why you're crying," I say in an even tone, feeling betrayed by her reaction. "Why are you upset? He left us and never looked back. He didn't love us, Mom. At least now I know he won't come around because he's dead and not just because he doesn't want to."

She cries harder. I'm shaking, trying to wrap my mind

around this.

"Catherine, I loved him! I had a child with him."

I understand loving a man who doesn't love you back—hell, I know it all too well. I can't fully understand since I never had a child with Neil—thank God for that. But for once I want her to put me before my father. Sure, at some point he was a good dad, but I barely remember that because the bad memories far outweigh any good ones. There's a small part of me that understands that once you love someone there is a piece of your heart that is always theirs. But doesn't the hurt and pain that he put us through for twenty years negate that love? Don't the months where we ate macaroni and cheese every night because it's all she could afford due to his disappearance and lack of child support dampen that? My head and heart can't find common ground with her reaction. I'm angry over his death more than anything. I will never get answers. I won't know why he did these things. Did he feel remorse? Did he think about me and wonder who I became?

My blood boils as my chest tightens. "Yes, and then he left!" I remind her as the anger takes hold of me.

"He was a good father—"

All the air is pushed out of my lungs as if I've been punched in the gut. Of all the things she could say—to side with him is more hurtful than anything. "Are you kidding me?" I shriek. This is insane.

"Catherine Grace Pope, you do *not* get to yell at me! I don't give a shit how old you are."

"Mom—"

"Don't you *Mom* me. He was my husband. Yes, he left, but I made vows with him. I loved him—very much. I know you don't feel the same. I've never asked you to. But don't you *dare* try to make me feel bad for being sad that someone I shared a part of myself with is dead." She starts to hiccup-cry again. I know better than to try to speak. My hands tremble with rage as angry tears flow down my face. She composes herself and starts again. "He loved you. Maybe he didn't know what to do or how to be a father after he left, but he did love you."

Apparently she forgot all the nights I cried myself to sleep begging for him to come home. The days I sat at the top of the steps with a bag, hoping he was going to come get me for the weekend. The thousands of times I would ask if Daddy was going to call or come back. Every birthday when I would cry because I would wish for him and he'd never show. Tears fall relentlessly as anguish slices through my heart.

"That's where you're wrong, Mom." I take deep breath. "I wasn't enough. I have to go." I press end, disconnecting the call, and throw the phone on the bed. I won't listen to her tell me he loved me. If I stayed on the phone, we would've fought more and I can't handle any more of it today.

The anger evaporates and all I'm left with is nothingness. Numb. All I feel is complete numbness. I'm not angry anymore, or sad. I couldn't give a shit less about anything regarding my mother or father. I open the balcony door and sit out there, enjoying the solitude. There's something about the ocean that's soothing. I hear my phone ring a few times, but there's no way I'm getting up. I'm enjoying this small sliver of peace. The smell of the salty air, the sounds of birds and the waves crashing, and the caress of the gentle breeze overwhelm my senses. Focusing on them, I melt into the lounge chair and just breathe. Time passes and I'm content and restful.

"Well, this explains why you aren't answering my calls or the door." I leap out of my seat at the sound of an angry voice.

Jackson is standing on the balcony to my right, glaring at me. Trying to slow my rapid pulse, I place my hand over my heart. Short of breath from the rush of fear, I gasp and try to speak. "You scared the shit out of me."

He pinches the bridge of his nose and closes his eyes. "I was worried. I had no idea if you left or were lost." He opens his eyes, straining to maintain his temper. "I didn't mean to scare you, but I didn't know what to think."

His concern warms my heart. I smile and shrug. "What if I was in the bathroom?"

"For an hour?" he questions in that raspy voice of his.

"An hour?" I ask, confused. I thought it was maybe twenty minutes.

"Yes. An hour of calling and then banging on your door. I came out to my balcony to see if maybe I could see you on the beach because I was starting to panic." He shakes his head and runs his hands through his dark brown hair.

"I came out for some fresh air. I didn't even hear the door. I'm sorry you were so worried." I walk over to the edge of my balcony to get closer to him. "You should know, though, I'm not as fragile as you seem to think." I smile, trying to reassure him.

Closing his eyes, he turns his head toward the ocean and mumbles to himself. Something about women being the death of him.

Using my diversionary tactics, I clear my throat to grab his attention. "Ready to go?"

He seems to collect himself and one side of his mouth quirks up. "Yeah, I'll meet you right outside your door."

"Okay. I'll see you in a few minutes."

I head back in the room. Grabbing my phone, I look at the call list: eleven missed calls. Two are from my mother and the rest are from Jackson. No wonder he was pissed and worried. I check myself in the mirror and groan at my appearance. I look like a bus hit me. Knowing that he's waiting and already irritated, I decide not to push my luck. I pinch my cheeks for some color and flip my hair a few times, trying to bring some life back to it.

As I open the door, I can't stop the smile that forms at the sight of Jackson. He's pacing with his hands clasped behind his head. When he hears my door shut, he looks over and walks toward me. Standing face-to-face, I tilt my head to look up and try to read his mood through his eyes. They give nothing away as he stares down at me. He shakes his head, letting out a short groan as he does so. I lift my eyebrow at the noise that escapes him and Jackson returns the gesture. Then we both start laughing at each other.

The moment of humor seems to have quelled our awkwardness. He puts his arm out in a gentlemanly way and I place my hand through it. He looks down, smiling as we walk and get on the elevator. "What am I going to do with you?"

"What the hell does that mean?" I ask, narrowing my eyes as I try to decipher what exactly his question is implying.

"Just what I asked."

"Yes, but what kind of a question is that?" I drop my arm from his.

"Clearly there is something happening here." He steps closer and I take a step back.

"Nothing is happening." I straighten and take another step back, trying to put distance between us.

His jaw tics at my statement and he takes another step toward me. He's hot and then cold—I can't keep up. He kisses me—a soul-searing kiss—and then acts as though it was a mistake. Needing something to hold onto, I grip the hem of my dress. Jackson's eyes snap down as I tug on the fabric and he grins.

"Catherine—" Before he can speak, the elevator door opens allowing me to get the hell out of here.

I don't reply or acknowledge him as I practically run out of the elevator. This man manages to suck the air out of any space we share. He makes it difficult for me to focus on anything other than him. The intensity between us is crippling. I continue walking through the lobby and outside, heading over to a bench to sit. *Think, Catherine!* I need to be able to do my damn job.

He sits beside me, not saying a word. I need to tell him that this has to stop. He must have sensed my apprehension at some point, yet he continues to play whatever game this is. It's my life he's playing with. My job pays me way too much money to screw this up. I also refuse to go through another agonizing breakup—as if we're even close to that. Ha! It's too much. I have to maintain control. Yeah, like there's a shot in hell that's going to happen with a man like Jackson. Regardless, I'm going to *attempt* to keep it together.

I glance at him and my heart squeezes.

He returns my gaze as the car pulls up. "Let's get to work," he says as he stands and walks over to the car. This time he gets in the front seat.

Good. We need physical distance. We need to resume the roles of client and consultant. No matter how charming he is, no matter how handsome, he's ultimately paying me to help his company. I need to honor that agreement.

We arrive at the production facility fifteen minutes later. I used our travel time to strengthen my resolve and plan how to get back to being the strong businesswoman I am rather than the girl who can't control herself over some guy. Hell, I never acted like this with Neil. Half the fun with him was kicking his ass in the business world, not fawning and tripping over myself.

I open the door and smile at Jackson, wearing my business mask. This time he keeps his hands in his pockets.

"Welcome to Raven Cosmetics," he says as I walk past him into the building.

"Thank you. I know our main objective is the successful release of the new line you have coming out. Will we get to see that today?"

"Yes. The older products are being handled for now. The new line is really what we want you to focus on." It seems Jackson has also found his professional mask. Thank God! When he's charming and flirtatious it makes it damn near impossible to keep my mind on task.

"Perfect. Can I ask why you brought in an outside company?" The more information I have, the better.

He looks away and stops in front of a door. "Do I look like I wear makeup?" he asks, dripping with sarcasm. My breath hitches at his sudden mood shift. Jackson has never been rude or nasty. It shocks me. "Sorry. I didn't mean it like that. It's been a real shitty day." He inhales and begins to speak in an even tone. "I never had control over anything that happened with the cosmetic company. I honestly couldn't tell you the first thing about what the hell went on here. So when—" He stops abruptly and looks up before continuing, "—the former CEO departed, I knew I needed help. That's where you came in." He turns and opens the door, holding it so I can pass through.

"I understand." I nod and smile tightly as I walk past him. I stop and turn back, adding, "I'm glad you chose CJJ."

"I chose you. Not CJJ." He reaches for my hand and places it in the crook of his arm, holding it there. I stare at his beautiful eyes, biting my lower lip. "Now let me show you all the girly shit we make here." He turns and pulls me through the hall.

Our tour lasts about two hours and I'm exhausted by the end. I've met all the people on the production team as well as a few people I'm sure I'll speak to when I start to get more involved with each product. I have a million ideas floating around about things I want to focus on. I also have a huge bag of products to sample. Jackson was friendly, funny, and playful with his employees. The rapport he had with them was amazing. Just as impressive was how obvious it was that they love him. He knew almost every person's name, which is rare in a lot of big companies nowadays. It's clear that he views them as people and not just numbers. For someone who's had little to do with the company, he's either learned fast or has been more involved than he let on.

After the tour, both of us seem to relax into our appropriate roles. Throughout the car ride, we talk a lot about what he wants regarding the company's growth and how he'll be hands-on but ultimately knows nothing about this market or how to handle the press. The amount of free reign I have on this account has me feeling confident, even a little giddy.

Once we get off the elevator at our hotel, Jackson's phone rings. He glances at the screen and grimaces. He looks at me, a frown marring his features as he takes the call. "Hi, Mark. Everything okay?" He makes a low grumbling noise in the back of his throat at whatever Mark is relaying on the phone. "Well, fix it!" he yells, clearly frustrated at the situation. "No, I don't ... fine. I'll be in the office in twenty minutes. You better have Tom, Aaron, and Dean on standby. I'm not fucking around this time." He disconnects the call and puts his phone in his pocket.

Looking over at me, he swallows and his shoulders drop. "I'm sorry, I have to go deal with this crap. I know we planned to go over some things at dinner, but ..."

Wanting to relieve whatever turmoil he's struggling with, and also understanding all too well the pressures of his position, I smile and place my hand on his arm. "No problem. I'm exhausted anyway. Today has been ... overwhelming."

His eyes look sad. "I promise I'll make it up to you." He gives me a small smile.

"No need, Jackson. Just go. What time is our meeting tomorrow?"

His eyes twinkle with mischief and his voice turns playful. "No meetings. I have other plans for us. Be ready by one o'clock."

My eyes widen and I start to twist my hands as my heart races. Do I continue to fight this? There's only one way this is going to end—badly—but I want to spend the day with him. I want to see if this is all my crazy imagination. I'm too tired to think anymore. I take a shaky breath and exhale. "Okay." My brilliant plan to keep things strictly business just went out the door. I know I should spend tomorrow working or alone, but I can't resist him.

"Good night, Catherine." And with that, he turns and walks away.

Too late to change my mind now.

chapter

thirteen

I SLEPT WELL, considering the absolute shit day I had yesterday. Between my dead father, the earth-moving kiss with Jackson, Jackson regretting said earth-moving kiss, and the fight with my mother, I'm surprised I can even function. The worst part is I'm more upset about Jackson than any of the other things. One minute he's seducing me with his magnetic eyes, sexy grin, and that damn dimple, and the next he's pushing me away and tormenting me.

I roll over and my eyes land on the clock sitting on the nightstand. It takes a second for them to focus, but when they do ... Holy shit I slept late—it's almost noon. I've always been an up-at-seven-no-matter-what girl, but not today apparently. Groaning, I get out of the extremely comfortable bed and start getting ready for whatever Jackson has planned for me. Looking over the outfits I threw in my bag during my pissed-off packing, I realize I don't have an outfit for *"I have plans."* I have no clue what to wear or where we're going. Instead of agonizing over it, I opt for jeans and a cute pink top. Luckily I brought my favorite pair, which hug my butt perfectly and accentuate my curves. The top that Ashton threw in is not a business top, but it's perfect for our *"plans."* The one shoulder gives a little sexy, but the loose fit keeps it looking casual. I have my hair in a loose ponytail with the ends curled. I throw on my white sneakers and hope for the best.

I've just sat in the chair and broke out my Kindle when I hear a knock on the door. Rushing over, I take two deep breaths, press the handle down, and open it. Jackson's smiling as he leans against the wall with his legs and arms crossed. My brain ceases to form rational thoughts. The sight before me takes my breath away—he's mouthwatering. I look down at the floor, trying to hide my blush and get my mind functioning again. As he uncrosses his leg and stands straight, I can't help but think that this man is going to be the death of me. My eyes slowly scan his body, absorbing as much detail as possible before I have to meet his eyes again. First thing I see are his dark blue track shorts, and above them a tight black shirt shows the ripples of his abs. My greedy perusal continues until I land on his face. That's when my knees buckle and I grip the doorjamb for support. His eyes darken. The intensity of his stare causes my stomach to clench and heat to pool in my center.

He steps forward so we're toe-to-toe and I have to tilt my head to look up at his smiling face. His six-foot-three frame towers over me and the sheer size of him has me parting and licking my lips. Jackson's expression changes as he follows my movement. He takes a deep breath and closes his eyes, letting me know I'm affecting him as much as he's affecting me. A thrill runs through me, increasing my desperation for his lips on mine. He pushes forward. Our chests are touching, my nipples pebbling at the warmth of his body and the thoughts flooding my mind of him taking me right here, right now. Jackson lifts his hands and cups my face, slowly leaning into me as we breathe each other in. He stills, our mouths almost touching, but I hold my ground. I want him to be the one to kiss me again. I need it to be his choice. I close my eyes, trying to make my intentions clear, silently begging. *Please, just kiss me!*

I feel his lips brush against mine before I hear, "Not yet, Catherine. But soon." Jackson's voice drops even lower. "The next time there won't be any mistakes."

He takes a small step back and I open my eyes, watching as

his gaze darts between my eyes and my lips, as if he's battling his own desire. I can't speak. I can barely process anything he's saying. He takes a deep breath and shakes his head. "First, we have plans, okay?"

No, it's not okay! I want him to push me down to the floor or up against the wall and take me. Damn him and all his self-control. I take a step out of his grip and respond in a breathless whisper, "Sure."

"Good. Grab your stuff. We only have it reserved for an hour. I think you'll have fun today." His voice is now playful, refocused and excited by whatever plans he's made for us.

The only fun I want to have doesn't include us leaving this hotel room. I walk over and grab my purse, shoving my phone in and gritting my teeth. So much for my own self-control—I have none when it comes to him. Not even two seconds after seeing him, I'm ready to strip and let him have his way with me.

Jackson turns to walk away, taking only two steps before he stops, grabs my hand, and weaves his fingers through mine. I can't help but smile at the small gesture. Great. Holding hands has reduced me to a schoolgirl.

"Oh, and Catherine?" The hair on the back of my neck rises at the deep rasp in his voice. "Today we're going to talk and figure this out."

I nod, praying that we can figure out whatever's happening between us before it destroys everything I've worked for. No matter what I'm feeling for him, he needs to know that I won't sacrifice my career for this, for him, for anything.

"Where are we going?" I ask, grabbing my driver's license out of my wallet as he requested. We're waiting in line to get through security.

"This is the Navy base. I thought you might have fun doing

something different," he replies, taking my license and handing it over to a guy with a rather large gun around his chest. I'm so confused.

"Wait," I say as he starts driving forward. "Did I miss something? Are you still in the Navy?" I narrow my eyes and he smiles over at me.

"No, but I'm a contractor, so I can still access the base. Also, I was a SEAL, so I called ahead to my friends and got all this cleared." His smile widens as we pull up behind a fence.

"These are our plans?"

Jackson doesn't say anything as he parks the truck. When he sneaks a peek at my expression, I can see the mischief dancing in his eyes. What in the ever-loving hell is he thinking? I'd be lying if I said I didn't love this side of him. I've never really enjoyed surprises, but he looks like a kid on Christmas morning and I don't want to spoil his mood.

I look around, trying to see exactly what he has planned for us on a Navy base. I can't see anything through the trees lining the fence, and my lack of information is quickly turning my excitement into anxiety. Jackson leans over the console and grips my hand. I'm both relieved and annoyed by how my panic starts to ebb at his small touch. He squeezes once and exits the car. I climb out of the cab and squint, trying to decipher what the large tree-house-looking building is.

"Ready?" I flinch, my heart accelerating at the feel of him behind me. I didn't even hear him approach.

"Stop scaring me! Jesus, don't you make noise when you move?" I ask, slightly flustered. He lets out a loud, carefree laugh as he comes around. The look on his face is priceless, and his dimpled smile melts my momentary irritation.

"I'm just stealthy."

"I have no words for you." I smile and shake my head. "Stop scaring me all the time."

"You're just skittish. Maybe you should pay closer attention to what's going on around you." He pulls me in by my hips, right up against his chest. My eyes widen and the air expels from my lungs at the sudden contact. In a flash, his expression changes. His eyes smolder and his voice is low and hoarse when he says, "Maybe soon you'll hear *all* the noises I make." I gasp as a shudder passes through me. He releases me without a word and walks toward the metal gate.

There are no words. I can't think of a single thing to say to him. Once again, Jackson renders me speechless. He's flirtatious and seductive one moment and then a smartass then next. He's unlike any man I've ever met. Shaking my head to rid the turmoil in my mind, I gather my wits and walk over to him.

"Are you ready for some fun?" he asks with an amused smirk.

I have no idea what kind of fun we're going to have in a gated, woodsy area, but for some reason I trust Jackson. I don't know if it's because of his time in the service or the fact that he owns a security company, but I don't believe he'd put me in harm's way. I take a deep breath and smile. "Ready as I'll ever be. Do you mind clueing me in to what this fun is?"

Jackson grabs my hand as we walk through the gate. What I see stops me dead in my tracks and I drop his hand absently. He's got to be kidding me! Through the clearing is a large four-story building. Long ropes stretch from the top of it to a huge pole across about a hundred feet of open air, with only a shabby-looking net under them. Off to the right are four tree trunks on their side with about a foot of space between the ground and the trenches dug beneath them. Farther down are large metal cylinders that you either climb through or over. What the hell is this place? As I continue to look around, there's more—ropes, walls, even a moat! Oh hell no! I'm in jeans—cute, expensive, skintight jeans—and a pretty pink top. He's insane. I look over to where he was standing, but he's moved about ten steps away. He's leaning casually against the gate, and judging from the look on his face, he's getting quite a kick out of my reaction.

"You're enjoying this, aren't you?" I ask him with a half laugh.

"What?" he replies innocently, a sarcastic grin plastered to his face. "You said you were stronger than I thought. I figured maybe you'd wanna put your money where your mouth is, Ms. Pope."

"I never said I was training to become a soldier!" I huff.

Jackson walks toward me and stops about a foot away. He has one brow raised and his voice is playful. "Sailor," he reminds me. "Hmmm, maybe you're too ..."—he taps a finger on his chin—"scared?" he taunts.

My jaw falls slack as I stare wide-eyed at his comment. I'm way too competitive to let that comment slide and somehow he knows it. Yet again he's found a way to bend me to his will. Who the hell does he think he is? Screw that! "I am *not* scared! I will own this course, *Muffin*." I glare and then soften as an idea enters my head. Giving him a taste of his own medicine, I bend and touch my toes, providing a little seduction of my own. I glide back up and cock my head to the side, pursing my lips and narrowing my eyes. "I hope you're ready to have your ass handed to you." I'm about to embarrass myself, but I will not let him beat me.

Jackson takes a small step forward. His cheeks raise and the crinkles by his eyes grow more defined. His eyes are sparkling and his voice is smooth. "Then by all means." He waves his hand toward the course. "I can't wait to have my ass handled by you."

"Handed! I said handed!" I throw my hand over my face. I fell right into this trap and now I'm going to look like an ass. If I'm going to lose, I will go down with dignity.

"Same difference." He laughs. "You should know this isn't my first time here. I also *never* lose, so if you want to back out, now's your chance," Jackson says, completely relaxed. He starts stretching, laughing at me as I glare at him.

"Nope," I say confidently. No way am I going to back out now. I'm in this—balls to the walls. I mentally roll my eyes at my false bravado. I'm so screwed.

I look over and realize I have no idea what the hell I'm supposed to do. Is there a safety harness or padding I can wear? Shit! I clear my throat and Jackson looks back with a knowing grin. "Ummm, how does this work? Do I start here or what?"

He walks me through the course, explaining whether to go under, over, through, or up. I keep shaking my head and huffing, each time earning a laugh or some other entertained reaction from Jackson. I sure hope he's enjoying himself because I'm freaking the hell out.

We end back at the starting point and he places his hands on my shoulders, brushing his thumbs across my collarbone, sending chills through my body. His finger glides up my neck, just barely touching my skin. Without permission, my head tilts into his touch, naturally gravitating toward him like a magnet. His eyes swim with emotion as I try to decipher what he's feeling. Jackson shifts forward and puts his lips to my forehead. My lids shut as I absorb the moment of intimacy. Inch by inch he backs away and I stare at him with questions floating in my head. One side of his mouth lifts and his low voice cracks through my daze. "Time starts now."

"What?"

"Clock is ticking. You're wasting precious time that you're going to need if you plan to ..." He looks pensive as he rolls his eyes up and taps his foot. "What was it? Oh I know, *handle* my ass." He leans down and whispers in my ear, "Remember, I never lose." He swats my ass and laughs.

I take off and start running, half surprised, half frustrated that his plan to get me flustered and then start the timer worked. Stupid boy and his stupid plan. I can't believe I'm actually doing this. The only thing keeping me moving is my need to win and the chance to watch Jackson run this damn course after me. I climb over the logs and then crawl through the metal tube. As I approach the huge building, I swallow nervously. Seriously? I have to climb this? Panting my way up the stairs, I make a mental note that the gym is now a daily requirement. It feels like someone's sitting on my lungs. I continue to climb but stop when I notice Jackson standing at the top, smiling. Asshat!

As I move toward the ropes, he steps forward and puts his hands on my waist. I don't have time for his stupid touch-Catherine-and-she-gets-flustered game—I have a challenge to win, dammit. "Place your hands on the rope," his deep voice commands. "Now swing your legs up and grab it with your feet."

My eyes widen and my mouth drops open. He's joking, right? There is no way I'm sliding down this rope. "Yeah, no thanks. I'll just slide down the net."

His loud guffaw reverberates in the woods around us. "Fine. Then I'll add two minutes on to your time." He shrugs as he returns to his spot against the wall.

"Yeah, that whole endearing thing is total bullshit. They lied." I narrow my eyes and then grab the rope, swinging my body forward but missing with my feet on my first try. I cast a quick glance at Jackson, who's trying to hide his smile. Bastard. I bite my lip and try again, managing to get my leg around the rope this time. I hold on for dear life and lean my head back, smirking at Jackson with an I-told-you-so look. Okay, now what?

As if hearing my mental question, Jackson walks toward the rope. I'm hanging upside down with my head still tilted backward, giving him a perfect view of my breasts. Though he seems to be trying to keep his eyes on mine, he's failing miserably as he glances more than once. A low grumble sounds from his chest and he closes his eyes. His voice is strained when he looks back at me. "Okay. Now, slide down the rope and keep your feet locked. If you fall, you lose."

I groan, slowly starting to move down the rope. There are times I truly wonder what the hell is wrong with me and why

I'm being punished. I look back at him when he grabs the rope and pulls himself up. It jumps and I clench my legs tighter, letting out a high-pitched scream. "Jackson!"

"What?" he asks innocently.

I'm not buying his act.

I slide lower down the rope, getting about halfway and feeling confident I can do this, when it jerks again and I bounce up and down. He smiles widely and I let him know what's about to happen. "I swear you're going to pay for this!"

He's a dead man walking. I continue to slide until I reach the end, where I promptly let go and fall on my ass. *Awesome.* That's going to leave a mark.

Running to the finish line, I hear his throaty laugh behind me as he claps his hands. "You did it!" he yells excitedly, moving fast in my direction.

My hands are on my knees as I gasp for air, trying to catch my breath from running and hurling myself all over this stupid course. People do this for fun? He moves toward me and picks me up, throwing me over his shoulder. I gasp and squeak, "Jackson! Put me down!"

He lets out a chuckle while carrying me over to a bench near the starting line. His voice is happy. "Nope. You need to sit and see how it's really done. Time to watch the master." He plops me down and hands me his watch. I stare up at him as I realize I get to watch him run it now.

"Master? What if my time is better?"

He laughs and quickly recovers. "Should we bet?"

"Are you sure you want to chance it?" I smile, goading him.

Jackson has a huge grin on his face as he stands in front of me, blocking the sun with his muscular body. "If I win, you have to have dinner with me in New York."

"But if I win, you owe me a spa day and a new pair of jeans."

Jackson smirks as if this is the easiest bet he's ever made. "Deal. This is going to be a walk in the park."

"I wouldn't be so sure of that."

He chuckles and grabs my hand holding the watch. "Okay, that button on the right is the timer. When I say go, you press it. Got it?" He smiles as I nod in agreement. Good thing he missed my finger twitch when I pressed it a moment ago.

"Oh, Jackson?" I ask innocently.

"Yes?"

I casually lift my shoulders and press my chest out to stretch my back, taking an agonizingly slow time with each movement. His jaw tics as he watches me roll my neck. I let out a gentle breath and drop my voice to a seductive whisper. "Did you enjoy the show?" My teeth bite on my bottom lip and I watch every moment, taking great pleasure in the way his eyes drop to my mouth and his Adam's apple bobs.

He takes a deep breath and rips his shirt off, stopping whatever game I was attempting to play. Holy fucking shit. He's standing completely still, allowing me to take him in. Each muscle in his solid body is toned and perfect. My mouth goes completely dry as I stare at his taut chest and the large tattoo covering the left side of it. It's a tribal sun that takes up the entire space over his heart. Greedily, my eyes graze lower to his rippled abs, all the way down to my favorite part of a man—the deep V. I find my way back up to his blazing eyes—the look he gives me cements me to my seat.

He takes three long strides and places his hands on the back of the bench on each side of me, staring intently into my eyes. I feel naked, the intensity of his gaze stripping me and baring my soul. I've never felt so vulnerable yet so desired at the same time. His breathing is labored and I'm completely still. Neither of us moves as my eyes start to drift, and then he makes a deep noise in his throat. My gaze quickly reverts to his turquoise eyes as they probe for something. Between the running, adrenaline, and the intensity that is Jackson I start to get dizzy.

He leans in and drops his head to the side of my neck, taking two deep breaths. I can feel the tension, the turmoil rolling through his body. I don't know what he's fighting. He runs his nose up my throat and my eyes roll back as I moan. "Keep making those noises and I'm going to get the wrong idea."

Abruptly, he's gone. He's at the start line looking back at me. "Ready for *your* show, Catherine?"

So damn sure of himself, isn't he? Leaning back, he lifts his arms over his head, which causes his shorts to drop a tiny bit. My eyes follow the indentation of his hips down to the tiny trail that leads to all things happy. My lips part and my breathing becomes erratic. I'm incredibly turned on right now. He gets in the ready position, waiting for me to tell him to go. I smile inwardly knowing that he's added about three minutes on to his time with his little seduction game. I lift the watch and yell, "Go!"

Nothing could have prepared me for watching Jackson run the course. Not only does he have a large tattoo on his front, he has one on his shoulder as well. It's black and looks like the skeleton of a frog. His body moves as if he was made for this—each leap graceful and precise, every step calculated. His body moves, his muscles tighten, and my mouth waters at the sight of him. There's no time for me to return the favor of climbing to the top of the ginormous building, so I decide to rush over to the bottom of the steps. Jackson still has a little time before he makes it over there, although with the way he's moving, it may be a lot faster than I'm anticipating. I get there before him and try to climb a couple flights, but the five-alarm fire burning in my legs prevents me from getting too far. I sit on the steps instead, trying to appear casual as Jackson starts to climb.

I lie across the step and rest my hand on my propped-up knee. He gets to my step and stops briefly, letting out a throaty laugh. "Nice try, babe." He leaps over me and laughs the rest of the way up.

I turn and yell in his direction, "Hey! Not fair!"

I look up and see him descending a rope faster than I thought humanly possible. Somehow when he reaches the bottom, he's not even winded. He sprints to the end, finishing without breaking a sweat. Jesus!

He yells back, "Done! Press stop!" as I gingerly walk to him, trying to lessen the throbbing in my muscles. Jackson heads toward me with a huge smile on his face as I press the button.

I place the watch in my back pocket. He's not getting it until I know my time. "So, Jackson, you tell me my time and I'll tell you yours. Then we can see who the winner is." I raise my eyebrow, smiling coyly.

He reaches forward and pulls me against him. "First, dinner. I'll tell you then."

"What?" I huff. "No! I want to know now." I purse my lips and push back from him.

"Too bad. If you want it, you have to have dinner with me. Besides, you owe me anyway."

"Ugh! You don't fight fair." He drives me insane. On the other hand, I haven't had this much fun since ... I can't even remember. He makes me laugh and feel special. There are worse ways to spend my evening than dinner with an extremely sexy and agile and funny and powerful and ... Oh man. This is bad. He's all of those things, but he's also my client. Still, he doesn't seem to be concerned with that little fact.

His low voice halts my mental debate. "Stop overthinking. It's dinner—we can even talk business. Plus, don't you want to know how bad you lost and if you get your spa day?"

I grab the watch, taking a picture of his final time with my phone. I clear the display and then hand it back to him. His time was outrageously long—that makes me smile. And now that I have the proof in my phone, there's no way he can deny it. "Fine. Dinner, but we talk about work. Then I'll show you just how bad you lost." I grin, walking toward the car.

chapter

fourteen

I CLIMB INTO the cab of the truck, laughing as I imagine his reaction when he finally sees his ridiculous time.

"What's so funny?" he asks.

"Oh, nothing. You'll see later tonight. Unless of course you're ready to share my time now?" I smile and bat my eyelashes.

He returns my smile and throws the truck in reverse. "Nice try, babe. But if I give you the time now, I'll have nothing to ensure you show up tonight."

"It's not like I can go very far." I really want him to tell me so I can watch his face fall when he sees how bad he lost. There's no way he beat me. Well, there is, just not with the amount of lead-time I added in. If he still beat me, even with the extra time, I'm not only signing up for a gym, I'm getting a personal trainer.

"No, I think I have you right where I want you." He winks and his cheek rises.

We start driving back toward the hotel, but it's a different way than how we came. When I look off to the right the shoreline is close. It's beautiful. The homes lining the street are all quaint little beach cottages with white picket fences and trees that cast shade over the road.

"This area is adorable," I muse.

Jackson looks over, smiling. "I lived on this side when I

was stationed here. It's the locals' beach on this side of the bay. You get to enjoy the ocean without the crowds."

"So if you still have your headquarters down here, do you stay in a hotel every time or do you have a home here?"

I wondered this before but wasn't sure how or if I should ask. Since he thought it would be entertaining to make me run an obstacle course, I think it's fair game. If it weren't for him, my legs wouldn't be throbbing and my arms wouldn't be numb.

"No, I sold my house when I moved up to New York. I kept the office here because it made more sense being close to the base. Plus, it gives me an excuse to come back to the beach and see friends." His hand grips the steering wheel and he puts his blinker on.

"Where are we going?" I ask, confused. The hotel isn't here, not that I know where here is. But still, there isn't anything here but trees. I look at the sign as we turn—another military base. No. No. No. I'm *not* doing this again. He's trying to kill me. "Ummm ..."

Jackson laughs but doesn't answer. He gives his ID to the guard at the gate and keeps driving forward. "Relax, this will be fun."

My hands are clenching the seat as I try to get a grip. Jackson reaches over and grabs my hand, pulling it onto the middle console as his fingers intertwine with mine. If he keeps pushing against that wall, soon enough it's going to crumble. Distance. I need distance. I try to pull away but he tightens his grip, continuing to look forward.

"I don't believe you. You said the same thing about the last base we went to."

"I had fun. Didn't you?" he asks.

"Fun? Sure, if you call aching joints, atrocious hair, and a dirt mark on my butt from falling fun. I would call it something else, but we can go with that." I smile even though I was going for sarcasm.

Jackson's loud laughter fills the truck as he parks. A little nervous and afraid to see where he's brought me, I decide to stare at him—the view is beautiful either way.

"You still look perfect even with messy hair and dirt on your ass—which I happen to be fond of." Jackson's brow raises and he shifts forward, coming so close our lips could brush. "I want to show you my favorite place in Virginia Beach, or would you rather go back?"

With his breath heating my face, I'm cognitively misfiring. He could ask me to strip and run the course again and right now, I would. "Here is fine."

His smile is brighter than the sun. "Good, let's go."

I climb, or more like hobble, out of the truck. The sea air assaults my nose and seagulls fly overhead. I look around and it's truly remarkable. The sand is a little whiter than by the hotel. There are no waves. It's calm and peaceful. But what causes my breath to catch is the huge brick lighthouse. It's very old but still perfect. The red is muted from years of wind, rain, and storms, but there she stands—steadfast and strong to guide the ships home.

I look at Jackson leaning on the hood of the truck, watching me take in the sights. He walks around and extends his hand. Instead of wavering, I eagerly give him what he wants, reveling in the way his hand engulfs mine.

"I used to come here a lot. Have you ever been to a lighthouse?" Jackson asks in a hushed tone.

"In Jersey there are tons of lighthouses. My uncle had a boat, and when I was young we used to fish right by one. I always thought they were magic." I smile and Jackson pulls me closer to him as we walk.

"Magic, huh?"

I shrug, not wanting to share too much of my heart with him. I loved the stories my uncle would tell me about sailors and the women waiting for them to return. He was a silly old man but he always made it seem so romantic, talking about how men would be lost for days until the lighthouse guided them home. And how the lighthouse keeper would ensure it was lit, helping sailors find their beacon. He used to call my aunt his light-keeper and say she was the light he'd always find his way back to. All my life I've dreamed of sharing a love like that.

We stop in front of the steps that lead inside. The wind whips my hair forward and I realize I have to climb my way to the top. I'm not going to be able to walk for a week. Maybe we can go back to the hotel where there's an elevator?

Jackson notices my body tense and rubs his thumb in small circles on the back of my hand.

I have two choices: either I suck it up and climb to the top to see the view, or I pout and go back to the car. Option two sounds like a better idea for my feet, but there's no way I want to miss this. Even back home I couldn't ever go inside the lighthouse.

I nudge Jackson as we enter the small building. "Just in case you're curious, no matter who wins the bet, you owe me a massage. And a new pair of jeans."

"Are you saying you want me to rub you down?"

I scoff and roll my eyes. "Let's go, Muffin. We have about four hundred stairs to climb." If he only knew how bad I want his hands all over me, I'd be in big trouble.

I hear him sigh deeply as I giggle to myself.

The inside is cramped and the spiral metal stairs are terrifying. I'm sure I'll have blisters all over my hands from gripping the railing so tight. My legs are quivering—not sure if it's from the previous workout or from fear of falling to my death. The only thing giving me any comfort is Jackson insisting on going behind me in case I lose my footing.

"How much farther does this go?" I ask.

Next thing I know I'm being hoisted over Jackson's shoulder.

"Stop wiggling or I'll drop you," he says with a short laugh, seeming unconcerned as he carries me up the steps.

"You're insane! You're going to drop me anyway!"

"Only if you keep moving. I'll put you down on one condition." Jackson's voice is loud and strong as he begins to lower me. He's very good at getting his way.

"What's that?"

"You let me carry you on my back."

What? No. "I can walk up the steps."

"Then you deal with being upside down," he says and starts climbing the stairs again, throwing me back over his shoulder.

Jackson climbs about ten more steps and I slap his ass, giggling. "Jackson! Put me down!"

"Nah, this is more fun," he says, gripping my legs tighter.

I can't take another second of being hung upside down, staring and feeling suspended over the hundreds of feet below. "Fine! I give up. You win."

For once, he doesn't make a noise but I can feel his chest bounce as if he's laughing. *Cocky bastard.* Instead of putting me down so I can climb on his back, he lowers me and scoops me in his arms. My arms naturally wrap around his neck as if it's the most normal thing to be carried like this. Never once can I remember having this happen in any past relationship. His strong arms hold me close against his chest and I feel his heart racing through his shirt. I don't say a word, afraid to break the moment between us. Safe and secure is the only way I can define this space in time.

Once we reach the top of the lighthouse, he sets me down. My arms fall to my sides as he leans forward and places a kiss on the top of my head. I swallow and try to regulate my breathing and slow my pulse.

He weaves his fingers with mine again and guides me to the windows.

"I used to come up here after my run in the mornings," he says quietly as we look out at the horizon.

"So you worked out and then climbed the stairs? By choice?" I ask with a raised brow.

His throaty laugh echoes through the building and he pulls me close. "Not all of us find exercise dumb. There are lots of activities that can be"—he coughs and smiles—"enjoyable."

Jackson's innuendo makes my cheeks flush. Him and his mouth!

"Well, only if you do it right," I say boldly.

He leans in conspiratorially. "I always do it right," he says in my ear. Then he walks past me.

"I'm sure you do," I mutter.

"What was that?"

Of course he heard me.

"Nothing. Just admiring the view," I lie and stare out the window.

We walk around the lighthouse, viewing the ocean from all angles. Times like this you realize how small you really are. Up here, looking out, I see endless seas and skies. Jackson and I are the only ones standing here, and as I take it all in I wonder who would light the way home for me?

I'm lost in thought when Jackson comes behind me, pressing against my back. His heat comforts me and I lean back a little. "Look over there," he says against my ear, pointing toward a huge bridge.

I look over but it's not the bridge that causes me to gasp. It's the huge aircraft carrier that's floating over where the bridge becomes a tunnel.

"Ships come in and out through there. You see the white?" Jackson asks.

I squint to get a better view. It looks like there's a white lining around the deck of the ship. I nod, still trying to get a closer look.

"That's called manning the rails. When a ship goes in or out of port for a deployment, they stand around the side of the ship and watch their home either go out of view or come into view," Jackson explains.

I wonder how many times he's done that. How many

families have watched their loved ones leave, knowing they were about to spend countless nights alone? How many have stood waiting, anticipating their love's return, serving as lighthouses to guide them home?

In the softest whisper I say, "See. Magic."

Jackson smiles and his eyes lock on mine. "Yeah, there's magic here for sure."

"I don't know what the hell to do!" I say into the receiver. Ashton is not helping and I *need* my best friend to help me right now.

I called her shortly after we got back from the lighthouse. Jackson and I spent about a half hour up there, laughing and talking about different stuff—what it was like for him going through boot camp, a little about my college experience and Ashton and Gretchen. I was nervous and quiet in the car after we left, unsure how to proceed with him and how to process what I was thinking. Jackson, however, was relaxed and completely at ease with our silent drive back. As we were arriving back at our hotel, another call came in from his security team. All I could hear was something about an issue with the contract in Afghanistan. Jackson apologized for being on the phone again and when we arrived at our rooms, he just gave me a wave and a wink, unlocked his door, and went in.

"See why I told you to bring pretty panties?"

"You know! You're not freaking helpful." I sigh and pace around the room. After crawling and running around all over today, I desperately needed a shower when we got back. But while I was enjoying the warmth and serenity, I remembered I was going to dinner with Jackson tonight. My nerves grew to the point that I had to do some deep breathing exercises to avoid an anxiety attack.

"Look, you like him, right?"

"Yes ... I think. I don't really know him. He could be a complete asshole."

"Or he could be perfect for you," she quickly replies.

"Again with the helping." I huff and continue to pace. "You're supposed to be on my side. Where is *my* best friend?"

She makes an obnoxious sound—a mix between a grunt and a snort. "I really hope you're kidding me, twunt. I *am* helping. You just refuse to listen to what I'm saying."

"Twunt?" I ask. "Seriously, did you make that word up?"

"Yes. Be jealous of my superior intelligence."

I laugh. "Wow, you *can* make up stupid curse words."

"Whatever." I can almost picture her rolling her eyes. "Let's get back to the issue at hand. He wants dinner. You're on a business trip. Go to dinner with your sex-on-a-stick boss. And if you didn't pack the right stuff, just go commando."

"The problem isn't the underwear. It hasn't been that long since things ended with Neil—"

She quickly cuts me off with a stern voice. "That shit was over long before you found out. Let's be real." Her voice softens a little but still sounds annoyed. "I'm gonna be brutal here. Neil is not the issue. You are. You get in your head and you think you're not good enough. Why?"

"Because ..." I trail off. I don't know why. That's the problem. I don't know why I can't accept that a man like Jackson would ever want to have dinner with me, let alone anything more. I've never felt special. I was always second best. But the worst thing isn't that people told me those things—the worst thing is that I believe them. The only place I'm worth a damn is at work. Sometimes when you're told something long enough you eventually believe it.

"Well, that's a great answer!" she screams, loud enough that I have to move the phone from my ear. "Here's the deal. Your dad did a real number on you, and I'm sorry. Your mom has always made you feel like it was your fault. And don't even get me started on Neil." She clears her throat and her tone softens dramatically. "Please listen to me this once." She takes a deep breath. "You're so much more than you give yourself credit for, but Jesus Christ stop for one goddamn minute. Stop being so deep in your head that you're blind to the fact that life is short and if you keep letting others influence your decisions, you're going to be that crazy bitch with a hundred cats. We all know a woman should only have one pussy."

"Ashton!" I laugh.

Her voice softens again. "I love you. You're my best friend. You're worthy and one of the best people in the world. You've always deserved more than the bullshit you always seem to get. So go and be the beautiful girl I know you are and live for the moment."

A tear falls down my face at Ashton's sincerity. If we were face-to-face, I'd hug her and never let go. "Thank you," I say softly, never more grateful for our friendship. "I should get ready."

"I love you, Catherine. Now, open the outside zipper of your suitcase, put what's inside on under your black dress, and get laid already!" She laughs and hangs up before I can say anything more.

Shaking my head, I walk over to my suitcase, open the compartment, and sink into the chair. I pull out a black corset, which I've never seen before. When the hell did she put this in my bag? I need to focus and pull myself together. I'll worry about clothes in a bit and finish getting ready now. I head into the bathroom to dry my hair. I style it with curls at the end and then do my makeup, making sure it's perfect. When I'm done primping, I walk back into the room where my dress and corset are lying on the bed, silently mocking me.

Picking up the corset, I hold it to my chest and look in the mirror. My eyes widen as I take in my reflection. I don't look like the same girl. My hair falls softly down my back. My eyes are rimmed in a chocolate color and my lashes are thick and long, which makes my brown eyes look big and sultry. I put the

corset around and hook each eye, pull up the matching panties, and stare at myself in the mirror. My breasts are pushed
up and it cuts in at the perfect place to give me an hourglass
figure. Satisfied with how I look for a change, I smile as I run
my hands down the silky fabric. Yeah, I'm definitely wearing
this tonight. Even with no plans of Jackson ever seeing it, I feel
sexy. I slip my black sleeveless sweetheart dress over my head.
It hugs each curve and tapers down, clinging to my legs, ending
right above the knee. I pair it with my open toe, strappy gold
heels.

I send a quick text to Ashton, thanking her for earlier and
letting her know that I owe her dinner for packing the corset.
Needing to keep moving, I clean the room a little and check my
makeup at least two more times. I have fifteen minutes before
I'm supposed to meet Jackson at the restaurant downstairs. He
texted me about an hour ago saying he had to run out and it
would be easier to meet there.

Pacing the floor and watching the never-moving clock, I
decide to go to the bar and get a drink to kill some time. I keep
telling myself this isn't a date, but in the back of my mind I
know I'm only fooling myself by saying this is a business meeting. Maybe Ashton is right—I need to see where this goes and
stop fighting my desires when it comes to Jackson. If we can
talk and come to an agreement, maybe it won't affect my career.

chapter

fifteen

*T*HERE'S AN OPEN seat at the end of the bar. I sit down, ordering my signature drink—lemon drop martini. As I place a ten-dollar bill on the bar, a hand presses over mine. I look up to a pair of deep brown eyes and a shy smile.

"Hi. Can I help you?" I ask timidly.

"Sorry, but a beautiful woman such as yourself shouldn't have to pay for a drink. Ever." His smile widens and he extends his hand. "I'm Pat. Nice to meet you."

Not wanting to be impolite, I return the handshake. "Hi, I'm Catherine. Thanks for the drink."

"So, are you from Virginia Beach?" He asks and takes a sip of his beer. Really? How original.

"No." I give a short laugh. "I hate to be rude, Pat, but I'm meeting someone."

"He isn't here though, is he?" Pat asks.

Before I have a chance to reply, a deep, sexy voice rasps, "Yes, he is," from behind me.

Chills run down my spine. My body tightens as my breath hitches. A warm hand slowly travels up my back and rests on my bare shoulder. Jackson's presence is so distinct. I know it's him even without turning around. His thumb rests on the back of my neck, rubbing up and down. The entire lower part of my body is warm and tingling from his possessive touch.

Jackson's voice is low and warning, and I can only imagine

the look he's giving Pat right now. "Catherine,"—he leans close and presses his lips to my temple—"sorry to keep you waiting. Our table is ready."

Pat's face is stoic as he returns to his beer. I smile at him and place the ten-dollar bill back on the counter. Poor guy. He didn't stand a chance.

I gather my things and hear Jackson inhale loudly as I stand. When I turn to him he's standing there with his jaw slack. I look around to see what has his attention, but he's staring at me.

I try to break his trance. "Jackson?"

"You look breathtaking. I can't take my eyes off you." He looks me up and down, stopping leisurely at my neckline before his eyes make their way back up to my face.

"Ummm, thanks." I don't know how to take his compliment, the way he said it, or the way he seems to be undressing me with his eyes. I'm suddenly very hot—and bothered.

"You don't see it, do you?"

"See what?" I ask.

"Every man in this bar wants you right now." He takes a step forward, never breaking eye contact. "Every man wants to be me right now." Another step. "And none of them see what I see." One more step. We're now toe-to-toe as I lift my head to stare into his eyes. My heart beats so loud in my ears I have to strain to hear his words. He places his hand on my hip, pulling me against him. "I'm going to kiss you now, and I don't know if I'll be able to stop."

He lowers his head and hooks his other hand around my back, slowly sliding it up as the gap between us closes. His full lips are only a breath away when my lids flutter and shut. Then I feel his lips, soft and warm, pressing against mine. He pulls me even closer, tightening his grip and intensifying the kiss. I thread my fingers into his hair as his tongue sweeps across my lips, seeking entrance. I've died and gone to heaven. This is one of those moments I'll remember forever. Every girl dreams about a kiss like this. I sigh and give him access as our tongues brush against each other. All too soon Jackson loosens his hold and ends the kiss. He lets out a soft breath and then presses a brief kiss to my lips once more. His voice is raspy against my ear. "That should've been our first kiss."

I'm afraid to open my eyes and face a repeat rejection like last time. I lower my arms, still holding on to his shoulders, and take a deep breath. Hesitantly, I open my eyes and look up. Intensity like I've never seen dominates his stare, and my doubts about him wanting me, about this crazy attraction between us, disappear. With that one look he's torn down every wall around my heart. All my futile reasons to stay away from him are gone, replaced by this undeniable pull toward Jackson Cole. They simply don't exist anymore, and I realize I never had a chance against him. I open my mouth to speak but can't find my voice. I've never known this kind of feeling. It's heady and intoxicating, filling me with fear and excitement. He gently places his finger under my chin, pushing my jaw shut, and the dimple I love so much reappears with his warm smile.

My smile is shy when I finally speak. "So ... dinner?" *Dinner?* That's my fabulous response? My cheeks flare red—I'm so embarrassed. He makes me so self-conscious. The confidence he exudes is hard to keep up with.

Thankfully, he smiles and nods. "Yes, let's eat and talk."

Jackson places his hand on the small of my back and I grab my drink before making our way over to the hostess. Once we're seated, I basically down my martini and order another one. My palms are sweating and I can't stop fidgeting.

The restaurant is beautiful. It's done in rich blues and greens, which reminds me of Jackson's eyes. There's a large oyster bar on the right wall and the entire back wall is windows overlooking the ocean. Our table is situated with a perfect view of the water. I look around, smiling at the opulence of the scenery and clientele.

Jackson clears his throat as a handsome man walks toward

us with a smile on his face. "Carter!" He stands. "How are you? It's been a long time," he says as they hug and clap each other on the back.

Carter glances down at me and back over at Jackson. "Yes, brother, it has been. Didn't mean to interrupt."

Jackson smiles and shifts his weight. "No problem. This is Catherine. She's the new publicist working with me on the cosmetics company."

"Oh, well, I thought maybe you were finally getting back out there." Carter places his hand on his shoulder and Jackson's eyes narrow as he subtly shakes his head.

Hmmm ... that's weird. Back out there? And what's with the head shake? My stomach plummets as fear grips my heart. A hundred scenarios race through my mind.

"I should get back to my dinner." Jackson's tone is flat, lacking the buoyancy it held moments before. "It was good seeing you. I'll call next time I'm in town."

"You know Mad—"

"See you, Carter," Jackson cuts in.

"Right. See you, brother. Don't be a stranger." He pats his back and Jackson returns to his seat.

He won't look my way. Gone is the warm and sensual man from a few minutes ago. I can feel the tension coming off him in waves. I want to say something but—well, I don't really know what the hell any of this is. I'm not his girlfriend or even his friend, really. I'm his publicist. He made that crystal clear. I'm such a fool. I knew it was a mistake to get all dressed up and think there could be anything more to this. Taking his cue, I straighten my back and decide to rebuild my wall.

The waitress comes over and takes our orders, and Jackson starts talking about the business. An hour and three martinis later, dinner is done. I want to go to bed. I'm upset and exhausted. I kept myself in check. I didn't get all gooey—I did good. It's not as if he was being charming anyway. We created a plan on where he wants to see things go. He asked a lot of questions regarding the market and buying behaviors, but we steered clear of anything other than the end goal and how he wants to handle the launch. I gave him my best suggestions on how we get there, but the entire dinner Jackson barely spoke other than to ask pointed business questions.

Resting my hand on the table and fiddling with the martini glass, I'm lost in my disappointment. Jackson blows out a deep breath and leans forward then back again. Looking into his eyes, I can see the turmoil churning. After a few seconds, he leans forward again and places his hand over mine.

Glancing at our joined hands, I pull mine out of his grasp and place it on my lap, refusing to look at him. I'm hurt and angry. Two times he's kissed me and two times he's rejected me. The last time was different but the pain is the same.

His deep voice breaks through my ruminating. "Catherine, don't pull away."

"I'm not." I say sharply. I didn't pull away—he did. And so what if I did? He's not anything more than a client and I don't have to get personal with him.

He narrows his eyes and places his hand on the table palm up. "Yes. You are. We need to talk about this. Please give me your hand."

I look down at his hand, open and waiting for me. All I want to do is place my hand in his, to feel his skin against mine. Yet I don't want to. I close my eyes and shake my head.

"Please. I want to explain."

I lift my eyes and see nothing but sincerity. His hand is just lying on the table, waiting, and I'm paralyzed. I remember my rule and promise—I won't allow any man to hurt me again, not that I can prevent it entirely. I place my hand on the table next to his, sending my own message. "Explain, then."

"I'm sorry. I didn't expect to see Carter. He was like a brother to me. There's a lot of history and bad blood between us, to say the least." He inches his hand closer to mine. "I wasn't sure what to say and didn't want you to be in the middle of it." I'm torn. I understand being surprised, but why wait until now to say anything? He places his hand on top of mine and his voice is apologetic. "I want us to figure out whatever this is between us. Can you forgive me for being an asshole?"

In all the years I was with Neil, I don't think he ever apologized. I've been around Jackson for two days and he's not hesitated once. There's something now, though, about how cold he grew that has me on edge. His hand glides up and down the back of mine, but it's his eyes that break through my trepidation. "I forgive you for being an ass. So let's talk." I sigh and he grips my hand.

"I can't and I won't lie to you. I feel something for you. I have since the first day we met." His eyes blaze as he gazes at me. "I think about you all the time. I want to kiss you every time I look at you. Every time I try to focus at work, somehow I'm distracted thinking of you. I can't explain it but I think you feel it too."

I look away, trying to gather my thoughts and express them in a way that doesn't make me feel stupid. How can I explain it to him when I can barely describe it myself? "I don't know how to fully put it into words." I take a deep breath. "I've been hurt. When we met, obviously, I was wearing a ring." His finger rubs across my naked ring finger. I look up and he has a small smile, but his eyes are urging me to keep going. "Anyway, he ... well, he wrecked me. To say things ended badly would be putting it mildly. But honestly, you're my client, Jackson. You could ruin *everything* I've worked for. I'm not willing to throw my career away." I hesitate before saying more. There's no way I'm ready to tell him what's in my heart. I already know where this is going. I'm on a one-way trip to more heartache. Every single man in my life has chosen someone or something else over me. Jackson will be no different.

"I wouldn't ruin anything for you. I'm saying there's something between us. Can you honestly tell me you feel nothing?"

Nothing? No, I definitely can't say that. His blue-green

eyes pierce through me. I'm searching, trying to read any emotion telling me I should turn him away. He smiles expectantly and I sigh. "No. But I don't trust myself with you. It's so intense sometimes and if I get caught up ... " I trail off, afraid to finish my sentence.

He flips my palm over and traces the inside of my hand, sending tingles through my body. "Look, I'm saying let's take it slow. Have some fun. No matter what, I wouldn't jeopardize your career."

"So, what? We date? I don't know what you're looking for. I don't want another serious relationship right now. I can't ..." Emotion chokes me. I'm not sure why all of a sudden I'm struggling. I guess I just don't want another Neil. I'm not strong enough to deal with it.

"Yes, we date. We'll be spending a lot of time together anyway. So either we keep fighting this ... pull or whatever this is ..." he trails off and runs his hand through his hair. "I don't want to pretend anymore. Being around you, seeing you, listening to you laugh, just makes me want you that much more."

I want what he's offering so much, but the other part of me is fighting it. "And what if this ends badly? How do we work together day in and day out?" It's a valid question, and it's really the last flimsy excuse I can voice to him.

He places his palm flat against mine and smiles tentatively. "We're both professionals. I already told you I wouldn't hurt your career." He chuckles.

"Why are you laughing?"

"I've never had to work so hard to get a woman to date me. I always thought I was a pretty good catch." He lets out a short laugh again.

"I guess it further proves I don't find you charming or endearing." I smile at my line of bullshit. He's absolutely charming, so much so that I'm fighting the urge to crawl across the table and into his lap.

Jackson stands and strides to my side of the table with his

hand extended. "Dance with me."

His strong hand engulfs my tiny one as he helps me stand. It's symbolic of how I feel when I'm around him—consumed. We walk to the middle of the small dance floor. Jackson places his hand on my hip and his warmth penetrates my dress. Slowly he lifts my palm and places it on his chest, right over his heart. I can feel its steady beating, the constant thrum as it calms my own. I close my eyes and sink into him as I listen to the singer croon about coming away with her for a while. If only I could get away for a while, ignore all the painful turns my life has taken. He leads us through the song as I replay the last few weeks. Somehow, Jackson has taken my life by storm. He's found a way to make me feel alive, as if a light switch has been turned on, illuminating all my dark corners. He sharpens my senses and fills me with so many different things—excitement, fear, humor, anger. It terrifies me.

The song ends and I look into his kind, warm eyes. He leans in purposefully and gives me a tender kiss.

I smile and a soft giggle comes out.

"What?" Jackson asks.

"Oh, nothing." I shrug. "Just rethinking—maybe you are charming."

"You haven't seen anything yet."

I bet I haven't.

chapter

sixteen

WE FINISH DINNER and head through the lobby, and over to the elevator. As we wait, I consider my options. Do I invite him in? I mean, we aren't a couple. We're agreeing to stop flirting around the fact that we have some serious sexual tension. I don't know if I'm ready to sleep with him, but if he kisses like that, I can only imagine what he fucks like. I'm not even going to let myself go there. I don't really have time to make a pros and cons list, but I'm pretty sure the pros would win. I'm also quite sure that I could make anything into a pro at this point. Regardless, there are cons and the biggest one is how badly this could end for me. Sure, he doesn't want to ruin my career, but how do I know I can trust him? Look how great my track record has been. No, there's no way I'm going to sleep with him. We decided to take things slow. I need to pace myself with him or I'm going to get burned.

When the elevator door closes, all the feelings I was questioning are amplified by a thousand. I peek at Jackson who appears to have the same thoughts brewing. Our eyes lock and for a moment neither one of us moves. Then, all at once, we reach for each other, colliding in a haze of lust. I couldn't give a shit about being burned—right now, I'd gladly turn to ash. Hands, teeth, lips are everywhere. Jackson has me pinned against the wall as his mouth greedily devours mine. There's no finesse, no tenderness—this is primal, raw, two people desperate for each other. This kiss is weeks of flirting, toying, and resisting the urge to rip each other's clothes off. His hands roam my body, groping, grasping, squeezing. I'm panting and moaning—I need *more*.

"Catherine ..." He sighs heavily against my neck as I claw at his back.

"Please," I beg. "Don't stop."

I hardly get the words out and his mouth is ravishing mine. Jesus Christ! Who am I? I no longer have the ability to form rational thoughts. All I am is desire, want, lust, and I can't stop. I barely hear the ding of the elevator, but I'm definitely aware of Jackson's absence.

I'm panting, staring incredulously at him as he leans on the wall opposite me. An older gentleman enters the elevator and looks at both of us with a knowing smile, clearly aware of what we were doing. Now I understand why he moved. My lips are swollen, and I can only imagine what my hair looks like after having Jackson's hands tangled in it. I fix my dress and try to regain some semblance of composure. I swear I've completely lost control. The girl who wasn't going to do this? Yeah, she's gone. We're like two teenagers going at it in an elevator—well, interrupted in an elevator, but I enjoyed every second of it.

The door opens with a ding, and Jackson grabs my hand and pulls me out of the elevator. His fingers intertwine with mine as we walk through the hall toward our rooms. He lifts our hands, kissing the back of mine. The feel of his calloused fingers brushing against me increases my need to have them everywhere. When we arrive at my door, the nerves coursing through me smother the yearning I was struggling to control. The fear of being hurt and vulnerable all over again is almost crippling.

Jackson speaks first. "Look at me." He places his hand under my chin and lifts my head. "I want nothing more than to take you to bed, but I'm not going to push you." There's so much honesty in his words.

I nod, unsure of what I want. The woman who wore the corset wants him to come inside. However, my sensible and responsible side says I'm being crazy and I should take things slow. There is an angel and a devil on each shoulder and I'm not sure which one I should listen to. I'm not even sure there's a choice.

He leans down and the instant his full lips press against mine, the sparks ignite into a raging fire that consumes every fiber of my being. I'm burning and I need him to extinguish the flames. His tongue explores my mouth and all I can taste is Jackson. Strong hands roam my body and pull me close, making me feel like I'm being branded. Fuck being sensible!

Somehow we manage to open the door while our mouths are fused together. Jackson's tongue swirls with mine as we stumble through the room. My legs hit the edge of the bed, halting our movement. His deep voice drips with sex. "Turn around."

Breathless, I obey his command. He lifts my hair and brushes it to the side, placing hot kisses against my neck. The anticipation buzzes from my head to my toes and back up to my stomach. *Oh God, I want him so bad.* Shifting my weight as the fire burns in my core, desperate to relieve the aching, I whimper as he pulls my zipper down agonizingly slow. Other than my erratic breathing and the teeth of my dress coming apart, there's no sound in the room. In a husky whisper I beg, "Jackson, please ..."

"Please what, baby?"

My dress pools on the floor and a long moan escapes my lips as he trails his tongue across my shoulders. The heat of his tongue in contrast to the cool room is wreaking havoc on my body. He turns me around and his breath hitches. With hungry eyes, he devours my body as I stand before him in my corset and heels. He steps forward and groans. "You are so fucking beautiful." His mouth slams against my swollen lips and he pushes me on the bed.

I claw at his clothes, needing to feel his skin against mine. He rips his shirt off and my fingers press against his abs. Jackson hisses as my nails graze his chest, feeling every inch of his perfectly toned body. At the same time, he grabs my ankle and his hands roam up my legs, pushing my need for release to a throbbing ache. "Jackson ..." I moan, trying to control the sensations his touch is educing.

"What do you want, Catherine? You're going to have to tell me."

"You—I want you." I groan as his hands make their way higher.

"Oh baby, you're going to have me." He leans down against my ear and slowly traces the outside shell with his tongue. "I'm going to watch you come. Over and over." I nearly shatter from his promise alone. His voice is low and primal, assuring all of what's to come.

His hands slide down my body and unhook each tiny eye of my corset. With every pop, my chest tightens instead of finding relief. Finally, the last hook is free and the material falls to the side, leaving me exposed before him. Jackson leans down as I grab for his neck, pulling him toward me and devouring his mouth. He breaks the kiss and moves down my neck and chest, licking and kissing, until he reaches my breasts. The swirl of his tongue across my nipple makes it hard. He pulls it in his mouth, sucking, while his hand pulls and teases my other breast. My eyes roll back and I moan in ecstasy. "Oh God ..."

Jackson groans and moves a hand to my panties. Moving them to the side, his fingers open my pussy. "Mmmm. So fucking wet for me." He moves to my stomach and then pulls the tiny black thong down so that I'm completely naked except for my gold heels. The hunger in his eyes knocks me off center—I've never felt as sexy as I do right now. I need him. I want him so bad it hurts.

I lean in and grab his belt, needing to feel him. I manage to get his pants off, but he grabs my wrists before I can pull his boxers off too. I look up and he smiles softly. "I won't be able to control myself if you do that. Lie down." I comply. "I need to taste you. Right. Fucking. Now."

He leans in and places slow kisses from my knee up to my thigh. As his mouth moves higher, I start to tremble. I close my eyes and fist the sheets as his tongue swipes at my center. It feels so incredible. He continues to lick and suck at the bundle of nerves and then stops. Then he starts again, bringing me closer and closer before suddenly stopping again. I'm almost to the point of tears. I need to release so bad it's becoming physically painful. I moan and beg, "Jackson! Please, I'm so close."

Jackson licks and sucks my clit, bringing me higher, almost to the breaking point. He inserts a finger, slowly curling it around, while he presses harder with his tongue. I detonate and my back bows off the bed as I repeat his name over and over, losing myself to the most intense orgasm I've ever had. Holy fuck!

I open my eyes as he crawls over me. "So fucking sexy. I'm going to enjoy watching you do that again."

I sit up and press him down against the bed, straddling him. He lets out a groan while grabbing the back of my neck. His tongue swirls with mine, allowing me to taste myself mixed with Jackson. I moan, breaking the kiss as my lips travel down his body. I lick and kiss every ridge from his neck to his stomach. I pull his boxers off, setting his impressive erection free. There is nothing small about him—anywhere. I glance up as I lick his cock from root to tip and grip my hand around him, stroking him.

"Fuuuck. You're about to unman me, Catherine."

I'm about to do a whole lot more than that.

I smile and pull my hair to the side so he can see me take him in my mouth. I lick the bead of pre-cum from his tip and circle the top before sheathing my teeth and taking him into my mouth. His fingers tangle in my hair as I hollow out my mouth and take him deeper. He groans as I pump him up and down, applying pressure with my tongue on the underside. I feel him growing larger as I take him in to the back of my throat. Trying to control my gag reflexes, I do it one more time and he pulls tight on my hair as he moans. I want to make him come apart. I want to see if I can make him lose control the way he did to me, to call out my name over and over again. I reach down and roll his balls in my hand.

"Catherine, you better stop." Jackson barely gets the words out and I do it again. "Baby, I'm gonna come."

He erupts in my mouth, pumping in and out as he rides out his orgasm. I swallow every drop as he says my name over and over with reverence. I've never enjoyed giving a blowjob but that was worth watching.

I roll over while both of us try to catch our breath. I'm still coming down from my orgasmic bliss, but as my mind catches up with what just happened, I start to shake. What did I do? I never do this. Ever. I was so absorbed in the moment and now ... there's no going back. Until tonight, I'd never taken a man home before at least two months had passed. I've always been the one to put the brakes on—this time I was begging. I freaking begged him. My mind is reeling and the emotions are so intense my chest tightens.

Suddenly, Jackson lifts me and I'm facing him. He brushes the hair off my face as he rests on his arm beside me. He's assessing me, watching each breath, watching how my eyes close as I try to mask my emotions. The way he's reading me makes me tense. My emotions are all over the place and I know he can see it. I look off to the side while I grip his forearm. When he turns my head to look at him, worry is etched on his face. "Hey, what's wrong?"

How do I explain this to him? "I just don't do this—random hook-ups and one night stands." I don't know whether I'm more mortified by the fact that we barely know each other or that I enjoyed it. I close my eyes and focus on how amazing everything felt, how during that entire time he made me feel good, beautiful.

Jackson's face softens and he smiles tenderly. "I never said this was random or a one-night thing, did I?"

"No." I shake my head and look away to hide the tears forming. I ruined everything with my dumb insecurities. "I'm sorry."

"You have nothing to be sorry for." Jackson rolls onto his back and I try to get up. He grabs me, pulling me against his chest and wrapping his arms around me. He whispers in my hair, "Can I stay tonight?"

What? He wants to stay even though I've ruined it? "If you want. Of course you can stay." I want him to so badly. I don't know why, but I want nothing more than to lie in his arms and fall asleep.

Jackson doesn't say another word. He just rubs his hand methodically on my back. I curl into him with my arm draped across his chest as I drift off to sleep.

"Mmmm." I moan as I feel strong hands knead my breasts. I arch back and my eyes snap open as I process that someone is in bed behind me. Someone with his hands on my breasts.

His deep, raspy voice breaks through my fog as he croons in my ear, "Catherine ..." Jackson pulls me against him as his hands roam my naked body. I guess this is a benefit to sleeping nude. He stayed. He didn't run when I spooked. He held me all night and gave me comfort.

I've never wanted him more than I do right now. He begins kissing my neck and moves to my ear. "Jackson, now. Please." I reach behind me and start stroking his cock.

"Soon enough, baby. I'm not sure you're ready for me yet." Jackson's voice is hoarse as he makes his way down, spreading my sex and inserting two fingers. Slowly he pulls out and uses his thumb against my clit, drawing a long moan from me. I'm desperate for him. The need crushes me, making it difficult to breathe. Jackson continues to bring me higher and higher.

He flips me onto my back and gazes at me with an intensity so fierce my heart skips a beat. He rolls on a condom and I take a deep breath.

"You have no idea what you do to me, how you make me feel," Jackson says as his jaw ticks, trying to control some unnamed emotion. "I'm going to take you now. Make you mine."

My eyes widen and my mouth drops open as he slowly enters me. Bliss—complete and total bliss. I can die a happy woman from this moment on. Nothing has ever felt this good. Every inch of my body is alive as Jackson claims me. I will never recover from him no matter how hard I try. "Oh my God," I say in a breathy moan.

"Not God, baby, but pretty damn close. Now open those sexy brown eyes and watch me." His rough voice is strained as he sinks deeper.

"Jackson." I sigh and try to keep my eyes open, but the pleasure coursing through my body is driving me insane. "More. Please," I beg, desperate for all of him.

"Just feel me. I want you to feel this moment every time you close your eyes." He pushes deeper, eliciting a strangled sob from my mouth. "Feel how deep I am inside your pussy. Feel how fucking hard you make me." He rears back and slams into me. "Feel it, baby." There's no way I couldn't feel it if I tried. He's everywhere—every sense, every breath, and every heartbeat right now. He owns me.

Jackson reaches between us and applies pressure to my clit, making me cry out and claw at his back. I grate my nails down and he pounds into me harder and faster. We're both becoming frantic, desperate. Meeting him thrust for thrust, my eyes are locked on his as I cry out and shatter into a thousand pieces. I ride out my orgasm, unintelligibly yelling as Jackson follows with his head buried in my neck.

I rub my hand down his back languidly for a few minutes

before he rolls over and heads into the bathroom. I look over at the clock and stretch. What a way to wake up. Jackson walks back over and I take a minute to appreciate the man before me. He oozes sex and confidence and for some reason, he's attracted to me. Out of all the females he could choose, he wants me? I shake my head as he gets closer to the bed.

"What?" he says, smirking.

I smile and bite my lip, embarrassed for being caught staring at this glorious man yet again. There's so much more to him than just looks, though. He makes me laugh and compliments me. He consoled me in the car after I got the news about my father. Unlike most men I've had in my life, he seems to care about others before himself. He climbs into bed and raises a brow. I sigh. "Nothing. Just thinking."

"About what?"

"You. Me. Us. I don't know. Everything." My heart is pounding as I relay more than I wanted to. It's like he forces the truth out of me without even doing anything.

"Don't overthink this. We'll take things as they come." He pulls me against his chest and tucks my hair behind my ear. "I want us to spend time together and stop fighting what we feel. I want to kiss you and not feel like I'm doing something wrong. I know we have a lot going on, and the fact that I'm your client complicates things. But we keep it professional at work and when I have you alone"—he drops his voice so it's low and seductive—"I make no promises." He rolls us on our sides so we can look at each other.

"I don't want this to affect my work. When we're in the client-publicist role, I need you to let me do my job." I smile and rub my hand across his stubble. "My career matters to me. I need to know you understand that."

"Do you think *my* career doesn't matter to me? I own and run two companies, one of which takes me away for periods of time. Though, I didn't want the cosmetics company. If it weren't for Danielle, I would have sold it by now." His admission takes me back a little. If he didn't want the company, why does he own it? And why does Danielle matter in that equation?

"I'm not sure I understand."

"Danielle is a long-time friend of the family. She's worked extremely hard to make Raven what it is today. She helped run the business when I was tied up with the security company, but her heart is in the lab. She really didn't want to handle the business end." He rolls back and puts his hand behind his head. "I entered the Navy when I was twenty-two. I did eight years, saved every penny I made, and invested it well. When—" He pauses and takes a deep breath. "Anyway, I got out of the Navy and invested in the security company. I didn't know it would do so well." I lie with my head on his chest and trace the tattoo there. I sense there's more he's not telling me about why he got out of the military. I can't put my finger on it, but I felt him tense when he got to that part.

I rest my hand on his chest and put my chin on it. "Why a security company?"

He smiles at me with a glimmer in his eyes. "I figured that was obvious. I mean, I'm pretty badass. I have to keep this persona." Jackson grins and taps my nose.

"So humble." I roll my eyes. I run my hands down his chest and give him a playful smile.

"What?"

"Oh, nothing, Mr. I'm a Navy SEAL who's charming, endearing, oh, and God's gift to women." I smile and remember his bullshit reason to get me to dinner with him. I sit up and pull the sheet around me. "Hey! You made me a bet, Muffin. I want to know my time from that insane course yesterday."

He pulls the sheet down, exposing my breasts, and rips it farther away when I try to grab it. "Muffin, huh?" He leans up and I try to hold my ground and not back away. "Are you sure you want to call me that?" His one brow raises and his eyes darken. Oh shit. I'm in trouble now.

Mustering my courage, I respond, "I'm pretty sure I

already did. Now I want my time!"

Jackson crawls toward me and I scamper backward. I'm smiling, but I know I'm going to pay for this. "Where are you going? You started this game, baby." I try to scoot back but I'm going to be off the bed in about two seconds.

"You owe me my time and a spa day."

He smiles and lunges for me. I laugh as he starts to tickle me relentlessly. "Jackson ... stop," I try to say through fits of giggles. "Oh my God ... Stop!" He doesn't let up.

"Will you call me Muffin again?" he asks while I try to catch my breath.

"Yes!"

The mischief is back in his eyes as he begins tickling me again. I squirm and writhe on the bed. He stills suddenly and I realize he's extremely turned on. I'm gasping for air as he brings his mouth down, stopping right before his perfect lips connect with mine. His eyes crinkle in the corners and I try to kiss him, but he backs away. So not fair! "Wanna rethink your answer?"

Two can play at this game. I raise my arms over my head and stretch. His eyes shift to my breasts and I smile. Good, it's working. "What if I called you a different muffin?" He doesn't respond, so I tilt his chin so he's looking in my eyes. "Jackson?"

"Huh?" The confusion is evident as his gaze shifts back to my exposed body before returning to my face.

I raise my eyebrows at his question.

Seeming to recover, he smirks and leans toward me again. "What kind of muffin are you referring to?"

"Oh, I don't know ..." I sigh dramatically. "You know, there are a lot of muffins. Corn, blueberry, chocolate chip, stud muffin—"

Jackson crushes his mouth against mine, effectively ending the conversation.

chapter

seventeen

$\mathcal{A}$FTER ONE OF the best mornings I've had in a long time, I kicked Jackson out so I could get ready. We're heading back to New Jersey late in the evening and I needed to get some work done. I managed to get some emails sorted and check my voicemails. All in all, I've been pretty damn productive. I don't think I've stopped smiling, and my cheeks are starting to hurt.

I hear a ding on my phone.

Jackson: Hey, I need to go to the office. We need to leave in 30 min.

Me: Okay. No problem.

There must me something serious going on. He's been on the phone several times, has gone in to the office, and seems tense when it comes to anything regarding his security firm. I start to pack my bags and close my laptop. Luckily, there isn't too much stuff to pick up. I close my eyes, remembering how Jackson was so reluctant to leave this morning, how he melted another part of my carefully constructed wall. It's so easy to be comfortable around him.

Twenty minutes later, there's a knock at the door. Grabbing my bags and giving the room a once over, my trepidation soars. What do I say or do? I'm not good at this crap, which is why I've always been in a relationship. I don't know what this is, so I don't know how to act. Another bang on the door. I can't hide since he's my ride home. I channel some inner strength and head to the door.

"Hey, gorgeous." He smiles and leans in, pressing his lips to mine.

Maybe this won't be so awkward.

"Hey." I look him over and grin. Now that I know what's underneath those clothes, it's virtually impossible not to stare. His eyes narrow and his dimple reappears.

"Are you mentally undressing me?"

Cocky ass.

"No!" Damn him and his ability to read me. "What time is our flight?"

He smiles and grabs my bag—always the gentleman. "We leave around six, but I may have to push it back depending on what I find out when I get to the office."

Letting my curiosity get the best of me, words tumble out of my mouth as we head to the elevator. "What's going on? Can I help?" He looks over with his head cocked to the side. "I'm not trying to pry." And here I go with my overstepping. I swear one day I'll keep my big mouth shut.

"You're not prying." Jackson's fingers interlace with mine and my heart skips a beat. Just the small physical touch he gives me is reassuring. "I told you we have contracts, but our contracts are very different. Basically, my company trains men and women to go to a war zone. They get paid a lot of money, but it's hazardous. We get funded by the government and we send a team to do various missions or security details."

"Wow, sounds dangerous."

"It can be, but we make sure our people have the best equipment, training, and anything else they could need while they're out there. It's why most of my team are former SEALs or prior military."

It's insane to think people volunteer to go to Iraq and Afghanistan when they aren't in the military. Ice shoots through my veins, freezing me in place. What if Jackson has to go? I'm sure he's been before and it's obvious he's trained, but still. Would he spend long periods of time there?

Jackson stops and cups my face. "What is it?"

Unable to articulate my sudden anxiety, I shake my head and smile. "Nothing. Sorry. I'm trying to understand why anyone would do that voluntarily." I'm not going to bring up that it's him I'm worried about. For all I know this relationship—or whatever it is—could be done next week. I break his hold and head toward the elevator. I need to shake this dread from the pit of my stomach. Otherwise, this thing we have might be over before it actually begins.

"Well, for a lot of us it's that we miss serving. But it's different for everyone."

I guess that makes sense. I'm hoping he doesn't have that same desire. I'm not sure I'd be strong enough to handle it. However, I'd rather not go there right now.

The ride to the office is quiet. About thirty minutes later, we arrive at Cole Security. I'm hoping to see a little more of what Jackson's world is like. We walk in and head straight to his office. A few people raise their hands but they're either immersed in paperwork or on the phone. I head over to the wall of photos and take a closer look. Mark is in a lot of them along with three other men. They look like they're really close.

"Jackson?" He looks up. "Who are these guys?" I ask, pointing to the picture of the five of them all smiling in their uniforms.

He walks over, smiling, and takes the picture down. "This is Mark." He points and then hangs the photo back on the wall. "The other guys were in my unit. Aaron." He points to the one guy in the middle. "He works for me here. But Brian and Fernando died on a mission." He runs his fingers through his hair with his eyes downcast. I want to console him but someone walks in before I have the chance.

"Hey, you're here. Good." A stocky guy with a goatee

comes in the door. I recognize him as Aaron from the picture. He heads over to Jackson's desk as he searches through the papers in his hand.

"Aaron, this is Catherine."

I smile and lift my hand. He smiles and looks back to Jackson. Okay. A man of few words.

"I talked to a few people at the base, but so far nothing. I think some of us should head out and oversee the team in place now. The information is sketchy and I don't like it. There's something that doesn't feel right." Aaron speaks so fast that I have a hard time keeping up. He keeps grabbing at his neck, obviously stressed.

Jackson clears his throat and starts to pace. After a few minutes of back and forth, and what appears to be a lot of consideration, he answers, "Talk to Mark. If you both agree, then fine, get a team together. I want you or Mark on point. I don't know what's going on out there, but we need to get it settled and I don't trust anyone else."

"I agree, Muff. I'm going to see who's on standby and also work some other angles. I don't want to head out there with Natalie so close to delivering, but I will if it comes to that."

"Fuck, I forgot she's due soon. Let's try to avoid anyone going if we can. See if you can work any more contacts and find out why their shipments are delayed." Jackson glances at me and then looks back to Aaron.

"Okay, I'll keep you in the loop." Aaron heads back out and I smile, nodding as he walks past.

I stand by the wall, unsure of what to do. There's something going on in his company and he's dealing with launching a new campaign with his other company. It's a lot to take on. How do I fit into all this? This question and my own uncertainties are always looming. I make myself a promise to keep this under control. Jackson brings out my strength and I'm going to find a way to let that show more. Looking at his friends and all the things he's done is astounding. He's a leader, a friend, and seems to be loved by many.

"Ready?"

"Ah!" I nearly scream as he scares the shit out of me. Lost in the photos and my own inner thoughts, Jackson's stealth mode catches me off guard yet again.

His deep, throaty chuckle is against my neck as his arms wrap around me from behind.

"Seriously, this is getting old." I mean really, am I that oblivious?

He runs his face against my neck, his stubble scratching against my skin. Leaning back into his embrace, he places chaste kisses on my shoulder and neck as he runs his hands up my arms and squeezes. When he stops, I turn to face him. His eyes are desolate—completely void—as they look at the photos on the wall.

"Jackson? Are you okay?" I ask apprehensively.

When he looks at me, he looks sad. He winces when I place my hand on his arm so I drop it. It's the same look he had the last time he glimpsed at the photos and, like then, I'm unsure how to proceed. I don't want to push him, but I want to know what's causing him pain. I try again by placing my hand on his face, rubbing it on his scruffy cheek. Our gazes lock and I watch his eyes gloss with unshed tears. Leaning up, I place a gentle kiss on his lips.

"I'm fine. I'm just lost in memories," he finally replies, giving me some insight into what's troubling him. I hate seeing anyone hurting, but for some reason Jackson's pain feels like my own, worse even. And that scares me—a lot.

"Wanna tell me about them?"

"Not today." He gives a small smile and places his lips against mine. I feel his tongue across the seam of my lips, asking for entrance. I grant him access and our tongues brush against each other. He kisses me slowly, tenderly, never rushing the kiss. It's sweet, almost timid. My hands roam up his arms and around his neck as his fingers gently tangle in my hair. Our kiss stays soft, as if he's pouring his emotion into me. Tears form as my own emotions are unleashed. My hurt, pain, sadness, and loss from the last few days bubbles up. His hands are sliding down my neck and then my shoulders when we hear a cough and a loud laugh behind us.

"Don't let me interrupt. I don't mind watching." Mark smiles as he enters the room. He plops in a chair and puts his legs on the table.

I laugh as my heavy emotions quickly change to embarrassment, which is surely displayed across my face. As I start to move, Jackson grabs me and pulls me close, glaring at Mark. "By all means, asshole, make yourself at home."

Mark looks around, smirking. "I need an office like this. You're never here. I think I'll move in after you leave."

"I think maybe I'll let Papa Smurf stay off the mission. You really could use some time in the sun," Jackson goes back at Mark.

I giggle. Seriously, what is with these guys and their names? I don't even want to ask who Papa Smurf is or how he earned that name.

"Did she just giggle?" Mark asks before snorting.

"Did you just snort?" I reply with a smile.

"Well played, Catherine. Well played."

I love when men think they can get one over on me.

"She got you, fucker," Jackson says while laughing and pushing Mark's feet off the table. "What do you need?"

Mark and Jackson start talking about the mission that's in trouble in Afghanistan. One of the trucks never delivered their second shipment of ammunition and they're both worried. The stress of knowing their friends are in harm's way must be insurmountable. No wonder Jackson was pissed the other day.

"Listen, Kitty." Mark leans in since he's finished talking with Jackson.

What the hell did he call me? "Kitty?"

"Yeah, I mean your name is Cat, so I figure Kitty is a good

call sign for you. You get all cute and cuddly, but I bet you could claw someone's eye out if they pissed you off. Right?" Mark laughs and raises his brow.

Jackson stands there with a smug smile on his face.

"Seriously, I don't need a call sign. I'm pretty sure I'm not going on any missions anytime soon."

"Nah, Kitty works. Plus, now that I know it pisses you off, this shit is going to be even more fun. Make sure fat ass stays out of trouble in New York. I don't want to have to come up there and kick his ass."

Jackson laughs, "Keep dreaming, fucker."

Mark walks out of the office, whistling the melody of "The Cat Came Back" as he goes.

I turn to Jackson with my mouth hanging open. This can't be real. He's just smiling away, completely amused. I start to walk over, narrowing my eyes, and he raises his hands in mock surrender.

"Catherine, Mark is a jackass." He starts backing away as I move closer.

"Yes, I've learned as much, but you—" I point my finger as I get closer. "You didn't even try to stop him." I smile and bite my lip as Jackson takes a step forward.

"Don't worry. You don't have to see him too much. Plus, if I intervene, it'll only get worse. Besides, kittens are cute." He reaches out, grabs me around my waist, and pulls me flush against him. My heart races and my breathing accelerates as he leans down and kisses me. He lifts me up and turns me, pushing my back against the wall. I wrap my leg around his waist as our mouths fuse together. Forcefully, passionately, he plunges into my mouth, claiming me. I moan, knowing that with every touch, with every kiss, I'm becoming his. The low flame that burns whenever Jackson is around turns into an inferno. I pull my mouth away, trying to push him back.

"Jackson, we have to stop." My voice is weak and breathless.

He ignores my futile attempt for space and puts his arms against the wall, not allowing me to move anywhere. "I told you, in private I make no promises."

"Yes, but we're not in private. Two of your employees have already made that clear. Plus, we have a plane to catch."

"I own the plane," he whispers seductively against my lips. "It'll wait until I'm ready. Tell me you don't want me," he commands and pulls his mouth back. I'm against the wall, breathless and unable to lie. I want him more than my next breath. "Tell me."

"I want you," I say, closing my eyes to the sound of my shaking voice. I'm so damn turned-on. I've wanted him since day one. Feeling his arousal on my stomach, I open my eyes and look into his. The lust in them spurs me on. I lean in and grip his shirt. He pulls back slightly and his cheek lifts in amusement.

"Good. Now we have a plane to catch." He leans backward, making it impossible for me to kiss him again.

"Jackson, you don't want to play this game, do you?" I say, dripping with desire.

"What game, baby? I'm just following your wishes."

"I don't think so. I want you." I snake my hand around his neck and yank as his eyes crinkle. I'm practically climbing my way to his mouth.

"You want me, huh?"

"I think I've said that already." I inch closer to his mouth. He pulls back but shifts me up higher on his waist.

"Too bad." He leans in and gives me a brief kiss.

It seems Jackson likes to play games. Good thing I never lose. He may not know it yet, but he has met his match.

I spent the entire flight keyed up from Jackson's teasing and subsequent refusal to quench my desire in Virginia. Then, of course, he found any way he could to continue the torturous game. He'd brush against my leg or just barely touch my arm, fueling the hunger coursing through my veins. In order to avoid begging him, I spent the flight plotting a way to repay the favor. Payback is a bitch and he's about to see how big of one I can be—in a nice way, of course.

We finally settle into the car and enjoy the comfortable silence. It's nice not to feel as though you have to always talk. After ten minutes Jackson shifts over, putting his arm behind my seat and pulling me against his side. I look up and smile.

"It's going to be a few days until I can see you again. I have a lot of shit to get settled at the office and there's still the situation in Virginia." He smiles and rubs my arm.

"I don't expect anything." If he feels like I'm going to be needy because we had sex, I need to squash that quickly. I need space to think about all that's already happened, plus I have work to do too. When I'm around him I lose the ability to say no, so it's a good thing we'll have time apart.

"Never said you did. But I don't want you to use this as an excuse to push me away again or get any ideas in your head that I'm avoiding you." His brow rises as he somehow reads my mind.

"I understand your job, just as I hope you understand mine."

The car stops once we reach my apartment, but Jackson's strong arm still surrounds me. I haven't addressed his last statement and I don't intend to. Slowly he lifts my chin, placing a tender kiss on my lips. Without a word, he exits the car and I press my hands to my mouth. It's tingling from the brief but warm moment. It's astounding to me how much he affects my mind and body.

Standing there with my bag, he tells the driver he'll be a moment. He grips my hand and pulls me into him, almost like we're dancing. I gasp as I stumble into his solid chest. He stares intensely and my body begins to quiver under his gaze.

"Tonight, when I'm alone, I'm going to think about how good your legs felt wrapped around me, how your voice sounded when you screamed out my name. I'll remember how it felt when my dick sunk into your hot, wet pussy." He leans closely and whispers against my ear, causing the hair on the back of my neck to stand, "And I'll be counting down the minutes until I have you again."

I let out a low moan as he presses his lips to the spot right below my ear. Oh. Fucking. Shit. Without thinking, I grip the back of his neck and crush my lips against his. His chest rumbles as he returns the kiss, giving and taking as his words spur an undeniable passion. His fingers wrap around my arms and he pushes me back with a cocky smile before turning to leave.

What? No way!

I grab his arm before he can escape. "You can't say shit like that and then freaking leave!" My eyes are wide and I'm practically panting.

"What? You don't like my dirty talk?" His eyes are liquid, showing he's affected as well.

"Oh, I like my Muff dirty, but you might want to remember two can play at this game." I smile, trying to quell the desperation I'm feeling for him right now.

Jackson leans in close and his lips whisper across my cheek. "I can't wait to show you how dirty I can get. That's to make sure you don't pull away." His warm breath washes over me, heating every part of me, before his lips reach mine. "Until next time. Don't miss me too much."

He turns, leaving me standing there, stunned and completely turned-on. Bastard. I'm going to make him pay for that shit. I see a serious case of blue balls in his future.

chapter

eighteen

I'VE BEEN HOME for a week and haven't accomplished a damn thing. The song for the Raven Cosmetics commercial is no longer legal to use. The approval I obtained beforehand expired, and now the music company is dragging their feet. Then Taylor told me the partners met yesterday about who would be given the promotion. It was a fifty-fifty split between Elle and me. So much for me being a shoo-in for the promotion once I landed the Raven account. They plan to wait until we both finish with our current clients to make a decision.

Jackson and I haven't seen each other since he dropped me off after our trip. We've talked a few times on the phone about what he needs to do to get ready for the launch and we made plans for this weekend. But he's not happy about the ad delay. Plus, Neil's been calling again. Worse than all that, though, is how I have to go for the reading of my father's will in three weeks. I keep trying to push it to the depths of my mind, but it keeps creeping up at the most inopportune times. In my life, when it rains it doesn't just pour, no—it's a full-on monsoon.

I grab my journal and decide to write again. It's therapeutic and helps me get my thoughts together. I've been so busy that I haven't really had much time lately. I miss it—I miss watching my heart bleed onto the paper.

I put the pen down when I hear a loud voice. "Biffle, time

for a drink." Ashton stalks toward me holding a bottle in her hand.

"Good." I shrug and decide not to fight her this time. "I need one." Or four.

"I'm not sure what to do with this attitude," she says with a cat-ate-the-canary grin. "Usually I have to threaten you. By the way, just-fucked is a better look for you. Maybe you should call him and get that taken care of. We need to make sure frumpy, nasty Cat stays away."

I groan and roll my eyes. She's been pushing me to go to him, to not let him get away. I'm not sure why she's so up my ass about it. "I don't feel like calling him. I feel like having my best friend pour me a shot and get me drunk."

"Well now *that* I can do. I've got bubblegum vodka or whipped. What's your poison?"

"Whipped, baby!"

We grab some shot glasses and get comfy on the couch, laughing about the new doctor in Ashton's lab. He's been hitting on her and my crazy friend is feeding it.

"Well he's ugly as all hell, but if he wants to keep buying me dinner, I'm not an idiot."

"Ashton! That's just so ... so ... wrong." I slap her arm.

"Maybe I'll tell him I'm a lesbian." She shrugs, laughing, and hooks her arms around me. "Wanna make out?"

"Oh good God. Get off me, jackass."

We've been drinking for a few hours. Ashton has analyzed my trip in great detail. I think she's falling in love with Jackson. It's kinda funny. We laugh and swoon, only stopping to refill our shot glasses. I know I'm three sheets to the wind since I can't feel my tongue anymore.

"Ash, I gotta pee." I practically fall off the couch and laugh as I try to stand straight. I'm completely shit-faced. I make my way to the bathroom and back by the grace of God. When I get to the living room, my eyes go wide. Either I'm hallucinating or Jackson is sitting on my couch.

"Catherine, aren't you a sight for sore eyes." He smiles as he gets up and walks over to me. When he leans down to kiss me, I quickly put my hand up to his mouth before he can touch my lips. "You can't kiss me," I whisper and look around. I'm still not sure it's really him. Maybe my mind conjured him up.

"Oh, why not?" He stares at me with one brow raised and that cocky smile I love so much. Awww, fake Jackson even makes the same gestures.

"Well, imaginary Jackson, I'll tell you." I lean in real close and somehow get the words out between giggles. "I like a boy and I don't think I should kiss you." Ashton is laughing hysterically and I join her, although I'm not sure why we're laughing.

"Imaginary, huh? And tell me, baby, what's this boy's name?" He leans close and places his hand on the back of my head, pulling me against his chest. I lean into him and take a deep breath. Imaginary Jackson even smells the same.

"He's not really a boy. He's *all* man, if you know what I mean." I slur the words and giggle.

"How much have you had to drink?"

"Ohhh, you know, six or eight. I can't remember." I close my eyes and rest against his strong, hard chest. My mind is a beautiful place right now. "How did you know where I was?"

Ashton speaks first. "I think you're cut off. Jackson is really here and you are gonna hate yourself tomorrow."

Imaginary Jackson pulls us to the couch, where I sink into him further.

"Nuh uh," I retort, drifting to sleep.

Next thing I know, strong hands are cupping my cheeks and lifting my face. My lashes flutter open and I'm staring into Jackson's—or imaginary Jackson's—gorgeous turquoise eyes. Damn he's hot. I so want to break off a piece of that again. He continues to gaze with a fierce intensity—it almost sobers me. Fuck! He's here!

And I'm drunk—really drunk.

His deep voice breaks through my alcohol fog. "Hi there."

"Hi," I say breathlessly.

"Hi! I'm going to bed in case anyone was curious," Ashton yells, and we all start laughing. "Jackson, it was a pleasure meeting you. Hopefully I'll see you in the morning." She winks at me and starts to leave, giving me a thumbs up as she heads to her room.

Jackson scoops me into his arms effortlessly and places a quick kiss on my forehead. "Where's your room?"

I point at what I hope is my door. "Ummm that one. I think." He laughs as he opens the door to the bathroom. Oops.

The next door he opens is my bedroom. "Lucky door number two." He walks over and gently places me on my bed. Crap! Jackson is here—in my room—and I'm not even sober to enjoy it. "I'm going to stay tonight. I'll be a gentleman," he whispers in my ear.

"Okay. But feel free not to be." I laugh since I've become a giggly, drunken fool.

I watch as he undresses. At least I'm going to enjoy this! His gaze as he pulls his pants off stops my urge to laugh. Nope. Nothing funny about that.

"I like your room," Jackson says, looking around.

"I like you naked," I say, then slap my hand over my mouth.

"Are you sure? Maybe you like imaginary Jackson better." His brow lifts and his dimple appears.

"I like *all* the Jacksons." I fall against my pillow as the room spins. Ugh! Please don't let me get sick.

"I'm glad. I was starting to wonder." I feel the bed shift as he slides his arm under my head. "Sleep well."

"Good night." I nuzzle into his neck as I pass out, suddenly not feeling so sick after all.

I crack my eye open and slam it shut again—too bright! My head is pounding and my mouth feels like I have a million cotton balls in it. I roll over and my hand slaps on a warm, shirtless, rock-hard chest. What?

"That wasn't very nice," a deep, husky voice croaks.

I slowly open my eye and see Jackson's wide grin. Ummm, why is he in my bed and when the hell did he get here? Well, I'm fully clothed so that's good ... I think. I open my mouth to speak but nothing comes out. Water. I need water. I look over at my nightstand and see two aspirins and a water bottle. I quickly sit up, groaning as I grab the side of my head.

"Not feeling so hot this morning, huh?" Jackson yells, or at least that's what it sounds like in my head.

"Shhh. Too loud," I whisper and reach for the medicine.

He leans over, swipes the pills, and places them in my hand. "I was whispering, babe. Here. Drink."

Hopefully this medicine is fast acting, otherwise I'm going to be worthless all day. I lie back down and try to recall what happened last night. We drank. I remember that much. I remember going to the bathroom and eyes ... I remember his eyes. I roll over and face Jackson, hoping he can fill me in. "So ..."

"What? You like imaginary Jackson more?"

"I ..." The puzzle pieces start to click. Imaginary Jackson! Please someone kill me. That would be a lot easier than the embarrassment I'm dealing with now. "Look, I drank a lot. Nothing I said—or did—can be held against me."

He rolls and faces me, pushing the hair back off my face. "You were adorable and nothing happened last night—well, at least not what I was hoping for." Jackson's grin is wide as his eyes shift toward my breasts.

"Hey!" I quickly cut him off. "I didn't mean that you did anything. I mean I vaguely remember a few things." My hand makes its way to his chest and I trace the tribal sun. It's so beautiful. The tattoo on my hip is more of a celestial sun, but his is huge and takes up his entire pec, completely covering where his heart is. My fingers roam the rays and he sighs, placing his hand over mine. "We both have suns," I observe.

"The sun is constant," Jackson states.

"I got mine on my eighteenth birthday."

"What made you get the sun?" he asks.

I could very easily give him a girly answer like I usually do, but I want to share this with him. The sun has great significance to me, even if it also brings a fair amount of darkness. "When I was a child, my father used to sing 'You are My Sunshine' to me when I was sad. I always remembered that about him. I still sing it when I need to calm myself." I sigh and look up with sad eyes. "It's probably the only good memory I have of him, or at least one I remember. He would either sing it or whistle it if he was upset with my mother. I carried on that tradition, which basically means it's my theme song."

"Tell me about him," Jackson says quietly and holds my hand steady against his chest.

"I don't really have much to say." I take a deep breath. "He left when I was nine, on my birthday, and I never saw him again. He walked away while I cried on the floor. Never looked back."

"I'm sorry. That must've been hard."

"Well, yeah. I was a kid. I begged him, literally hanging onto his leg." I pause, remembering how desperate I was for him not to walk away. Unfortunately, that was only the beginning of my heartache. "I would write letters and beg my mom to take me to him. But she didn't know where he was. He disappeared. It was awful because before he left, he adored me. He told me every day how much he loved me and how special I was. Then he just ..." Tears start to leak as I recall my childhood. "I cried a lot in the beginning. Then I would tell people he died because it was easier than explaining he didn't love me."

He smiles sadly and presses his lips to my forehead, giving me the strength to say more. I haven't even touched the surface of the years of damage his absence caused.

"I never understood it. How do you love someone so much

and then walk away?" I take a shaky breath and continue, "I wanted him to *want* me. Or explain why he deserted me. If he didn't love my mother anymore, I could handle that, but to not love me anymore—I still don't fully comprehend it. I don't have kids, so I don't understand a parent's love. But I've seen my friends and there is nothing they wouldn't do for their children. I thought a parent's love was supposed to be unwavering." I hate thinking about this but the floodgates have opened and they don't want to close. Jackson lies here, staring at me with compassion as he holds my hand and gives it a small squeeze. I sigh before going on.

"There was a time I used to hope he would return and we could just go back to the way things were, but I realized it was never going to happen. I blamed myself for a long time. I thought I did something wrong to make him leave. If I was good enough, or if I didn't cry all the time, maybe he wouldn't have left." Jackson's calloused thumb catches one of my tears. I've never told anyone other than Ashton these things.

"I'm so sorry, Catherine. But you didn't do anything wrong. *He* fucking decided how to handle it, not you."

"I know I didn't do anything wrong *now*, but he really fucked me up for a while." And then it hits me out of nowhere. The reality comes crashing down around me, smothering me. "He's really dead. He's never coming back. I'll never get any answers. Do you know what kind of crushing guilt I'll carry forever because I never tried? I could've tried as an adult. Searched for him. But I didn't. I gave up."

Jackson's arms encase me and he pulls me close as I start to cry in earnest. Tears fall like rain and the last week of emotions pummels me. My dad is gone. I'll never get a chance to reconcile with him. There will never be a chance of him being a part of my life or my future children's lives. He'll never know who I am and I'll never be able to let this go. I'll have to carry around all the hurt and pain of an unloved child because he was too selfish to try. He broke me and I'll never be fixed because he's dead.

Jackson simply rubs my back and lets me unload years' worth of unshed tears. After a few minutes, I lean back with red-rimmed eyes and he places a small kiss on my lips. He hasn't said a word, but there's pain in his eyes as he closes them. "I'm sorry you're hurting, baby. I know more about guilt than you can ever imagine."

I lean on his chest and place my hand on his cheek, gently stroking his face and enjoying the way his stubble feels against my skin. "What do you mean?" I ask timidly.

"I'll talk about it at some point, but not today. You've had a lot to process," he says as he rolls onto his back, taking me with him. I curl up on his chest.

"Will you tell me about your parents, then?"

He lets out a half laugh. "I'm afraid my story isn't very interesting. My parents are pretty boring and still happily married. My dad is former Air Force, so he was gone a lot. Even when I was a kid he always emphasized that hard work is essential to any man and I should get used to it.

"My mom is your typical military wife. She was mother, father, friend, disciplinarian, and everything in between. She cooked, cleaned, made sure my sister, Reagan, and I didn't kill each other, and then she'd replace the alternator in the car when it went out."

"She sounds like an amazing woman," I say, looking at him as his grin spreads across his face. I love watching those eyes crinkle when he's truly happy.

"She really is. She could kick my ass and then turn around and bake cookies for my class. I feared my dad—but Mom, she was a force of nature. You know how mothers always say, 'Just wait till your father comes home?'"

"Yeah. Ashton's mother invented that phrase. We heard it a lot. We were kind of a handful. I'm sure you find that hard to believe." My brow rises, waiting for him to challenge me.

"Not you!" He laughs and tickles my sides. I squirm before

he continues on. "Anyway, my mom never said that. It was my dad who probably could've said it. She still scares the shit out of me."

"They sound great." I'm happy that he has such a wonderful family. No child should grow up without love. It's obvious his parents have done an amazing job with him.

"Don't get me wrong, there were times when my dad being away was rough. He missed a lot of birthdays, Christmases, and other holidays. My mom had to make sure Reagan and I didn't notice or at least that it didn't fuck up the whole day if we did. That's the life of a military kid, though. Dad was a pilot, so even when he was home he was usually doing work-ups."

"Wait. Your name is Jackson and your sister's name is Reagan?"

"Yes, why?" He looks confused at where I'm going with this.

"I'm noticing the dead president theme going on with your family, that's all. Am I missing something?"

"Out of everything we just talked about, that's what you want to ask me about?"

"If my name was Thelma and I had a sister Louise, you would think it was funny too!" I laugh and shrink back.

He grabs me and flips me on my back, hovering over me. I love the playfulness dancing in his eyes. "Are you making fun of me?"

Batting my eyelashes and tilting my head to the side, trying to feign innocence, I smile. "Who, me? Never."

With a warm smile playing across his lips, he leans down and gives me a long closed-mouthed kiss as he grips my leg and wraps it around his waist. Enjoying where this seems to be heading, I push up into the kiss. Jackson rolls me so I'm on top of him. The alcohol fog has completely dissipated as the kiss deepens. Our tongues volley back and forth—I couldn't care less about my head throbbing or anything else. Right when things are about to get better, he stops and slaps my ass, hard.

"Owww!" I laugh, rubbing my butt, and he rolls off to the side, matching my laughter. "Jerkface."

"That'll teach you to be such a smartass. Now, what else did you want to know about my nonpolitical parents?"

I crawl back to my former position and nestle in. "How did your dad feel about you going into the Navy?"

"He didn't care, honestly. He thought I was fucking insane for wanting to be a SEAL. When you know the life and what we really go through, it's different. There is no idolizing." He runs his hand through his hair and pulls me close.

"Did you always want to be a SEAL?" I wonder.

"There was never a doubt. Dad was adamant I finish college first. So I went to school and double majored in finance and criminal justice. Then I enlisted as an officer, but I knew I'd be a SEAL. If you're going to join, might as well be the best. And that's what we are—the best." He smirks and juts out his chin, showing his arrogance a little.

I can see why he's proud. He's accomplished something many have failed at.

"Pretty sure of yourself, aren't ya?"

"Well, what's there not to be sure of?" He laughs and kisses the top of my head.

"Your humility needs some help. Your head gets any bigger, I'll need to get a larger apartment so you can fit." I laugh and he chuckles.

"I speak the truth."

I shake my head and lay down against his chest.

We both grow quiet, comfortable with the silence between us. Nuzzling into him, I close my eyes as my head throbs from the night of drinking I'm still paying for. The onslaught of emotions probably hasn't helped either. My mind drifts, thinking of a young Jackson and how it must have been difficult knowing his dad was away but wanted to be home.

"Hey," he says quietly. I must've fallen asleep. "You awake?"

"Yeah, I'm up. Sorry. Between the hangover and crying I guess I was beat."

"I need to get going but I want to take you out tonight. On a date," Jackson says against my neck.

Before I can respond, my cell phone rings. Jackson reaches over, grabs it, and hands it to me. Neil again. I roll my eyes and huff. I'm pissed he's still calling—there's nothing left to say. I silence the phone and put it down. Jackson gets up and starts getting dressed. He looks over and smiles, then heads out of my room. Maybe he saw the name? He doesn't know who Neil is, though. I hear the voicemail alert and decide to check it real quick.

"Hey, Cat. I need to talk. I know you see me calling." He takes a shaky breath. "I understand why you're not answering, but please—I need you."

I slump on the bed and put my phone on the charger. Simple things I can handle, but Neil? No, not today. My chest is tight and I'm suddenly nauseous. He didn't need me three months ago, hell, seven months ago when he made his choice to sleep with Piper. He didn't *need* me when he told me I wasn't enough. Screw him. He can need *her* for all I care. Yet, somewhere deep in my heart, I know I'll cave and answer my phone or call him back at some point. It's unlike him to sound desperate. Something could be seriously wrong. Whatever. Not going there.

I get up, put my sweatshirt on, and head out to get coffee. Despite my tearfest this morning and the stress of this Neil predicament, the medicine kicked in. I lean against the door and watch as Jackson and Ashton laugh together. It warms my heart to see them getting along. I can't recall if I ever saw her talk to Neil when I wasn't around. Smiling, I walk over and start my coffee, allowing them to keep talking.

"Good morning, hot tits." Ashton laughs as I roll my eyes. Please don't let her embarrass me again. She turns to Jackson. "So you were about to tell me about your sexy, available friends, right?"

I bust out laughing and grip the edge of the counter for support. Of course she's trolling for men. "For real? You're trying to score a hot friend?"

"Hey, I'd enlist if I knew I could look at guys like him all day. I'm cooped up in a lab with nerds who think they're hot." Her grin is wide as she leans in, tilting her head to the side. "Don't get all stabby." She returns her attention to the sexy man sitting at my table. "Well?"

Jackson smiles and leans back in his seat, patting his leg. Grabbing my coffee, I smother my trepidation and snuggle into him. He looks at me brightly. "Why don't you answer her? Any of my friends hot?" Oh sure, make me say it.

Deciding to play coy and give Jackson a taste of his own medicine, I say, "Well, there is this one guy." I smile, turning my back to him as I lean on the table with both hands holding my head. "He was *so* dreamy. Almost made think twice about Muffin over here."

She plays along. Her eyes widen and she grins devilishly. There's nothing Ashton enjoys more than taunting people. "So he's like super hot, then?"

"Oh yeah, I'm talking off the charts." Jackson leans against my back and his body heat pulses through my sweatshirt. His hand grips my hip before slipping underneath the hem and splaying across my bare stomach. I gasp.

"What's wrong, baby?" he asks as I turn and look at him over my shoulder incredulously. "Just curious who you think was off the charts?" Slowly his fingertips trail against my stomach. The shirt is baggy, so hopefully Ashton can't see anything that's happening.

I bite my lip and lean back against his chest. "It's hard to say—" My words cut off when his finger slides against the underside of my breast.

Ashton smiles. "What's wrong? Cat got your tongue? Or is it that Jackson's feeling you up?"

Jackson leans back, laughing hysterically. Busted! My face is painted in red as I get up and put my mug in the sink.

Ashton yells at my back as I walk to my room. "Oh c'mon, hot tits. I'd touch them too if I were him. Don't be like that."

"I hate you both!" I yell back, laughing. Out of nowhere I'm airborne and squeaking as Jackson lifts me and throws me over his shoulder. We laugh as we make our way back to my room.

"I'm going to head into the city and get ready. I want us to go out and have fun. Pack a bag. You can stay at my place tonight," he says with a serious look.

"What time?"

"I'll text you details. I need to make some calls." His lips press against mine and I lean into him. I don't think I'll ever tire of kissing him. Even though we've just started whatever this is, it feels like it's been so much longer. It's like every day I'm with him, a little more of the broken me mends, making me whole again.

chapter

nineteen

FTER SPENDING THE next three hours agonizing over what to wear, I finally settled on my red, one-shoulder, A-line dress. My hair is curled and swept to the side and I'm pretty happy with the overall turnout. I've packed my overnight bag and threw my nude heels in there since I have to take the train into the city—there's no way I'm running around in heels. Ashton is going out later, so she agreed to drop me at the station on her way.

Stepping out into the living room, I ask, "Well, what do you think?" She lets out a whistle.

"You look holy shit hot! Wow. He's gonna be tenting all night long."

"What?" I ask, dumbfounded.

"You know, be pitching a tent in his pants." She giggles and nudges me.

"Grab your keys. I'm nervous enough without your as-inine comments." I huff and nudge her back. My nerves are out of control. I don't know why since we've already slept to-gether. We had a rather powerful talk today, but this seems so different—probably because our date is actually planned and I wasn't roped into it.

We exit the house with Ashton's arm around my neck. "No need to be nervous. You need to be you and he'll see how spe-cial you are. I'm pretty sure he already does."

"Just … I don't know. Things got heavy this morning," I say to her as we get in the car. "I don't mean sexual heavy either. I kind of had a huge breakdown about my dad," I admit reluctantly. It's weird telling her this. Ashton and I share everything, but there are parts of my relationship with Jackson I want to keep to myself.

"Wow. You never talk about him. But he still wants to take you out, so it didn't scare him off. Jackson seems like a good guy. He came over last night to see you. You were plastered and he stayed. He's obviously into you." She takes a deep breath while the words sink in. "I know it's hard for you to see, but please don't push him away. Let him see what I see." She places her hand on mine and squeezes, offering me comfort I'm reluctant to receive.

"Thanks, Ash. I guess I'm just waiting for the proverbial shoe to drop."

"Well that's no way to live. Live for the moment." The car stops as we arrive at the train station. Ashton turns to me with her lips pursed. "I know this is hard for you. Here's the thing— nice guys like him don't come around twice. From everything you've told me, he's only been good to you. Yeah, he's intense, but you guys have this insane chemistry. Stop fighting it!"

I lean over and give her a kiss on the cheek. "I'll try. Love you, Ashypoo!"

I run to catch the train. Thankfully I get on just in time. Grabbing the first seat available, I sit and text Jackson.

Me: On my way. Where am I going?

Jackson: A car will be waiting with your name. See you soon.

I smile at his gesture. He really is a good guy, and I'm going to try to relax and enjoy tonight. The train ride is only about ten minutes, so I don't have time to do anything other than change my shoes and check myself over once. Exiting the train, I find a tall man in a suit holding a sign with my name on it.

"Ms. Pope, I'm Xavier. I'll be your driver for this evening."

"Nice to meet you." I smile and follow him to a sleek black limo.

Wow, he really went all out.

"Do you know where we're going?" he asks curiously.

My eyes widen at his question. "No, do you?"

He lets out a throaty laugh and opens the door for me. "Yes, ma'am." I take a deep breath and scoot into the back. "It'll only be about ten minutes to our destination. There's champagne chilling in the bucket if you'd like a glass."

"Yes!" I say, almost too eagerly.

Get a damn grip.

I take a small sip and the bubbles tickle my nose. Jackson's thoughtfulness warms my heart. Even though we saw each other a few hours ago, I'm excited to see him again. It appears he managed to plan quite a bit in a short amount of time.

We arrive at what I'm assuming is a restaurant. Xavier comes around, opens my door, and sweeps his arm to the side where I see Jackson walking toward me. He looks breathtaking. I know that's not the manliest way to describe him, but there is no other word. He takes my breath away.

My eyes eat him up and I'm pretty sure I lick my lips at the sight of him. He's dressed in a black pinstripe suit with a white shirt, the top button undone, and his eyes burn even in the darkness. I can see the blue shift to green and deepen as he approaches me. That may be a trick of light and shadow, but I like to think it's lust making those eyes change like that. The same lust that has my heart racing a mile a minute right now. His smile is wide when he reaches me, but he doesn't say anything.

Finally, after an eternity—or what feels like it—his low, rough voice breaks the silence. "You look beautiful."

"Thank you for this. The limo, last night, everything. It's too much. I never really thought of you as a limo guy."

"I'm not, but you deserve to feel special. So no, it's not too much. It's only the beginning." He takes a step closer and extends his hand, giving me a single stargazer lily. Does he know they're my favorite?

Between his words and now this gesture, I'm liquefying. "I love lilies. How did you know?"

"Ashton," he says matter-of-factly. Of course she would know, but it surprises me that he thought to ask.

"I think you'll like these plans better than the last." Jackson grins and grips my hand. Hell yeah. I won't be climbing any walls in this dress.

We begin to walk forward when suddenly he stops. He turns and tenderly grabs my face with both hands, pulling me gently until we're an inch apart. "You really are beautiful, baby." Before I can respond, his lips are on mine. My eyes flutter closed and I grip the lapels of his jacket. His strong arms wrap around my lower back, pulling me into him. What may have started as a tender kiss turns into a passionate exchange. Jackson pulls that out of me. He consumes me, making me forget where, sometimes who, I am.

Dropping his hand, he squeezes my ass and I giggle. Well, that's one way to stop it. And very Jackson-like. My hand slaps him playfully across the chest as I shake my head at his antics.

"Come on, Muffin. Let's go eat."

"Keep it up and I'll show you how much you'll pay for using that name."

"I don't take lightly to threats, Muff." I smile and walk forward. He growls and wraps his arms around my waist, pulling me flush against his chest.

"Well, wait until I show you how fucking good it feels when it's no longer a threat," he murmurs seductively, staring straight into my eyes.

My stomach clenches and I tremble from the timbre of his voice before he releases his hold. Could he be any sexier?

I'm grinning ear to ear as we enter the restaurant and are seated. It's beautiful. Candles sit on all the tables and huge chandeliers hang in the center of the room, creating beautiful rainbow prisms everywhere. The walls are deep burgundy and almost look like fabric, which only adds to the ambiance. Everything seems so upscale. It doesn't surprise me Jackson would choose a place like this. He's rugged but sophisticated—a walking contradiction.

"I've ordered for us already. The chef is a good friend. He's making us something special."

Typically, I would be less than excited about someone deciding my meal for me—I've had enough of that shit to last a lifetime—but with Jackson it feels different. He's not trying to take away my choices. He's simply being kind. "Thank you for all of this, Jackson. It's very sweet."

He leans forward. "You're welcome. I'm just lucky you fell into my chair that day."

I laugh and turn my head to the side, hiding my embarrassment. Not one of my finest moments. When I finally recover, I look up to find him smiling warmly. "Thanks for reminding me."

"Hey, look where it got us."

"Where exactly is *this*?" Because of my constant self-doubt, I need him to spell it out for me. I don't want to get too attached to him and have the rug pulled out from under me. Jackson is a man any woman could easily fall in love with, and he seems to have a direct line to my heart.

"I don't know where it is, but I know I want to be around you. I know I've thought about you every day and every night since we've met. There are a lot of things we need to learn about each other. But you fell into my life and I won't let you fall out. So whatever this is … it's ours."

My eyes swim with emotion. It takes everything inside of me not to cry. That was the best answer he could've given me— it's honest and real. I sigh and look at him with a hopeful heart. "I want us to get to know each other. I never thought we'd be here."

"Why?"

"Because I thought you were like all the other guys I've met—cocky and looking for one thing." I shrug and smile. "Not to be a bitch, but you were so intense. I'd never felt anything like that before. Then you turned out to be my client. You keep breaking my rules." It's true. Each time I tell myself I'm not going to do this or that, he finds a loophole and I no longer care about my rules anymore.

We fall into a comfortable silence as we let the words settle around us. There are a lot of truths yet to be told. I don't know how to tell him about what Neil did, or that one of his trusted consultants is a part of my past. There's no way to know for sure if he heard what she said that day in the conference room. I don't even know if Piper's still working with Raven. Regardless, it's going to come to light at some point.

Throughout dinner we talk and laugh. He tells me more about some of the antics he and his sister, Reagan, got into as kids. We talk about my mother a little and how I haven't spoken to her since the phone call in Virginia. Jackson makes me nearly fall out of my chair laughing when he tells me the story about Mark and Aaron when they first became SEALs and some of the prank wars they had.

"Okay. So you seriously glued ketchup packets to the toilet seat?" Insane. They're all insane.

"Fuck yeah, we did. And when Mark sat down, you would've thought a bomb went off in the head. There was ketchup everywhere." His eyes are filled with humor.

"And what did he do back? I can't see him being like, 'Good one,' and letting it go."

"Oh hell no, there's no backing down. Mark has one thing I don't."

"Which is?" I ask.

"Patience. So he waited until my guard was slightly down. My truck is my baby—you don't fuck with my F150. Mark, being the prick he is, decided I needed to really suffer. So he took my license plates and flipped them upside down, but then he somehow got into the cab." I smile and roll my eyes at the talk of his precious truck. As he remembers whatever his friend did to repay him for the bathroom casualty, his smile fades. "It was December and cold as shit. The motherfucker took pepper spray and soaked my floor mats and my air vents. Every time I turned the heat on I couldn't see because my eyes watered so bad."

Laughter erupts from my chest and there's no chance of stopping it. My hands fly over my mouth, trying to contain it as I imagine Jackson crying every time he got into his truck. Tears are running down my cheeks, and the look on his face only makes me laugh harder. "I can't breathe."

"No, baby, I couldn't breathe. I had to ride around in the freezing fucking cold with my windows down so I could see. It was hell. But payback's a bitch and Twilight learned that shit quick." He smiles again, laughing at the memories as I swipe the tears from my face.

"Oh God! What did you do?"

He steeples his fingers and his devilish grin grows. "It was a multilayered attack. Phase one was all about making him think it was coming. So there were small, subtle hints. I had the gate guards search his car every time he arrived on base, which takes about twenty minutes out of your day. Not a big deal, but he was late a few times and he got his ass chewed." I'm starting to see how much he must have enjoyed this. His eyes glimmer and he's lost to the memory. "Phase two was a little more ... difficult."

"Difficult how?"

"I had to make sure it would work perfectly. I needed other people's help, but they didn't want to be the next casualty of our war. After watching some of the shit we did, no one wanted to play. We didn't fight fair. I plotted very carefully and also had to be ready in case I was on the other end of his attack. Plus, if he fucked with my truck again, he'd be on the missing persons list."

"I'm seeing that this truck is worth more than friendship."
I laugh and sit back in my chair, wondering how their war finally ended.

"You don't mess with a man's truck."

"Okay, I get it. Please continue."

His eyes are excited as he gets back to his story. "Mark had done a few small things, but nothing really epic. We all had lockers that we kept our gear in, so I had the supply guys open his for me." He lets out a small laugh. "I rigged it so when he opened it, a glitter bomb exploded. It went everywhere! Him, all his gear—everything covered with glitter!"

"Holy shit!" I gasp. Glitter gets everywhere. I can't even imagine the mess that made.

"But wait!" He leans in and smiles ear to ear. "I didn't stop there. Fuck with me and there is no limit to the lengths I'll go for payback."

"Seriously, I'm a little worried."

"We were leaving for a training mission the next day, so Twilight literally had to scrub his shit before he could go. *Hours* it took him and it still didn't come out. But while some would think that was enough retribution, I didn't agree. When we were out on the mission, I put glitter in his shampoo and body wash."

"Oh Jesus." My eyes widen as he sits back, arms crossed over his chest. I make a mental note never to get into a war with him because I'll lose—epically. "I would say you won, huh?"

I'm so engrossed in the story I don't notice the waitress standing at our table.

"Can I get you anything else? Dessert?" she asks.

"No way, I couldn't eat another thing," I smile and Jackson shakes his head and grabs the check. "Everything was delicious, Jackson. Thank you for tonight."

"Tonight's not over." Standing before me, he extends his hand tentatively. Without any hesitation I place mine in his.

Was he afraid I'd say no? There isn't a damn thing that would stop me. The feel of his hand surrounding mine makes my heart skip a beat. Almost like the world has righted itself. I'm in trouble. I'm falling fast.

We exit into the cool night air and I shiver. "Hey." He stops and encircles my waist. "Thank you for letting me break your rules."

"Of course." Leaning in, I place a brief kiss on his lips. Passion erupts the moment our lips meet and the kiss becomes more frantic. His hands grip my sides as his fingers dig into my hips. I welcome the feeling. His need pushes my own. I feel his arousal against my stomach and suddenly couldn't care less about the rest of our evening. Jackson pushes me back against the car as his mouth devours mine. Time is irrelevant. Everything else fades away. Once again, he overtakes me and I'm lost to him. All I hear is the sound of his breathing, his moans. All I feel is him around me—touching me, wanting me, making me fall faster. He pulls away and turns, rubbing his hand roughly down his face.

"Fucking Christ," he mumbles. "I can't control myself when I touch you."

His words stun me. They're exactly how I feel. As soon as his skin meets mine, I lose all self-control. I need to get a freaking grip. The constant battling of emotions when I'm around him is draining. One minute I can't get close enough, and the next I'm fighting to keep my heart safe. Why does this have to be so damn difficult?

Once he's composed himself he walks back up to me and opens the car door. "In." My body obeys him without hesitation.

Jackson takes a minute outside the limo and tells Xavier where to go. I roll the window down and look at him. The air between us is charged, and though he's listening to something Xavier is saying, his unblinking eyes are locked on mine. The depth of his stare is almost too much. My yearning grows and

I lick my lips, gripping the bottom one between my teeth as he opens the door. Before it even clicks shut behind him, his mouth is on mine again. I can't get close enough. I've never been this girl. I've never desired a man as much as I do at this moment. It's primal, raw.

Our lips are fused and the need to be closer is unbearable. It's clear Jackson is fighting the same urges. He pushes me flat on the seat, and hovers above me. My heart is pounding, my lips are tingling, and all I want is to ease the aching between my legs.

His eyes shift from lustful to resolute and he pulls me back up. We're both breathing heavy as we recover from the rush of the moment. I would have let him fuck me in this car. With the window open for all to see! What the hell is wrong with me? I turn and look out the window, thankful for the cool air as I try to reel in my libido.

Jackson grasps my hand and I look over. "If you think I don't want you, you're wrong. I promise I'm going to do that and so much more, but we need a lot more time than a ten-minute drive." His brow lifts as his dimple appears.

I bite my lip at the hunger evident on his face and the promise of things to come. The longing to kiss him is too great to fight. I lean in and brush my lips against his.

"Not that I'm complaining, but what was that for?" He smiles.

"For everything." I shrug and return to watching the city pass by.

Not even a minute later, the car stops. We're on the Upper East Side of Manhattan, right by Central Park. I love this area of the city. It's gorgeous—and extremely expensive. Jackson's hand extends as he exits the limo. He pulls me forward as Xavier retrieves my bag. I look at the huge apartment building and it hits me—we aren't going to the park. He lives here. Ashton and I looked at a few apartments on this side of the city, but even with both our incomes it was out of our price range.

I shouldn't be surprised. He does own two companies, but he never seems to flaunt his money.

"Catherine?" he says softly, causing me to jump. "Ready?" I swear one day he won't be able to sneak up and scare the crap out of me.

We enter the building and I'm surprised by its contemporary design. Everything is clean lines, reminding me of his office in Virginia.

"How long have you lived here?" I ask.

Jackson rolls his neck and drops my hand before answering. "About a year."

"It's beautiful. I love this part of the city."

We enter the elevator and head to the twentieth floor. Jackson's hand snakes around my back. "I do too."

"I wish our office were closer to the park. I've always wanted to go there for lunch and just people watch." Central Park is spectacular. Sometimes it's a little scary, but for the most part it's wonderful. My father took me to the zoo there a few times. I always thought it was amazing that this little piece of the wild was placed in the perfectly manicured park in the perfectly chaotic city.

"Every morning I go for a five-mile run in the park."

"I'm not surprised you run every day." There will be none of that for me.

"We can wake up tomorrow and go." He smiles, knowing damn well that isn't happening.

"You're funny. The only way I'm running is if someone or something is chasing me. And even then, I might say screw it. I'd much rather eat a bag of Doritos, thanks."

"I bet you'd do it if I made you." His brow lifts as he leans in close.

I scoff and throw my head back. "Never gonna happen, babe. Besides, you owe me my time, Muff. Until I get that, there will be no more obstacle courses or stair climbing happening here."

"Who said anything about stairs?"

Before I can retort the elevator dings. My stomach is in knots. You'd think this was our first time being alone or intimate. This is the last barrier we have. He already knows where I live and work. Now both of us will have stayed at each other's homes. I'm excited to put together another piece of the puzzle that is Jackson Cole.

We reach his unit on the twentieth floor. He smiles and opens the door, allowing me through. "Welcome to my home."

While my apartment is modern, it has nothing on his. Jackson's place is masculine, but a woman could easily fit in.

"This is it," he says with a shrug and places my bag in the middle of the living room.

I take my shoes off and walk into the middle of the room. "It's amazing. I love the architecture and the color choices."

He slowly walks toward me. I stand rooted, unable to move an inch. Once he reaches me, his rough hands graze down my bare arms and I briefly close my eyes. "Let me show you around."

It takes a second to process that he said something. "Sure." As long as the tour ends in the bedroom I'm completely fine with it. My body is still humming with lust from our hot and heavy make out session outside the restaurant and in the limo.

Jackson shows me around the rest of the apartment. Every room has the same feel, like fire and ice—cold blues against warm reds. However, it's all somehow in perfect harmony. We enter his bedroom and the view ... The view is magnificent. The bedroom is warm and romantic, its ambiance completely different from the rest of the house. The massive king size bed faces windows that overlook the park. Jackson turns on the wall-mounted fireplace and the tension from the car returns full force. Desire courses through my body. Fire, heat, and lust are all I feel.

"I had other plans for the night," he says smoothly as he walks toward me.

"What happened?"

"You did." Jackson stops. He stands still, illuminated by the flames. I take a step toward him.

"Me?" I whisper, and he takes the final step so we're within reach.

"Yes. You, Catherine." His hand cups my face as his thumb rubs across my bottom lip. My head naturally tilts into his palm.

Please don't hurt me, I silently beg.

His eyes are warm and even though I'm fully dressed I feel completely naked. "I told you before, you do something to me. I need you and I haven't allowed myself to need anyone for a long time." He leans down, pressing his lips against my cheek. His voice is low and gruff. "When I'm around you all I can think about is being buried deep inside you." Jackson's lips graze the corner of my mouth as he continues his seduction. "I see you and all I see is every beautiful inch of the skin I know is underneath your clothes. I watch you talk and I think of what your mouth looks like wrapped around my cock."

I moan as his hands slip around my back and unzips my dress. No man's ever talked to me like this. I'm so aroused I could come from his words alone. He's speaking to every part of me—my heart and my core. I try to reach for him but he steps back.

"Stay still." His voice is strained as he makes the demand.

My body is begging for him, needing to touch him, yet I stand still as he circles me. His right hand stays in contact with me as he approaches my back and slowly pulls my hair to the side, opening my unzipped dress and pushing it off my shoulders. I stand facing the fire, so I can't see when he steps away from me, but I know just the same. The loss of his body close to mine is unmistakable, even in the heat. It feels like forever since he's moved or done anything and I can't take it anymore. I have to move. I need to see him, touch him. It's too much to fight.

I turn and he's standing there staring at me with fire in his eyes. My dress was too tight to require a bra and I chose not to wear panties since I didn't want lines. It seems to have worked in my favor. Now it's time to turn the tables on him. I shimmy out of my dress completely and approach him as his eyes drink me in. It's unnerving, yet I'm empowered by his silence.

"You know..." I pause, letting the statement hang out there while I reach for the top button of his shirt. "You aren't the only one who's turned on." My hand drops to the next button. I make sure to take my time with my words and my hands. His eyes are locked on mine as I start to seduce him. "I think about you all the time. I have to fight the urge to beg you to take me." After undoing the final button, I slide my hands back up his chiseled chest and his head drops back. I glide them under his shirt and push it down his toned arms, feeling every muscle tense beneath my touch. His reaction makes me stronger. It's exhilarating to know I elicit the same reaction he pulls from me. "You're impossible to resist." I tug on his belt and pull him closer to me, unbuttoning his pants and sliding them and his boxers down, trailing my fingertips on his legs as they descend. We're both bared completely to each other now, and I stand back up before speaking my last words to him. "But when you touch me, I'm lost to you."

His head snaps up at my admission and I realize we're both fighting the same temptation, both fighting something neither of us can explain—a connection that's powerful and scary. I see the emotions I'm feeling mirrored in his eyes.

His lips inch closer to mine and his words are soft and dripping with honesty. "You're never lost, Catherine. I'll always find you." His mouth crushes down on mine as his words resonate through me, bringing tears to my eyes. And there he is—my hero.

There's no more time for talking as we express what our hearts are feeling with our mouths and tongues and hands and bodies. He hooks his arm under my legs and carries me to the bed. Tenderly, he lays me down and hovers over me. This time is different for me. A part of my heart will be his tonight, and I'm willingly giving it over. I know I'm not in love with him yet, but he's breaking my defenses slowly but surely. I fight him and myself all to no avail. It's only a matter of time.

Our entire night was foreplay and now, I'm aching for him. "Jackson, don't make me beg."

"No need for begging." His head drops to my neck as he kisses and licks the sensitive skin behind my ear.

I start to shift and squirm, desperate for him to fill me and make me whole.

"Stay still," he says as he pins my arms down and restrains me.

"I need you. Now."

Instead of responding to my pleas, he releases my hands and glides his tongue down my side, purposely avoiding my breasts. Making his way farther, I grow anxious as he continues across my stomach and then up my other side. I'm going fucking crazy! His strong arms keep me still and my body is tight, vibrating with need. When he makes his way back up to my ear, I've lost all control. I can't take another second.

I've finally snapped. "I want you to fuck me. Right. Now."

"I have all intentions of it, but first I'm going to drive you absolutely fucking crazy. Just like you do to me. This has just begun. The more you beg, the more I'll make you wait." The combination of his words and the timbre of his voice when he says them is too much. My muscles contract and deep-seated need courses its way through me, calling for him to take me and claim me.

He pushes up and puts the condom on, moving me higher on the bed. Lifting my leg, he pulls it to his mouth and makes his way down to my core. I lie there watching as he gets closer and closer, and my breath hitches as he avoids the one place I need him most. His tongue trails to the other leg and I groan and throw my head back. My breathing is erratic. I'm going out of my mind. We lock eyes as his tongue swipes up my center. My eyes close from the intense pleasure of finally being touched only to have him stop.

"I want you to watch me. If you look away, I'll stop." His low voice is fierce and commanding.

Keeping our eyes locked, he leans back down and licks my pussy again, stirring an involuntary shudder. I watch as he begins sucking and licking over and over again. I'm fighting the urge to close my eyes. If he stops, I might combust, so I keep my eyes trained on him. It's the most erotic thing, watching him. He looks up as he inserts two fingers, pumping, and my body tenses. Every muscle is locking, ready to finally release, and my eyes slam shut. Immediately, I feel his loss. *No!*

"I told you keep your eyes on me." I nod, unable to speak from being so close and then having it taken away.

Jackson wastes no time as he sucks on my clit. When I feel his teeth bite down, I'm gone. I shout his name over and over and writhe in a pleasure only he gives me. I splinter into a million pieces as he pumps his fingers, drawing out my orgasm until I finally settle and become coherent.

When I open my eyes he's above me, waiting for me to come back to reality. I bite my lip as I feel the tip of his dick brush against my sensitive clit. I spread my legs and press the heels of my feet on his ass, pushing him into me. His jaw is tight and he seems to be fighting his own needs. I push again but he's so much stronger than me, so he barely moves.

"Please, fuck me," I beg softly.

"I'm not going to fuck you this time," he says in a hushed tone. "I'm going to go slow." He leans down and kisses me deeply, swirling his tongue with mine as I moan, begging for more. "I'm going to show you how sexy and irresistible you are, how you test my patience." He nips at my ear and then runs his tongue over where he just bit. "Then I'm going to fuck you until you beg me to stop."

I rub my hand against his rough cheek. Once his eyes meet

mine I groan and say, "Then do it already."

His eyes blaze as he slowly fills me, stretching me and then pulling out fully. He enters me again and my eyes are heavy-lidded as he stares through to my soul. With each thrust he's tearing me apart and then putting me back together again. Quickly, he flips our positions so I'm on top. I push against him, grinding down and enjoying the intense fullness while he holds my hips and sets the pace. I lean back, bringing him impossibly deeper. He rubs his thumb on my clit and I lose my breath as the force of my sudden orgasm rips me apart. My body takes over, riding him harder, and I hear Jackson groan as he orgasms, both of us riding out the bliss together.

chapter

twenty

'M SPENT.

Completely and totally useless.

I'm lying against his chest, still unable to catch my breath. He runs his fingers lightly against my back before shifting me to go clean up. I groan and stretch as my muscles loosen from the aftermath of our intense sex session. The tightness reminds me of the obstacle course and how much my body ached afterward. But this is the kind of physical workout I welcome.

Jackson returns and flops on his stomach, giving me a view of his perfect ass. He really is magnificent. I kind of want to pinch myself—surely this can't be real. He turns his head toward me with a smile and I place my hand on his back. I've never gotten a good look at the art on his shoulder. It's really remarkable, so intricate, and has so many different parts to it. In the center are the bones of a frog. Its body wraps around from the front of his shoulder and ends with the head facing down on his back. In the frog's hands is the trident of Poseidon, only the three spears of the trident aren't spears, they're names. Brian, Fernando, and Devon are written in an elegant script and the number four serves as the handle. It's surrounded by black tribal ink. My finger grazes the frog and the labyrinth of tribal markings around it. Below it is the most beautiful quote.

We have this hope as an anchor for our soul, firm and secure. – Hebrews 6:19

It's profound and speaks to my heart. There's meaning behind each word. Hope is something we all have, and it's often the only thing we can grasp when our world is shattering. I hoped for my father to return. I hoped for Neil to be faithful. Neither of those things happened, but that hope is what kept me going every day.

Jackson rolls and faces me with sad eyes, so different from just moments ago. I reach up, placing my hand on his heart, and he pulls me in, close enough so I can see the front of the tattoo. "What does your tattoo mean?" I feel him tense.

"It's the tattoo you get when you lose someone on the team," he says matter-of-factly.

"Is that the loss you've mentioned?"

"Some," he replies and laces his fingers with mine, holding our clasped hands between us.

I want to push him to tell me. I want him to share with me—more like I want him to *want* to tell me. I'm just not sure I should try to force it.

"Why a frog?" My curiosity gets the best of me. I don't understand some of his world.

"SEALs are referred to as Frogmen." He smiles and squeezes my hand gently. His eyes are warm and he continues on, "I got that tattoo to remember my three friends who died on a mission."

My heart swells that he's opening up, but aches for the pain of his loss. "I'm so sorry."

He removes his hand from mine and wraps his arm around my middle. I scoot closer and return his hug, placing a small kiss on his chest. My mind begins to wander as the silence persists. Do I push again?

Jackson takes a deep breath and begins to speak. His voice is low, pain threading through his words. "It's my fault."

Pulling back, I look in his eyes. The agony there is evident. "What's your fault?"

Jackson struggles to hide his emotions, but I watch each

one play like a movie—sadness, anger, guilt, hatred—before his expression goes void. "Their deaths—I was in charge of the mission."

"Jackson, I doubt that," I say softly, hoping he'll hear the disbelief in my voice.

He tugs me back against his chest. I'm not sure if he's done talking or if he wants to hide from me. Giving him what he's silently requesting, I wrap my arm around him and stay quiet.

Right as I'm starting to drift to sleep, feeling safe and content in his arms, I hear his deep voice. "When we were in Iraq, we got into some heavy firefight. I was in command of my team." He pauses and runs his fingers up and down my spine methodically.

I look up and his eyes are closed tight as if he's fighting an internal war. Every part of him is rigid and tense. I bring my hand to his face, brushing my thumb across his cheek. "Hey," I whisper.

His eyes are vacant as he speaks. "There were six of us and we had bad intel. Something wasn't sitting right, but I had my orders." He takes a deep breath and his voice is distant. "So we deviated a little, hoping it would give us the element of surprise. I split the team in half. Mark, Aaron, and I took to the left." He pauses again and I watch as pain lances through his features. Every single bone in my body is aching for him, but I stay still and quiet as I wait for him to go on.

"Brian, Fernando, and Devon took to the right of the village. I knew something was wrong. I had that sinking feeling but we didn't have a choice. We had to fucking go and do our job. When we split up, it made it easier to pick us off. I heard the gunfire, but we couldn't get to them quick enough. They were shot and killed. I was in charge—it's on me."

"Oh, Jackson." I gasp and pull myself up.

I want to comfort him. I'm just not sure what to do. The pain in his voice, the torment in his eyes, it's lashing through me. I want to take it from him, carry the burden so he's not hurting, but he keeps going.

"By the time our extraction team got in, it was too late. They were already dead. Mark and I were both shot. Aaron was the only one who got out without getting injured. Mine was on my arm." He points to a faint scar on his bicep. I lean over and kiss him. He smiles weakly at me, but there's nothing but sadness in his eyes. "I carry their deaths on my shoulders."

I can't imagine how much the tattoo hurt, but the agony of reliving that memory while someone permanently etches it into your skin ...

"I'm sure no one blames you. I mean Mark works with you and so does Aaron. Surely, they know what an amazing man you are."

Anger flashes in his eyes at my statement, like it couldn't be true. "They don't need to. *I* blame me." He bangs his fist on his chest. "It was my call. Their wives had to bury them, Catherine. They had to go to their funeral. They had to tell their kids that their dads would never come back again. Had we stuck together, we all would have lived." He shuts his eyes on the memory and me.

"You don't know that. You can't know that if you stuck to the plan, or together, that all of you wouldn't have been killed." My voice is small but strong. I'm trying to give him the other side of things.

He doesn't respond. I know it's futile to try to argue. Ashton tried to tell me hundreds of times that my father probably had a reason to leave, and how Neil might not be the best guy for me. Sometimes it doesn't matter because you can't see past the image in your own heart.

We lie here together, unspeaking. Two broken ships trying to find a way through rough seas. I close my eyes and settle back on his chest, listening to the steady thrum of his heart as he tenderly holds me. And though I feel for his loss, I'm grateful he was spared.

He kisses the top of my head, and I move back so he can

see the truth in my eyes. I need him to really hear what I'm saying. "I think you're a wonderful man. From what I've seen you're kind, loyal, trusting, and wouldn't purposely put anyone in danger. You've comforted me and I saw how worried you were over the situation at your company."

I grab hold of his face, forcing him to look at me. He shouldn't carry guilt over something that wasn't his fault. "You, Jackson Cole, are a man worth following. Those men wouldn't want you to carry their deaths on your shoulders."

"Those men should be alive," he says almost inaudibly. Then he tries to move his head out of my grasp, but I'm not having it. I'm not done.

"True, they shouldn't have died. No one should have to die, but would you have taken the bullet for them?" I raise my brow, already knowing his answer.

Without hesitation, he responds forcefully, "In a heartbeat."

"Well, don't you think they would do the same for you? I know loss too, Jackson. I'm living it now."

I know he's upset and hurt, but he's failing to see that he wouldn't want them to suffer if the situation were reversed. If it were Ashton and, God forbid, something happened and I was gone, I wouldn't want her to live with that kind of guilt. I would want her to pick up her life and live on.

"You're not telling me anything I haven't heard before. Bottom line—I was there. I lived it." His eyes narrow in anger. "I watched it happen and I couldn't stop it. I fucked up and no one is going to tell me different. Their blood is on my hands. Did you kill your dad? No. So don't compare." His voice is cold, fused with frustration and defeat.

"You didn't kill them either," I whisper and drop my hands. A tear forms and I try to choke it down and hide my face from him.

I'm hurting for this entire situation and for my own guilt. No, I'm not responsible for my father's death, but I never tried to find him either. I wrote him off. Some may think I was justified. Whether I was or not, I'll never get that chance now. And now I've brought all of Jackson's pain to the forefront. Regret is a shitty thing to live with and it seems both of us have an entire truckload of it.

"I'm sorry." I feel him shift and his strong arms encase me.

"You have nothing to be sorry for."

"You're crying." He releases his hold and turns my head to look at him.

What else is new? I'm emotional. With all the stress of the last few months and my lack of sleep, I'm a little frayed. The impending reading of my father's will is wearing on me too. I want to get past all of this so I can get back to who I once was.

Swiping the tear from my face, I smile and retort, "No, I'm not."

"I didn't mean to be an asshole and ruin our night."

"You didn't, Jackson. I'm sorry I pushed." I smile and place my hand against his cheek. "But I'm going to keep telling you how incredible you are, okay?"

His smile is soft, placating. It's clear he doesn't believe me. I wish he could see what I see. I shrug and give him a quick kiss. I'm not giving up on him.

"Come on, let's go to bed."

I put my finger up and hop out of the bed. "One minute. I just need to brush my teeth and all that good stuff."

Seeing Jackson's shirt on the floor, I grab it and throw it on, then enter the bathroom. I try to fix my now disheveled hair and quickly brush my teeth. I take a few extra minutes to get my head under control. He's seen and been through so much. Are we both too fucked-up to work? No, if I think like that, I'm doing exactly what I always do. He's not fucked-up, nor am I. We just have some healing to do.

Climbing back into bed, Jackson pulls me against his solid chest. "You look good in my shirt."

I chuckle and smile at him. "You look good in your shirt

too."

His voice is low and oozes sexual promise. "You look even better out of my shirt."

I laugh and shake my head. He effortlessly lifts me so we're eye to eye and leans in to kiss me. It's a slow, easy, and careful kind of kiss. It's the kind of moment your heart will never recover from because you're both saying so much. My head is spinning. I try to hold myself back. Between all the details tonight—the dinner, the earth-shattering sex, and then him finally opening up to me—Jackson has obliterated my walls.

He finally releases me, settling me into the crook of his arm. "Good night, baby."

I smile even though he can't see me. "Good night, Muffin."

chapter

twenty-one

OUR NIGHT TOGETHER put us over some imaginary threshold. We've talked almost every day and we saw each other for lunch a few days ago. It's been two weeks of laughter and falling into a nice rhythm together.

I grab the subway and head to his apartment, where he has another day of surprises in store for me. He's standing outside waiting, and the sight of him causes my pulse to spike. His dark brown hair is in sexy disarray and his white T-shirt is tight, which lets me see his defined muscles perfectly. Butterflies stir in my stomach. It astounds me that we're dating—he's magnificent, commanding, sweet, and so many other things. I can't keep my eyes off him when he's around. The chemistry between us crackles like flames on a log. My body comes to life when he touches me—it's a heady feeling.

As I approach he gives me a lopsided grin. "Hello, gorgeous."

"Hello yourself." I smile and he immediately reaches out, pulling me flush against him. "Do you always have to manhandle me?"

"Well, baby, I'm all man and I sure as hell love to handle you." His eyes glimmer with humor.

Hell yeah he's all man—every single fantastic inch of him.

"You're ridiculous." I shake my head.

"Yet you keep coming back, so I must not be that bad." He

smirks and gives me a long, panty-melting kiss.

Right here on 5th Avenue in New York City, he has once again rendered me helpless. Shoppers, families, cabs, and bikers all fade away as his lips move with mine. Jackson pulls back and wraps his arm around my shoulders.

I love how physical he is, almost as if he can't keep his hands off me. It's such a contrast to anything I'm used to. Whether it's holding hands or something as simple as touching legs when we watch television, those small moments say so much. They're unspoken words that show the true depth of what we're both feeling.

"So what's on our agenda today?" I ask with a light heart.

There's happiness dancing in his eyes when he responds, "The park."

My face falls at his answer. Jackson told me to make sure I was comfortable today. No heels, no dresses. He said to be sure I wore sneakers. I made him promise no military training exercises, no entering me for some kind of race or marathon, and no other strenuous physical activity that would have me aching for days after completion. After my ribbing about his love of running and exercise in general, I was a little hesitant, but he swore I would love today. I trusted him—first mistake.

"Why do I think I should've stayed home in bed?" I groan.

He laughs and pulls me tighter. "I wasn't in bed with you, so that's reason enough to get up," Jackson jokes in my ear as we walk. "One day I'll get you to agree to a mud run or something, but you'll be happy to know I kept my end of the bargain today. They don't have an obstacle course in Central Park—yet. And there's no marathon."

"Yet somehow that doesn't comfort me." I smile and nudge him.

We keep walking until we stop in front of the Central Park Zoo. My smile is so wide I can't contain it. I leap into his arms, wrapping my legs around his torso and pressing my lips to his. His eyes are bright and full of happiness.

"Jackson!" I squeal, hugging him tight.

"Happy?" he asks with an irresistibly devilish grin.

I've thought it before and I'm thinking it now—Jackson can read my mind. Or we're just that in sync. The zoo. This is one of the few places that holds any kind of happy memories for me and my dad. I love that he brought me here.

I let him see it all in my eyes, allowing him to see how very much this means to me. My whole heart is open to him as we stand wrapped around each other. After a few seconds or minutes—I don't know which—I give him another kiss and untangle myself.

"Come on, babe. Let's go inside." His husky voice wraps around my heart, warming me from the inside out.

Our fingers lace together as we enter through the brick archway. I pull him around the zoo, looking at all the animals and laughing with him throughout our miniature safari in the city. We walk and catch each other up on the days we were both swamped and couldn't talk. Jackson informs me about his upcoming trip to Virginia in the next few weeks. I tell him about Ashton's newest fling. When we approach my favorite animals, I'm practically bouncing up and down.

"I love the camels!" I shout, pulling him to the fence. "They're the most underrated animals."

Jackson's laughter peals through my cooing at the camel in the back. "You're kidding. This is your favorite animal?"

"Whatever! I think they're cute. They have the humps and they're strong." I stare through as the one I'm wooing comes closer.

"I like to hump and I'm strong. I'm sensing a pattern." His brow lifts.

My brain blanks out as I envision Jackson doing a variety of things in the bedroom. I need to move off this topic quickly before my thoughts go further in the wrong direction.

"Anyway. They're my favorite." I smile.

"I seriously can't believe this is what you wanted to see.

I mean, how 'bout a lion? Monkey? Something cool," he says with humor and a trace of incredulity.

I shake my head at his indifference toward this beautiful creature.

"They're cool. They even have a song about them." I raise my brows.

"What song?" he asks, laughing and clearly confused.

"You know, 'Sally the Camel has Five Humps,'" I say in a singsong way. Back in college I babysat a child whose favorite show played that counting song all the time. It was annoying and repetitive and would inevitably get stuck in your head and drive you crazy. If he thinks I'm going to sing it to him, he's lost his damn mind.

"I have no clue what you're talking about, but by all means feel free to sing it." Jackson's smile lights up his face.

"No, I don't think that would be enjoyable for either of us." I laugh, returning my gaze to the animals. "If I lived on a farm, I'd own one."

"They're gross and they smell. Plus, I've ridden them plenty during deployments. I promise there is nothing special about a camel. Now, you want to talk about a tiger, I'm all for it." He grins, enjoying his teasing.

The camel walks over to the fence and a young boy lifts his hand up, feeding it from his palm. I giggle, but Jackson looks like he's disgusted.

"See. You couldn't feed a lion from your hand." I tilt my head, toying with him. The machine to get food for the camel is a few feet away. I dig through my purse for the quarter I need as Jackson scoffs.

"No, but—" Before he can finish his sentence, the camel spits and it lands not even an inch in front of him.

I bust out laughing. Tears stream from my eyes as he stands there looking like he wants to climb the fence and teach it a lesson, which only makes me laugh harder. Jackson stares at me before his own grin and chuckle break free. "Oh my ... She showed you!" I barely get out.

"So not funny." He rushes toward me and grips my hand, pulling me away from the animal, which clearly does not like him. "Fucking thing almost got me."

"If only my beautiful Jessica had better aim." I giggle and wrap my arms around his torso, trying to control myself.

"You named the camel that tried to spit on me?" Jackson asks, sounding wounded.

"Jessica the camel. She only spit because you were being an ass and talking shit about her." I wink.

"Glad to see where your loyalties lie."

"Jessica and I have a strong bond. Sorry, babe, Jessica and I are like this." I say and hold my crossed fingers up.

We stop in front of the next animal and he wraps his arms around my waist, pulling me against him. I gaze at him, breathing in this moment in time. I love the way he makes me laugh, smile, and enjoy a normal day. Jackson brings out parts of me that I'd buried after Neil. But I don't have to pretend with him. I can just *be*. Knowing that he doesn't want to change me, that he wants to be with me as I am—it's liberating. I snake my arms up his taut back as my mind drifts to all the ways Jackson's infiltrated my heart and soul. I think of him as soon as I wake up and before I go to bed. He's in my dreams too. He's wrapped up with every aspect of my work life, but even when I'm not looking at the launch, someone will say something that brings me back to him.

Jackson's eyes bore into mine. "I don't know what I did to deserve this chance with you." His fingers tenderly brush a loose strand of hair back behind my ear. "You're beautiful, smart, funny ... I can't get enough of you. What's going on in that gorgeous head of yours?"

I'm taken aback by his intensity and what he's saying. He thinks he's undeserving? It's me who doesn't know how I somehow have him.

I place my hand on his cheek. "I think you have it mixed-up.

It's me who's lucky. I keep waiting to wake up and realize you're a dream." I rub my thumb against his stubble. He's real. We're real. No pretending, no dreams—only us.

"Believe it, baby. I'm not going anywhere," he says softly before his lips meet mine.

We continue our day walking through the zoo. He refuses to let me say good-bye to the camels, no matter how hard I try. We walk through the park hand in hand, stopping to grab a dirty water dog and pretzel from the hot dog truck. It's your typical day in New York City. No fanfare or crazy planning. It's perfect. Every single solitary second is all I could ever want.

"How about we head back to my place and watch a movie?" Jackson asks.

"Sure. Only if I can pick it." I smile, happy that he wants to spend the rest of the day together.

I note that he didn't answer, but he's crazy if he thinks I'm going to let him win—again. We head to his apartment and memories of the last time I was here flood back. The way he seduced me, touched me, brought me to the brink, and then opened up about the mission. How in the morning there was no awkwardness. We had breakfast and I headed back to my apartment, floating on cloud nine.

"Pick something good," Jackson warns as we head into the living room.

"You didn't give any contingencies, so you get no say." I smirk and head over to the wall of DVDs. I could be a total pain in the ass and pick something I know he'd hate, but then again his selection doesn't exactly give me many options. Scanning the endless rows, I find one and gasp.

"Oh my God! You have *Empire Records*?" I grab the DVD and rush over to put it in the player.

"You know this movie is cinema gold," Jackson says as he brings over popcorn and settles into the couch.

"This is the best movie ever!" I exclaim and snuggle into his side. "Okay. Before we start watching, if you could be anyone, who would you pick? I'd be Lucas. He's hysterical." I smile and grab the bowl, putting it on my lap.

"I guess Joe. He's the boss."

I laugh at his choice. Of course he'd pick the one who's in charge. Joe is pretty badass, though.

"I think you'd be a great Rex. Oh Rexy, you're so sexy." I smirk and push play as he scoffs.

We spend the next hour laughing and reciting lines. Just as Rex Manning and Gina are getting it on in the copy room, Jackson runs his fingers up and down my arm. Suddenly I'm not so interested in the movie anymore. I shift, trying to stifle the lust bubbling up, but he moves his hand to the back of my neck and starts making small circles on my skin with his fingertips. My breathing becomes heavier as the pad of his finger rubs the spot right below my ear. Every caress increases my yearning. Heat pools as he makes his way back down my neck, lingering there.

I move my hand higher up his leg and hear him swallow loudly. The urge to touch him, to feel him, to make him come apart in my hands grows with each beat of my heart. Slowly I turn to look at him. His eyes drink me in before his mouth crushes against my lips with savage intensity. He shifts us and swings me on top of him. Feeling his erection against my core causes my arousal to rage like a storm.

His lips lower and his tongue traces my neck and shoulders. "Jackson, I want you," I say in a breathy whisper.

"Understatement of the year." He pulls the strap of my tank top and bra down, exposing my breast to his hungry mouth. Jackson pushes me back as his tongue circles my nipple.

My lids close as I absorb the sensations of his warm breath and mouth on me. His hand glides up my back and tangles in my hair as he tugs, exposing my neck and arching me forward to give him easier access. I try to sit up but he grips my hair and pulls harder, bringing my chest closer to him. He sucks and nips as I writhe in his lap. His other hand digs into my ass, gripping, kneading, and pushing me into his cock.

Using his teeth, he pulls the other strap down and pays the same attention to my other breast. The scruff on his cheek grazes my already sensitive skin, sending tingles from my head to my toes.

I push forward and pull his shirt off before fusing my mouth to his. Our tongues tangle as the kiss becomes aggressive and desperate. God, I want him so bad. I'm dripping with need, aching for him to fill me. I rake my nails down his arms, extracting a low rumble from his chest.

Breaking the kiss, my tongue grazes his ear before I say huskily, "I want to fuck you."

He groans before pushing me up and tearing my pants off. I hastily pull his off as he reaches over and puts a condom on. I'm straddling him when he says, "Then fuck me, Catherine."

I slide down on him as he fills me to the brink. So fucking full. He's so deep his cock is hitting every nerve inside me. Jackson's eyes close and his head falls back against the couch. My hands grip his shoulders as I start to move.

"Your pussy feels so good." His voice fills the room and he groans louder.

Every breath, every moan goes straight to my core.

Gripping my hips, he sets the pace. Raw passion spreads through me at the sweet friction of his bare skin against mine. Watching him lost in my touch, in my body, as I rock back and forth is incredible. Our eyes connect, awakening something deep within me. His fingers dig in so tight it's almost painful, but we don't drop our eyes. The unrestrained emotion behind his gaze mirrors mine. With each thrust, each caress, each kiss, we're both giving each other everything, all the good and bad. I don't know where he ends and I begin. I ride him hard and fast, embracing this intimacy, climbing my way toward ecstasy.

Jackson slips his hand between us, applying pressure to my clit. I lean against his chest, absorbing the heat from his body. "Let go," he groans against my neck. "I want to feel you grip me. Ride me harder."

"Don't stop," I pant as he continues to draw pleasure from me.

He rubs in small circles, keeping pace from below, pushing me harder and faster so every nerve surges with liquid heat. I lose control at the intense pleasure and sink my teeth into his shoulder, biting down as my orgasm tears through me.

"Holy shit!" Jackson calls out as he pounds into me, taking control of my movement.

I lean back with a seductive gleam in my eyes, but it's nothing compared to the fire burning in his. My heart clenches. He's either angry or extremely turned-on. Jackson lifts me off him and places me on the floor, gripping me from behind as he lifts my ass in the air. Definitely turned-on.

"You fucking amaze me," he says, low and raspy as his hand glides up my back. Then he grabs my shoulder, entering me roughly. "This. Us. You. Your body—was made for me. You're mine."

"Oh my God, yes." I moan as the feeling of him deeper than he's ever been overtakes me. He tangles a hand in my hair as he plows into me, hard. My breasts hang heavily and the sound of our bodies connecting over and over fills the room.

"You look so fucking sexy." Jackson's voice is strained as he slams into me. His fingers wrap around my hip, gripping me so tight. He shifts his position, hitting the sweet spot inside me. The sound of him slapping his body against mine only drives me higher. "I want to fuck you all day and all night, so all you see is me. When you walk, I want you to remember where I've been and how good it feels when I'm inside you."

His words go directly to my core, reviving my previous orgasm. My mind is a sponge soaking up every syllable. Jackson reaches his hand around, finds my sensitive clit, and rubs it, bringing my orgasm closer.

"I'll never get enough of you. Mine goddamnit. All fucking mine."

That word: enough. Only this time he's telling me I *am* enough. Telling me he wants more.

I shatter, crying out his name as he continues to hit every sensitive spot in my body. My bones are melting from the sheer force of it.

He pumps a few more times before following. "Catherine ... My Catherine."

We both crumple to the floor, exhausted and sated. I look up at him as he rubs his shoulder where I bit him. Oh my God, I bit him. I actually sunk my teeth into him because I was so far gone.

"Sorry about that." I smile as my cheeks flame with embarrassment.

He smiles back at me. "You can bite me." Jackson's lips find purchase on mine. "Any fucking time." He lies on his back and shifts me closer.

He's everything I could have wanted but never knew to ask for. We enjoy and entertain each other. The one thing my grandma always said was to find someone who makes you laugh. We can be serious or playful, and either way it works. As scared as I am, right now I feel content, happy. I close my eyes and listen to the rhythm of his heart.

He kisses my head. "I've got you, baby." The sound of his voice lulls me and I drift off, hoping we can handle whatever comes our way, because the thought of losing moments and days like this scares me.

chapter

twenty-two

IT'S BEEN THE week from hell. Nothing has gone right. My car broke down and I spilled coffee on my shirt first thing this morning. Worse than anything, Jackson and I haven't seen each other much. He's coming with me today to the reading of my father's will, which is also causing me extreme stress. Ashton wanted to be there for me, but she's working on a breakthrough and it's been keeping her in the city for the last week.

I'm working on the final version of Raven's ad campaign today since the approvals finally came through. It's been the only thing Jackson and I have argued about. I scheduled a few press releases, but he's been fighting about getting in front of the camera.

"Cat," Taylor's sweet voice comes through the intercom.

"Yes?"

"I have Neil on the line. He says it's urgent." Taylor sounds as irritated as I am at his calling.

He's been relentless. He calls or texts almost every day, but this is the first time he's resorted to calling the office. He's wearing me down and my patience is already nonexistent.

"Tay, I can't do this today. Tell him I'm out of the office or whatever." I drop my head on the desk, making a loud thump. Fucking Neil. Will this ever end?

Taylor comes in after getting rid of my annoyingly

persistent ex. "He said he would try again later." She's wringing her hands as she sits to go over the Raven account.

"I don't want to take his calls, so don't even let me know anymore. Just don't put it through. Okay?"

"Sure, no problem." She smiles and nods her head.

"I have a meeting on Wednesday that I need the video ready for, so let's get to work." I return her smile and open my folder.

We have so much left to do to get things to where I want them. I'm an overachiever by nature, but I'm borderline obsessive on this one. It's different when you know the client, even more so when you know them intimately. My need to please people is always a problem, but with Jackson it's kind of scary. I want him to be blown away by what I've done.

"It's almost time for you to leave," Taylor reminds me. "Do you want to finish up Monday?"

"Oh shit! Yes, let's plan to be in the office late next Monday and Tuesday. I need to have a few meetings with some magazines and meet with the marketing team. Plus, I need the print ads done before the release and the photo shoot." I stand and smooth my black dress. I figured black would be appropriate. Even though I'm not going to a funeral, in a way it's my own personal version of one. I'm saying good-bye to my father today in more ways than one.

"Sounds good." She shifts her weight and looks away.

"What's wrong, Tay?"

She doesn't say a word as she walks over and wraps her slender arms around me. After a moment of her squeezing, she inhales and swipes at her eye, looking forlorn. What the hell is going on?

"Are you quitting? Is that what this is?" I ask, panicking.

"No! I felt like you needed a hug. You've had a lot happen in the last few months, and I can't imagine today is going to be easy for you. I know you've been trying to pretend this isn't happening. I'm just glad you won't be alone."

I didn't want to tell Taylor or anyone in the office about my relationship with Jackson, but I trust her. That, and she saw how happy I was after the trip, so she knew something was going on. She knows what a risk I'm taking, but she's genuinely excited about Jackson and me. This is the kind of person I want in my life. People like her remind me not everyone is awful. I didn't even put two and two together as to what had her bothered, and come to find out it was concern for me.

"Thanks. I'll be okay. Maybe I'll finally get some closure." I muster a small smile.

I hear someone clearing their throat and turn to see Jackson leaning against the door of my office with a huge grin.

"Jackson! What are you doing here? I thought I was meeting you at the lawyer's office." I smile as he walks toward me, taking in his perfectly tailored suit. He brushes my hair off my face and stares at me. All I can do is smile back in wonder. I'm so far gone—I'd be a fool to think otherwise.

"I was close. I figured I'd ride there with you," he says, wrapping his arms around me.

Suddenly aware that we're in my office, I quickly step back out of his embrace. It's so easy to fall into a pattern with him and forget he's my client. He may not care about my rules, but the bottom line is I can't risk losing my job.

"Jackson, not here please," I whisper, looking over at the wide open door.

Hurt flashes in his eyes before he recovers. "You almost ready to go?"

I step forward but keep a professional distance, allowing my eyes to convey all I can't show him physically. The thin line between being his publicist and girlfriend can hurt both of us if it isn't clear.

"You know how badly I wish I could wrap my arms around you? But you're still my client and you promised. My assistant is outside the door and my boss could walk in at any moment. So I'm not trying to push you away. I'm asking you to think about how it would look."

My heart stutters when I think about how thoughtful he was to come here and make sure I'm not alone on the ride over. Once again he's giving be something I didn't know I needed. He knows me. He gets me. It baffles me that he's wormed his way through all my layers without any resistance. Well, very little resistance.

A slow, sexy smile glides across his features. "It's fine, baby. In about three minutes we won't be in your office. Remember, outside of our business relationship I make no promises."

Returning his smile, I can see he wants to kiss me, but instead he strides out of my office.

Taylor and Jackson spend a few minutes talking and laughing while I clean up my desk. I grab my phone, unsurprised that I have a few missed calls from Neil, a text from Ashton, and another from Gretchen.

Ashton: Be strong and remember you're loved.

Me: Thanks Biffle. I love you. See you tonight.

I check the next message from Gretchen and smile.

Gretchen: Call me if you need anything and text me a picture of the new hottie. Ashton said I'd shit myself.

Me: I will! Can't wait for you to meet him.

Gretchen: Where's my picture?

Me: You'll get one soon.

I look up as Taylor glances over, eyes wide and mouth agape as she points to Jackson. I resist the urge to laugh—he is ridiculously gorgeous. But more than that, he sees me. He sees everything I am and doesn't run.

I glance at the clock and close up my office. We only have about twenty minutes before we have to be there. "Come on. Stop flirting with the office staff."

Taylor laughs and we say our good-byes. Jackson has

a town car waiting downstairs for us—another sign of his thoughtfulness. We climb in and he clasps my hand in his. A sad smile spreads across my face. I'm glad he's here with me. But as far as we've come in the short amount of time we've known each other, I can't shake the feeling that it's only a matter of time until Jackson walks away. It's like there's this barrier around him that only permits me to get so close, and I have a nagging feeling that he's hiding something. I can't put my finger on what exactly, but it's there in the way he breaks off his thoughts sometimes or the forlorn look he occasionally gets when he thinks I'm not paying attention. It keeps me from trusting my emotions. I want to give myself freely, allow him into the deeper parts of me, but I need the same in return.

"Hey, you're quiet. What's going on?" Jackson says, breaking my inner thoughts.

"I'm just thinking. A lot could happen today."

My nerves are all over the place. I don't know what to expect. It's not like I have anything to go off of.

He rubs his thumb across my soft skin and my heart flutters. "Did your father have any other relatives?"

"I honestly don't know," I mutter. "I don't remember much about my father or his family. I know he had a brother, but I don't think they were close."

"These usually aren't long. It's really a formality," he says and looks out the window, taking a moment to himself. As he faces forward again, I notice his eyes, glossy with unshed tears. Releasing my hand, he grips his pants, looking uncomfortable.

"You okay?"

Quickly he glances up, giving me a half-hearted smile. "Yeah. Sorry. I hate lawyers. Will your mother be there?"

I want to call bullshit but something holds me back. I hate a lot of things, but most don't make me emotional. I take a moment to weigh my response. As much as I want to press him, we don't have enough time and my head isn't clear enough for anything too deep. "No. I didn't even tell her about it. I don't really want her to be there. Let's just say our relationship is strained at best."

"Were you always like that?" he asks.

No, sadly we weren't.

"There was a time when we were close. She worked hard throughout my childhood to make sure we had the basics— food, shelter, clothing. Eventually, it wore on her. Being a single mother and having to raise me alone with no financial or emotional support from anyone else was hard. I remember my grandmother being around when my father first left, but she died when I was twelve. That was when everything fell to shit. My mother started trying to replace my father and I became irrelevant.

"There were times we had fun. I remember a family vacation to Florida, and I clung to that memory when I was younger. But the older I got, the more and more bitter she got, until I left for college—which she refused to help me with. She thought I was an idiot and wouldn't make it through year one, let alone get a degree. I really hated her during that time. But I proved her wrong. I busted my ass and got grants and loans to pay for my education. I refuse to fail and school was no different." I look away, embarrassed by my rant. I didn't mean to tell him all that. A simple no would have sufficed.

The car slows and comes to a stop in front of a tall building. This will be the final piece to my father's part in my life. The moisture builds in my eyes as I think of the few good memories I have of him—the times he showered me with adoration, when he sang to me, when we played games, and when he helped with my homework. It surprises me that I remember any of them since they weren't a large part of my life. Still, they were all I had to cling to during my darker times.

Whatever's showing on my face gives Jackson pause. "Catherine, what's wrong?" The concern in his voice chips away at my resolve.

"I'm fine." I turn away, trying to gather myself so I can face this. Suddenly it feels like the car is closing in—I need to get out of here. Practically falling out of the car, I right myself and clench my hands. *I can do this.* I can go in there, find out what I need to be here for, and leave.

Jackson is behind me in a heartbeat, turning me around to face him. "If you're fine, then why do you look like you're about to pass out?"

"I'm just ... nervous." I try to shrug it off so I can get this over with. Am I scared? Yes. Am I ready to lay to rest a piece of the puzzle that's been missing since I was a child? Yes. I close my eyes, shake my head, and gather all the strength I can.

"You don't have to do this. We can come back if you're not feeling well."

"Jackson, I have to do this now."

"No, you don't." His jaw is set and his features appear angry, yet his voice is filled with empathy and understanding. "You need to be sure you're strong and ready to face it. Let's go up and reschedule. When you rush trying to get it over with, it only leaves a mess afterward."

I glance at him curiously, wondering about that last statement. "No, I'm doing this today. If I leave here, I'll never come back." I take a step closer to him, grasping his hand in mine. My eyes soften and my heart swells from his concern. I need him. I need his strength even if it's only him sitting beside me through this. "Please, I can't do this alone."

His body stiffens at my plea, but he doesn't answer. I beg with my eyes as he looks away and releases my hand. He takes a deep breath and grips the back of his neck. Though it's my father whose affairs we're here to settle, by the way he's acting you'd think Jackson was just as upset by this whole thing as I am. I can see how hard this is for him, but I don't understand why. It goes beyond his worry for me. It's personal. What inner struggle is he battling right now?

He takes a step forward. "I'm not going to make you do this alone. I promised I'd be here. If this gets to be too much, you say the word and we're gone."

I manage a half smile as I lift my head. Another piece of my battered heart was claimed by Jackson Cole.

"Thank you," I say. Our fingers interlace as we enter the building.

Jackson lifts my hand, tenderly pressing his lips against my fingers. The whisper of his voice radiates to my heart as he gently says, "Of course."

He lifts me up and keeps me safe. I hope he doesn't let me fall.

chapter

twenty-three

ENTERING THE UPSCALE Manhattan law firm of Coogan, Goldstein & Leibowitz, the fear of the unknown is choking the life out of me. I have no idea what to expect or what my father could have left for me. All I keep thinking about are the possibilities—I could get answers today, or more questions. Why was I required to come to the office? Why couldn't they have mailed me the paperwork? Is there something here I need to see? I can't answer any of these questions, but they keep coming. What if he left some kind of video? Will I want to watch it? With each new thought comes a sickening feeling in the pit of my stomach. My fight or flight reflexes are in high gear, and if it weren't for Jackson holding my hand, I'd be fleeing back into the elevator and getting the hell out of here.

Jackson gives my hand a small squeeze and I look at his apprehensive face. "I know you said we should do this today, but you're pale and shaking."

I'm shaking? I didn't even notice.

"I'm just nervous because of all the possibilities. I don't know what to expect. What if he had another kid and they're here?" I somehow manage to choke the words out.

Stopping, he releases my hand and moves to cradle my head. My heart rate slows at his gentle touch. His eyes penetrate my fear and his voice is tender. "I'll be here the whole time. All that's going to happen is the lawyer will read the will, you'll find out what you were left, and then we'll go. No matter who else is here, if you don't want to deal with them, you don't. Okay?"

I give him a nod, trying to keep myself together while drawing strength from him.

We enter the office. It's nondescript and simple—and empty. More than anything I'm grateful for this because if there were a long lost sister sitting here, I might have collapsed. Jackson's strong hand grips mine. He's pretty focused on making sure I'm not having an emotional breakdown. As long as he's here, I'm okay.

Mr. Goldstein enters and shakes our hands. "Catherine, I'm Avi Goldstein. I'm the lawyer in charge of your father's estate."

"Nice to meet you. This is Jackson Cole, my ..."

"Boyfriend," Jackson finishes matter-of-factly.

My head whips around to look at him. Boyfriend? Well that was unexpected. After the last date we had, I guess it's true, but it still shocks me. He didn't hesitate or question, he seemed proud to say it. The smile on his face rocks me. I'm sure it mirrors mine, and I'm also sure my heart grew to twice its size.

Mr. Goldstein clears his throat and begins. "Nice to meet you both. I'm very sorry for your loss, Ms. Pope. I know these proceedings are hard, especially when you lose a loved one suddenly. Whether it's a father, mother, or spouse it's never easy. I hope you can find peace and closure." Jackson's hand releases mine abruptly. When I look at him, he seems anxious, uncomfortable. The loss of his warmth and support leaves me bereft. Jackson shoves his hand in his pocket and looks away.

"Thank you, Mr. Goldstein," I say with a tremble in my voice. There will be no closure because I've gained no answers. I don't even know how you close something that was never opened.

"Please, call me Avi. I assure you this is the least favorite part of my job. I was on your side not too long ago when my wife passed, so I'll try to make this as easy as possible," Avi says with a smile.

Suddenly Jackson gets up and walks over to the window. I can see his chest rising and falling powerfully.

"Jackson?"

He looks over with sadness in his eyes before returning to his seat.

"You were saying, Mr. Goldstein," Jackson says. Any trace of sadness is gone, replaced by the mask of determination I've come to know so well.

Avi nods and begins. "I'll get down to it. Your father's estate is rather simple. You're his next of kin. There are no other living relatives, so everything he possessed when he passed is now yours. There is a house in New Jersey as well as some cash and stocks. You were also named as his beneficiary on his life insurance. However, I asked you here so I could give you a letter from your father. His wishes were simple. You are to read this when you're ready. He mailed it to me in a separate envelope with a letter asking for me to personally ensure you received it." He stands, extending the letter to me.

A letter. From him. I stand and move forward. My hand is unstable when Mr. Goldstein places the letter in it. As I clasp my fingers around the envelope, a single tear escapes. This could contain all the answers to my doubt, or it could break my heart even more. Placing the letter on my lap, I cover it with my hand, holding on to the last piece of my father. Dread, pain, sadness, wonder, and so many more feelings seep through my veins at all the possible things this letter could say. Did he write it to tell me why he left? Why he never looked back? Will it tell me that I just wasn't that important to him? All my insecurities come forward full force as the fear of what it could hold nearly cripples me.

"Ms. Pope, I didn't know your father very well, but I met him a few times. He was a wonderful man. I truly hope he's at peace." Avi smiles kindly. "I'll try to keep this brief. You are due to inherit quite a bit. All your assets total around $300,000 plus whatever the property is worth. His life insurance will need to be dealt with separately, but his policy was around half a million. It's obvious he wanted you well cared for. Were you close?"

I glance at Jackson, completely overwhelmed. He extends his hand and I eagerly accept the warmth and solace he's offering. Lacing my fingers with his, I try to fight back the tears as my heart shatters a little more. "No, Avi, we weren't close. I haven't spoken to my father in about twenty years. This is very overwhelming for me. I don't really understand why he left me anything."

"Well, I can't answer for him, but maybe his letter will give you the answers you're looking for. I just need you to sign the paperwork. I have the key here for the house and if there is anything else, I can call you."

I place the letter and key in my purse and take a moment to collect myself. Walking over to the desk, my hands shake. This is it. The end. The finale to my father's life. I'll have no chance of finding out more. There are no living relatives, no family to ask. Whatever's in the letter is all I'll have.

The pen is shaking so hard I have to stop twice to try to get my hand under control. Tears stain the paper, and my heart plummets as I finally finish my signature. I let out a strangled sob and press my hand to my mouth to stop the pain trying to make its way out. Somehow I manage to smother it. Squaring my shoulders, I wipe away the tears staining my face.

Avi shakes my hand and places his other on top. "Catherine, even though you didn't know your father, I know he loved you. My clients come to me because they want their loved ones to find peace and move on. Even when they're gone they are always a part of us. We never have to truly let them go. They live in our hearts and memories forever."

Closing my eyes, I absorb his words. "Thank you, Avi. I ..."

I shake my head, unable to speak, but the understanding in his eyes tells me he doesn't need a response. He releases my hand with a sad smile and I gather my belongings.

Jackson stays quiet off to the side. As I approach, I notice his furrowed brow and the way he keeps gripping his neck as if he's uncomfortable.

"You ready?" he asks.

"Yeah, let's go."

Once we're out of the building, I take a deep breath and let the tears roll down my face again. It's over. I have nothing left. I'm empty. All I want to do is rewind the last ten years and change it all. I want to know who my father was, why he made the choices he did, go back in time and rewrite my story—but I can't. I miss a man I didn't even know. How is that possible?

Jackson sees the tears and takes a hesitant step toward me. "I don't want you to be alone. I'm staying with you tonight. No arguments."

I couldn't argue if I wanted to—which I don't. If Jackson's close, maybe I can keep it together long enough to read the letter burning a hole in my purse.

The train station is only a few blocks away, and I could use the walk. All I want to do is curl into Jackson, but since we left the office he hasn't touched me. Even with my scattered mind, I've processed that much. Wherever Jackson is, it's not here. Oh my God. I didn't take into account how hard this might be for him with his history of loss and grief. Of course bringing up death would push him away. He's never felt this distant to me. Now I know why. It was selfish to ask him to be with me today.

The two blocks seem to take forever, and with each step it feels like miles separate Jackson and me. He's stiff and keeps his hands in his pockets while he processes whatever he's feeling. I want to slap him and force him to talk because his silence is shredding me. Not because he's doing anything wrong, but because I need to stop my mind from racing over what just happened. Both of us walk in silence until I can't take it anymore.

"Jackson?" I ask tentatively.

He looks up but doesn't respond. Every indication, from his tight jaw to his rigid posture, is saying he wants to be left alone.

"Forget it." I look away, taken aback by his aloofness.

Neither of us says anything else as we approach the train. Where I was quiet and sad a moment ago, now my frustration is growing. If he didn't want to be with me, then he shouldn't have said he was coming to my place. He could've gone back home and left me alone. I could've processed this on my own instead of having him brooding next to me and adding to my stress. I need his arms, his strength, but right now all I'm getting is nothing.

I can't take another second of this. "Are we going to talk or keep ignoring each other?" My voice is full of the annoyance I'm feeling. Part of it is directed at him, part at this entire day.

"What do you want to talk about?" he says with narrowed eyes.

Apparently he's irritated by my approach. Good. "Oh, I don't know. The weather? Why you're being so quiet and haven't said a word since we left the office? You can choose." I'm being a total bitch, but at this point I really don't care.

"Nice to see you haven't lost your attitude." Jackson huffs with a sarcastic smile as the train approaches.

"*You* said you wanted to come back to my place. I didn't ask you to."

His answer comes fast and angry. "I know that."

"If you didn't want to be around me or whatever, you didn't have to." I throw over my shoulder as I board the train. Fuck him. He wants to be a jerk, he can do it alone. I'm going home, pouring myself an overflowing glass of wine, and finding the courage to read this freaking letter.

Just thinking about it makes me nauseous. There are so many things it could say, some of which I'm not ready to face. But I know myself well enough to know I'll never sleep if I don't get it over with soon. His attitude isn't helping.

I'm facing the window, refusing to look at him, when the seat next to me moves. He doesn't say a word, but the warmth of his hand on my leg stills me and a tear falls from the corner of my eye. God! I'm a mess! One minute I'm livid, and then he touches me and I cry.

"I want to be with you. That's why I'm here." His voice is low, full of the strength I've come to rely on.

I turn and face him, hopeful that he means that. "This isn't easy for me, you know? Trusting you, letting you be here for me. You don't understand how hard this is."

He wipes the tears from my face and gently cradles me to his chest. "I know more than you think."

"How so?" My voice is barely a whisper, but I know he hears me when he lets out a long breath. I sit up and stare at him through blurry eyes, waiting for his answer.

The pain that lances across his perfect face erases all my anger.

"You know about the fucking hell I've been through, Catherine. Do you think I wanted anyone around me? I hated myself. I hated everyone who talked to me, touched me, or made me feel. I wanted to die with them." His hand touches his chest and then moves to his shoulder. "You can't imagine the man I was during that time. Anger?" He scoffs before going on, "Baby, you can't imagine what angry looked like. So you want to be mad at me, be mad."

The train stops, halting our conversation. I don't fully understand his withdrawal. He's the one who's pushed me repeatedly, and now suddenly he's retreating? And yes, I'm mad. I'm mad at him, at my father, at my mother, and anyone else who made me this way.

As we exit the train, my mind begins to wander, thinking about the pain he must have been in. Losing people you know and love, people who understand you and stand beside you ... I can't think about any of this right now. My brain can't contain any more. I want to change into my comfy clothes, drink a bottle ... errr glass of wine, and forget this day ever happened.

Standing here, facing each other, the silence stretches for miles. Both of us trying to read the other. Both lost in some form of grief. Gripping my hips, he pulls me close. I close my eyes and relish his embrace. Here I feel okay. I'm safe when his arms are around me, protecting me, but is my heart? In this moment I don't care. I mold to him, allowing his strength to surround me.

"I won't let you fall. I'll be here, but sometimes I'm going to be a dick. Sometimes I'm going to say the wrong thing. But if I didn't want to be here with you, I would've walked away."

I look up and the sincerity on his face matches what I heard in his voice, but the last thirty minutes did nothing to allay my fears. If anything, my doubts have intensified. "Then why were you so distant before?" I ask.

He speaks in a low, hushed tone. "Today brought up a lot of memories for me. Memories I've tried extremely hard to forget."

Jackson takes a deep breath and places his hand on the small of my back as we start walking to my apartment. He's silent for a few minutes and I sense he needs the time to collect his thoughts.

"I just want to he—" I stop short when I see someone in front of my apartment complex.

Neil. Why the hell is he here? Today of all days. My stomach drops as the reality of my past and present collide. I've tried to get rid of him. Ignoring him hasn't worked, so now he's apparently going to stalk me. Great. My body begins to tremble, shaking uncontrollably as fear, anger, and hate overtake me.

"Catherine?" Jackson asks, looking for whatever caused me to freeze.

Neil steps forward with his eyes fixed on Jackson. "Well, it seems you didn't miss me all that much, did you?" he sneers.

"What do you want?" I return acidly.

"I've been calling. We have to talk. You have something that's mine," Neil says.

Obviously he's been calling and I've been avoiding him. I swear he wasn't this stupid before. Or maybe he was but I was too blind to see it. Either way, I don't think I can handle this confrontation today.

"I have nothing of yours," I say, trying to step around him.

Jackson moves next to me, angling his body so he's between us. "Who the hell are you?"

Neil steps to the side, blocking me from getting past him. He jerks a thumb toward Jackson. "Who's this guy?"

Jackson takes a step closer to Neil, who huffs and steps back.

"I'm her fiancé," he says with a sardonic smile.

"No, you're not!" I scream. "Are you fucking kidding me?"

He's purposely trying to ruin my life. Why? What the hell did I ever do to him? He broke my heart and I didn't do a damn thing to retaliate. I didn't steal from him, hurt his precious career, cheat on him, or anything else. Now he stands in front of my apartment, trying to take something else from me. Rage pulses through my body with each heartbeat. The first good thing I have he's going to try to ruin. I look to Jackson whose eyes are wide. No! He can't believe this.

Jackson stands there and crosses his arms across his broad chest as he lets out a mocking laugh. "Care to explain?"

I'm struggling not to cry. The emotions I've been swallowing all day are making their way back up. "Jackson, this is my *ex*-fiancé. He's a liar and a piece of shit!"

"Don't let her fool you," Neil sneers from behind me.

I'm unable to control myself anymore. I'm done. I'm lost. There's no stopping me as I unload my anger in Neil's face. "Shut the fuck up! You cheated on me! Why are you here? We haven't been together for months! Go away!" I'm breaking. Every single part of me is falling apart.

I turn back to Jackson. The look on his face makes my

stomach clench. He looks like he's wavering between anger and pride. Both of us are dealing with too much right now, but I desperately need him to listen me.

"None of this is true! He's with another woman. He's lying!" I yell, feeling my sanity slip away. "This is Neil Mullins. He works for Boyce. We *were* engaged and then he cheated on me with *Piper*." This is definitely not how I planned to talk about my ex, if I ever decided to talk about him at all. I implore him to believe me with my eyes. "Jackson, please. We've been over for months!"

Neil barks out a laugh. "Your memory is a little off, love. You stole my numbers so I left you. I should've had the Raven account. Now, I want my fucking ring and the money you owe me back."

Jackson steps away from me. He curls his lip while flexing his hands and glaring at Neil. "Wait a fucking minute," he says and then looks at me. "Neil? From Boyce, the other PR firm?"

I nod, trying to choke back the tears that keep spilling down my face. This is the worst day of my life. It feels like my heart is being ripped out of my chest.

"Since you know who I am, I'll ask again. Who the fuck are you?" Neil says, puffing out his chest.

Jackson glares at Neil. "I'm Jackson Cole."

Recognition registers on Neil's face as his angry smile grows. "Well, that explains everything. You fucked the client, Cat. I didn't think you had it in you." He steps toward me, his eyes hard and cold.

Jackson pushes me back behind him as anger rolls off him in waves. You can smell the testosterone in the air. His knuckles are white from clenching his fists so hard, and the vein on the side of his neck is protruding. I need to calm him before this gets out of hand. I place my hand on his shoulder and move around him, but his arm grips my waist, keeping me safely behind him.

From behind Jackson, I yell at Neil, "You need to leave.

Now!" My entire body is trembling. I'm not sure if it's anger or hate or any other emotion you can name.

Neil steps forward and Jackson tenses. Neil isn't a small guy, but he's no match for a man Jackson's size. Not only that, but I'm pretty sure Jackson is trained to kill him in one move. *Could this day get any fucking worse?*

Jackson clears his throat and pulls me against his side. "She told you to leave. I suggest you go." His voice brokers no argument. He's reached his max.

"Right, well this is between me and Cat. So I think I'll just finish what I came here for." Neil smiles and moves closer.

Jackson's reaction seems involuntary as he steps forward and pushes against Neil's chest, sending him backward. The commanding sound in Jackson's voice scares me. "I don't think so, asshole. You're going to fucking leave right now—either by free will or by force. But I promise—you don't want to fuck with me."

I step between them, trying to get Jackson to calm down. The tears have stopped, but fear has taken over.

My voice is strangled as I plead with them both. "Please! Stop! I can't take any more." I step toward Neil with narrowed eyes. "You need to go! I don't have anything of yours, and I don't have anything left to say to you. Just leave!"

Neil snaps. His nostrils flare and his lip pulls back. He barrels toward me. The noise from his throat is a guttural roar. "You owe me my fucking ring! So you can either get it, or I'm going to do everything in my power to ruin you." He grips my arms, squeezing them painfully.

Before I have a second to process anything, Neil's on the ground and Jackson's on top of him. The sound of their bodies hitting the pavement echoes around me.

He hits Neil in the face and blood splatters on the sidewalk at the impact. "Stop!" I scream, trying to stop the madness in front of me.

Punch after punch he lands on Neil. Neil manages to get a

fist to Jackson's face, but it only seems to stoke Jackson's rage. I rush over and pull at his arms, but he shakes me off easily, continuing the onslaught, undeterred.

"Motherfucker! You don't touch her!" he says as he hits him again, his fist finding his mark. With each blow, the sound of his knuckles connecting with Neil's face cuts through the night air.

"Jackson! Stop!" I yell over and over. My voice falls on deaf ears as they continue to assault each other. Tears are pouring again, and my entire body is running on adrenaline.

I lean down, grabbing for Jacksons arm, finally snapping him out of his rage. He towers over Neil lying on the pavement. "I'll fucking kill you if you ever touch her again," he says, his voice venomous.

Jackson turns and looks at me. His expression shifts from anger to pain to worry when he sees the tears streaming down my face.

"Are you hurt?" His hands grasp my face as I pull away from his touch.

It's too much. I can't do this. All I can do is shake my head back and forth as I pray my legs don't give out on me.

"Catherine, talk to me. Please." His voice breaks on the last word and my heart goes with it.

Neil staggers to his feet and Jackson's back stiffens as he readies to protect me again. "You better have a damn good lawyer, Cole. This isn't over." He swipes the blood off his mouth and turns with vengeance in his eyes.

I squeeze my eyes shut and pray for strength because I don't have any left.

chapter

twenty-four

*T*EARS ARE STREAMING, leaving rivers of black mascara on my cheeks. Jackson's strong arms encase me, holding me tight as I crumble. I breathe in his scent, which usually calms me, but right now it does nothing to help my state. My eyes close and the numbness takes hold. I'm floating, completely weightless—I've finally lost it. I think we're moving but can't be sure. I'm enjoying the peace and serenity my mind has given me, the reprieve from all the hell that broke loose a few moments ago. Images of Neil and Jackson brawling blur before my eyelids, and I fight for the numbness again.

When I open my eyes, I'm shocked to see we're in my apartment. I don't remember walking, but then again I'm almost positive I've snapped. Jackson holds me in his arms and tries to speak to me, but I don't hear him. I barely register his touch. His warmth is absent.

Maybe, like everything else, he's gone cold, the tenderness he once felt for me destroyed by the display on the street. He's been distant all night. Maybe Neil just sealed the deal. The thought sends a wave of panic through my body, but I'm too defeated to fight it. He'll take the last remaining part of my heart and shatter it. I knew it would happen. He'll do what every man in my life does—leave.

His arms wrap tighter around me, but I don't want his arms. I don't want anyone. I'm better off alone, making a clean break now before I fall further. I need to protect what's left of myself. He's already claimed parts of me that I'll never get back. I wish I could get the numbness back. I want to stop feeling so much all the time. It hurts—everything hurts.

His grip tightens, but I need to get away. I step back, pushing against his chest. His arms reach out as if I'm falling and he needs to catch me. But I'm done falling.

I place my hands in front of me to stop him. Gone is the uncertainty I had hours ago. All my resolve is back with a vengeance. Stifling the tears, I take a deep breath, ready to salvage what's left of myself. I look over to see his unsure face and posture. Ensuring my voice is clear, I answer the questions in his eyes. "You should go."

"What?" He steps back with a shocked expression.

"Leave, please," I croak out and point to the door.

He looks at me cautiously, like I'm a wounded animal. Tilting his head, brow furrowed, he responds, "Why would I leave? I'm not going anywhere. I told you I was staying." He stands defiantly, ready to fight me on this.

"I don't want you to stay here. I need to be alone," I say with as much steel in my voice as I can gather. There's a small part of me that knows pushing him away could be a mistake, but at this point I can't trust myself. He's already taken so much—I'm already in too deep. The last time we made love, he owned me. I knew then I'd never be the same. He's going to destroy me if I don't put an end to this now.

Jackson takes a step closer, shaking his head at my request. "I'm not leaving you."

There's no way he's going to walk away on his own—it's not who he is. This is the man who'd stand in front of a bullet and bear the pain so someone else wouldn't have to. But I don't need a hero. "I'm not asking you, Jackson. I'm telling you to leave. I want to be alone. I can't deal with anything else right now."

He strides toward me with his lips pursed. "Don't push me

away. Don't make me the bad guy here." He reaches for me, but I take a step back.

I throw my hands up. "Really? Push you away? You pushed me away back there before the fight. I didn't do that—you did. I needed you! Do you have any idea what this was like for me today? Huh?" I step forward and push against his chest, but he doesn't budge. Instead he stands there and lets me unleash my fury. "Did you think about how this would be for me when you beat the shit out of him? Did you hear me screaming and begging you to stop? My God! Do you get it now? I was engaged to him. He was supposed to love me and cherish me! But instead he pushed me away, cheated on me. He left me for someone else because she was better than me!" I slap my hand against his chest, broken and hurt, but he doesn't move. He takes it. "I need to be more than that, Jackson. I need to be someone's everything. I deserve that! I'm tired ... I'm tired of being hurt. I want to be *enough* already!" I take a few steps back, needing some space.

Jackson takes another step, but I put my hands up to stop him. No. He can't touch me. He's already shown me what all the important men in my life have told me—I'm not enough. Not good enough to open up to. Not enough to share himself with. Will I ever be enough? "Don't touch me." Jackson's face contorts as if I've slapped him.

"Really, Catherine?" He shifts forward and clenches his jaw.

I take a shaky breath before continuing, "In the last two hours, I've had to face every fucking man in my life who's ever meant anything to me—my father, Neil, and now you. I can't do this. Please, just go!" I shake my head over and over, trying to grab on to the anger instead of the crushing pain of pushing him away.

"You think this has been easy for me? I've never made you feel irrelevant. I haven't cheated on you, or hurt you. No, I've been there for you, giving you everything I could. I held you when you cried and listened to you. I didn't make you feel cheap or worthless." His hands are shaking as he pauses to take a deep breath. "I've tried to be the man you say you deserve. Tell me what I did to make you think otherwise! So I pulled away on the train—we got past that. Did I get pissed off and beat the shit out of your fucking asshole ex? Yes! And if he fucking touched you again, I would've killed him. Is this about him? Do you still love him?"

I gasp and press my fingers to my lips, shaking my head back and forth in disbelief. How could he think that? "This has nothing to do with him. But it has everything to do with me."

"So you're going to take this out on me? I deserve this?"

We stand there in the middle of my living room, staring at each other, trying to get the resolution we're each fighting for. I look away and glance at his shirt. The blood there reminds me of everything that's happened.

"I just need time." The faint whisper of a voice I manage to get out sounds so broken—even to me.

His head tilts back as he grips his hair. "Fucking time? Time to what? Push me away and convince yourself that I'm like *him*. Are you sure you want me to leave? You're ready for me to walk away?"

"I need some damn time. I can't think with you around!" I turn away from him.

"You want me to walk out so you can hate me and blame me for leaving you. Well I won't let you play some fucking bullshit game with me."

I let out a breathy laugh and roll my eyes. "A game? You think this is a game for me? What do I win, huh?"

"You tell me. You're the one telling me to leave. I can't fucking believe this." He throws his hands up and then claps them against his legs. "If I walk out this door, I won't come back until I know you want me here."

"I'm used to watching men walk out the door." I say bitterly.

"Maybe you should stop pushing them out, then."

My heart stops as his words rip my chest apart. The pain is dragging me under, but he's standing there, watching the tears fall, watching how deep his words cut. "You don't know a fucking thing."

"I know you're fighting me because you're afraid. You think I'm like every other man. Have I hurt you? Have I lied to you?"

"Not yet!" I cry out.

Jackson takes a step closer. His breathing is heavy but he's trying to keep his tone soft. "You've already sentenced me for someone else's crime."

I weep into my hands because he's right. "You can't expect me to process all of what happened today with you here. My feelings for you ... they scare me. You make me feel too much! Every time you're around or you touch me, I lose something inside," I say earnestly.

"You think it's any different for me? I fought against this! Every time you walked in the room, I fought the urge to take you. If you think you're the only one who loses, you're wrong." His voice grows warm and seductive. "Somehow, at every turn, you've made me feel more than I've wanted to."

He closes the distance and I'm unable to fight him anymore. I allow his arms to hold me one last time. After this, I won't let him back in.

"Please," I cry into his chest as he clutches me to him. "Please, if you care, let me have time to think."

His arms fall from my back and he slowly moves to hold my face, tilting it so we're staring into each other's eyes. Jackson's expression is pained, but his eyes express so much more. "Fine. You win. I'll go." His eyes close as though the words are bitter in his mouth. When they open again he looks fierce and determined. "But hear me. You're it for me, Catherine." His thumb brushes a tear from my cheek. "I'm not walking away from you or us. I wasn't ready to love again when you came crashing into me. But you made me want to try again." Our lips touch briefly. When he looks back up, his eyes are intense. "Leaving you right now goes against every fucking thing I want. I'm going to let you push me away this once. But I mean it, when I walk out it's up to you when I come back. Don't make me wait too long." He leans down and places a long, tender kiss upon my lips. Our eyes meet again and he waits for a second before continuing, "I told you I'll always find you, but you have to want to be found. Let me find you, Catherine."

Without another word, his hands disappear. I want to beg him to stay, but I need him to go. It's as though someone is sawing me in half. I'm fighting against the pull, but I honestly don't know what I want anymore. He opens the door and hesitates, turning back to give me a sad smile before walking out.

When the door closes, I fall to the ground and let out a strangled sob. What have I done? Why does this always have to be so hard?

You're it for me, Catherine. His words repeat in my head.

I crawl to the couch and curl up, letting the tears come, hoping they'll wash away the pain. He asked me not to push and I basically shoved him. I fight the urge to run after him, to beg him to stay and hold me. Hoping I made the right choice, I curl into myself and rock back and forth.

What if I'm the reason they leave?

Maybe you should stop pushing them out, then.

If I truly pushed them all away, what does that say about me?

You've already sentenced me for someone else's crime.

Have I?

I lie here, soaking the cushion as I let out twenty years' worth of devastation. I cry until my tears have dried, but the hollow feeling in my chest has grown. I'm truly alone. There's no one here. What I wouldn't give to go back a few hours and skip ever going to the lawyer's. I would've waited for Ashton to go, or I'd go back even further to when I first met Jackson and not give in to him. Then I could live my life and not have to suffer all over again. If I thought the pain of losing Neil was bad, it's not even a tenth of what I'm feeling right now. Jackson took pieces of my heart with every kiss, every gesture, every smile, and I'll never get them back. Though, as I sit here and replay everything that's happened, I wonder if maybe that's not true. Yes, he claimed those pieces, but not to keep. He used those moments to put my heart back together. And then I made him leave.

I need to find my phone. I need Ashton. As I grab for my purse, it tips over and all the contents fly out. Why not? At this point I'm not surprised the hell won't end. I reach for my phone and see my father's letter on the floor. Every bone in my body freezes and my heart plummets into my stomach. Am I ready to read this? I reach for the letter and hold it in my hands. It's now or never.

Sitting on the floor, my finger slides under the lip and I gently tear the envelope open. I hesitate for a moment. Once I read this I can't unread it. My eyes water again but I stifle the tears. I'm tired of crying. Tired of feeling weak and not in control of my life. My heart is racing and the tightness in my chest is making me dizzy. I say a silent prayer as my fingers gently tug out the letter. Slowly, I open it and begin to read my father's last words to me.

My Dearest Catherine,

I'm sorry you're reading this letter and not hearing the words from me. It means that I was never brave enough to come find you. I'm a coward. I want to try to explain, and I hope that someday you'll forgive me. You see, I loved your mother very much, but we couldn't make it work. You were never to blame. Ever. Not one single thing that ever happened between us was your fault. I'm sorry for hurting you. I know my absence must've caused you a lot of pain, and for that I'll have died bearing that burden on my shoulders. I thought about you every single day since I walked out that door. I wondered about you, hoping you grew to become a beautiful woman, never doubting you did.

I'll start at the beginning. When I left that day, you broke me. Your tears ripped through my heart. The pain of having to pry you off my leg destroyed me. Having you beg and promise to be good ... I can't describe my emotions because there aren't enough words to do so. You couldn't have been any better—you were already perfect. I didn't know how I was going to walk away. The agony was almost more than I could bear. At first, it was easier to stay away than imagine having to watch you hurt every time I had to leave. You were my world, Catherine. You gave me something I never knew I was missing. When you were born, you stole my heart. Then your mother and I realized it wasn't working, and I had to make a choice. That choice changed the rest of our lives. After I walked out the door that day, I knew I could never do it again. I couldn't walk away from you. Your tears, your hurt—they were caused by me that day and I've never forgiven myself for it. If I close my eyes, I can still see the anguish on your face. I can hear your pleas as if I'm right back there again. That does something to a man. When he sees the face of his daughter breaking, it forever changes him. I'm not excusing my absence because there is no excuse. I stayed away because I couldn't see that again. I didn't want cause you any more pain. I regretted that decision every birthday, every Christmas, every holiday, and every event that you've ever attended that I missed. A father I was not. A man I was not. Because I was too scared.

I want you to know I did follow you. I went to your dance recital when you were thirteen—you were an amazing swan. You were breathtaking in your prom dress—your date was a lucky guy. I attended your high school graduation. You looked beautiful—I was so proud. Standing in the back as they called your name, I realized how wrong I'd been. You, Catherine, deserved more. You should've had a father who was sitting in the front row, clapping for his daughter, not cowering in the back of the room. At that moment my shame and self-loathing was never clearer. I didn't deserve you. Which is why I continued to stay away after that. You were doing so well without me. If I came back into your life again, it would only confuse you. I'd already done enough of that.

When I was diagnosed with cancer, I started to re-evaluate my choices. I spent days in the hospital alone, contemplating how stupid I was. I couldn't call you and ask you to be there for me. I'd never been there for you. I wouldn't expect it and I couldn't ask you to do it—it was my penance. I still don't know if things would have been different, but please know I'm sorry, Catherine. More than I can ever fully express. I am so sorry. I'm sorry I wasn't the man you needed. I can only hope that as you read this you see that I loved you. One day you'll marry and he won't be good enough for you, because you, my daughter, deserve nothing less than perfection. I hope that he will love you with his whole heart and not make the same mistakes I did. I hope he'll show you every day just how special you are. I hope he'll be the father to your children I was never able to be to you. He should fight every day to show you how worth it you are. There will come a time it will get tough, but if you truly love each other, you'll find your way.

If you're still reading this, I want you to know that I'm looking down on you and smiling at the woman you've become. I wish I could turn back the hands of time, but I can't. I can't take all the hurt away, but I hope you understand that it was me. It was never you. I'm sorry. I want you to know the last person I'll think about when my time is up, is you. Every time the sun shines down upon you, I hope you'll think of me keeping the gray skies away. I love you, Catherine.

Love,
Your Father

It's too much and yet not enough. I place the letter down, lie on the cold floor, and cry myself to sleep, hoping for blackness to take hold. But there's no darkness, no absolution from the pain.

Even in my sleep I can't escape it. My dreams shift and change, haunting me with what I never had but always wanted. I wake up feeling nauseous, my headache now a throbbing migraine. Crying yourself dry of tears will do that. I glimpse at the clock. It's only nine thirty. Sheer emotional and physical exhaustion is all I register. I hate that I couldn't even sleep past midnight. At least then this horrific day would've been over. It's seriously the day that's never going to end.

Shaking my head, I try to clear the remnants of my bad dream involving Jackson, Neil, and my father. I grab the letter and my phone and head into my bedroom. Grasping my father's farewell, I curl myself around my pillow and text Ashton that I need her before passing out, letter and phone still in hand.

chapter

twenty-five

WHEN I WAKE up, I roll over and hold back a yelp when I realize someone is in my bed. For a moment I allow myself a sliver of hope that Jackson came back, but when I see the deep crimson hair, I know it's Ash. She must have come home and crawled into bed with me knowing something happened.

"Ash," my voice croaks as I wake her.

She groans and turns over, facing me and opening one eye. "Morning, lover."

It's as if I'm back to how I felt five months ago all over again. My lip quivers as the agony of last night returns full force. "Ash ..."

She pulls me into her arms and rubs my back. "Shhh, Cat. It'll be okay. Tell me what happened."

We sit and talk, going over the previous day's events. She listens and offers support, never saying more than a few words or pulling me back into a hug. I show her the letter and Ashton sobs as she reads the words my father wrote. Her pain is my pain and my pain is hers. We're like sisters—she knows how much this means to me. There are no secrets between us. She's fully aware of how hard my childhood was.

"How do you feel about what he wrote?" she asks, swiping tears away.

His words heal, but hurt a little more. I've longed to hear

them from him, but they've come after so much damage has been done. Growing up, feeling unloved and alone for years, and then having another man I loved abandon me ... For the longest time, I truly believed I was unworthy. I still believe that. "I'm not sure. It's all a little late, don't you think?"

"I don't know. It's obvious he thought of you and felt a lot of remorse."

"But why not come and find me? Why not make amends before he died?"

"He was scared, Cat. I can't imagine how he would have just shown up after twenty years. Would you have given him a chance if he did?" she asks.

I sigh and think about whether I would have been able to. A part of me wants to say, "Yes, of course," but I was angry for so long. I was furious to the point that I would have probably slapped him and told him to leave. His absence hurt, which caused my mother to lash out at me in turn. She would always say things about how *we* weren't good enough for him.

"It would have depended, but he never tried." I shrug.

I continue recounting the rest of the night and Ashton grows more and more furious. She stands and then sits several times when I tell her what Neil did. She doesn't hide her anger easily. I start to shake as I recall his rage.

"I'll fucking kill him!" Her eyes narrow into slits as I show her the bruises.

"I think Jackson threatened the same thing."

"Well, good. He's at least trained and could probably get rid of the body. No one would miss that piece of shit." She stands and starts to pace. "I swear to God, Cat, he's going to pay for this. We need a plan."

I can see the wheels in her head turning. "Ashton," I warn.

"Don't *Ashton* me! He comes here and assaults you over his ring? No! I wish I majored in biochem. Then I'd have access to the good stuff in the lab." She continues to pace, formulating her revenge.

"Seriously, he's not worth it." I try to break through her plotting.

Ashton continues as if I haven't even spoken. "Maybe we can ..."

I stretch, lifting my arms over my head as I arch my back. Ashton's eyes go wide and she gasps.

"What?" I ask.

She rushes over and holds my arm up. "Look."

When I look down, I can't believe what I see. I have huge bruises on my arms where Neil grabbed me.

She sits on the bed, takes out her phone, and starts snapping pictures of my arms. "You need photos in case this gets ugly."

I nod, wishing I'd thought about that. Whatever brought Neil to talk to me in the first place hasn't been addressed. Now there's the fact that he got his ass kicked, knows who Jackson is, and is angry—not good.

"It's already there, Ash."

"I'm sorry I wasn't here. I got tied up at the lab. When I finally got home, I came right in here when you didn't answer my text." She softly rubs my back.

"I understand. You couldn't have known this was going to happen."

Ashton lifts my chin. "Now tell me why Jackson's not here."

I rehash the entire argument with tears forming, but somehow I manage to keep them at bay. She doesn't comment on my fight with Jackson, she just shakes her head. When I tell her how I threw him out, however, her blue eyes grow darker. She's pissed but is choosing to keep her thoughts to herself, which definitely surprises me. I sit there and wait for it, but she looks off.

"What? You can't tell me you have nothing to say," I say after her silence drives me insane.

She smiles as she places her hand on mine. "I don't know

what to say, Cat. I think you were on emotional overload. You'd had one of the worst days of your life. Do I think you made a mistake? Maybe." She shrugs before she goes on. "Jackson may have been a little distant, but I don't think he did anything wrong. I think Neil has some serious issues and Jackson protected you."

"He's going to leave me," I choke out and wrap my arms around my center, trying to hold myself together.

"You made him leave." Her voice is soft and nonjudgmental. She understands, but I can sense her disapproval.

"I had to."

She lets out a sad sigh, shaking her head. "No, honey, you didn't have to. Not every man is going to leave you. You need to take a few days and really think about how you feel about Jackson. Remember what you felt when you were with him. Then think about whether you can let go of the past and find a chance at a future. If it's not Jackson, it'll be the next man. You've always questioned if you were good enough, never considering that they weren't good enough for you. But Jackson? Well, that's for you to decide."

"What if he wrecks me? What I feel for him is so intense. I've fallen for him so fast. It scares me."

Ashton gets up without answering my question. She grabs something off my dresser and places it on my pillow. Before I can grab it, she puts her hand over it and looks at me.

"I don't think you're the only one that's fallen." Her brow rises and she places a kiss on my forehead. "Now, it's up to you. Is he worth the fall and possible heartbreak, or is he strong enough to catch you?"

Without another word she leaves my room. I look over at the small, torn paper, curious as to what's on it. Lifting and turning it over, I see Jackson's handwriting.

I spend the weekend pretending nothing happened, trying to come to grips with my emotions. Ashton leaves me alone most of the time, giving me space to sort it through. There are so many times I almost cave, call Jackson, and beg him to come back, but I know I'm not ready. His shutting me out really hurt, but more than that I'm terrified of how much I care for him. I fear the way he stormed into my life and churned up my emotions.

When I wake from my second nap on Sunday, there are multiple text messages from Neil threating his lawyer, but not one from Jackson. I'm not sure whether I should be relieved or disappointed. His message was clear when he left—I have to choose him, fight for him. Instead I've been fighting against it. Fear grips my soul. It smothers me, and I'm not sure how to get past it. I would rather be alone than go through another devastating loss.

Much to my chagrin, I call out of work on Monday. My eyes are swollen and I want a day to wallow—alone. Ashton rolls her eyes, giving me an earful before leaving for work.

"So you're going to stay home and mope?"

"No, I'm staying home because I have a migraine," I retort.

She huffs and narrows her eyes. "I know you better than that. Funny, you didn't miss work after Neil. In fact, you became almost obsessed with your job. What gives?"

"Well it didn't hurt this bad. And my staying home has nothing to do with Jackson." I grab my coffee and try to leave the kitchen.

Ashton follows behind me. "Then what does it have to do with?"

"Everything! It has to do with everything, dammit. I'm so tired of it all. That letter ... I don't even know what to do with it."

Ashton continues, unfazed by my outburst. "Why don't you sit down and reread it? You've had a few days to digest it now. But I don't think that's really the issue." Her brow rises. "I think it has to do with a certain sexy SEAL who you're in love with."

"Jesus!" I throw my hands up. "This has nothing to do with him. Do I miss Jackson? Yes. Are you happy now?"

"Are you?" she fires back with a calm voice.

"Do I look happy?" Again with the damn tears!

She leans against the wall, casually sipping her coffee. "No, but one phone call would fix it. So what else is making you skip work?"

"I ... ugh!" I grip the sides of my head, irritated with her.

"I think you're making yourself live a lie. You need to look deep down and figure out what you're willing to walk away from. If you can look me in the eye and tell me that you don't have some serious feelings for him and he doesn't make you happy, then fine. Good riddance. But from the look on your face right now, I don't think that's how you feel. Fear is going to drive away the one man who's strong enough to walk through this with you."

Without a word I head to my room, slam the door, and lock it. I'm batting a thousand right now. Is there anyone in my life I'm not pissed at? Why does she always push me so damn much?

I hear my phone ringing, but the number isn't one I know.

I hesitate and calm myself before deciding to answer it.

"Hello?"

"Ms. Pope. This is Avi Goldstein."

"Hi, Mr. Goldstein. Is there a problem?"

"No, nothing serious. Sorry to bother you, but I received a call regarding the property in Scotch Plains," he says, seeming distracted.

"Scotch Plains?" I ask, confused.

"Yes, it's the house you inherited. I'm afraid I didn't give you the address when you were in my office. Anyway, I received a call stating there was a door open in the back of the house. Nothing has been damaged, but you might want to go secure it until you decide what to do with the property."

"Oh. Ummm, okay. Can you give me the address?"

"It's 198 Mueller Court. I'm sorry, I have to go. I'm due in court in ten minutes, but please don't hesitate to contact me if you need anything, Ms. Pope," Avi says before the line disconnects.

I guess my day of wallowing in self-pity just went down the drain. Scotch Plains is about an hour away. Determined to avoid rush hour traffic, I grab my keys and head out the door. All I want is to shut my brain off. I think it's time for some chic rock music. Blaring my radio, I get lost in the sounds of angry, scorned girls singing about how much they don't need a man.

As I get closer to the house, I start to feel a familiar pang of nerves. The last few days I've realized how strong I am. During all the tears and pain, I've held it together for the most part. I ate, I showered—which Ashton was impressed with—and I functioned. Even so, the aching was still there, hovering behind the bravado.

I contemplate why I called out of work and if there's any validity to Ashton's claim that it's because of Jackson. If I'm being completely honest, yes, it has a lot to do with him. I miss him. I haven't spoken to him in three days and every time my phone beeps, I pray his number will show. Even if it makes no sense—since he's doing exactly what I asked—the emotions are still there.

Pulling up to the address, my heart starts beating faster. The street is adorable. It's filled with cute little Cape Cod style homes with plush green lawns. Exiting the car, I look at number 198 and sigh. It's a muted yellow with white shutters. There's a large oak tree and some overgrown bushes against the house. As I approach the door, I stop myself from dreaming of what it could've been like living here. It could've been worse than what I grew up with.

"Hello? Can I help you?" A quiet old voice stops me before I can put the key in the lock.

"Hi," I respond.

"I'm Mary. I live in the house right over there." She points to the house on the left and then takes an unsteady step toward me. Mary is beautiful even in her old age. She must be around eighty, but you can see the youth in her eyes. She has an aura around her that makes you want to smile.

"Nice to meet you. I'm Catherine. I guess I own the house now. I received a call I needed to check on things."

Mary clasps her hands together as if she's praying. Her smile is bright and warm. "Oh! I'm just ... Catherine." She walks a little faster to reach me. "Let me see you."

My eyes widen. Somehow she seems to know who I am. "I'm sorry, do we know each other?"

Her smile doesn't fade when she reaches me. "No, dear. I knew Hunter—your father—for a very long time. I always hoped I'd get to meet you."

"Me?"

"Yes, of course. Come. Let's go inside and you can tell me all about yourself." Her grip is surprisingly firm as she takes my hand and pulls me inside.

When I enter I try to take it all in. It's nothing like the home I grew up in. The rooms are large, but everything is stark—bare white walls, hardwood floors. It lacks any warmth. Everything is ... cold. There's a small television in the corner with a recliner and a small sofa situated in front of it.

I continue on as Mary walks through the hall into another room. The outdated kitchen has a card table with four chairs around it. On the wall there's a calendar and a phone list. I look through the names, most of which are doctors.

"Would you like some tea, dear?" Mary asks while filling the kettle with water.

"Sure," I say with a smile. I don't drink tea, but she seems so kind and she knew my father, so maybe she can answer my questions. "So how long did you know my father?"

"I've lived in that house since the day I got married. It was my late husband's wedding gift to me." You can hear the smile in her voice as she places the kettle on the stove. "My husband, Ray, was a wonderful man. He served in the Army," she says with pride.

"He sounds wonderful. You're a very lucky woman."

"I was," she says, holding out the chair for me to sit. "We were married for sixty-two years and we were blessed with four boys. They've all grown and now I have beautiful grandchildren that I get to spoil. But enough about me." Mary places her hand on mine. "You want to know about your father, don't you?"

"Yes, ma'am." I look around the room at the house he lived in. If I were to judge how he lived based on what I've seen so far, the one word I can think of is *empty*. There are no photos, nothing adorning the walls, it's merely a house.

"Well, he moved here around fifteen years ago. It took him about a year until he warmed up to us. Ray was good at forcing him to come out of his house by asking him to help fix things." Mary looks away wistfully. "Ray could've done the things he asked for help with, but Hunter couldn't say no to an old man." She chuckles. "Eventually, he opened up little by little."

The kettle whistles and Mary and I get up to make the tea. She already set out the cups and tea bags. Listening to how she knows him breaks my heart. I'm jealous of the woman who knew the man I so desperately needed. However, I'm grateful in a sense for people like her and Ray, who were there for him. He wasn't completely alone. And neither was I—I had Ashton, Gretchen, and my mother.

Once we have our drinks, we sit back down. "Thank you." She takes a sip before beginning again. "I came to learn about you from your father. He was very sad in the beginning. At times he would talk about a girl named Catherine, but didn't tell us you were his daughter. Anyway, one day I asked him to tell me about her. He sat with me for quite some time, telling me all about you."

"He left when I was nine." My voice is tiny and I'm not sure that Mary heard me.

"He told me. He wasn't proud of what he'd done. I think as the years went on he convinced himself that it was for the best. But then he'd show us a photo or tell us about something you did. There was always such pride in his eyes when he spoke about you, dear."

My eyes lift to hers and I read the truth behind them. He said he'd followed me. I guess he'd shared what he learned with Mary. I'm conflicted by the years of hate and anger now turning to sympathy. He said he stayed away because he wanted to protect me, and initially I thought it was a cop-out. Now I'm confused. Maybe everything he wrote in the letter wasn't a lie.

"He wrote me a letter while he was sick. Did you know that?"

"No, he never mentioned a letter." Her gray brow rises. "When he found out he was sick, he changed a lot of things. He didn't suffer for long. It was very late in the disease when he was diagnosed. He talked a lot more about you and what he gave up toward the end, though." Mary pats my hand, giving me a warm smile. "You know, when we know our time is running out, we think more about the choices we made. I'm sure his letter was sincere." She gets up from the table and washes the cups before she returns to sit with me.

"I don't know what to think anymore. It feels like everything I knew was a lie." A tear drops as the sadness returns. "I blamed myself all my life. I always felt like I'd done something as a kid to make him leave. Then I get this letter saying it wasn't me, it was him. My entire life I've believed I wasn't good enough for him to come back for."

Mary places her hand on my arm. "The heart knows the truth. When times are hard, we have to rely on the voice in our hearts. Trust yourself, Catherine. I do know the Hunter I knew would've never left because of you."

"I wish I'd known him." I sigh and look away. That's the bottom line. I know nothing about him. I don't know how he lived, if he was sad or happy, if he wished things were different—although his letter says he did.

"There's an office down the hall on the left. He spent a lot of time in there. There are probably some things that might give you some peace." She wipes the tear from my cheek. "Sometimes the heart and mind don't work together, but a child is never to blame for the errors of the parent. We all make mistakes, but forgiveness sets the soul free." Mary rises from her seat and I stand as well. "I'm going to lie down for a bit and give you some time alone, but promise you'll come back and visit soon."

"I promise," I say as she walks out the door, giving me time to absorb everything.

I walk through the rooms, looking around and trying to figure out who he really was when I come across the office she spoke of. There's a small desk and a bookshelf inside. I gasp and my hands cover my heart when I see the top shelf. It's lined with photos of me. Every picture is in chronological order, from my infant photo at the hospital all the way through third grade. There are even some where I'm older. My high school graduation picture and my newspaper engagement announcement are framed. He has little bits of my life all around the room.

I make my way to his desk and look around. He was so

alone. It has papers and bills, but the photo sitting on top causes a sob to break free. It's a photo of us on my birthday. He's standing behind me right as I'm inhaling to blow out the candles on my cake. The love in his eyes shines as bright as the flames.

Overloaded with varying degrees of heartache, I rush out of the room, gasping for air. Nothing makes any sense. The world seems to be shifting, but I'm not shifting with it. I can't wrap my mind around why he chose to keep that door closed. He could have come to me and talked to me, tried to explain. I might have been mad, but we could've had a chance at *some* kind of relationship. So much wasted time, so many tears that didn't need to be shed. He was there for parts of my life even though I never knew.

Is this the life I'm heading toward?

I lock up the house and make sure everything is secure. I need to decide what to do with the house, but not today. I feel a sense of peace settle around me. I've gained some answers or at least some insight. Getting into my car, I allow the silence to surround me as the sun shines upon on my face.

chapter

twenty-six

TUESDAY MORNING ROLLS along, and I know I have to get up and get it together. I have a job to do, one that ultimately will force me to deal with Jackson again. This was what my fear of getting involved with him was all along. He promised it wouldn't affect my career, and now it's time for him to prove it. I stroll into the office in my black slacks and coral top, hoping the bright color will draw attention away from my swollen eyes.

"Good morning," I say with a forced smile.

Taylor stands and follows me into my office. "Morning, Cat. How are you feeling?"

"Fine. We have a lot of work to do. Can you see where we are on the advertising piece getting released to the press next week?" I say quickly.

I don't want to talk. I don't even know what to say. *Hi. I had a mental breakdown. My ex and my current boyfriend got in a fight. Oh, and my dad, who I haven't seen or heard from in over twenty years, wrote me a letter telling me he loved me. But the best part is I threw Jackson out after he told me I was it for him. And I still refuse to call him because I'm a chicken shit.* Yup, that about sums it up.

"Okay," she says slowly while glancing around. "I'll get the graphics people on the phone."

Great. I've made her uncomfortable. With a smile, I try to

ease her tension. "No, I think I'll just go there and check it out myself. If you can get the schedule for the next month of potential accounts coming up, that would be great."

Her eyes widen as her head tilts to the side. "For upcoming clients? I thought we had another month or two on the Raven account?"

I know I'm not making sense, but moving forward is all I have. I debated sending Taylor in my place on Wednesday and letting her give over all the finalized plans, but I'd lose my job. I could always hand it over to Elle and simply state the client and I weren't agreeing on how to proceed, but the idea of Elle's breasts and her lack of clothing anywhere near Jackson makes me sick. So, I'm stuck. I need to put my big girl panties on and deal with it.

I'm fighting the real problem, which is how much I miss him. The thought of losing him makes it hard to get through the day. I imagine running into him with another woman on his arm, kissing her, touching her, and telling her he loves her. Pain radiates from my heart out through my body. There's no way I could handle that. Why does he have to be so damn irresistible? And why do I have to be so stubborn?

"Cat?" Taylor breaks me from my thoughts.

I shake my head, drawing air into my lungs before pushing it out loudly. "Sorry, you're right. I wanted to see what was coming up, but it's fine."

"I can grab them, no problem. I just—"

"Seriously, not a big deal." I smile, trying to ease her confusion. "My head is all over the place."

Taylor steps forward and sits in the chair. She doesn't say anything as her eyes assess me. "We're friends, right?"

"Of course," I respond.

"Then, no bullshit. What's wrong?" Her eyes are soft and caring. It's the same look I got from her when I opened up about Neil's affair. Taylor sits with her hands in her lap, patiently waiting.

As much as I want to take this moment and lay it all out there, I'm not sure I want to hear a lecture. Every minute that passes, I'm less convinced I did the right thing by throwing Jackson out. Also, I'm realizing my feelings for him run far deeper than I've allowed myself to admit. He's given me strength but never made me feel weak, and along the way he's embedded himself in my heart.

"Let's just say that my weekend was less than stellar. The night of the reading of the will was horrific. I've got a lot on my mind. I'm sorting it all out."

She smiles sincerely. "I'm sorry. It's not like you to call out of work. You're usually here no matter what."

"It was a good thing I wasn't. I needed to take care of some stuff regarding my father. You know me. I'll be fine."

"If you want to talk, I'm here."

Taylor is one of the few people I know I can talk to without fear of judgment. She listens with an open heart. When she moved to New York, she vowed not to let the big city take away her country roots. She's innocent but not naïve, which allows her to cut through the drama. She has an old soul, one of the purest of anyone I know. And her best asset—even at her young age, she sees and understands things people three and four times her senior wouldn't. It's an exceptional gift, but one I have no desire to take advantage of at the moment.

Before she uncovers it all, I cut her off. "I'll be downstairs with the design team. Page me if you need anything."

She nods, pressing her lips into a fine line. "Sure thing. I'll just be out here doing my job, pretending you didn't just try to deflect."

"Good. Pretend away." I smile and head out of the office.

I spend an hour downstairs checking in on the marketing and graphic side of things to get the first press release ready to go out. It gives me the small reprieve I needed from my mind. No Jackson, no Neil, no thoughts of anything else but work.

Once I'm content with everything, I decide to head out for

lunch. It's a beautiful day and I think an hour to myself will help my mood. I grab the subway and head to Central Park. I walk toward an empty bench and kick my heels off. Taking a deep breath, I close my eyes and embrace the sun and fresh air. The park is tranquil even in its chaos. It's never empty, but you can always find your own section of heaven.

During the first few minutes, I clear my mind and focus on everything around me. I hear the birds making beautiful music, the leaves rustling in the tree above thanks to the gentle wind blowing through them, and the sound of running feet pounding the pavement, moving forward with each stride.

My mind drifts to Jackson. I imagine him here in the mornings jogging, running through life and finding the courage to keep going. He's strong in the face of adversity and has found a way to rise above his grief. Every day he cares for the people in not one but two companies. More than that, he cared for me. Jackson's strength kept me together even when he wasn't there. I pushed him so hard because I couldn't take another man leaving. I thought if I shoved him out the door, I'd be protecting myself. As I sit here thinking of the runners and their path through the park, I consider their options: they can stay on the paved road, on solid ground, or they can take a dirt trail and see where it leads. Sure, the road less traveled is bumpy and may be scary, but it could also be amazing.

It applies to me. I can keep on handling things the way I have with Jackson and protect myself, push him away, and keep building the fortress around my heart, or I can rip down that fortress and see where it goes. If I give him the benefit of the doubt instead of assuming he'll devastate me, we might have a chance.

I glance at my watch. I've been enjoying this serenity for over an hour. With a little lighter heart, I trudge back to my office to finish securing my position in the company. Time to be epic.

"Did I miss anything?" I ask Tay as I walk past her.

She jumps a little, holding her hand against her heart. Taking a second to recover, she responds, "I forwarded a few calls to your voicemail. Also, I grabbed the upcoming accounts in the cue, in case you wanted to look." She smiles and hands me a few papers.

"Perfect. Please hold my calls for the rest of the day. I have a ton of stuff to get done before for tomorrow."

"No problem," she replies.

With the door closed, I gather the latest sales figures and start getting everything together. We have a press release going out this week and need to finalize everything, which means I'll see him again tomorrow. I'm terrified. When he's around it's hard to keep things in perspective or focus on anything but him. And he has a way of seeing through my mask, so I know I'll need to be extremely careful.

Closing my eyes, I remember his touch, the way he says my name, and his smell. I can almost feel his hands moving over my skin, touching every part of my body as I give myself over to him. I remember the feel of him filling me over and over, the sound of his voice calling out my name as he came.

The door bursts open, pulling me from my erotic memories. I look up to see Piper glaring at me as Taylor tries to stop her from entering. Well, this is unexpected and unwelcome.

"Catherine, I'm sorry. I tried to stop her!" Taylor says quickly.

I stand, needing to be on equal ground with her.

"It's fine. She wouldn't have listened anyway. She obviously has no class or tact," I tell Taylor.

"Do you want me to call security?" she asks, glaring at Piper.

While that's probably the smart thing to do, Piper must be desperate to come to my office and barge in like this.

"No, I'd love to hear why she felt the need to show up unannounced." I give Taylor a small nod. "You can go ahead and close the door. I'll yell if I need you."

My gaze returns to Piper as Taylor closes the door. "Why are you here?" I ask coldly.

She walks forward and sits in a chair, seemingly unaffected by my glacial tone. Piper looks around, picking at her fingernails. "You got me fired." Her eyes lift as she purses her lips.

"I have no clue what the hell you're talking about." Clearly I'm thrown by how she figures I have anything to do with her losing a client.

"Right," she scoffs. "You had nothing to do with your boyfriend firing me? I doubt that."

"Piper, I don't have time for your shit. You come to my office—uninvited—and start talking about something I have no knowledge of." I roll my eyes at her ridiculous riddle, but I have a feeling there's more to this. Considering everything that happened on Friday, she could be using this to try to get information. Subtly, I reach for my phone. I press the voice recorder, hoping it works. I don't trust her at all and I won't leave her any chance to spin this meeting.

She steps toward me with her hands on her hips. "You owe me a client. A big one."

I don't try to hide the short laugh that escapes me. Owe her? I don't think so. "I owe you absolutely nothing. And it's not my problem. Maybe you can talk to your boyfriend and he can get you a new client. Plus, I've never spoken to Jackson about you." I give a snide smile. "You're not worth my time."

Taking another step, she leans on my desk. "Here's how I see it. Not only did your boyfriend assault Neil, he then fired me because I refused to sleep with him." Piper leans back and smiles. "I hope he has a fantastic lawyer because I'm going to bury him."

Right. This is absolutely insane. No matter what she says, there's no way I believe Jackson tried to sleep with her. If he fired her for any reason, it's because she's incompetent.

"Gosh, Piper. I'm so sorry you lost your client, but I couldn't give two flying fucks. And you *really* don't want to threaten me or Jackson." I smile, sarcasm oozing out of my mouth. I start to walk toward her. With each step I find more strength to confront her. She's on my turf, in my office, and there's no way she's going to make me cower. "If Jackson—sorry, I mean Mr. Cole. Isn't that what you called him?" I ask petulantly. "Well, if Mr. Cole fired you, I'm sure there was a good reason. Maybe he didn't like the fact that you,"—I wave my hand in a casual way as if searching for the words—"oh, I don't know, are a complete idiot and a liar."

Piper steps back with each step I take in her direction. "He came on to me. How does it feel to have two men you've slept with want me instead of you?"

For a half-second I *almost* believe her. It would be so easy to think it's true. She's trying to use her words like knives, but this time they're not cutting. She's desperate and it shows. I don't think Jackson would purposely hurt me that way. He told me I was it for him.

"If I believed you, that might've actually hurt. But since I don't and I can see you're grasping at straws, I don't feel a damn thing but pity." I give a cynical laugh.

"Fuck you and your pity," she yells back.

"Oh Piper, you poor, poor girl. It must suck to have nothing. Your workload just got a whole lot lighter and you're dating a cheating asshole that can't fight. And here I am with my dream job, an extremely sexy boyfriend,"—I lean in and whisper with a huge grin—"who's a hundred times better than Neil in *every* possible way, if you know what I mean." I wink and move closer to the door.

God, it feels good to say this to her. I'm completely calm, enjoying Piper's unease. She's got nothing and for once I have it all. She doesn't know Jackson and I aren't speaking, but *he* fired her. No matter what his reason is, it feels good to see karma finally making the rounds to someone other than me.

Piper sneers but recovers quickly. "You don't have to believe me. The truth show itself in time. But don't say I didn't warn you." She smiles, walking toward the door. "You could've avoided all this." Piper shrugs, patting my arm. "Just remember, all you had to do was get me a client."

I grab the door handle, opening the door as Taylor looks up. "Tay, could you please take out the trash?"

"Sure thing." She smiles and turns to Piper. "Right this way, Ms. Carlson." She extends her arm, showing Piper where to go.

Piper stops, turning back toward me. "It's only a matter of time and you'll be alone. Again."

I step toward her, trying to make sure I don't cause a scene in my office. "I'd rather be alone than be with a man who cheats, steals, and assaults women." I take a step back with a plastic smile. "Have a great day, Piper."

I make it back into my office feeling strong. Jackson fired her. There could be hundreds of reasons, but I want to believe it's because he learned the truth. He saw who she was and was protecting me in some small way. Or it could be because she really screwed up. Whatever the reason, it's one more way she's gone and out of my life. I have too much to get done to sit and ponder over Jackson's decisions. I stop the recording and check to make sure it worked. I hear some of it and shut it off. I didn't want to hear what she had to say the first time and I certainly don't want to hear it again.

I take a few minutes to refocus. There are papers all over, I've got to return about a hundred emails, and I still need to get my notes done. Time to kick a little ass. I immerse myself in my project, putting everything else in the back of my mind.

Time goes by, but I have no idea how long it's been when Taylor buzzes through on the intercom. "Hey, Cat, it's almost seven. Did you still need me to stay?"

Wow. I didn't notice it was so late. I pick up the receiver. "I don't think so. I'm going to head home to finish this. Ashton is staying in the city again this week, so it'll be quiet. I can proba-bly get a lot of this done there," I reply.

"Okay, I'll see you tomorrow," Taylor says sweetly.

"Have a great night." I smile and hang up.

Sighing, I gather all my papers to take home, prepared to get this done.

chapter

twenty-seven

WITH A LARGE box filled with everything I needed, I made it home before the rain started. My table is now covered in papers and diagrams while the storm rages outside. I've got my music going, comfy clothes on, and copious amounts of coffee in a gigantic cup. I never should've called out on Monday. This meeting will be a disaster because I'm not prepared. Looks like an all-nighter is in my future. My phone keeps ringing. It's the fifth time in the last hour, but I don't have time to deal with it.

Finally, after the tenth missed call, I grab it and see Jackson's name across the screen. My heart starts pounding and my throat goes dry. With shaking fingers, I swipe across the screen.

"Hi," I say softly.

"Hello, Catherine. Sorry to call so late but I just got out of a meeting." His tone is all business.

Hearing him is a shock to my system. I've missed the sound of his voice. The way he says my name—it's like home. However, he doesn't sound like he returns the sentiment.

I straighten my back, hoping to grab on to my professionalism. This is business. He's not calling because he missed me or wants to talk. "Not a problem. What did you need?" My voice sounds weak, even to me.

He takes a deep breath before answering. "I know we

planned to finalize everything tomorrow, but I need it tonight."

"Tonight?" I look around at all the incomplete papers. I can't have it ready tonight! I already needed to work well past midnight to get it done.

"I'm in New Jersey. I'm assuming you're home since you didn't answer your office phone."

"Yes, I'm home but I don't have everything with me. Some things are still in the office. But I can get it to you tomorrow. Besides, it's storming," I say, trying to stall him. Shit!

"I'm going out of town tomorrow and I'm not sure when I'll be back. I won't have time. It has to be tonight," he says, clipped and almost angry.

"You're leaving?" I ask, confused. He was going to leave and not tell me. I know we're not in the best place, but it still hurts to hear it.

"I need to go to Virginia. I would've called earlier but, like I said, I've been tied up. I'll be at your house in twenty."

I look at the clock and then at what I have done. While most would be satisfied, I'm not. It's not my best work and the idea of giving it to Jackson unfinished makes me nauseous. There's no way he's going to be impressed. I'm shaking my head and trying to find another excuse when I hear him clear his throat.

"Jackson," I sigh. His name rolls off my tongue while tearing a hole in my chest. "I can meet you tomorrow morning, before your trip. I have some stuff in the office that would complete the press release and the other items for the launch. I don't want to give it to you incomplete." I close my eyes. He feels so close, almost like I could touch him through the phone.

"I won't have time tomorrow. I'll take what you have and you can have the rest sent."

If he wants to treat me like a business associate, then he should know showing up at people's apartments at night isn't exactly professional.

"I'm not happy about this. It's late and I—"

"If I could help it, I would. I have to leave early in the

morning, and I need this set in motion before I get back. So you can either have me come get it now, or you can bring it to me in New York tonight." He takes a long pause. "I was trying to make it easier for you since I'm in New Jersey."

"Fine, but just know you don't have everything."

"See you in a few," he says and disconnects the call.

I throw down the phone and blast into action. I quickly put a bra on, pick up some dishes and other things lying around, and try to make some kind of sense of the paperwork. I only have about ten minutes until he's here and I'm starting to panic. I snatch the phone and call Ashton.

She answers on the second ring. "Hey."

"He's coming here," I say quickly.

"You called him? Finally!" Ashton sounds ecstatic.

I huff, pressing the phone to my shoulder so I can keep cleaning. "No, he called me. He needs his project early because he has to leave for Virginia tomorrow. I don't know, Ashton. Why am I freaking out?"

"Because you love him and you know you fucked up? Just a hunch."

"No, I—" I stop unable to complete the sentence.

Do I love him? No, it's too soon. Isn't it? We've only begun getting to know each other, but he makes perfect sense. He's everything I want, everything I need.

Ashton breaks through the silence as I stand shell-shocked. "You just had your epiphany, didn't you?"

I hear a knock at the door. "I gotta go," I say and disconnect the phone. I don't have time for a damn epiphany.

After a few deep breaths, I walk to the door. He's right there on the other side. He said he wouldn't come back through this door if I didn't tell him I wanted him here. And I do want him here. All I want is Jackson. But that fear of losing him is always looming, making its way into my head, causing me to second-guess everything. I'm out of time and now Ashton's made me even more nervous.

Another knock.

I press my hand on the door and rest my head against the cool wood grain, trying to settle my pulse. I'm brave enough for this. Maybe.

Enough stalling.

Time to be strong.

I open the door and freeze when our eyes lock. Jackson's even more devastatingly handsome than I remember in his black pants and light blue shirt with the top two buttons undone. His hair is disheveled, but all I see is perfection. The stubble on his jaw is much thicker, making him look darker, more mysterious and dangerous. He looks tired, but I see the underlying emotions as his gaze travels my face. Despite the dark circles forming beneath his eyes, he still looks flawless.

When he gives me a small smile, everything in my world shifts. That grin and the perfectly placed dimple cause an explosion around my guarded heart. It hits me. I love him. It's a different love than what I had with Neil. It doesn't feel forced. It's strong and hopeful. He doesn't want to take from me—he gives. My weaknesses don't scare or bother him and he doesn't want to exploit them. No, he wants to make me stronger. And when I can't be, he'll be strong enough for the both of us.

I take a step forward, but before I can speak, he grabs me and pulls me against him. My eyes widen and a second later his lips crash against mine in an angry, hot kiss. Jackson's arms wrap around me, holding me close. It's almost crushing, but I couldn't care less. My fingers tangle in his hair, pulling him closer even though we couldn't get any more attached than we already are. I breathe in his scent—all male and pure sex. I try to pull him into the apartment, but he won't budge. He breaks the kiss, but hovers over my mouth. I whimper at the loss of his lips.

"Do you want to let me in?" His deep voice goes straight to my core.

I nod yes, but he doesn't move. Every cell in my body is

awakened. I need his touch. I want him to fill me up and make me whole again. But I know that's not what he's asking.

"I told you when I walked out of here the last time—"

I cut him off, leaning up and pressing my lips against his. It's pure survival. His lips are breathing life into me. Our time apart has me desperate for him. I want to ingrain this moment in my mind in case things don't go the way I'm hoping.

Jackson grips the side of my face and pulls back. *Bastard.* He has the height advantage. He smiles when my lip juts out in a pout. Looking into his eyes, I know I can't walk away from him. The last few days were hell, but now that the truth of my feelings is clear, I know the pain of really losing him would cripple me. I will fight all my fears for him.

His gaze doesn't break, but his voice does. "You need to make a choice."

The words tumble out of my mouth effortlessly. "Find me."

With his hands cupping my face, his lips press against mine as he crosses the threshold. When the door slams closed, the energy changes—three days of anger, longing, and doubt rip through us. Jackson's hands hold my face tight as he pours himself into the kiss, giving me every emotion through his mouth.

The growl emanating from his chest travels straight to my core. Every part of me is alive and desperate for him. I grab at his shirt, unbuttoning it as we move into the house. I want to feel his skin, need to feel the warmth and heat of his body against mine. But he has other ideas. Jackson twists his fingers in my hair and tugs, causing a loud moan to escape. He doesn't hesitate as his tongue enters my mouth roughly, each stroke edging my need up and out of control. He's pushing me back as I'm pulling him closer. I grab onto his shoulders. I've missed his touch.

Jackson slams me back against the wall. He breaks the kiss, ripping off my shirt and drinking me in as his tongue slides across my lips. My hands reach out to grab him, but he grips my wrists and holds them above my head. Jackson crushes his body against mine. The ache to have him grows with each second.

"Did you miss me like I missed you? Do you know how hard it was every fucking day fighting the urge to see you? How many times I had to stop myself from coming here and breaking down your goddamn door?" he asks against my ear, causing goose bumps to form everywhere.

Before I can respond, his lips are pressed against me, tongue probing for the answers I wasn't able to give. He has me pinned, completely at his mercy, and there's nowhere else I'd rather be. It baffles me how I could've turned this man away.

Jackson moves his knee between my legs, further restricting my movements. Warm lips descend to my neck as he nips and kisses. I hear his phone ring but neither of us stops or cares. All I'm thinking about is him touching me. I rub against his leg, trying to create some friction to relieve the pulsing between my thighs.

He grips my hips. "Not yet, baby."

With my hands now free, I begin to roam his body. His shirt is still half buttoned. I grip the sides, ripping it open and sending buttons flying across the room. My fingers trace the hard, taut planes of his chest, enjoying the feel of it rising and falling heavily. Leaning forward, I use the tip of my tongue, running it from the middle of his chest up to his ear. He braces his hands against the wall as his head drops to the crook of my neck. Jackson's breathing is labored and I'm savoring how much I'm affecting him. It's a heady feeling to have such power over a man like him.

I reach his ear and graze the edge. "Jackson," I softly whisper, "show me how much you missed me." I smile against his ear before he becomes ravenous.

His tears my bra off, then lifts me with his leg and rips my pants and panties down. I quickly remove his pants and start to push him toward the bedroom, but he grips both wrists in his one hand, pressing me back on the wall. His other hand slips between us as he circles my clit.

"I'll fucking show you, baby. You're soaking wet for me." Jackson moans as he slips a finger into my pussy. "Did you miss me, Catherine?"

I try to pull my hands away, but he grips them harder, keeping me at his mercy. "I want to touch you."

Jackson inserts a second finger. My legs buckle, but he holds me up easily. "I'm going to make you remember why you're not allowed to run anymore." His voice is primal and demanding. "You want to be found, baby?" Jackson's thumb presses against my clit, eliciting a long moan as my eyes roll back.

Does he actually want me to answer? I'm incapable of speaking let alone answering any questions right now. With his one hand still restraining me and the other doing incredible things to my pussy, he leans forward and licks his tongue around my nipple. He brings it into his mouth, teasing and sucking. I writhe against him but get no relief.

"Jackson, please!" I'm begging for everything. I feel everything, everywhere, and I need to release. It's too much. My head falls back as the sensations threaten to overwhelm me.

"Are you going to push me away again?" he asks forcefully while he twists his fingers and presses on the bundle of nerves with his thumb. My vision becomes fuzzy as he increases the pressure and bites down on my nipple.

"Oh God." I'm so close. My impending orgasm is right there and I'm desperate. I move my hips, trying to get there. Jackson releases his thumb and withdraws his fingers. My eyes open in protest.

Jackson releases my hands, grasps my legs, and lifts me while rubbing his cock against my sex. "Wrap your legs around me. I want you to come when I'm inside of you." I comply as he thrusts his dick inside me. His eyes roll back and he takes a second before he begins to move. "Fuck. You feel incredible."

His voice is thick with pleasure.

Incredible doesn't begin to explain how I feel. I'm in complete ecstasy. All the days of being apart are gone. I've never been more with him than I am right now. We are one. Our bodies are connected and I'm giving myself to him in every way. My heart will never be mine again. Every fiber of my being is screaming *I love you*. The three words are on the tip of my tongue, but I bite them back. It's too soon to tell him how much he owns me. With every push, I fight hard to keep them to myself. But I hope one day he'll feel the same.

Jackson pushes deeper, slamming my back against the wall. It's pleasure and pain combining, taking me higher toward release.

"Are. You. Going. To. Run?" He enunciates every word in between thrusts. "Tell me. Tell me you're mine!" It's anger mixed with hunger and need. When I don't respond, he stops moving and stares into my eyes. "Don't fucking run from me again!"

"Jackson!" I call out as he pounds again, harder. I swear I'm going to black out from the pleasure overload. As soon as I reach the brink, he slows, holding off my orgasm. "Please," I beg.

"Answer me," he demands, holding me against the wall and refusing to move.

"I'm yours!" I cry in out in frustration. "Now move!" Each nerve in my body is burning. I'm shaking, on the verge of tears.

"Damn fucking right you are." He lifts me slowly, gradually increasing his pace and adjusting his hips to ensure he hits every nerve while his cock rubs the sweet spot inside of me. He grinds his teeth, trying to hold off his own orgasm. "Let go, Catherine."

As my muscles coil, Jackson rears back and plunges hard, causing my orgasm to rip through me. "Yes! Jackson!" I shriek over and over as he fucks me until he finally releases.

I'm pressed against the wall as we both try to slow our

breathing. That was the best sex I've ever had. Then I realize why it felt so different—no condom. Jackson slides out and kisses the top of my nose. I love when he does that. It's sweet and tender. Our eyes meet before I go to the bathroom to clean up. When I come back, Jackson's sitting on the couch with his head in his hands.

"Well that was one helluva a hello." I laugh as I sit beside him.

His shoulders are hunched even after I sit. "I didn't plan that."

"I'm not complaining." I raise my brow, giving him a playful smirk.

He pulls me against his chest with a chuckle. "Good to know. Also, I'll make a mental note—you're more agreeable when I fuck it out of you."

"Asshole." I feign anger and slap his chest. "Maybe next time I'll refuse to answer."

"Go ahead. It'll just make it that much more fun to get you to agree." His smirk reaches his eyes, fully erasing the expression he wore when he first arrived.

Jackson gazes at me with reverence. It warms me, offering reassurance in my decision to let him in, find happiness again, and stop running from fear. Some of my newfound peace comes from dealing with my father's death. Another part is because I did push Jackson away and it forced me to see how life without him would be.

His thumb whispers across my lower lip, releasing a flurry of butterflies in my belly. A simple touch says so much. "You felt so fucking amazing. I couldn't think straight." He looks away with regret in his eyes.

My lips part as I kiss his thumb, enjoying how his eyes close at my touch. I look up from beneath my lashes. "We probably should've talked before this, but we're good. I'm on birth control." I smile.

Jackson gives a crisp nod. "Yeah, we probably should've."

"Well neither of us thought about it, so I guess we both fucked up."

Lacing his fingers with mine, his voice drops to a sad whisper. "We need to talk."

"About?" I try to keep my voice steady. My heart begins to race as doubt seeps through me. Please tell me we aren't going to go back now. I told him I was his. He pushed me to answer him. I've allowed myself to admit I love him. This would devastate me.

His phone rings again, but he silences it.

"The last few days were horrible. I know you thought you needed space, but I won't be pushed away again. If you push me, I'll push harder. I'm not your piece of shit ex who's going to run away like a pussy." His eyes pierce through me as he squares his shoulders. "I meant it. You're it for me." The sincerity rings clear in his voice.

I want to tell him. Tell him how I won't run. How I can't run away anymore. I love him. I love how he makes me feel. My heart clenches as I gather my strength and prepare to lay it all out for him.

"Jackson—" His phone rings again, halting me from saying anything more. He groans at the incessant ringing. "Go ahead and grab that. I'm not going anywhere." I give him a reassuring smile.

Jackson stands, walking toward the window as he answers the phone. "What?" he says in a clipped tone.

I get up to gather the clothes we shed by the door when I hear him slam his hand against the wall. Looking over, I see his shoulders are slumped as he listens to whoever's on the other line. "An IED?" He stops talking for a moment. "Casualties?"

I stop moving. I watch Jackson, waiting to hear what happened. It happens so fast. Jackson rears his fist back and punches a hole in the wall. My mouth is agape as I watch him continue to slam his hand against the wall. His face is contorted in pain. He looks ... defeated. Do I comfort him? I don't know what's wrong or why he's so upset.

He yells into the receiver, "How fucking many?"

The pain in his voice breaks me. Something's wrong—very wrong. I walk over to him, but he puts his hand up to stop me.

His entire body is shaking and his voice cracks when he asks, "Aaron?" A short pause. "Fuck! No ..." The sound that comes from his chest tears through me. It's a cry and a scream all mixed into one, and I'm sure it's the worst thing I've ever heard. Immediately, tears begin to form in his eyes. I want to go to him, but he turns his back to me.

I start putting the pieces together. Aaron is his buddy that works for him. He was also on the mission in Afghanistan, the one where they lost friends. He was going to maybe handle something overseas? My hand covers my mouth as I start to draw conclusions.

His hands fist into his hair as he leans forward with his head against the wall. I pray this isn't what I think it is. He can't lose another friend.

Please, God, don't do this to him.

"I can't—" he says but stops as a tear falls from his eye. "No! I'll call her. Get the fucking plans in motion. We leave tonight! I don't give a shit what you have to do. Wake everyone— we're wheels up in three hours." His phone tumbles to the floor as he stands there with a vacant look.

Jackson's chest is heaving with exaggerated breaths. Hesitantly, I take a step toward him.

"Jackson, what happened?" I ask quietly. He turns, eyes glistening with tears, but he doesn't respond.

I watch as he crumples to the floor. Every part of his body is quivering. I rush over, wrapping my arms around him as he sobs. He's breaking. My chest is cracking open watching the man I love fall apart. Tears fall with every strangled, broken sound that Jackson releases. All I can do is hold him close while he unloads his grief.

chapter

twenty-eight

"TALK TO ME. What happened?" I croon softly, not releasing my hold. "Hey." I lift his face, trying to get him to look at me.

He shifts, pulling away from my embrace. I feel the loss everywhere and see the change as soon as he stands. He's shutting down. Two steps forward, one step back. The mask of indifference has secured itself.

With eyes closed, he takes two deep breaths before speaking. "What happened?" Jackson asks sarcastically. He pushes the air from his lungs in frustration. "I'll tell you what happened—I did it again!"

"Did what again?" I ask quietly.

He throws his hands in the air and begins to pace the room. "I fucking knew it."

I start to approach him, trying to keep my tone calm. "I don't understand. What did you know?"

Jackson stops moving. His eyes widen as if he forgot I was here. The harshness in his voice slices through me. "I'm no good for you."

"Why would you say that?" His statement stuns me, especially since he just said he'd fight for me. What the hell happened on the phone to make him think this?

"Don't you get it? Everyone I love dies!" Jackson approaches but stops. "I can't let you be the next one. I'll die before I let that happen."

I'm lost. "Jackson, talk to me." I place my hand on his arm, but he shoves it away. The rejection burns through my veins. "Don't push me away. I'm trying to understand," I urge him. "I'm not pushing you away. I'm saving you!" he yells and walks over to grab his phone. "I won't let it happen to you too!" "Let what happen? You're not making any sense!" I say to him as he heads toward the door. "Stop! Talk to me!" I beg him. He made me promise not to run but that's exactly what he's doing.

It's like we've gone back to three days ago, only now I'm on the other side. He's breaking and I can't stop it. Desperate to get him to listen, I run in front of him, placing myself between him and the door and hoping it will stop him. His eyes are un-focused and void as the storm rages within him. He's going to break my heart right here. The irony is not lost on me—I gave it to him only to have it shattered. My stomach churns as I see the truth of that reflected in his eyes. Whether I'm standing here or not, he's walking out this door. I've already lost him.

His face is ashen as he chokes out the words. He's speak-ing but not to me. "How many more tattoos do I have to get? Huh? How many ways do I have to mark my mistakes?" Jack-son looks at me, desperation flashing across his face. "I'm pro-tecting you, Catherine. I won't let you love me."

A tear cascades as the words fall out. "Too late."

His eyes snap up at my admission and his nostrils flare. He quickly pushes forward. "Don't! Don't say that!" The muscles in his neck are pulsing with rage and frustration.

"I will say it because it's true. What did you think was going to happen? I knew I was falling for you. Then you told me ... you told me I was it for you! Don't walk away. Don't give up on us."

Leaning close to my face, his warm breath washes over my cheek while my tears fall freely. Ever so slowly, his hand lifts. He gently removes a droplet of pain from my cheek only to have more follow in its path. His lips tenderly find purchase on my temple. "I'm not giving up. I'm giving you a chance."

I refuse to move from the door. If he leaves, I'll never get him back. I can't lose him. My pulse is racing, but I stand strong. I have to do something to make him see me.

"Jackson, I love you! Give *us* a chance," I beg him, praying he'll listen to me.

His arms wrap around me, dispelling my fears and the breath I was holding. With my eyes closed, I take this moment, finding the tiniest bit of relief in it. He didn't leave. I told him I loved him and he's here, enveloping me in his warmth. I could stay in his arms forever. I feel his lips press against my forehead. When I look up into his eyes, hoping to see him recovered, the color drains from my face. There's no love or recovery there, just determination. It rolls off him like thunder.

"No ..." The strangled sound of my voice doesn't register.

Jackson's hold disappears along with my hope. With each step he takes, the floor falls a little further down, and my heart follows. He doesn't stop or look back.

No.

His hand touches the handle and my breath hitches.

Please don't do this.

I want to tell him, but the words won't come out!

Dammit, Jackson, stop!

"Jackson." I say his name like a prayer.

He stops but doesn't turn as his hands clench the door jam. "You said I shouldn't run." The pain lances through me, fueling my anger to flames. "You lied to me! You're doing what you promised you wouldn't—leave." Still he says nothing, so I step toward him. "Fine. Be a coward! Go! Walk away just like they all do."

His hands drop but he doesn't turn. Shoulders slumped, defeated, broken—he's not the man I know. Jackson is strong, a fighter, loyal, and I'm desperate to get him back.

"Coward? I'm fucking saving you. The only thing I'm afraid

of is losing you."

"I can't do this again, Jackson. Please don't walk out that door after I've told you how I feel."

I watch his head shake from side to side and everything inside me rattles. Jackson remains in the door with his back to me, his voice quiet and strained. "I can't lose you like that. I'd rather walk away."

Anger that was simmering beneath the hurt is starting to boil. How dare he do this? He comes here, fucks me, tells me not to run, and then he's going to do exactly that? I'm pissed. I'm talking volcano erupting, fire burning, hulk smashing kind of pissed the fuck off.

"You're going to listen to me, goddamnit. Four days ago, when we went into that lawyer's office, I was falling apart. Everything in my life felt out of control. It was *you* who held me together. I drew on your strength to get through that fucking day from hell." I close my eyes, remembering what came after that. "But after everything else, I was terrified. You could hurt me so much. I was falling in love with you weeks ago, but that day I saw it all vanish. I ran because I was so afraid you'd let me go. I thought if I pushed you away before you got rid of me, it would be better. But it wasn't!"

Jackson turns and looks at me, the battle still raging inside him. "I'm not running, Catherine. Aaron is dead. I'm going to collect his fucking body and deliver it to his pregnant wife. Guess whose fault it is again? I give up trying to fight a war I'll never win."

"It's not your fault."

He goes stone-cold, every muscle rigid and tense. The blue-green eyes I love are black and glossy. "Try telling Natalie that. I leave tonight for Afghanistan to get his body and bring it home. I'm done arguing with you. I'm just ... done."

If I don't get this out now, I'll find a reason to hold back. I'm trembling from adrenaline as well as the fear of him walking out this door.

"I'm ready to fight for you. For so long I thought it wasn't my choice if things worked or not with any man. But with you—it's different. You told me I was it for you. Well, same here. I love you." I look into his eyes, completely vulnerable. No walls, nothing to hide my emotions. I'm giving him the truth with everything I am. "So you choose, Jackson. You tell me now if you want me to walk away. You walked through my door today. It's up to you to keep it open. I'm not talking about going to do what you have to do. Please, don't close the door on us."

The silence surrounds us, giving me the answer I was dreading. I drop my head while I struggle to keep the tears in check. When I feel his hand on my chin, my heart sputters. Once I look up, I'll have to face the truth. My gaze drifts as my chin glides toward his eyes. His face gives nothing away. My emotions are like a dam about to break.

"Say something, dammit!" I yell with tears in my eyes.

Jackson's hand drops from my face, leaving me bereft. "I've said it all already. You're not listening."

"That's your answer?" I ask, defeated.

He looks up, shaking his head, then exhales. "Everyone I love or care about dies. I'm protecting you."

"No. You're protecting yourself. People die, Jackson. It's tragic, but it happens."

His fingers sweep the hair off my face, lingering in my hair. "You know that night we met in the restaurant? It was so intense. I'd never felt so connected to someone so quickly. You walked away. Then, by some miracle ..." Jackson's hands cup my face. He takes a moment with his eyes closed. "You found your way back. I won't allow anything to hurt you. Including me." Releasing a heavy sigh, he drops his hands.

"The only thing hurting me is you leaving."

"I don't have a choice." He grips the back of his neck and looks at the ceiling.

There has to be a way. If I can keep him talking, maybe he won't go. "Of course you have a choice! Please. I'm begging you. Stay tonight, fly out tomorrow—please stay with me. We can figure this out. You're too upset to drive or be alone. I want to be here for you, but you're pushing me away."

Jackson stares at the window, unwilling to look at me. "The plane leaves tonight."

If he has to leave because he needs to deal with whatever is going on, fine. But he's leaving and planning to end things. If he walks out the door, I fear it's truly the end.

"I won't give up on us. I know you're hurting and I understand you have to handle this situation, but you can lean on me. Let me carry some of your burden. *Talk* to me, Jackson. Let me in."

Our eyes meet for a moment before his lips crush against mine. I'd give everything up right now if he'd keep me in his embrace. His tongue demands entrance and my lips part, allowing him access. Every organ clenches as he pours himself into the kiss. I give him everything right back. All the love in my heart, my body, I offer him at this moment.

Needing an answer, I break the kiss. My heart is pounding so loud I'd swear he could hear it. I take a deep breath. "Don't kiss me if you're going to break my heart."

He looks at me with a mix of fear and regret. Then he closes his eyes and whispers, "Good-bye, Catherine." Jackson walks out the door without a backward glance.

I stand there, waiting to wake up from this nightmare. Surely that didn't happen. I'm asleep—that has to be it. I'm at my kitchen table with the papers strewn everywhere because *that* did not happen. Only it did. I look around my apartment, at the hole in the wall where Jackson punched it in anger. The door he walked through is still open, waiting for him to walk back through. I stare at the space he walked away from. It seems to be growing smaller, shrinking into itself as time does the same. He doesn't return. The thunder booms outside, snapping me from my haze. The tempest within becomes a hurricane.

He's gone.

He walked out on me after he promised he wouldn't. My heart splinters like glass on the ground—jagged and raw and ready to cut with all its sharp edges. I knew this was going to happen eventually—I'd hoped not to fall, but I guess it's too late for that now. I've crested the mountain only to fall down the other side, and no one is going to catch me.

CHAPTER
TWENTY NINE

JACKSON

Seven days later-Afghanistan

"FUCK. I DIDN'T miss this shithole!" I glance over at Mark, who's looking out at the village on the left, checking for anything out of the norm.

"Need to clean the sand out of your vag, Muff? Does Kitty know you're this big of a pussy?" Mark taunts like the douchebag he is.

I scoff at his sorry attempt at a jab. "Kiss my ass. Try not to sparkle too much while we're here. You might draw some hijab attention." I give him the finger and he starts laughing. "Also, don't talk about Catherine."

"Touchy. Have you told her yet?"

"No," I say with no room for further discussion. He's already told me I need to tell her about my past, but I wasn't going to drop that shit on her lap and rush off to deal with the mess here.

Mark and I didn't speak for the first leg of the trip, both of us dealing with the loss of yet another member of our team. This shit is fucking with both of us. We started with six—and then there were two. When you're active duty, you know your time is numbered. Once you're out, though, that's not how you think anymore.

I look to the left, take a deep breath, and regret doing that immediately. The Humvee smells like shit, but we've been traveling for five long ass days, so we aren't any better. We flew into Spain and waited there for two days. Rota reminded me of the trouble we got in during the last deployment here. It was a fucking joke. We drank, ate, drank some more, and worked out. Made bank and went home.

Then we flew into Dubai for another two days. At least in Dubai there's a ton of shit to do. Of course, it was only supposed to be a five-hour layover, but when you're flying on Navy equipment, you expect the unexpected. Which is a nice way of saying prepare for that shit to break.

Since we've hit the sandbox, it's been nothing but constant bullshit. Our convoy never met us at the base we flew into. I had to call a bunch of old friends to get someone to come get us, then take us to Camp Victory so we could claim Aaron's body. Normally that's not how it works, but I don't give a fuck. He's our brother and we weren't leaving him to fly alone. Mark had to pull a few strings to get it done, but he felt the same way. We owed Natalie that much.

Now we're heading to the IED site. Another favor I cashed in. Whatever. At this rate, I just want to get some damn answers on how they fucked this up.

"By the way, asshat, this doesn't count as my vacation," Mark lets me know through the mics on our helmets.

I adjust my Kevlar so I can breathe. This shit didn't get any lighter. We're fully loaded and tacked out. "You said you wanted the sun and the sand. I delivered."

"Funny." He laughs.

We approach the site and my guard instantly goes up. I slip right back into battle mode.

I get out first.

"Hey, Muff, watch your six," Mark says seriously. We've done enough missions together to know when the tone changes, it means something's not right. "I have a bad feeling about the mountains up on the left," Mark says, pointing to the rocky terrain.

"Yeah, I have a bad feeling about this whole fucking place. Cover me."

I hear the door close behind me. The debris is cleared for the most part. Considering we're a week behind, a lot of the intel I could've gotten is pretty much gone, but you never know. I've seen insurgents sing like canaries for a soda. Everyone has a price and today, I'm the banker.

I scan the area. So far there's a few kids playing soccer and a woman standing by the fence, talking to another child. Ahead of me I see what looks like some pieces of the explosion. I lean down right as a ball comes flying in front of my face. The kids are laughing at the almost collision. I grab the ball and smile—I've just found my bargaining chip.

I crouch low to the ground and sling my gun onto my back. Probably not the smartest move, but I need the kids to come close. Plus, Mark's behind me along with the other two guys we grabbed when we rolled out. "Want the ball?" I ask, holding it out.

The two kids nod and walk over.

This might be too easy.

I hold the ball out and the little girl gives me a huge smile. She's cute as hell. I place the ball between us and pull it back. She giggles and reaches out. We do this four times before I hand it over. "Do you speak English?"

We didn't bring a translator with us, so I'm on my own. We may have to draw pictures in the dirt.

She nods but doesn't speak.

"I'm Ja—Muff. What's your name?" I almost told her my real name like a fucking idiot. It's bad enough we're in uniforms with our names on them. I get to walk around bumfuck Afghanistan with my last name on me. Perfect.

She stares at me and finally responds, "Cat."

My eyes go wide. What the fuck? Cat? I don't know if it's her name or if it's the only English word she knows.

I shake my head and go back to the little girl. "Your name is Cat?"

She holds her ball and nods her head yes.

I smile and think about Catherine, going back to the day I left. The way she looked. How I was so blind with rage I couldn't even talk to her. She has no clue what it was like for me to walk away from her. It was bad enough when she pushed me away, but to know it's me this time—it's fucking killing me. She captivates me, makes me want to try again, to feel things I swore I'd never allow myself to feel. Those brown eyes get me every time. It's only been a week, but I miss her. I wish I could hear her voice and beg her to take me back. Something's kept me from calling her, though. It's better this way. I don't care if someone thinks it makes me a pussy. I'm far from it.

Suddenly the little girl turns and runs back to her brother, who's screaming her name.

Fuck.

I turn back to Twilight, who's staring off at the perimeter. I kick myself for thinking the little girl would give us any answers. Mark was right when he said this was stupid. There's no court of law and no one gives a damn here, but I couldn't let it go. Again, because of me and my choices someone else's blood is on my hands. It was my fucking mission—I sent him. I made *him* go, even though his wife was seven months pregnant, because I was dealing with the stupid cosmetics shit—which I never wanted in the first place. It was never supposed to be my job. It was for her. Now it's my goddamn mess. Running one company was responsibility enough, but two?

As I walk to the detonation point, the air shifts.

My entire body goes still. Not a muscle moves.

The hairs on my arms rise. I take a breath as everything around me becomes crystal clear and moves in slow motion. The tree on my left is moving. A bird flies to the north. A sense of calm washes over me as the sound barrels toward me.

I can count the seconds. I know it's coming.

The heartbeats of time pass.

Until it hits.

The bullet rips through my skin and muscle before exiting the other side. I jerk back from the impact of the gunshot. Everything stops as my body registers what my mind was prepared for. I've been shot.

Pain. Numb. Pain. It crushes together.

I hunch over as another bullet shreds through my body. I buckle and crumple to the ground as the agony becomes too much. Holy fucking shit! I curse and yell as the sound of bullets rains down.

"Shots fired! Shots fired!" I hear from a distance.

Yeah, no shit shots fired.

"He's down!" I hear Mark call out from behind the Humvee.

The bullets hit the ground around me. The sound of each one bouncing on the dirt just inches away from me vibrates in my head.

I start to crawl toward the truck for cover.

Another bullet hits.

"Fuuuuuuuuuuuuuck!" I scream out as it tears through me.

"Don't move!" Mark yells franticly as I try to roll and grab my gun.

"On the roof! Sniper on the roof," I cry out.

Pop. Pop. Pop. I hear them over and over. Heavy gunfire fills my ears as Mark continues to yell at me. All I see is red. My vision fades in and out.

Black.

Red.

White.

"Kill them and let's go!" Mark's loud voice says over the sound of bullets. "Up on the ridge. There's another one!"

I return fire, trying to shoot my way to safety. The sounds

of screaming and gunfire are all I register.

"Muff!" Mark calls out as my vision starts to fade. The pain is unlike anything I've ever felt before.

Everything becomes foggy. My eyes. I'm so tired. But then I see her. She's beautiful. Her dark blue eyes pierce through the pain, giving me numbness. Her long blond hair is exactly as I remember. She walks toward me with her hand outstretched.

"Madelyn." Her name rolls off my tongue effortlessly. She steps closer as I extend my arm. Closer and closer, her eyes stay locked on mine.

"Jackson, no! Stay with me," I hear. Catherine's voice. The sound of it jolts me and I drop my hand.

"Catherine," I call out to her.

Opening my eyes, I see Mark's face contort as he continues to shoot. "Motherfucker! Move!" Using my arms, I try to crawl closer.

I see him throw his gun down and rush toward me.

"Mark," I croak. My vision is hazy.

I'm weak. I can't hold on.

The pain is taking over and I can't fight the black.

I close my eyes. There's no fight. I'm too tired. She's here, waiting for me with her long brown hair and chocolate brown eyes—she's perfect. It's too much. In the dark, I see her. In the dark, there's no pain, no guilt—just her.

I focus on the warmth in her eyes and succumb to the numbness.

TO BE CONTINUED ...

acknowledgements

IF I FAIL to mention someone I'm eternally sorry. Some of you kept me afloat when I felt like I was sinking. Some were my cheerleaders, some were a little more forceful making me write when I wanted to sleep, but all of you have made my life complete.

Cara, what do I even say to you? Because really ... there aren't enough words to express my gratitude. No amount of thank you's can suffice. From day one you stood behind me and pushed—hard. You made me laugh and then bawl my eyes out but it was expected and needed. The jokes and laughter regarding my incessant rewrites and "wait don't read that version" kept me desperate to keep you on your toes. The backroom deals, the quest to find Jackson, letting me talk to myself with you on the phone. #NMCNMM

Mandi, you "got" their story. Your support and honesty was invaluable. Thank you for not letting me try out for American Idol when I couldn't sing and for loving Jackson. Most of all thank you for keeping me grounded. You gave me your time, love, and wisdom when I needed it. You are my Muffin and no one loves him more than you and Cara! #IlovemyMuffDirty

Betas, I have no words to fully express the appreciation I have for you. Livia, Roxana, Stacia, Jennifer, and Lisa ... you pushed me to do better and made me laugh, cry, and shake my head in awe of your genuine love and support. Thank you for dropping things to read and not backing down. For the refusal to let me put out anything less than my best and not allowing me to get away with anything. Beta reading is hard and I appreciate how honest you all were. but I know you all came from a place of love and for that I thank you so much. A huge thank you to my test readers: Alison, Letty, Donna, Jessica, Keisha and Tara. You gave me so much feedback on the finished product and blew me away. It meant the world to me.

Angie, thank you for all of you support, love, and friendship. For taking your time to make sure I had a successful release. You held my hand when I was afraid and gave me words of wisdom when I needed it. I love your face!

Lisa, it's not everyday you meet someone and just "click". Our friendship was never forced, it just happened. Your snark, sarcasm, and love of Jackie has brought us closer than ever. I love ya!

Rose, you are my inspiration. You pushed me to see the courage I had when I didn't think it was there. You forced me to do better day after day. The tears you virtually wiped and then literally wiped I will never forget. Thank you for being my wifey and never letting me down. There are certain people who enter our lives for one reason or another and I'm thankful everyday you are one of them. Our friendship is beyond all of this and I'll cherish it always.

Emmy, Kristy, and Laurelin, if it weren't for you three I wouldn't have had the guts to write in the first place. When I told you this is what I was going to do you all stood behind me and made me go forward. You read my first drafts and said, "keep going". I love you all as writers and friends.

Faith, you made me a better writer and challenged me to listen to my characters! I can't tell you how much your friendship means to me. Every single day I'm grateful I met you. While it may have been a complete fluke that we met you've become one of my closest friends that I rely on more than you may know.

FYW: I can't even say enough about you ladies. During times of doubt, struggle, joy, and happiness we've come together. It has been so special to me and I love every one of you.

To my editor, Megan Ward, you are so much more than

an editor. You took a hold of my story and cared for it. Your attention to every detail, every word, and every emotion was astounding. This process was exciting and remarkable because of you. You achieved your goal of making this fun. I can only hope every writer at some time or another gets to work with you. Thank you for empowering me to push harder and see what was there. I will forever laugh when I see anyone wink.

My cover designer, Najla Qamber, thank you for making it perfect. I love every single thing about it. You are truly an amazing artist.

Christine from Perfectly Publishable, you stepped in and saved the day. I appreciate your professionalism, attention to detail, and making this a painless and wonderful experience.

Bloggers – I have so many to thank because without you none of this would be possible. Some of you may not realize what you give to authors ... a chance. You take time away from your loved ones to read and then even more time to tell your fans how you felt. It's appreciated and truly respected. I know the dedication, sacrifice, and time you spend. From the bottom of my heart thank you for taking the time to read and review!

Heather Maven, thank you for your friendship, love, and always making me laugh. Everyday I am grateful for you in my life.

To my friends and family, some of you didn't know I was writing *Beloved* so if you're reading this ... surprise! Thank you to my mother who won't ever read this but stood beside me every step of the way. You gave me life, then made sure I lived it to my fullest. I never felt unloved or unwanted because of you. My Aunt Donna, you took me to the zoo and made sure I had these memories. You taught me that just because I was hurting didn't mean I had to be alone. I pray that every person in this world has someone like you, because you are one in a million.

The SPQ, There are few people who mean more to me in this world than you. There are so many things you probably picked up on just for you. You stood beside me when I wasn't sure. You pushed when I wanted to quit. You joked when I needed to laugh.

To my beautiful children...Thank you for your daily dinner talks asking how much I wrote. You both are the reason I kept going when I wanted to cry some nights. I know it wasn't easy when mommy was crazy glued to the computer and I love you both so much! To my son who tells everyone his mommy wrote a book even though I pray he'll never read it. To my daughter who told me she was so proud of me for following my dream and would take the laptop and sit next to me and write her own story. You both are my beloved.

I want to thank my husband for his undying love and support. You love the broken in me and have never given up. Our love has never been easy but it's ours. We've gone through so much and still come out on top. Deployments, moves, kids, more deployments but you've always been my constant. Most of all, thank you for being my anchor in the storm. You're it for me, babe.

To my readers ... Wow! The fact that I'm even sitting here writing to you is overwhelming. I had a dream as a little girl to write books, and because of you reading this right now it's no longer a dream, but a reality. I don't even know how to thank you because it's surreal. For some reason you choose to pick this up and read. For that I'm eternally grateful. I know you have kindles filled with books to choose, and a never ending supply of books coming—so thank you.

about the author

Corinne Michaels is an emotional, witty, sarcastic, and fun loving mom of two beautiful children. She's happily married to the man of her dreams and is a former Navy wife. After spending months away from her husband while he was deployed, reading and writing was her escape from the loneliness. Beloved and Beholden conclude The Belonging Duet and she's currently working on three spinoffs.

connect with corinne

www.corinnemichaels.com

Connect on Facebook
www.facebook.com/CorinneMichaels

Connect on Twitter
https://twitter.com/AuthorCMichaels

Connect on Goodreads

Connect on Instagram
http://instagram.com/authorcorinnemichaels

CPSIA information can be obtained
at www.ICGtesting.com
Printed in the USA
BVOW00s1925261016

466102BV00028B/512/P